The Enigma of Treason

MISSION POINT PRESS

Published by Mission Point Press
2554 Chandler Rd.
Traverse City, MI 49696
(231) 421-9513
www.MissionPointPress.com

ISBN: 9781958363577
Library of Congress Control Number: 2022923898

Printed in the United States of America

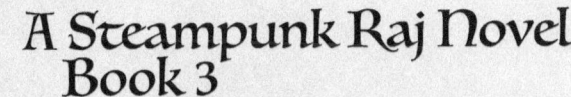

A Steampunk Raj Novel
Book 3

The Enigma of Treason

J.R. SEEGER

Mission Point Press

The man that hath no music in himself,
Nor is not moved with concord of sweet sounds,
Is fit for treasons, stratagems, and spoils

William Shakespeare, "The Merchant of Venice,"
act 5, scene 1

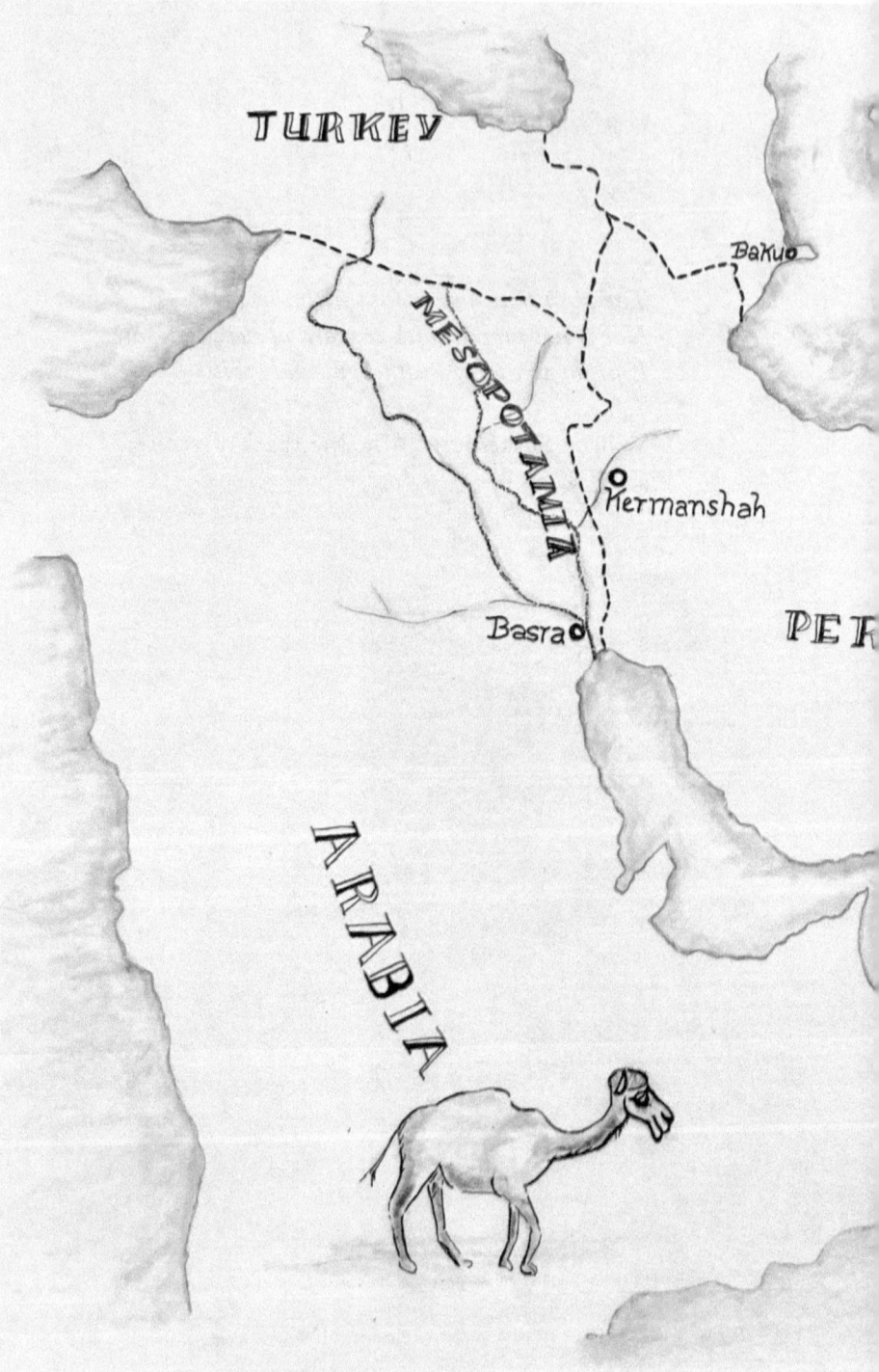

Part One

Tournament of Shadows

INDIA

Back Bay

Bombay Harbor

Gymkhana

Taj Mahal Hotel

ISLAND OF BOMBAY

St John's Church

Ḣunting the Underground

Bombay, September 1914

ELIZABETH BANKROFT WAS TAKING TEA IN THE SEA LOUNGE OF THE TAJ
Hotel in Bombay. She wore her khaki military uniform of
wool jacket and skirt over a white silk blouse. A row of colorful ribbons ran along the top of her left breast pocket and
her shined insignia identified her as a member of the Field
Ambulance Nursing Yoemanry. The medical identity offered
reasonable cover for a female intelligence officer who traveled in and out of military offices in the city. Indian Army
or Royal Navy officers would be surprised to see a young
woman in uniform, and would assume she was "just a nurse"
who belonged to the local hospital.

Elizabeth Bankroft was absolutely not a nurse and did not
see herself as "belonging" to anyone in Bombay.

It had been a late monsoon and afternoon rains were
beating against the windows that overlooked the port. The war
that started in Europe just one month ago had now become
a world war affecting the entire Empire and, most especially,

British India. The Marine Lines that had been occupied by foreign travelers and sailors from around the world were now filled with Royal Navy and Royal Marine personnel. The Arabian Sea patrol had grown into a full squadron of ships including one cruiser, a half dozen destroyers and a dozen patrol boats of various sizes. As Elizabeth looked north toward the end of the Navy docks, she could see three airships tethered to steel frames. The airships were now in full use as long-range patrol craft monitoring German warships. Warships that Elizabeth helped identify over the past six months.

When she learned that the German Navy was actively raiding in the Bay of Bengal, Elizabeth was shocked. Eventually, the reporting from military intelligence identified the German craft as the light cruiser *Emden*. Elizabeth had enough experience in the shadow world of espionage that she had expected some sabotage from German spies and their Indian revolutionary colleagues. But she had not expected German warships so far from the real theatre of operations in Europe raiding India! It reinforced to her that this was quickly becoming a world war with many different theatres. It also reminded her that her job was not simply an intelligence game. It was a job where lives were at stake.

One of Elizabeth's earlier adventures before the war had revealed a German military base in East Africa. She supposed once the *Emden* completed its raid, it headed to temporary rest and refitting at that base. Where it would go next was a mystery, but if Elizabeth could find out, she intended to do so. Unfortunately, most of Elizabeth's work since the declaration of war had been focused on countering German subversion in Bombay, but she remained convinced that any German raid against Bombay would come from the sea and would have its origins in Africa. She suspected that this link would include the Portuguese colony of Goa, on the Indian coast a few hundred miles away. There were many complexities to this entire question of defending the west coast of

British India. Elizabeth knew of few local British military or civilian leaders willing to talk about this subject and fewer still who would listen to what they saw as a very young, very inexperienced girl.

This level of prejudice meant little to Elizabeth since her commander was Colonel Gareth Winslow-Heath, the Indian Army intelligence chief for western India. Based in Rawalpindi, Winslow-Heath was both her direct supervisor and a long-standing family friend. He always seemed interested in whatever Elizabeth collected as well as her interpretation of the intelligence. Yesterday, she received a message by enciphered telegram. Hand delivered to her by a Royal Navy seaman, it took her an hour to decipher the message which read:

E,

Your work is critical to the security of India. Do not be bothered by those who do not understand. They are mostly policemen or sailors who have no experience in the complexities of our trade. The former are men who spent their time hunting murderers and smugglers. The latter are men who wish to engage the enemy in great sea battles. You cannot expect them to understand the nature of the German commitment to attacking the Raj. Continue to develop your network and report directly to me. Carry on!

W-H

After she read it, Elizabeth folded the paper in the approved accordion fold taught at the Viceroy's College and then burned the message in the ashtray in her room. As the paper flamed, Elizabeth smiled at the thought that her work was important enough that Colonel Winslow-Heath wrote to her directly. Heady stuff for a girl not yet twenty. Of course, she knew there were men her age facing far more serious problems on the battlefields in France and Belgium. One thing

3

was certain: the message meant she was on the right track in focusing on both Bombay and Goa.

After musing over her own success, Elizabeth's thoughts turned to the rest of her family. She knew her parents were safe in Odessa. On arrival at the Russian port, Elizabeth's mother had sent a brief telegram saying that they had arrived and were awaiting orders. Elizabeth could imagine her father like a caged lion wandering the streets of Odessa awaiting a new challenge. Elizabeth's most recent worry focused on her brother Conrad. His unit was recalled from the Bolan Pass on the Afghan Frontier and sent to Karachi to await deployment to some distant warzone. Where would her brother end up? And, after years of operating against bandits and tribals, how would he survive against a modern enemy? The thought of her beautiful brother facing German guns terrified Elizabeth.

In her hotel room that evening, Elizabeth began a transformation. The FANY uniform came off and was hung carefully in the closet. It was replaced by what Elizabeth had come to think of as her "work clothes." First, a cotton undergarment with small pockets that carried tools including powders that might incapacitate a man or might open a lock through a refined chemical reaction. After that, she donned grey shalwar pajama pants. The pants were modified with belt loops at the waist and buttons at the ankle to keep the pants tight. Next came a pair of shoes that looked like any other woman's shoe but were unlike anything that came from a store. They were designed by the boffins of the Intelligence Bureau quartermaster to be both supple and resilient. The shoes had rope soles that made her steps both silent and secure.

After her shoes, she laced a heavy leather belt through the belt loops. The belt included two leather pockets on her right hip, a holster for her pistol located in the small of her back, and, finally, a four-inch dagger in a sheath sitting on her left hip. Elizabeth jumped once or twice to insure the items were secure and made no sound. Then, she pulled the grey kamiz long-tailed shirt over her head. While a normal kamiz was designed to emphasize modesty, Elizabeth's version of the garment contained various slots at the waist that would allow her access to all the concealed weapons. She reached into the armoire and pulled out a shoulder bag which earlier in the day she had filled with groceries. Finally, she wrapped herself in a burgundy dupattā scarf that covered her hair and, when looped properly, covered her face up to her nose. Elizabeth walked over to the mirror on the door of the armoire. The transformation was complete. She was no longer a young British woman. She was now a local woman heading home after a long day at work as a servant for British citizens or elite Indians.

Elizabeth moved through the early-evening crowds in the Lalbagh Spice Market. She added to the shoulder bag various spices, dried beans and dried fruit. Her real purpose was to visit a spice merchant named Riv Ambali. He was one of the most successful of the spice traders, with contacts in India, the Persian Gulf and even the Horn of Africa. He was also Elizabeth's newest recruit, identified by Rawalpindi as Z-9 in their files. Elizabeth previously met with him before she went on her recent operations in Baluchistan and, once she returned, she formalized the relationship with her spice merchant so that he was now aware of his job supporting the Empire.

When Elizabeth revealed her interest and her role as an intelligence officer, Ambali was quick to agree. "These young men interested in independence ... what do they think that means? We are part of a powerful empire. It means trade. It means law. It means protection from the most powerful navy on earth. If I can help, I will. Elizabeth, it is not because I like you. It is because it is in my self-interest. As a trader, I need to stay in the Empire."

With that, Elizabeth pushed Ambali to build a small network of reporting sources both inside the standard shipping community and inside the smuggling community. Elizabeth was looking forward to his latest reports from both sets of sources.

Later, Elizabeth realized that her enthusiasm for the meeting might have translated into a less careful approach to Ambali's store. Per their previous arrangements, he closed his shop when she arrived, swinging the wooden doors shut and locking them from the inside. They would eventually leave from the back door after an hour meeting punctuated by a pot of Ceylonese tea and samosas Ambali ordered from his favorite food stall. First, they talked about family and the economy and, of course, the war. Ambali was far better informed than Elizabeth on the war. His trading contacts were already reporting signs of German raiders in the Arabian Sea. Ambali's description made it clear that the German Navy had at least one light cruiser prowling the ocean waters between India, East Africa, and Arabia as well as two submarines and a strange aircraft that no one seemed able to describe. Ambali's spice network covered these areas and he was most worried that the Germans would focus on sinking the large and small cargo ships that followed regular routes in the Arabian Sea. Elizabeth wrote down the description of the ships seen by Ambali's contacts. As she did so, she reminded herself that she needed to learn more about the German Navy so that she could do more than just nod and take notes.

Next, they focused on the revolutionary underground simmering in Bombay. Ambali was dismissive of the revolutionaries. He thought they were nothing more than young men who were far too well educated for their own good. He noted that these individuals were all graduates from British Indian colleges and, in some cases, attendees at British or various European universities. Elizabeth admitted she was jealous of anyone given the opportunity to attend university. She told Ambali that she hoped someday to do so herself.

"Daughter, do not become captured with envy of those who attend high levels of learning — whether it is a British school, a Hindu ashram or a Muslim madresseh. It is all about the person and not about ideas the instructors pound into the heads of their students. These revolutionaries return to their home with no more skills for life than when they left. They may quote complex philosophies and international dogma on economics and on the benefits of freedom, but they don't know what it means to have a paying job. In fact, they don't try to get jobs. Instead, they congregate in tea shops all day long, planning and plotting against the Raj. It is enough to make you weep."

Elizabeth said, "Where do they go and if they don't have jobs, who pays their bills?"

Ambali put his right index finger against his nose. He smiled and said, "And that is the best news of all. I have found at least two places where they meet, and it seems that their bills are paid by a Portuguese trader from Goa. He has open accounts at the two tea shops and allows these useless children to spend his money. Here are the two places."

Ambali began to unwrap a hand-drawn map of the city. Elizabeth already knew the parts of the city frequented by Indian civil servants and British administrators, but the deepest, darkest sections of this ancient city were hard to find when city roads became little more than sidewalks and then evaporated altogether into unnamed alleys and small gullies where the seven islands of ancient Bombay joined.

7

From the back of the room, a voice shouted, "Traitor! You are a traitor to our people!"

The voice transformed into three men as they moved closer to the circle of lamplight where Ambali and Elizabeth sat with their tea. Elizabeth was closest to the intruders and Ambali tried, unsuccessfully to place himself between the newcomers and Elizabeth. Elizabeth placed a hand on his chest and used a carefully modulated mesmerism voice with her friend. "Please stay here, Ambali." He stopped in his tracks under the spell of the waking dream.

Elizabeth looked at the intruders. All in the late teens. All well-fed young men in western dress: black trousers and white shirts. Two were armed with hooked blades used in farm fields. The third held a four-foot wooden rod that resembled the wooden police staffs called lathis. Lathis were used by the Bombay policemen to keep the peace on the borders of the various Muslim, Hindu, Parsi, and European ethnic communities. Elizabeth had to force herself not to smile. She suspected the men with the two harvesting hooks had never used them for their real purpose and probably didn't know precisely how they planned to use them tonight. She also wondered how high they would climb on the ladder of consequences before this confrontation was over.

The martial-arts instructors at the Viceroy's College made it clear that intelligence officers were not being trained to be fighters. Rather, the instructors said, "If you can retreat, then retreat. If you can't retreat, do your best to talk your way out of a confrontation. However, if you must fight, be confident that you have done everything you could to avoid violence. This is called the ladder of consequences. You must give your adversary every opportunity to avoid climbing the ladder. However, if they choose to do so, then you must dispatch them quickly, thoroughly and without any guilt. They were the ones who chose the fight. The fact that they are going to die is their responsibility."

Elizabeth used her most powerful mesmerism voice and said, "Gentlemen, I was talking to my uncle. Why have you interrupted us?"

Elizabeth noted the leader of the three was the man with the lathi standing in the shadows behind the other two. He spoke with a perfect, clipped British accent. He said, "He is a traitor to Mother India and if you are his relative, then you must be a traitor as well." His voice offered nothing but venom. Elizabeth was certain he would climb the ladder before they were done.

She looked into the eyes of the first intruder. He was clearly confused by the confrontation with a young woman dressed in modest Indian clothes but with ice blue eyes and light skin. Elizabeth said, "Tonight is not the night to do anyone harm. You should go home."

The intruder looked at his partner on his right as he lowered his harvest tool. He said, "I think we have made a mistake. We should go home."

As the second man lowered his tool, their leader swung his lathi against a shelf in the back of the shop. The shelf rattled and dozens of glass bottles fell to the floor filling the room with a mix of scents of pepper, cumin, coriander and turmeric. The floor was now awash in orange spice. He shouted, "She is a spy and he is a traitor. You need to kill them both. JAI HIND!"

Elizabeth could see that the first two men would be no problem. It was the man in the back of the shop who was dangerous. The phrase, "Long live Hindustan," was a call to arms for various revolutionary groups. His use of the phrase indicated that he at least understood the purpose of the confrontation, even if his understanding was only marginal. Unfortunately, the narrow space in the shop limited her options. Elizabeth bowed her head in supplication and said, "In your hearts you know this is not correct." As she bowed, she had reached under her kamiz into one of the secret pockets of her undergarment. She recovered a small flask filled with a sleeping drug which was a mix of highly refined opium and multiple aromatic spices that she bought from Ambali.

As she stood up, Elizabeth could see the two men were torn between what they could see with their own eyes — an old man and a young woman drinking tea — and what they were being told by their leader. It was confusing and they delayed just long enough for Elizabeth to step toward them and blow the sleeping drug into their faces. The drug took immediate effect. They dropped their weapons and fell to their knees and then onto the floor among the broken vials and spices.

Elizabeth stepped over them and confronted the third man. Now that she was closer, she could see that he was older, easily in his twenties, and not from Western India. Perhaps a Bengali? Or even from a family in Burma? He remained angry, that was certain. "What have you done to my comrades? Are you some sort of witch?"

Elizabeth smiled and in her most powerful mesmerism voice said, "First you accuse me of being a spy and then a witch. Do you really know what you think anymore?"

What Elizabeth was projecting into his mind was a ghostly image of a mature woman, perhaps seven feet tall, with long white hair and a pale complexion. She hoped that this just might prevent what she feared was inevitable. The man backed away and swung the lathi back and forth, crashing into spice jars and earthenware jugs of oil. He slipped on the oil and fell to the ground. He began to wonder about his sanity as the tall ghost looked over him. She seemed to be floating above him. Suddenly, there was the smell of an aromatic herb and he felt as if he was sinking into the floor. He was afraid, and yet, he did not feel as if he was any longer attached to his body. He only knew that he needed to obey the ghost.

Elizabeth thought the leader was fully under the spell of her mesmerism and the substantial dose of powdered opium that she had blown into his face as he swung the lathi, breaking Ambali's stock of oils. In the back of her mind, she heard a voice saying *He is easy prey. Kill him now.* Elizabeth could not be certain who had entered her mind but it was neither her mother's voice nor Guru Naismith's. It seemed to be both inside her head and coming from outside. It was neither male nor female. Elizabeth confronted this mental antagonist with the thought, *He is a foolish man who will now be mine to control. Why would I want to kill him?*

The internal voice said, *Because it gives you pleasure every time you unleash your power. Because this sort of man will never respect you!* Elizabeth shook her head to clear it of this strange voice.

She leaned over the third man and said, "Do you want to live?"

The man said in a croak, "Please do not kill me. I will be your slave."

"Slave you shall be then. Your name?"

"I am Bipin. Bengali by birth, English by education."

"Bipin, you will call me Nana. I will be your guide. You will have great success and you will be pleased to serve me."

"Nana, I will be your slave. I will do whatever you order."

Elizabeth smiled. She now had three new members of a network and she avoided harming anyone. It would be a successful night before it was over. She said to Bipin, "First, you must clean up the mess you made. Give me the lathi."

As Elizabeth stood and turned back to face Ambali, she heard the swoosh of the lathi being swung toward her head. She ducked just in time and turned to face Bipin. He screamed as he charged toward her, "WITCH! Do you think a bit of opium would protect you from a dedicated man? Do you think your soft words would change my hard heart? It is now your turn to learn a lesson."

Elizabeth parried the second lathi swing with an upraised forearm. The lathi slid along her arm and crashed against the wall. The strike did not break her bones as intended, but it did hurt and she knew it would raise a large welt by morning. When Bipin raised the lathi again, Elizabeth put out her left hand as if to appeal for him to stop. She extended her *chi*, that power of mind and body. The force of her *chi* stopped the lathi in mid-strike as if it had hit some invisible wall. The shock of the stopped lathi extended down through Bipin's arms, nearly tipping him over. Elizabeth could see in Bipin's eyes that he remained determined to continue his attack. He dropped the lathi, drew a small blade from a sheath on his belt and rushed at Elizabeth.

Elizabeth misjudged his speed and his first slash cut across her kamiz and opened a small wound on her midriff. The pain was enough for Elizabeth to change her mind and listen to the voice that had spoken earlier. She held out her left arm with her hand open as if she was pushing on a door. Again, her *chi* extended out from her hand. But this time it hit Bipin in the chest. Elizabeth heard three of his ribs snapping one by one. The noise of the broken bones told her that she had rendered Bipin helpless. Elizabeth's face transformed from the young woman to the grim visage of one who could kill. She reached under her long shirt and pulled out the dagger. She walked up to Bipin, parried his attempt to hit her and then slid the dagger under his ribs and directly into his heart. Bipin dropped to the ground a very dead man.

The voice inside Elizabeth's head said, *This is the way to handle men. Killing is always the cleanest answer. He almost killed you. You need to listen to me next time.*

Elizabeth turned back to the collapsed shelves and broken pottery in the spice room. Who had spoken these words? No one seemed willing or able to speak at all. Ambali had sat back down, resting in the waking dream of mesmerism. The two young men were still collapsed against the far wall. The drugs would last at least another hour. Perhaps, the voice was just her imagination.

Elizabeth had to decide how to proceed. The next steps would be easy enough, but they wouldn't be pretty. She thought about the voice. Perhaps it had been right all along. She couldn't trust her good nature. This was a war and, in war, men died.

Gunfire at Night

Odessa, October 1914

FRANCIS AND MARY BANKROFT SAT ON THE LARGE PORCH OF THE DACHA overlooking the Russian Navy port of Odessa. They were drinking sweet tea served by their Albanian man servant, Bektashi Bey. The late afternoon sun still provided enough heat that they were comfortable in the wicker chairs wrapped in light wool blankets. It was a quiet interlude before their upcoming overland trip through the Caucasus to join the British intelligence teams working in Persia. After their quick escape from Constantinople and the uneventful sail across the Black Sea to Odessa, they had settled in the family dacha of their new Russian ally, Alexander Naglieff. Mary Bankroft was accustomed to well-appointed houses based on her background as the daughter of a senior British Army officer, but Naglieff's family house was something to behold. "Sasha" Naglieff had been their adversary only a few years ago and now he was their ally and their gracious host.

Naglieff walked onto the porch. He was dressed in the

14

new Russian Army field uniform. It was a khaki green color with a leather sword and pistol belt. He was wearing a peaked hat of the same color. His Colonel rank was marked on his epaulets. It was not at all like the colorful uniform that he had worn during his time as the Russian military attaché to the Ottoman Empire. The only items in his uniform that matched his time in Constantinople were his tall, highly shined riding boots. Mary turned to him and said, "Sasha, please have a seat and we will take tea together and watch the sunset."

"Mary, that would be lovely. It may be the last time I have a moment of peace."

Francis Bankroft had been especially restless over the past two months as they waited for instructions from the Intelligence Bureau of the Indian Army. He knew the Empire was at war with the Germans. He knew there were efforts on the part of the Germans to attack the Empire across the entire Middle East, Africa, and India. And he knew that he had to wait for orders from Rawalpindi or, perhaps, even London before he could participate in the conflict. It had made him especially grumpy with both Bektashi and Mary. Both understood the reason for his unpleasant demeanor, but that didn't mean they put up with it. Mary had chastised him multiple times over the past month and even Bektashi had made it clear to Francis that he did not need work with an unpleasant household. Francis apologized several times, but the waiting wore at him like a blister in an ill-fitting boot. He said, "Sasha, you have news?"

"I have been called back to Moscow for new orders. The intelligence service leadership seem committed to keep their secrets even to those who must deliver on their plans. It seems to me they could have sent an enciphered cable and be done with it. But, no. They want to see me in person."

Mary offered, "Perhaps because you are a member of royalty, they want to tell you in person?"

"It has never been so in the past. Why should it be so now when time is of the essence. We are already at war with the Germans and there are many places I could go that would help create chaos behind the German lines. The longer I am delayed, the harder it will be to get behind those lines."

Francis grumbled, "Well do I know your frustration, my friend."

Naglieff smirked and said, "Oh, did I forget to tell you a message came for you today?" He reached into his pocket and pulled out a single sheet of paper with 100 groups of five letters. An enciphered message!

Mary said, "I don't suppose you have read the message."

"How could I? It is enciphered."

Mary smiled and said, "So, what does it say? Naglieff laughed. "Your encryption system is very simplistic. Our Naval Intelligence team took about five minutes to defeat the cipher. I didn't even ask, they just did it more for their own amusement than anything else."

Francis said, "I can always use my code book, but what is the point? What does it say?"

Naglieff said, "Since you asked so politely, I will tell you what it says and more! It is dated 20 October. You are both instructed to travel by fastest means possible to Baku where you are to transit the Caspian Sea to meet one of your colleagues in Tashkent. The message only gives his designation, S230. Of course, we already know that S230 is your intelligence officer Percy Sykes who is traveling with his sister. According to our security service, he is headed to Western China. Heaven only knows why, given the fact that we are at war with Germany and his background in Persia. The Persians have oil and your navy needs that oil. What in the world do the Chinese have out in the mountains? Sykes is already traveling by train across Russia to get to Tashkent."

Naglieff took a moment to enjoy how perplexed his guests

were over his knowledge of the British Indian Intelligence operations.

"I remain even more puzzled why your service might send you to China," he continued. "Still, orders are orders. Personally, I recommend you travel by ship to Sochi and then directly to Baku, but I can get you on a carriage to Rostov and then you can travel the circuitous route by our less-than-comfortable and totally unreliable Imperial Rail system to Tashkent. The Russian Navy Squadron here in Odessa has a gunboat headed to Sochi tomorrow. It will be in Sochi at the end of the month. I can arrange a Cossack patrol to support you across the Caucasus since we are at present in control of the northern, Armenian lands of the Ottoman. Of course, if you do not need my help, then I will defer to you on when you wish to leave. It is entirely up to you!"

Francis stood up, spilling his tea over his blanket and grabbed Naglieff by the shoulders and pulled him to his chest. Naglieff was nearly the same height as Bankroft but easily 20 pounds lighter. Mary noticed he disappeared in the embrace of her husband. "Sasha, you are a treasure! When do we need to be at the docks?"

"I arranged for you to be welcomed by the captain of the *Donetz* tomorrow morning. You will be expected at 9 hours. They intend to make steam and leave the port shortly after that, so please do not be late."

"This calls for a drink!"

Mary nodded, "At least one before we all begin to pack."

As they began to assemble their items in preparation for departure, Francis realized that some items that had come from Constantinople via their sailboat probably would not be allowed on a Russian gunboat. He was standing on one of these items, a large Turkish carpet, when Bektashi walked

17

J.R. Seeger

into the room. He cleared his throat to let Francis know that he was in the room.

"Bektashi Bey, what can I do for you?"

"Sir, I wish to know if you are really going to leave on the Russian ship tomorrow."

"My friend, the proper statement is that we are all going to leave on the Russian ship tomorrow."

"You intend to take me on your adventure into the Caucasus?"

Francis was slightly distracted. He was still trying to determine if he could fold the carpet small enough that they would be able to fit it into a bag. He said, "Why not, Bektashi? Are you afraid of the mountains?"

The Albanian stood up almost at the position of attention. He said, "An Albanian afraid of mountains? You must be joking!"

"Indeed, Bektashi. I just wanted to know if you wanted to go. There is no obligation and it is a very long trip and we still do not know our final destination."

"And who else would take care of Madame on such a trip? You will need assistance!"

Francis reached down and started to fold the carpet into thirds. He did not want to insult his Albanian friend by pointing out that Mary Bankroft was more than capable of keeping herself safe. Instead, he said, "That is why I hoped you would come."

"Sir, what exactly are you doing?"

Francis looked up and said, "I am trying to determine if this carpet can travel with us."

"OF COURSE, sir! Leave this to me. I will make this the smallest of parcels. Heavy, but small. I will carry it along with my own bag, so do not worry. The carpet must travel with us to remind us of our time in Constantinople. Now, other than our weapons and our traveling clothes, what else will we take and what must we leave behind?"

18

Francis smiled. After years of traveling on the Afghan frontier, he needed little in the way of clothes. He would have to wear a formal uniform tomorrow so that the gunboat commander acknowledged his rank. That meant that he simply needed one set of traveling clothes — wool pants and a wool overshirt, a sweater, his leather vest and his sheepskin coat. The rest of his clothes would be left behind. He was certain that Naglieff would distribute the remainder to his staff or to the Russian Orthodox Church nearby. Winter was coming and someone could use the clothes. He said to Bektashi, "I will sort my clothes. What I need you to do is to sort our weapons. I will need my pistols and my Mauser and the long knife."

He pointed to the Khyber knife that was hanging in its sheath and belt on the open door of his armoire. "Madame will need your help sorting her weapons as well. You will take one of my rifles. We will only have one bag each, other than our weapons and tools. Any ship, whether Russian or British, will have little room for travelers or their kit."

"It will be done, sir. What time do you want morning tea?" Bektashi was looking down at the large pocket watch smothered in his huge left hand.

Francis knew that Bektashi was proud of the gold, hunter timepiece that he had gifted the Albanian before they departed Constantinople. Whenever there was any sort of plan, Bektashi would pull out the watch from his cummerbund and ask what time he wanted this or that accomplished. "I believe we should take tea at precisely 6 hours, but you should check with Madame to ensure she agrees."

"As you wish, sir."

With that Bektashi disappeared, headed to the dressing room where Mary was pondering her own traveling bag.

Francis thought about all his traveling companions over the years. These included Abdul Rashid the Uzbek as well as Mirza Khan, who died in Mazar-e-Sharif protecting him from assassins. The irony was those assassins had been in the pay of Sasha Naglieff. Now, they were allies and Sasha was doing everything he could to support the mission of his two English colleagues. Bektashi was another perfect ally in this world of shadows. He was loyal, he was very capable in a fight, and he didn't ask too many questions. Francis had not worked with Albanians in the past, but Bektashi seemed more like his Uzbek colleagues than any of the Indian intelligence operators, known as pundits, who were loyal to the Empire. He was pleased that Bektashi was traveling with them. Once they landed in Sochi, the trail would be long and hard. A steadfast subordinate would be critical to keep them all alive.

Mary was lying awake. She noticed over the years that no matter the level of chaos or concern, Francis could sleep without difficulty, and he was lying next to her snoring gently. Mary was thinking about their children. They were both committed to service to the Empire and both facing new challenges as Britain went to war. Their son, Conrad, was now a captain in the army based on the Afghan frontier. While the Indian Army remained in India defending the frontiers, Mary knew they would be called upon eventually to serve the Empire in some distant war zone.

Mary had no idea where their daughter might be. Months ago, when they last saw Elizabeth, she was headed back to Rawalpindi to receive instructions for her next assignment with the Intelligence Bureau. They escaped Constantinople shortly afterwards and had been in Odessa for weeks as the world faced a great war between the Empires of Europe. At this point, each member of the family would have to face the challenges on their own. It was most worrisome.

The screams of shells flying over the dacha woke Francis up. He rushed to the window in time to see naval gunfire crashing into the docks and into the ships in the harbor. On the distant western horizon, he could see flashes from some warship. Two small destroyers were approaching the port at full speed. He turned to Mary and said, "War has come to Odessa."

"And, I suspect our plans have changed."

Another set of artillery shells hit the port facilities, igniting buildings and oil reserves. In the light of the fires below, Mary could see several ships sinking. As they watched the fires, Francis pointed over to the military docks. The only Russian military ship in the harbor, a gunboat, exploded from what must have been a torpedo attack synchronized with the naval gunfire. It had to be the *Donetz*. "Our previous plans are sinking in the harbor. The real question at this point is how the Germans brought warships into the Black Sea."

Naglieff and Bektashi entered their bedroom at the same time. The Russian was already wearing his military trousers and boots. He was pulling his leather suspenders over his long-sleeved undershirt. He said, "Just when I thought our Navy had learned its lesson from Port Arthur, they have proven unable to protect themselves from raiders even when they know we are at war. You would have thought they would have put a screen of patrol boats to warn us of these sorts of actions. Apparently not."

Almost as punctuation of his comments, another set of rounds screamed over the dacha and landed in the port. "I need to report to my headquarters," he said with a shake of his head. "I believe you need to leave the city as soon as possible. This attack will create panic and there will be shortages of everything."

Bektashi stood behind Naglieff in a long, embroidered robe and what at present looked like a matching embroidered nightcap. He said, "Sir, I arranged for five horses yesterday and have had them stabled in the compound. As you have pointed out to me before, the only successful plan is one that is prepared for changes. I did not expect this sort of change, but I have no love for modern ships. Their engines seem to always fail when you need them the most. So, I thought horses might be useful. Also, if there were not, they would have been a reasonable parting gift for our Russian host. I know little about ships, but I know much about horses. These are fine horses and will carry us well on our travels."

Naglieff laughed and said, "Bektashi, are you sure you don't want to go with me? I could use a man like you."

Bektashi did a quick bow and said, "Your honor, I am sworn to the Bankrofts. I will stay with them to the ends of the earth."

Francis said, "We need to get started." He walked over to his Russian host and took his hand. "Sasha, thank you for all your hospitality and I wish you the best of luck. I suspect we shall see each other again."

"Francis, it has been my pleasure. I hope we can see each other in better times."

Mary walked over to the two men. She reached over to Naglieff and pulled him close and whispered in his ear. "Sasha, please stay safe. It is a dangerous world."

"Mary, I suspect my way will be less dangerous than yours. Still, we can be certain that we have God and our Emperors on our side."

The three intelligence officers were quiet for a moment. Naglieff turned on his heel and headed to his part of the house to finish dressing and head to his offices near the port.

Mary looked up at Francis and said, "An honorable enemy who became a friend and an ally. It is a strange world."

"Strange indeed in this new version of the tournament of shadows."

Quid pro Quo

MICHAEL O'CONNELL STOOD IN FRONT OF THE POLISHED WOOD DESK ONCE again. This time, he was in the uniform of a German cavalry officer: Grey wool tunic and riding trousers; polished black boots. Tucked under his arm was a service cap with a polished brim. He knew it was necessary, but it was too much frippery for him. Following his previous two missions for the German military intelligence, he had received a formal, albeit "staff" commission in the Imperial German Army. Over the last few months, he had received a second promotion to the rank of captain, second class. Again, a staff officer rank, but Michael could have cared less. He was a street agent, accustomed to multiple disguises and the loose garments of the Arab. He had no intention of serving in the Imperial German Army.

His father, James O'Connell, stood next to him dressed in a formal black suit, starched collar, and black-and-red striped tie. His father's voice resonated in his head. *Michael, you need to remember that this is just another disguise. We are negotiating for our own goals. The Germans are just here to help us along the way.*

After years of working with his father, Michael accepted that their most careful conversations were done through telepathy. They trusted no one and, as such, spoke little even when they were alone in their own house. As the Persians said: The walls have mice and the mice have ears. Michael replied using his own telepathic skills, *Father, I know. But this uniform itches.*

Son, all European dress clothes itch. Do you think I am any more comfortable than you?

Michael did his best not to smirk at the last comment.

At last, the two German officers they awaited walked into the room by way of the door to the right of the oak desk. Michael's primary German supervisor, Colonel Manfred von Trier, entered the room first. An old-style Prussian cavalry officer, von Trier looked the part with his polished boots, his grey uniform with two rows of military award ribbons on his left breast, his short-cut hair and the dueling scar on his cheek. Michael noticed his normal aura of blue-green confidence was tinged with an orange halo. Von Trier was nervous. He stopped and came to attention and said, "Herr Baron Field Marshal Colmar von der Goltz. Commander of the Kaiser's forces in the Ottoman Empire!"

As required by protocol, both Michael and his father came to the position of attention. Michael looked at the aged man in front of him. He walked slowly as Michael would have expected for a man in his late 60s. Thinning hair was pulled across his round head. He wore small glasses and seemed to have a perpetual squint or, perhaps, a sneer. He wore the uniform of an Ottoman general, dark blue, almost black. His shoulder boards were also of Ottoman design revealing that he was both a German field marshal and a "Mushir" which was field marshal in the Ottoman military nomenclature. He was wearing a small number of very high-status German awards including a blue and pearl cross known informally as the Blue Max though officially called "Pour le Merite" as well as the Knight's Cross of the Black Eagle. He also wore the Ottoman Order of Distinction with diamonds over his heart. Michael knew this was a significant award issued exclusively by the Ottoman sultan himself. The field marshal's aura was one of extreme blue confidence. Here was a man who was used to obedience from any and all men in his sight.

James O'Connell sent a very simple telepathic message: *Watch out son. This is a man who is exceptionally bright and exceptionally hostile to what he sees as modern, weak men. He has been called back from retirement to manage the German operations here. He is dangerous.*

The field marshal sat down at von Trier's desk. He looked up from the files on the desk and spent a period staring at both of the O'Connells. After a full minute, he finally said in a deliberate and very Prussian accented High German, "So, these are your two spies, eh Manfred?"

Von Trier nodded. He said, "Yes, Herr Field Marshal."

"What exactly have they done for us so far?"

"Sir, James O'Connell has identified over a dozen Arab officers who were traitors to Ottoman Army based in Damascus. They have been eliminated by the Ottoman *Tash-kila'at Mahsusa.*"

"Effective unit. I helped to create it when I was here in my past mission. Amusing that they simply call it the *special organization*, eh?"

Michael had been gently probing into von der Goltz's mind while standing at attention. He found a very clever man, fluent in multiple languages, and certain of his own views on the world including views that the German Empire needed to revive its martial spirit and cleanse itself from the liberalism that came from the prosperity of Empire. Michael realized his father was correct. This man was exceptionally dangerous.

"And what does this young one do for us?"

"Sir, along with helping his father manage the espionage ring that uncovered the Damascus traitors, Captain O'Connell has conducted two long-range reconnaissance missions. One targeting British spies operating in Carchemish and one targeting Arabs in the Nejd. In both cases, he provided intelligence that was critical to our understanding of the threat to our Ottoman allies."

Von der Goltz nodded. He said to von Trier, "And why do they do this for the Empire. They are both British, no?"

Michael was about to say something when his father used telepathy to say: *DON'T!*

Von Trier said, "Sir, they are Irish. They are an occupied nation of the British Empire."

"So, not traitors, but freedom fighters. Interesting." He looked up again at the O'Connells as if seeing them for the first time. He spoke first to James O'Connell. He addressed him in Persian. "Agha, what do you think of our Turkish allies?"

James O'Connell responded in Persian. "Excellency, the Turkish soldiers are warriors to the bone. They can fight for days without food or water and will kill without pleasure but also without mercy. There are other members of the Ottoman Army who are not Turks who are not to be trusted."

Von der Goltz nodded. "It is as I thought as well." He then turned to Michael. The light from the window caught his glasses in such a way that Michael could not see the Field Marshall's eyes. Instead, there were two silver circles where the eyes should be. Von der Goltz spoke in Arabic, not perfect Arabic but the language used by soldiers and Arab leaders. "What do you think of the Bedouin?"

Michael responded in carefully modulated Arabic. "Excellency, the Arabs are interested only in their desert and their own feuds. They will fight among themselves using the guns that we give them. Their loyalties are with tribe and clan.

They do not see their desert world as land to be owned any more than sailors see the oceans as someplace to own. They see the desert as nothing more than a battleground."

Von der Goltz nodded again. He turned to von Trier and said, "I am satisfied." He stood up and walked stiffly out of the room. Michael noticed that the most relieved person in the room was von Trier.

Once the field marshal was out of the room, the colonel sat down at his desk. He reached over and rang a small bell at this desk. Immediately, an Arab servant came through the main doors. "Yes, effendi?"

"Coffee for three." The servant disappeared for a moment. He reappeared with a small, wheeled cart. On it was a large brass coffee pot with a curved spout, a brass serving tray with a sugar bowl and three glass cups placed inside engraved brass cup holders. The servant poured the first cup for the colonel, added a lump of sugar and a small brass spoon and placed it on the polished desk. He then turned and walked quietly out the door.

Von Trier said, "Please help yourselves, gentlemen and then have a seat."

Michael moved to the cart and assembled the first cup of coffee for his father. He turned and walked to his father who was now seated in a high-backed chair in front of the desk. James nodded to his son as he took the coffee. Michael returned to the cart, made his own cup, took a lump of sugar and placed it inside his left cheek and returned to the open chair next to his father. He waited for the colonel to take the first sip of coffee before he took his own sip. After years in the region, Michael was always prepared for poison served in gracious hospitality.

Von Trier said, "We know you are interested in returning to Ireland and we also know that we have use for two men such as yourselves in Ireland. We hope that you will be as effective in building a revolutionary network in Ireland as you have been in destroying the Arab revolutionaries here in Damascus." Von Trier paused to take another sip of his coffee. Michael stood and poured the colonel more coffee and offered more sugar. Once he was back at his seat, von Trier continued, "We need one more thing for you to accomplish before you are dispatched back to Berlin and then on to Ireland. *Hauptman*, we want you to accomplish a mission which will require you to return to Arabia. Mr. O'Connell, we have a small job for you to do before you depart. That job will be easily accomplished here in Damascus."

Michael and James nodded their assent.

"Now, here is what you need to accomplish. Consider it a quid pro quo for your travel to your home country."

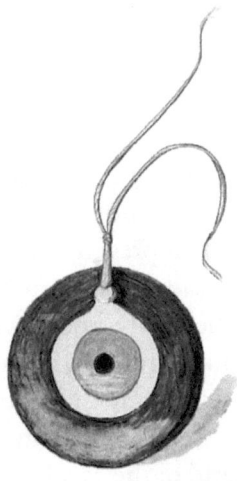

Fighting a Shadow War

Rawalpindi, January 1915

LIEUTENANT COLONEL BURGESS NAISMITH SAT BEHIND A DESK IN THE offices of the Western Command of the Military Intelligence Bureau of the Indian Army. The office was smaller than the one where he served as the master of the Viceroy's College in the mountains north and east of this ancient city. In September, the Western Command had told him it was a temporary move. At that time, no one except Naismith's direct superior Colonel Winslow-Heath expected the war with Germany to last a few weeks. Then the battles on the Western Front staggered to a halt and soon there were trenches from the North Sea to the Alps. And, in November, the Ottoman Caliph declared *jihad* against the allies and the Ottoman Empire entered the war on the side of the Germans and Austro-Hungarian Empire. The government of India and by extension the Indian Army suddenly faced a longer-term threat.

Over afternoon tea, Winslow-Heath turned to Naismith

and said, "We knew all along this was going to be a long fight, eh? Naismith, our work and most especially the work of your people is going to be critical if we intend to keep the Empire intact."

Naismith had already come to the same conclusion. He nodded and said, "Sir, the reality is far more grim than the mandarins in New Delhi and Whitehall presumed."

"That is the problem with our leaders, Naismith. They have never faced shot and shell. They only know war portrayed on maps. And, sadly, I think many of our generals don't understand that this is now a war where technology has overwhelmed intrepidity and dash. The machine gun, barbed wire and artillery have ended the world of the cavalry charge."

Naismith thought for a moment. Both he and Winslow-Heath had served in colonial wars and, as they said in the officers' mess, had "seen the elephant." In his most recent operations with his team of commandos known as the Ravens, he travelled by airship, watched machine guns wipe out a company of Afghan cavalry, and sat in an observing station while an airship bombed a German submarine. Winslow-Heath was right. This was a truly twentieth century war with all the horrors that one might expect from technology gone mad. Still, his own memories of previous wars were hardly without their own terrors. Death on any battlefield was neither honorable nor just. It was simply death. Naismith knew this better than most of his colleagues. He had been close and personal when he killed men. "Sir, along with technology, we face an implacable enemy who is determined to undermine our society from within. The Germans have been working on this effort for years."

"Too right, Naismith. That is why our work is so important. We must stop the Germans before they tear our Empire apart."

The Enigma of Treason

From his office down the hall from Winslow-Heath, Naismith now worked non-stop to build intelligence networks at the far reaches of the authority of the government of India. Networks that he hoped would dull the revolutionary blade that the Germans held to the throat of the Empire. Once Winslow-Heath convinced the Western Command leadership that this would be a long war, Naismith moved a small portion of his library from the College to the military cantonment. Most of the books focused on the numerous cultures and languages of the Raj. Some were memoirs of earlier Raj officers who worked against mutineers, revolutionaries, and bandits. And, some were the works of his adversaries who long ago published their plans. Few in India read them. Naismith was one of the few. If he was asked, Naismith would also admit that his books helped him feel comfortable in his new quarters even if the office still did not feel like his own.

One other thing that Naismith requested to bring with him from the Viceroy's College was his most senior instructor, Marian Sandusky. She had served as his partner in numerous training programs. Before that, she had served the Intelligence Bureau along the Tibetan frontier. Naismith knew that if he was going to be responsible for intelligence operations during wartime, he would absolutely need a deputy he could trust. Marian was that person.

Naismith understood his current mission was nothing like his previous job. Instead of training future intelligence officers to be dispatched to the far reaches of the British Empire, he now directed these same students in a world war of intrigues and treason. Just before the war began, his own work and the work of his students uncovered multiple efforts by the German Empire to undermine the authority of the Empire. A raid on a German compound in Gwadar in Baluchistan just before the war revealed the extent of German efforts to create a revolutionary movement inside India. The records they took from the compound included numerous reports from Berlin focused on this effort. The Germans understood, perhaps far better than the British people, that the wealth and power of the modern United Kingdom came from the economies and manpower of the British colonies and, most especially, India.

Naismith stood up from his desk, took his porcelain teacup and walked over to a map table tucked into the opposite end of his office. Marian looked up from her desk on the opposite side of the room. She said, "Guru Naismith?"

"Marian, come over to the map. We need to consider the nature of the problem." He stood over a map of the world, looking at the small flags that he had placed in strategic locations. "The largest of the flags represents Berlin. As you recall, we received a report last Fall from Elizabeth. She has uncovered letters from Berlin sent across India to various revolutionaries. The letters came from a newly established organization called the Berlin-India Committee. According to reports from Whitehall, this committee was attached to the German General Staff and included Indian exiles who were committed to the destruction of the Raj and to a plan that would establish them as autocrats in charge of India."

"So, it seems the challenges with the revolutionaries are based on a larger German policy, not just a bit of regional action."

"Exactly. This is a small part of a larger German program designed to undermine the entire British Empire. The Whitehall report details the program created and supervised by the well-respected German orientalist, Baron Max von Oppenheim, and his staff at the Intelligence Bureau for the East. Von Oppenheim is a linguist, an archaeologist, and apparently a cunning adversary." Naismith looked up from the map to the bookshelf. "I have always struggled with the German language, but von Oppenheim's two volume travelogue *Vom Mittelmeer zum Persischen Golf* is the work of a committed Arab scholar. And published in 1895 at that! It seems that von Oppenheim visited Constantinople in November 1914 just as the Ottoman caliph declared *jihad* against all infidels controlling the Muslim world — including British India. It is no coincidence."

Naismith ran his hand down the map to Constantinople. "Marian, this flag represents another German expert: Field Marshal Colmar von der Goltz. He understands the Ottoman military better than any European. Better still for the Kaiser, von der Goltz understands and has influence over the seniors of the Ottoman government run by the Committee for Union and Progress. We call them the Young Turks, mostly because they are far younger than the standard Ottoman bureaucrats. They are determined to create a modern Ottoman Empire with few of the shortcomings of the fraying Ottoman bureaucracy. If ever there was a man who was dedicated to the foreign adventures of the German Empire, von der Goltz is that man. A decorated soldier who fought both in Europe and in the German colonies, he solidified German control of the Ottoman Army over a decade ago as the German military advisor in Constantinople. Now that the Ottomans have joined forces with the Germans and the Austro-Hungarian Empire, he is back in Constantinople guiding both Turkish and German forces throughout the Ottoman lands."

Marian nodded, "What little reporting we get from the Sirdar in Khartoum suggests that the Germans are involved in several different revolutionary plots in their areas as well. In the last month we received reporting that Senussi tribals in North Africa might revive their raiding on Western Egypt. Everything about the Senussis' sudden interest in raiding Egypt argues that it is a German plot. More than once, you have told me never to accept coincidence as an explanation."

"Luckily, North Africa is not part of our problem set, Marian. Still, it does argue that the Germans have a strategic plan attacking our entire Empire. We don't yet have such a unified strategy. The British leadership in Whitehall have decided in their wisdom that the government of India will be responsible for the Persian Gulf and Mesopotamia, but the British government in Egypt and Sudan will oversee the Red Sea and the Suez Canal. Arabia remains a buffer zone between the two. Unfortunately, any effort on our part to consolidate the intelligence operations against the Germans in the Middle East will be stymied by the natural competition between the two British commands and their commanders."

Marian interjected, "More the commanders' egos than any strategic reason behind the competition."

"Indeed, but that is the nature of the world we live in. Sadly, the Germans face no such division, and their unity of command makes it far harder for British intelligence officers. Britain had its own experts for the region, but they are not empowered by Whitehall, Cairo, or New Delhi the same way the Germans empowered von Oppenheim and von der Goltz."

Naismith considered his own experience as an Anglo-Indian officer who had faced prejudice and disinterest in his expertise for most of his military career. "There seems to be a hostility inside the British military to expertise and a willingness, actually a pride, in muddling through," he said. "Regional experts were not considered helpful when they argued bold military plans would face the reality of the East."

"Lucky for us that Winslow-Heath is not in that camp."

"Indeed, Marian." Naismith took a sip from his tea and said, "Our agents in Baghdad report that the Germans are establishing iron-fisted control over the region. Between the Germans and the Turkish security services known as the *Tashkila'at Mahsusa*, the distant reaches of our collectors face a danger not seen for decades. Many of the reporting sources developed in Damascus and Baghdad have been arrested and executed."

Marian said, "And Beverly and Jonathan barely made it

out of Baghdad alive. Their last communication said they were alive but on the run heading toward Russian lines near Kars."

"I have reached out to the Bankrofts to help. They are in Baku, or should be shortly. I sent a message to Mary Bankroft for Francis and Mary to help the Mansfields."

"Ciphered telegram?"

Naismith smiled, "To the Bankrofts, yes. To the Mansfields, a more secure method — telepathy."

Marian nodded. While she was adept in some of the mystic arts, she had never achieved Naismith's level of skill. Of course, he had been practicing the arts for years before she was recruited by the service. It made sense that if the Mansfields were on the run, there would be no good method other than telepathy. It was one of the advantages gained by graduates of the Viceroy's College.

Naismith ran his hand across Mesopotamia and into Persia. "The Persian shah accepted years ago that he faced two implacable adversaries: the Russian and the British empires. The Qajar Shah decided to accept his fate and negotiated with both empires to ensure he remained on his throne. The Russians focus their influence on the Caspian Sea and we focus on the oil fields in Bushehr and the Baluch tribesmen who travel back and forth across the border between Persia and India."

Naismith pointed to another flag. "Here we face yet another adventurer: Wilhelm Wassmuss. Our reports identified Wassmuss and two dozen German riders headed back to Persia. Wassmuss is a capable German diplomat and an even more capable spy. He has caused no end of trouble in Bushehr and, if the reporting is accurate, he has authority from the Kaiser himself to create unrest throughout Persia. Persia's neutrality remains crucial to the conflict. After all, it is Persian oil powering the British Navy. Unrest in Persia would panic the Admiralty and that is not something we want in our already full plate of concerns from New Delhi and Whitehall."

Marian looked at a flag far closer to their current location. There was a red flag in Afghanistan. "I thought we resolved the German problem with the raid in Gwadar."

"One of the last reports from Jonathan and Beverly Mansfield was about a German mission to Afghanistan. A young captain, Oskar von Niedermayer, is leading the mission to convince the Emir in Kabul that there are benefits to siding with the Kaiser. Our requests for neutrality are words with little meaning within the intrigues of the Afghan court. German gold and guns will be tempting. Afghan hostility to British India is nearly a hundred years old on the border we now call the Durand Line." Naismith shook his head, "The Durand Line is nothing more than a mapmaker's trick. The Afghans have tribal allies and adversaries on both sides of that line and they still remember Peshawar as the winter home of Afghan kings. The Germans would need very little influence to create a conflict on the border. That conflict might have very little to do with Indian Army operations in the larger world war, but it would be a costly distraction that would bleed away men and material and distract the Indian Army command from the battlefields of Europe and the Middle East."

Marian said, "Honestly, some of our work seems better suited for the Indian police, most specifically, India Special Branch, rather than the Indian Army. Our people are trained in languages and cultures that allowed them to attack the problem at its heart — the Germans and their regional allies. They are not trained to be investigators of young, educated Indian men convinced that the only solution for their future is to side with the Germans and overthrow the British authorities across the Raj."

"Too true, Marian. But long ago, I learned a lesson from the ancient history of Great Britain. That lesson as simple: If you take the King's salt, you fight the King's wars. It means, we fight our battles wherever our masters choose. I have little sympathy for the revolutionaries but I can understand their anger. The police only see them as criminals and there is very little chance that they will make any effort to determine the nature of the German threat. That is our business. We are good at understanding the subtleties of the problem."

Marian nodded. She could imagine that Naismith, as an "Anglo-Indian," faced some of the same prejudices as these young revolutionaries and he could understand their anger. Luckily for the Raj, Naismith clearly did not accept their willingness to side with an enemy who was at war with British soldiers and sailors around the world.

Naismith said, "It is a complex problem and one we must solve. The raid on the German compound in Gwadar proved to me the only way to defeat this German effort is to go to the source. The only way to win is through offensive action. Our operations must focus on attacking the enemy plots at their heart. That means attacking the German and Ottoman headquarters for these subversive operations. It means we need to recall the Ravens and begin planning a new strategy. I'm not entirely certain that Winslow-Heath will agree and I am certain the mandarins in New Delhi will hate the idea, but it is the only way to fight this shadow war."

As he walked back to his desk, he said, "One bit of good news. I have recalled Elizabeth from Bombay. I need her to know the challenges we are facing and her role in the effort. She will be the first of the Ravens to return."

Marian smiled, "I look forward to seeing her. Her reports are excellent and she has matured more quickly than I expected."

"She faces her own demons, Marian. I need you to help her with that battle."

Marian was surprised at Naismith's comment. She had no

idea what demons Elizabeth might have. She said, "Guru, I am absolutely here to help."

When Naismith lowered the gas lamp in his quarters that evening, he intended to use a yoga breathing technique to relax and leave the problems of the day behind before he retired to his bed. As he started counting breaths as a relaxation technique, a voice thundered into his head: *So, human. Your world is turning to ashes. Do you honestly think there is any way you can prevent the destruction? Do you think there are ways to prevent the end of the world as you know it?*

Naismith shook his head to drive the voice out. He knew precisely where the voice was coming from and who it was. He thought: *Chodak. Why do you think there is no hope? Why do you still bother me when I killed you years ago?*

Human, if you think the end of my physical body was the end of my existence, you are even more of a child than I thought. The wheel of reincarnation spins and powerful minds come back to your world from the higher plane.

Naismith allowed himself to ponder, for a second, whether Chodak was simply a creation of his own mind. Chodak responded to that thought. The voice echoed in his head: *You really doubt my existence, human? There are those you have trained who not only accept my existence but are willing to bow to my guidance.*

At that point, Naismith could feel his astral presence pulled from his body. Chodak dragged him away from his office, from Rawalpindi, from anything he understood to be the real world. He looked around to see nothing but blue-grey shadows and mist. Facing him was a grinning white skull. Chodak's voice came from the skull: *Look about you, human. Do you see anything that suggests this is somehow a creation of your own mind? I think not. It terrifies you, no? And now, look down on the thousands of men who are killing each other for no reason other than their kings and emperors and tsars say they must do so. It is in this chaos that I and my fellow demons thrive. Do you surrender to the chaos, human? Or, will you still fight me? Feel free to use your logic and your science to explain this world.*

Naismith was distressed by his condition. He seemed to be floating in this miasma of the astral plane. He could not identify up or down, right or left. The lack of focus created nausea. The only reference point was the white skull in front of him. Naismith turned his mental energy inward and concentrated on his *chi*, his life force. He closed off all senses and concentrated. He focused on his *chi* which he imagined as a candle flame. The flame was weak and sputtered at first, but eventually grew in strength. Chodak's voice disappeared. The mist and shadows disappeared. His bedroom reappeared. He sat in a cold sweat. He still wondered if he was going mad or if the astral plane his gurus described really was inhabited by demons as well as gods of the mountains. It took him a half hour of deep meditation to clear his mind of the terrors inflicted in the previous few minutes.

Eventually, Naismith stood up and stretched. There would be little chance for sleep tonight. He turned to the small gas burner in his room and lighted it. A pot of green tea would help him concentrate. There was a worldwide conspiracy, and he must counter that conspiracy with a small number of well-trained agents operating in pairs or as singletons across most of southwestern Asia. A small number by any measure, but certainly agents with special skills. That might make all the difference in the world. No matter what Chodak might say, these were men and women of honor and determination. Years of facing the Russian threat to the Raj taught Naismith that he had to focus his resources on projects that could be accomplished rather than wasting resources on projects that had a low chance of success. Now that the Empire was at war, the long-term efforts that had been standard practice for the Intelligence Bureau were no longer appropriate. It would take some thought and he didn't have a great deal of time. His direct supervisor, Colonel Winslow-Heath, expected a plan and he expected it soon. If he could just keep Chodak at bay for some time, he might just be able to design a plan.

War in the Nejd

Central Arabia, January 1915

MICHAEL WAS NEVER COMFORTABLE WITH BEDOUIN TRIBESMEN OF THE Arabian desert. Their leaders were aged fighters who had cut more throats than Michael had sliced loaves of bread. They considered treachery simply one of the many ways to profit. Their world was harsh. Too little water and almost no grazing land for their sheep, camels, and horses. They fought their cousins and other tribes over the rare oases that dotted the landscape. These oases were the only green places in seemingly endless stretches of brown and grey. For their amusement and for plunder, the tribal leaders periodically raided the villages that stretched along the fringes of the desert. Young men Michael's age were considered infants until they had been bloodied in some raid or died trying. Arab guides often decided there was greater profit in killing their travelers rather than taking them to their planned destination. It meant that he could never relax. He had to maintain some control over their minds to ensure they were convinced it was in their own interest to take him and his German companions to the camp of the Rashidis. That focus was exhausting.

This was day ten of their caravan into the desert. The trip from Damascus to Baghdad was manageable, but as they headed south into the desert on camels, Michael knew from previous experience that it would be a very difficult and painful journey. While summers were beastly hot, desert winters were still warm in the daytime and exceptionally cold at night. The sun was so bright that he had to squint to see anything during their travels, and by sunset he was nearly blind. Then there was the sand of the desert: A mix of powdered alkali that invaded everything, and pebbles that found their way between boots and feet. Only the camels seemed unbothered. At sundown each day, Michael, his two German Army companions and their five Bedouin guides would stop, first for the Arabs to pray and then to make camp.

As soon as the sun dropped below the horizon, the temperature dropped and meals were eaten by a fire made from camel dung and what few twigs could be gathered. After the meal, Michael retreated to the black tent that served all three of the foreigners while the Arabs watched the stars and slept near the fire. If Michael could share confidences with anyone, he would have spent day after day complaining about the conditions and his fate. But, Michael was traveling with a pair of young Prussian hussars who would not want to share his complaints. In the best of times, Prussians barely tolerated other Germans and viewed anyone other than Germans as subhuman. This was not the best of times. Michael realized that the only saving grace for him was they had received orders directly from Colonel von Trier to support this foreign ally. They understood they had to succeed on this mission or face the consequences.

Based on the best guess of his Arab guides, this was their last night alone. Sometime tomorrow, they would be in the camp of the Rashidis. Michael's job was simple. He needed to find a way to kill a British intelligence officer named William Shakespear. When von Trier told him to eliminate Shakespear, Michael was sure that he had misunderstood his nominal supervisor. It took some time to understand that this was not the British playwright and poet who had been dead for centuries. It was a well-trained, highly successful British intelligence officer, Arabist and explorer. And the Germans wanted him dead.

In the last ten years, Shakespear had traveled throughout the Persian Gulf and established himself as the senior British envoy to the Kuwaiti sheikh. The sheikh had a very long and very productive relationship with one of the most senior tribal leaders in the Nejd, Abdul Aziz Ibn Saud. Ibn Saud's tribal authority was based on his reputation for raiding skills as well as building alliances among the tribes in the central desert of Arabia. He was also the leader of a strict sect in Islam known by the name of their original, 18th century founder, Mohammed Ibn Wahhab. The Wahhabis were profoundly conservative in their interpretation of Islam and more than willing to fight any Muslims who they determined to be "infidels" because of less conservative practices. The mix of charismatic leadership and exceptionally loyal fighters operating in Arabia raised real concerns among the regional Ottoman pashas. When they received word the leader of this ruthless fighting force regularly hosted a British advisor, the Ottoman pashas were terrified. They could imagine well-armed zealots raiding cities throughout Arabia and even into Turkey proper.

Von Trier was less terrified of any group of Bedouin raiders. He said to Michael, "The Bedouin are always revolting. That is their nature. However, we simply can't have the pashas fretting over something that is of no importance when we face the threat of a British army attacking Mesopotamia and another one waiting on the west of the Suez ready to attack Palestine at any time. We need them to concentrate on fighting the British. So, *Hauptman* O'Connell, your job is to end this relationship between Ibn Saud and Shakespear. I need you to end it permanently."

The challenge was not as difficult as it might seem in Damascus. Michael spent time the previous year with the Rashidi tribe, sworn enemies of the Ibn Saud. On that trip, he was part of a small training team that delivered modern rifles to the Rashidis and spent time with the sons of the tribal leaders. The Rashidis would remember that level of support from the German Empire. They understood the value of rifles. It shouldn't be that hard to encourage them to fight Ibn Saud. If they did, Michael was confident that he could find a way to eliminate this Englishman. If only von Trier had been willing to explain the entire mission to Michael's two companions. Von Trier said, "O'Connell, your mission will be unacceptable to the average Prussian officer. They have no problem imagining a battle where a hundred, perhaps even a thousand soldiers would die in one hour or one day. They would consider the murder of one man to avoid that battle simply not proper. They will not understand that in this new world, any opportunity to save lives will be essential because we can expect thousands, even tens of thousands, to die even when we do our best. I will order them to travel with you. I will not be able to tell them why. You will have to manufacture a credible reason for your travel." Michael had saluted and accepted the challenge.

Michael's colleagues came into the tent after a final check of the camels. Michael was sitting against his camel saddle, writing notes in his journal by candlelight. Lieutenant August von Lettow sat down against his own horse saddle and began his end-of-the-day personal maintenance. Von Lettow was a proper Prussian Hussar officer who had made every effort over the last six days to keep his uniform clean and his boots polished. Michael elicited from von Lettow that he was from a family of officers in the Imperial Army and a distant cousin was the commander of German forces in East Africa. He proudly pointed to his cousin's successes against the British and he hoped to join his cousin in East Africa after this mission. Michael had no idea what was happening in Africa and couldn't care less about what happened to this Prussian lieutenant after their mission was completed. But, he was pleased to see the lieutenant spent the greatest amount of time cleaning his Luger P08 and his Mauser K98A carbine. There was no guarantee that their travels would be without danger. In fact, Michael was nearly certain that his mission would take them directly into the line of fire someplace in the Nejd.

Michael's other German companion followed the lieutenant into the tent. Hans Freihart, a thirty-two-year-old senior sergeant, settled against his own saddle, lit a candle and started cleaning his K98A. After a thorough cleaning, he opened the same book he had been reading since they started their journey. During a previous conversation, Michael learned that Friehart was the second son of a farming family near Linz. The family was wealthy enough that both sons and even Friehart's sister received a formal education. The sergeant knew early on that his elder brother would inherit the farm. His options were to join the priesthood like his uncle or join the army. He chose the Imperial Army. He was good with horses and with mathematics and had hoped to serve in the Imperial horse-drawn artillery, based on the stories his father had told him of his experiences in the Franco-Prussian war. Instead, he was assigned as a dispatch rider for the German General Staff. It was while on the staff that von Trier identified him as a man of education. He brought Freihart with him in 1912 when he was assigned to the Imperial Army support team to the Ottoman Empire. Freihart was quiet, diligent, and committed to whatever job he had at the time.

When Michael asked him at the beginning of the trip what he was reading, Freihart seemed puzzled. Michael read his mind. He wondered why an officer would care what he was reading? Eventually, he admitted that he was interested in the great German philosophers and he was reading Friedrich Nietzsche. "Sir, much of what he says I do not understand. My father is a farmer and my uncle is a priest. What I can understand very well is Herr Nietzsche's view that a man must accept his fate, good and bad and that it is mostly hardship that forges character. That much I have seen in life, and it is good to read something that tells me I am not so wrong about life."

At that point, Michael realized that Freihart was more than a simple soldier. He would be a good ally in the worst of times and an amusing colleague in less serious times. While he was less interested in the goals of young lieutenant Lettow, he was pleased that the lieutenant did not appear to be bothered by the fact that his commander for this trip was neither royalty nor German. For the first time in his young life, Michael felt as if he had colleagues with whom he could share wishes and desires. Of course, up to a point. After all, he knew very well that his life would never be simple. He intended to use his skills to free Ireland from the British. Unlike Lettow and Friehart, Michael was fighting for a country he had never seen. For him, Ireland was more of a dream than a country. A dream where he and his father would fight for freedom from Britain. His loyalty to his German masters was nothing like the loyalty that his two colleagues felt for their homeland.

Just before Michael snuffed out his candle, Lettow asked, "Sir, is our mission important? I understand that our mission is secret, but I would like to know that our mission is important."

Michael thought for a moment. Important? Well, it was

certainly important to him. Would the success of the mission have any impact on this worldwide conflict? Or, even this theatre of operations? He had no idea. He decided the young lieutenant needed to believe it was important, so he told him so. He used his reasonable German language skills and his well-practiced mesmerism voice on both of his tent mates. "Our mission was important enough that we were dispatched by Colonel von Trier and, before I received my orders, I was interviewed by Field Marshal von der Goltz. You were selected to support the mission based on Colonel von Trier's personal assessment of your skills and your courage. I think that says much about the importance of our mission. More than that, I cannot say."

Both of his tent mates looked convinced. Now, all they had to do was find the Rashidis tomorrow and start a fight between that tribe and Ibn al-Saud's people. Based on what little intelligence von Trier had, that would be the easy part. Finding and killing Shakespear would be a different story. If they were lucky, they would succeed and return to Damascus. Lettow would receive praise and perhaps a medal. Friehart could return to serving as a courier for von Trier. And, Michael and his father would go to Ireland. If not, then it really didn't matter what von Trier promised.

As Michael drifted off to sleep, a voice reached into his dreams: *Michael, do you know that it may be necessary to kill the Britisher yourself?*

Michael's dream-self answered, *Of course. Anything to make sure father and I end up in Ireland.*

Anything, Michael?

Anything. We need to return to Ireland.

And then, Michael? Will you kill in Ireland if you need to?

Michael's dream-self nodded. *Yes.*

In the astral plane, Chodak smiled.

47

They arrived at midday. The war camp of the Rashidis was a mass of tents in a wadi in the desert. Their guides took them to a black tent at the outer ring of tents set up specifically for the German visitors. Michael knew that they would have to wait in this tent until invited for an audience with the tribal leaders and his commanders. Inside the tent was a large brown and black striped carpet surrounded by four large, rough woven pillows. Against the tent walls were three red-and-black carpets, three rolled wool blankets and three more pillows. In short order, their Arab guides brought in their saddles and small traveling bags. Michael knew that the guides would feed and water their horses as befitting guests of the sheikh.

As they settled into the tent, Michael explained to his traveling companions. "Gentlemen, we are now in the world of the Arab Bedouin. Their rules are strict and punishment is both harsh and immediate. Hospitality is central to the desert culture and we can expect to be treated well so long as we respect their rules and know our place. Please follow my lead when we finally do meet the leaders. I have worked with them before and we have the advantage of our history of providing modern rifles and ammunition to the Rashidis. That said, we are absolutely foreigners and, more importantly, infidels so the best we can hope for is a single, formal audience. After that, we will be allowed to travel somewhere inside the war party as it approaches the upcoming battle with the tribesmen of al-Saud. We may be able to help but I suspect our advice will be ignored."

Lettow asked, "Sir, then why are we here?"

"Lieutenant, we are here because Colonel von Trier ordered us here to observe this battle and, as best we can, to ensure the Rashidis do not decide at the last minute to ally themselves with the British. Ibn al-Saud has decided to take English gold and that has made our Ottoman allies nervous. We do our part to convince the Rashidis that they need to stay on the Ottoman side. We can be certain that the Rashidi tribal leaders are currently negotiating with the al-Saud leaders to determine if there is more profit in partnership than in war."

Michael was not surprised that Friehart asked a more interesting question. "Sir, are these tribesmen really allied to anyone except themselves?"

"Excellent question! We really don't care if these Arabs choose to fight themselves forever. We just don't want them using our guns or English guns against our Ottoman allies. I have brought with me gold from our command. I just hope it is enough gold to keep the Rashidis on side."

Lettow said, "So, we are here to observe and report."

"Precisely, Lieutenant. And, if allowed to do so, to make sure the Rashidis win this battle. Now, I recommend you rest. If we do get an audience with the tribal leaders, it is almost certain to be sometime in the middle of the night. We need to keep watch, but we also need to rest. Friehart, you will take the first watch. Lieutenant, you will take second watch and I will take the night watch. Clear?"

Michael's colleagues nodded. As he finished speaking, an Arab boy came into the tent carrying a brass tray with dates, flat bread and tea. He placed it on the rough woven carpet, keeping his eyes focused on the ground. He backed away, facing the foreigners until he left the tent. Michael was not certain this was a sign of honor or a concern on the part of the young man that the three foreigners might kill him and eat him. Certainly, the young man's aura of yellow-orange argued the latter. Michael walked over to the tray and took a handful of dates, poured himself some tea and sat back down. He said, "Enjoy the dates. It is likely all you will be served for some time."

They were invited to the tribal leader's meeting tent early in the morning the next day. It was pitch dark when the young man came to the tent. After putting on their uniforms, they followed him out into the darkness. The only light was from the crescent moon. Michael took a look at the radium dial of his large pocket watch. 0215hrs. It was as he expected. The Rashidi leadership had enjoyed their dinner and held a long debate about their upcoming fight with the Nejdi tribals. Somewhere in that debate, they had raised the question of whether they wanted the infidels to observe or simply stay in their tent awaiting the results of the fight over the "lake" of Jarrab. Michael had spent some of the evening using his illusory body to listen to the discussion. He knew the battle plan and he knew the level of perfidy that would make it possible for the Shammar to win on the morrow. He used a small bit of mesmerism to convince the tribal leader Abdul Aziz al-Rashidi that it would be best if the infidels were able to see their success. So, as they walked across the sand, Michael already knew the end result of the discussion even if he didn't know how long or involved the debate would be. Before they left, he warned both Lettow and Friehart that they had to appear interested even though they would be completely witless of what these Arab leaders were saying. Michael concluded by saying, "Just trust me. We will be in the fight tomorrow."

At dawn, they were indeed in the fight. Michael was surprised how quickly the tribal leaders acknowledged the help from the Germans. He expected endless cups of tea and conversation with the taciturn elders. Instead, the tribals received them politely but briefly. Michael was relieved. While he was used to the back and forth as Bedouin established consensus, he was concerned that his two German colleagues would be impatient and try to interject something into the conversation. They were in the main tent for no more than the absolutely required three cups of bitter, green coffee and one cup of tea. Michael made the obligatory acknowledgement of the courage and honor of the Rashidis and the tribal leaders made a similar, insincere acknowledgement of the importance of German Mausers and German gold. Michael apologized that he had no more rifles, but he did say that he had additional funds for his Rashidi friends. At that point, the Rashidi elders looked to Abdul Aziz al-Rashidi. He nodded and said, "We look forward to your attendance as we defeat the Nejdis. We only ask that you wear our clothes. We do not wish our people or our enemies to think we must have foreigners to help us fight."

Michael bowed and said in his most formal Arabic, "It is most proper. We shall dress accordingly and stay to the rear. We ask only to enjoy the pleasure of your victory." The elders nodded and Michael and his two colleagues were dismissed.

One of the servants of the elders followed them back to their tent and picked up the two heavy sacks of German minted gold coins. After the exchange, Lettow asked, "Sir, what just happened?"

Michael smiled. "We were just saved from hours of negotiation and endless cups of tea. We will be with the Rashidis tomorrow. Our only limitation is that we must wear thobes and gudras rather than our uniforms. The Rashidi leadership does not want to acknowledge our role and, honestly, I know that both Colonel von Trier and Field Marshal von der Goltz could care less what uniform we wear so long as the tribal leaders take our gold and our guns."

Lettow was astonished. "You have met the field marshal?"

Michael decided to play up the connection to ensure Lettow's obedience on the battlefield. "Lettow, he was the one who created this mission and who picked our team. We are serving as his eyes and ears."

Friehart said, "I have not worn the Arab dress before. Is it uncomfortable?"

"Not at all, Friehart. And, better still, it will make us invisible to the Nejdi's riflemen. We will be just three more Arab men. Far better for us to travel unobserved in the ranks so that we can report back to the colonel, no? Now, try to get another hour or two of sleep. It is going to be a long day once we mount up."

The horizon was just turning from black to grey when they dressed in Arab garb and mounted their camels. The Rashidi camels were lined up ten deep and thirty across, banners waving in the wind. Another, smaller group of horse cavalry were to the left flank. To the right flank were another set of riflemen mounted on camels. They would move to a small set of hills overlooking the valley floor where the fight would take place. Michael could see that the order of the day was sabers versus sabers on the dry lake bed with German Mausers serving as the primary fire support. While Michael generally did not fall prey to whimsy, he had to admit watching the Rashidis advance as the day began reminded him of the stories he heard as a young man both from his father and his ayha in India. His father told him of the early Irish rebellions and his ayha told him of Moghul conquests. In both cases, the stories always started with a dawn ride into battle. Now, he was in the middle of a similar story, but this time, it was his story.

Just before they dressed and left their tent, Michael used his illusory body to observe the same sort of formation taking place on the opposite side of the Jarrab dry lake bed. The Nejdis were ready for the same fight. Michael was amused as he watched William Shakepear leave the tent of Abdul Aziz Ibn Saud dressed in British Army khaki and a cork helmet known in India as a topi. As he watched, Michael thought: "This one is going to be easy to find and even easier to kill."

As his illusory body wandered among the Nejdi forces, he felt more than heard the presence of disloyal conversations among the Nejdis. He focused his attention as he floated among the various Arab tribals. Finally, he identified the center of the tensions. An Ajman tribal leader named Dhaydan Bin Hithlain. Michael noted this Dhaydan was frustrated that Ibn Saud treated him as a subordinate rather than a tribal equal. He was also less than pleased with the strict nature of the Hanbali religious rules that Ibn Saud and his followers insisted on in their camp. Michael reached deep into the mind of Dhaydan. He said, "These Nejdis have no support and they will not win today. The Shammar are supported by the Ottomans and have German Mausers. The al Rashidis will welcome an alliance and will respect the Ajman. Who will you choose to support?"

The Ajman chief stood in front of his tent looked out over the hillsides that would soon become the battlefield. He thought for a moment about what the voice in his head just said. Was it a premonition? Was he receiving advice from some djinn who knew the future? Could he ignore this voice? He knew even if the Nejdis won the battle the Ajman would receive no booty. Perhaps if he switched sides, the Ajman would profit. As Michael listened to the inner workings of the Ajman tribal leader, he added one more sentence. "The Shammar have German gold. They will be grateful for any allies on this day."

With that last poison pill placed inside the Ajman's head, Michael left the Nejdi camp and returned to his resting body in the black tent. An hour later when they rode into the sunrise, Michael was certain of the Shammar victory and certain that his mission would be a success. It only took a moment and a lucky shot. And, if luck was not possible, then he would make the shot himself.

Michael and his German colleagues pulled their camels up to a ridge line overlooking the lake bed. On the ridge were two dozen Shammar riflemen, each armed with a German Mauser. Michael turned to Lettow and Friehart. "Gentlemen, if you would like to assist our Arab allies, I think they would appreciate it. However, I think you will find they are perfectly good riflemen. Their only problems might be working the Mauser internal magazine. You won't need Arabic to help them with that. I will be walking the line offering my own small assistance. If you need an interpreter, please let me know."

With that, Michael crawled up to the edge of the ridge and pulled out a brass field telescope. He began to scan the opposite side. He smiled as he saw Shakespear standing behind the Nejdi riflemen. The British khaki stood out against the grey mix of sand and stone and, unlike his Nejdi riflemen, Shakespear was standing. Visible to anyone who might want to take a shot.

The Shammar were under orders to hold their fire until they saw their leaders ride into the lake bed and attack. Michael considered this Arabic chivalry to be nonsense, but he reminded himself that he was an observer, a guest of the sheikhs. Their way of fighting was simply their way. He turned and watched as the Shammar raised their mix of white and black flags and charged into the lake bed. On the opposite side of the lake bed, he watched as the Nejdi's raised their green flags and charged as well. Now was the time for the riflemen to do their duty.

Michael spoke in the rough Arabic of the streets. He said, "Our sheikhs will kill the Nejdis with blades, we need to kill their riflemen. Look over there!" He pointed to the far ridge line, a good two hundred yards away. The Mausers could do the distance. He wasn't certain that the Arabs could. That was until he watched the Shammar riflemen begin to pick off their Nejdi counterparts, one by one. Michael said, "Look!

They have an infidel with them. Kill the infidel!" Half of the riflemen fired at once. Michael watched through the telescope as Shakespear went down, hit by multiple rounds from the Mausers. Michael could only think: Mission accomplished.

Lettow had his own telescope focused on the battle between the two camel troops. He seemed hypnotized by the swirling dust and shining blades. He turned to Michael and said, "Sir, look. It appears one of the Nejdis' allies have switched sides! Look, horsemen coming from behind the Nejdis and attacking them from the rear."

Michael nodded. He tried to stay calm as he watched the battle unfold. He noticed Lettow begin to stand so that he could see the fight. Michael said, "Stay down!" He was about to add, "you fool." But it was too late. Two rounds from the Nejdi riflemen hit the young lieutenant. Once in the chest and once in the head. He died as he collapsed in the sand.

Michael looked over at Friehart as he crawled to Lettow's body. He shook his head. Michael said, "He died a soldier. We will be certain that his family knows that."

Friehart said, "It is the best one can hope for in this life. A warrior's death."

Michael thought to himself that Friehart and Lettow were living in a different century. He had yet to see any honor in violent death. He also knew that he was a long way from home with only Friehart to help him get back to Damascus. He used his best mesmerism voice to soothe the sergeant. "That is so, Friehart. We have played a role in today's victory and Lettow's family will know that his role was greater than ours."

Friehart nodded. His eyes were slightly glazed, the sign of the waking dream. He said, "He controlled this fighting force and died just as we were victorious."

"Exactly."

Michael noticed the gunfire had slowed. He peeked above the ridge to see the Nejdis in retreat. The Nejdi riflemen were on foot. They would not survive the onslaught from the Shammar and the Ajman cavalry. Somewhere in the mix would be Shakespear's dead body dressed in British khaki. Another soldier who thought there was such a thing as an honurable death for king or country. Michael knew otherwise.

In the Shammar encampment that night, there was celebration and dancing by firelight. Captured Nejdi rifles were fired into the sky, swords flashed as young men relived their first encounter with death. Older men sat together and plotted their next moves. Michael and Friehart sat alone watching the Arabs. Just before sunset, they had dressed Lettow in his German uniform, wrapped him in a shawl that he wore on the battlefield and buried him with the Shammar dead. There was no way to maintain Lettow's body on the long ride back to Damascus. They marked his grave with his sword. Abdul Aziz al-Rashidi spoke to his men warning them that any man who took that sword faced the anger of the Shammar as well as the powerful djinns of the infidels.

As they watched the celebrations, the tribal chief walked over to Michael and acknowledged the importance of the German Mausers in the battle. Michael responded by thanking the tribal chief and crediting the victory to the bravery of the Shammar tribesmen. Michael continued that he would pass on the story of that bravery to his leaders in Damascus. He watched as al-Rashidi's aura turned a bright blue. He took the praise as absolutely his due, but he still valued the flattery from this German envoy.

A young man walked up to al-Rashidi while he was talking to Michael. He whispered in the tribal chief's ear and handed him a canvas bag. The tribal chief smiled for the first time Michael could remember. It did not transform the chief's face, but simply exaggerated the wolf-like demeanor of the man. In the firelight, his dark skin stood out against the white robes he had donned for the celebration. As he handed the bag to Michael, Al-Rashidi spoke in his most formal Arabic. "We have a special gift for our Ottoman contacts in Damascus. Will you carry it to them for us? We need a trusted messenger and I have no men to spare if we are going to continue to raid the Nejdi encampments."

Michael accepted the bag with as much grace as possible. It was very heavy. The tribal chief smiled and said, "Please look into the bag. It is most important you know what you are carrying."

Michael looked into the bag to see the severed head of William Shakespear still wearing his British Army sun helmet. He heard the full-throated laughter of the tribal leader and his entourage who had all watched to see Michael's reaction.

Part Two

Unconventional War

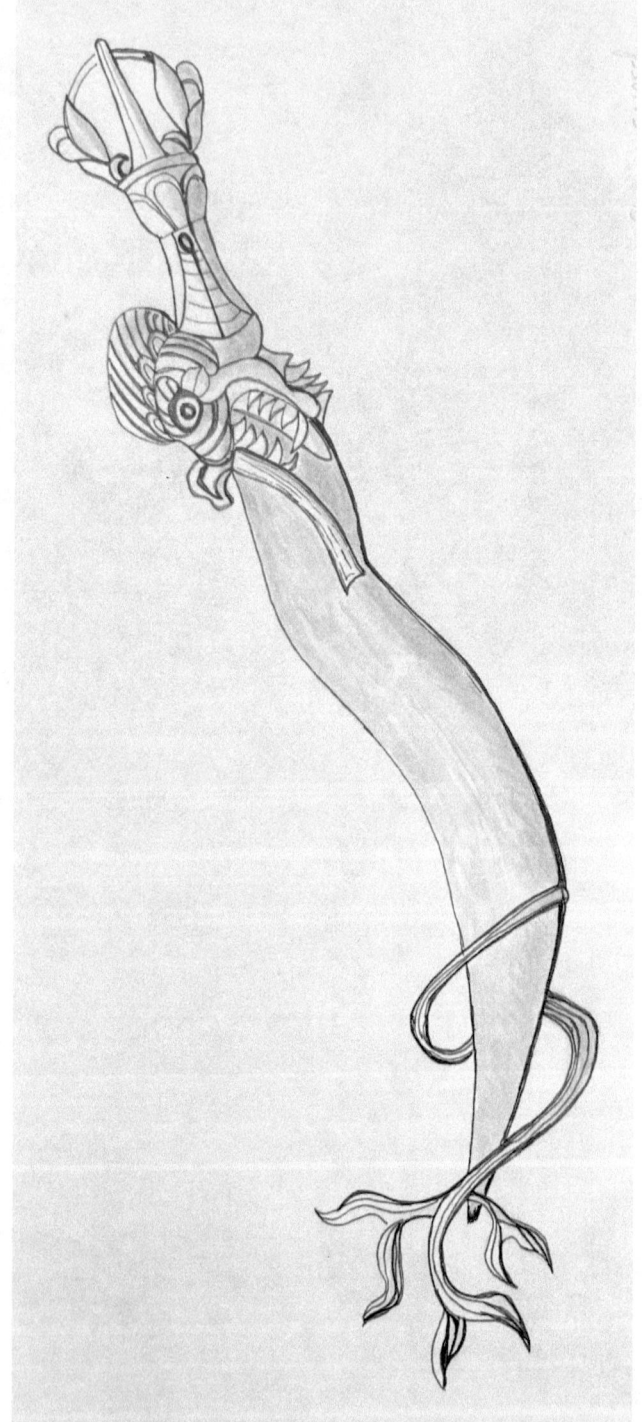

Search and Rescue

Baku, Russia, January 1915

BEKTASHI PADDED AROUND THE SMALL APARTMENT PREPARING THE FIRES AND starting the water boiling for tea and for his own coffee. January in this port city was cold, at least as cold as Istanbul. Bektashi thought: "At least we are no longer traveling on horseback."

The apartment might be small, but it was well furnished and well stocked. Francis Bey explained that this was a guest house maintained by his service to ensure there were always places for travelers in need of a room. Based on his time with the Bankrofts, he knew that the "service" his master identified was a secret service and the travelers who used this apartment were either secret agents on a mission or secret agents on the run. It mattered little to Bektashi. He had good employers, they treated him like a member of the family and he would fight with them and, if needed, die with them.

"Bektashi Bey, is the tea ready?" Mary Bankroft's voice echoed from the single bedroom in the apartment.

"One minute, madam. Soon coming."

"And coffee?"

For as long as he worked for the Bankrofts, Bektashi had yet to get used to how silent his master was. Francis Bankroft was at his shoulder. The man was like a djinn. One minute he is one place and, the next, someplace entirely different. Bektashi understood that's what made Francis Bankroft such a good agent. It still made him nervous. "Yes, master. Coffee is cooking in the pot."

Francis Bankroft was completely dressed. He had just come in from the street. A long wool coat and a karakul hat made him look like the locals, though Bektashi was certain few locals were as tall or as strong as his master. He also knew that under that long coat were various weapons that Francis Bey carried with him. "Master, do you need my help with your coat and hat?"

Francis smiled. "Bektashi, focus on tea for madam. I will worry about my kit and my coffee."

Bektashi nodded and prepared the small tea tray. He carried the tray into the room expecting to find Mary Bankroft in bed under several layers of quilts. Instead, he found her dressed and sitting in a chair staring at a candle on a table. If they were not djinns, at the very least the Bankrofts were Sufis. Bektashi was certain of that.

He placed the tea tray down on the bed and walked out. On his way out, he bumped into Francis Bankroft. In his left hand was a small coffee cup. Bankroft put a forefinger of his right hand to his lips to emphasize they needed to be silent. Bektashi nodded and disappeared.

Francis sat down in a wooden chair across from his wife. He pulled out his large, hunter pocket watch. It was just after nine in the morning. He was never sure if Mary used the morning to communicate telepathically with their daughter Elizabeth or with their former guru, Burgess Naismith.

Either way, telepathy required a degree of concentration that he acknowledged he never mastered.

"You just need to practice, dear."

"Reading my mind again as well as working in the astral plane, Mary?"

"Almost impossible not to read your impatience when I see you holding your watch and drinking coffee. And, let's accept the fact that telepathy is the only way we can communicate safely in Baku where we do not know friend from foe."

Francis nodded. Since they left Odessa, they had been on their own working through bandit country in the Caucasus and now in a city filed with criminals, mercenaries, and spies. Baku might be a cosmopolitan city from oil wealth, but that same wealth meant there were enemies around every corner. He said, "Messages from our masters or from our daughter?"

"Neither. You already know our mission based from the coded telegram from Naismith that arrived yesterday. He wants us to find two of our colleagues who are on the run from the Turks." She watched as Francis focused. The offer of action was always to his liking.

"When we decoded that message, it seemed vague to the point of useless," he said. "Where are they and how do we find them? Are the Turks in hot pursuit or can we plan to simply gather them up and bring them to this little safehouse on the Caspian?"

"If you will give me a moment to gather my thoughts and have a cup of Bektashi's tea, I will tell you. In the meantime, anything to report on the streets of Baku?"

Francis walked over to the bed, poured tea into a glass cup, dropped a single sugar cube into the cup and stirred it with a spoon on the tray. He handed his wife the tea and kissed her on the forehead. He walked back across the room and sat down before he started his report.

"Agent N21 reported that the German propaganda is working. There are dock workers who are considering how they should join the *jihad* against the British and Russian infidels. It doesn't help that we haven't had a strong presence here for two years. The network is still in place, but it needs minding. We can keep it running, but it needs a permanent presence. N16 said that the Turks have sent at least two spies to Baku to find us. Who knew they even cared?"

"Francis, my dear. You forget the small bit of harm we did to the Turks in Istanbul. They will not forget that we killed the men sent to kill us. It was both embarrassing and annoying for them. They could have cared less about the assassins. It was just the principle. Their special service succeeds as much due to reputation for omniscience as to their actual ruthless operations."

Francis thought about their last days in Istanbul. They fought assassins in their own house while hosting their colleague, Gertrude Bell. It was an ugly fight but one where there was never any doubt of the result. Francis, Mary, Elizabeth, Gertrude Bell and Bektashi all ended the lives of paid assassins. Francis realized those deaths would have bruised some egos inside the Sublime Porte. He nodded and said, "I will make sure Bektashi is on guard."

Mary laughed. "Dear, Bektashi is always on guard."

"Too true. I reached out to one of Sasha's counterparts this morning. He offered the necessary assistance for our return to the mountains." Francis took a sip from his coffee before it grew cold. "Now, tell me what details you have on our two colleagues."

"They are Alexander and Beverly Mansfield. Graduated after us but before Elizabeth. Both are Ravens. They were working with local Armenians in Eastern Anatolia reporting on the operations of the Ottoman Third Army when their operation was compromised. They have been hunted for nearly two months while the Ottoman and Russian armies have been fighting in the mountains east of Koprukoy. They skirted the fighting by heading toward the Black Sea. At that point, they came upon the start of an operation by the *Tashkilat Mahsusa* focusing on the Kurdish and Armenian populations. The Ottoman secret police are convinced the Armenians and the Kurds are loyal to the Tsar and not to the caliph and the CUP."

Francis interjected, "And when have any of these mountain folk ever been loyal to the Sublime Porte or St. Petersburg?"

Mary smiled and gently admonished her husband. "Are you going to let me finish?"

"My apologies, dear."

Mary continued, "The Mansfields are now four days' ride southeast of Baku. I have been in telepathic contact with Beverly. Our mission is to find them and bring them here. As we know from Winslow-Heath, once we accomplish that mission, we are supposed to all move into Persia. There is a German agent provocateur named Wassmuss that we are to find and capture."

"So, a rescue mission to find a pair of agents on the run. We find them, bring them to safety and then find a German agent in Persia and capture him. Easy enough, no?"

"Sarcasm does you no favors, dear. According to Winslow-Heath, we are the only agents in the area."

"You seem well ahead of me with your telepathic skills."

Mary smiled and offered, "You have other skills, dear."

"Well, I had best start using those other skills. I will let Bektashi know to prepare for another Caucasian adventure."

"I told him an hour ago."

"Really? So, what do you need me to do?"

"Bring breakfast and Bektashi. I have a plan."

AFTER BREAKFAST, MARY OFFERED HER IDEAS. NOT EXACTLY A PLAN, MORE like a general outline of the situation. Mary started by saying, "Our first mission is to find the Mansfields. We know in general where they are and will use some of our established agents to gain further … clarity."

Francis realized that Mary was not about to reveal to Bektashi that she intended to use her telepathic skills and, perhaps, even her ability to project her mind into the astral plane. Another skill she shared with their daughter: the projection known as the illusory body. Even Francis had trouble imagining how she did these things. Better to simply tell Bektashi there were agents out there who would help.

It was as the service always recommended: Completely true, just not truly complete. Bektashi was probably too polite or too loyal to ask how they were expected to find these lost agents of the Empire. He just wanted to know when they needed to leave and where they were going to go.

Mary continued, "We will need to ride southwest again into the mountains. Bandit country to be sure, and there will be more than a few bandits willing to sell us to the highest bidder."

Francis had anticipated something like this requirement so he interjected, "Once again, our colleague Naglieff has offered his assistance. He is sending twenty riders from the Persian Cossack Brigade to serve as our protectors. Twenty riders with a Russian commander."

Bektashi shook his head. "You trust them?"

Francis laughed. "Not in the least, Bektashi Bey. I only trust the three of us. However, we simply can't ride into bandit country without additional manpower. Remember, Sasha provided some riders to keep us safe when we rode here; he is offering the same assistance again. Even if the Persians are not trustworthy, just their presence should reduce the risk of a random raid. They are mercenaries in the pay of the Russians. They will be paid half when we depart and the second half of their pay after we return. I talked to our Russian contacts here in Baku. The Persians know their families are hostage to our safe return. And, if they prove to be enemies while on the road...."

Francis moved his forefinger across his neck. Bektashi nodded and understood completely. It was the way of the East.

Mary continued. "We will need to depart today. Bektashi, how soon can you get our horses ready? We will travel light, so all we need are basics for cold camps along the way and some supplies in case our colleagues need new kit. After all, they have been on the run for some time."

Bektashi thought for a moment. "Madame, I will have four horses in addition to our own. Two for supplies and two spare horses. As the master has told me before me in the past: two is one and one is none." With that, he stood up and pulled the gold hunter watch from the recesses of his blood-red silk cummerbund. "All shall be ready by 12 o'clock."

Bektashi bowed to Mary, saluted Francis and left the room. He moved at a brisk pace, but not in a rush.

Mary said, "He is a marvel."

"Indeed he is."

"The other riders?"

"As I said, Persians, serving as scouts for a Russian-led Persian Cossack Brigade. I talked to their Russian officer this morning. He is preparing them for whatever future missions we might require. I have some confidence in them and even more confidence in your ability to read their minds and convince them to stay loyal."

"I may be a bit distracted as I try to locate the Mansfields."

"Then Bektashi and I will focus on the Persians. It will not be a problem."

Mary smiled. "It never is when you are in the game."

A Job for the Ravens

Rawalpindi, February 1915

NAISMITH SMILED AS HE LOOKED OVER HIS MUG OF TEA AT HIS PROTÉGÉ, Elizabeth Bankroft. He had been in regular message contact with her, but this was their first face-to-face since the start of the war. He noticed she looked more mature, more confident, and, perhaps, older. Her face was thinner than he remembered. Perhaps maturity, perhaps the pressure of the job? Her hair was longer and pulled into a tight bun at the base of her neck. As he studied her, he realized her entire body was lean. Not emaciated, but simply the body of an athlete in training. Of course, he expected he looked far older than when she last saw him. Long hours, late nights, and the pressures of sending his students and friends into harm's way had added grey to his beard and dark circles under his eyes.

"Guru, don't fret. We all look older under the strain of the war."

Naismith smiled. Elizabeth had clearly developed another

skill: mind reading. He wondered how her telepathic skills were developing. He thought: *And do you feel older as well?*

Elizabeth responded: *Far older than I felt a year ago.*

Have you used your illusory body in Bombay?

Not as much as before. Once I heard mother and father were safe in Baku, I focused on work. There is so much work to do in Bombay to support the Crown. Just the Royal Navy taskings are enough for three of me!

Naismith smiled and decided to return to simple conversation. As he did, Marian Sandusky walked into the office. Elizabeth beamed. "Guru Marian, it is so good to see you!"

Marian smiled and said, "Elizabeth, now that you are a full member of the cadre, you should call me Marian. Or, if you want to be formal, then Major Sandusky."

It was Elizabeth's turn to smile. "Marian will be fine."

"Excellent. Now, why don't we let Guru Naismith continue with his briefing."

Naismith nodded and said, "Elizabeth, I wanted to see you in person to discuss your insights based on your assignment in Bombay. I wanted your opinion on whether we should focus our attention on the revolutionaries who are supported by the Germans, or the German Navy that threatens our fleet. It seems clear to me that we cannot do both." Naismith was about to offer his view when he realized that it would be better to leave the question open for Elizabeth. If she was reading his mind, she already knew what he thought.

Elizabeth took a sip from the mug of tea at her side and a small bite from the tea biscuit offered to her by Marian. The delay gave her time to assemble her thoughts. Finally, she said, "I have thought about this often enough. The military and civilian police personnel in Bombay are diligent though not terribly imaginative. They have no interest at all in what I might have to say because they want to capture saboteurs and revolutionaries who are breaking the Crown's laws. They don't want to hear from me about our source reporting on plans and intentions."

Elizabeth watched as Naismith's aura changed from blue to green. Had she been too forthright? She looked over at Marian Sandusky. Her aura had remained a royal blue. She decided Naismith had asked the question and deserved an answer even if it was an answer he would prefer not to hear. Just before she continued, Elizabeth realized that six months ago, she would have held her tongue. Now, she was confident enough of her own views that she felt she must say what she thought.

She continued, "I think the skills of any graduate from the Viceroy's College are wasted on this police work. Especially since the police do not want our help. I think we need to focus on targets outside of India. Assuming you want me to continue my work in Bombay, that means I should be focusing on the German Navy and their operations in either East Africa or the Arabian Sea. I don't know precisely how I would do that, but I think that makes the most sense." Though she might not have realized her action, Elizabeth punctuated her final comment with a vigorous placement of the mug of tea on the plate that had previously held tea biscuits. The clink of the china mug hitting the china plate startled her.

Naismith smiled and came close to laughing out loud. Elizabeth was growing into a confident intelligence officer and that made him both proud and excited to consider how she might be used in this world war. He looked over at Marian. She nodded. He decided to pull on the string of thought that she offered. "How would you manage intelligence operations for the Navy?" He paused and asked sincerely, "Will you need a ship or a plane?"

Elizabeth laughed. "I would very much like to use a seaplane for my operations. Alternatively, the Royal Indian Marine runs coastal operations from Bombay, but I suspect

Commodore Lumsden would not think a lieutenant in the FANY's should have one of his ships on call to support her operations."

Naismith smiled. "I didn't mean you would be given a ship of the line to do your bidding."

Elizabeth laughed again. "I didn't expect so."

"I simply wondered if you had contacts in the area who had fishing or cargo trawlers that we might … borrow? In either East Africa or Arabia, I do believe we might be able to arrange a delivery and recovery if that was needed." Naismith paused for a moment to sip his tea. He needed to direct Elizabeth's focus in an entirely different direction and that would take some effort. "First things first. Do you have any information on German operations in Mesopotamia or Persia?"

Elizabeth thought for a moment. Her network in Bombay included several distant reporting sources connected through the trading networks that linked India, Arabia, and Persia. She knew already the Royal Navy was very interested in the Abadan oil fields in Persia as the ships of the line transitioned from coal to oil. She started cautiously. "After our raid in Gwadar, I encouraged several of my sources to stretch their networks into Persia and southern Mesopotamia. They have reported further efforts on the part of Germans in southwestern Persia to build a revolutionary network in Persian Baluchistan. These same Germans are led by a German intelligence officer named Wassmuss. Have you heard of him?"

Naismith nodded. "Indeed I have, Elizabeth. He has worked in the region for years, is a fine Persian linguist, and an expert in what you might call revolutionary warfare. That is, he convinces tribals that it is their best interest to revolt against the central government. Since most tribals are hostile to any control other than their own, they are susceptible to his approach," Naismith paused to sip his tea. "And, susceptible to German rifles and German gold."

Elizabeth nodded. Wassmuss was clearly a target for

intelligence collection and possibly disruption if they could capture him. She said, "What would you recommend, Master Guru?"

Naismith understood and accepted Elizabeth's enthusiasm for an East African adventure. After all, the German cruiser Emden was somewhere out in the Arabian Sea and had to be making port calls somewhere on the coast of the German colonies of East Africa. She had previously identified submarines and even an advanced German seaplane operating from the African coast. However, it would be a long and involved effort to dispatch Elizabeth or her comrades to ... where? Naismith knew that British authorities in Nairobi had reported to the government of India and to Whitehall that they were more than capable of handling the Germans themselves. That confidence seemed misplaced, but Naismith was a practical man. He had a small number of resources and a military theatre in Mesopotamia and Persia that needed help.

He said, "I think we will have to let the Navy handle Africa for now. Instead, there are more pressing dangers in southern Persia and southern Mesopotamia. It turns out that you have worked with one of the officers who will be tackling the threat from Wassmuss. The Indian Army has a contingent in Abadan in Persia and has just captured Basra and Qurna in Mesopotamia. There will be fighting in both areas and we will be needed to help the army understand the threat from any German-inspired rebellion. The good news is that we may have some assistance from a Persian scholar who you know. Percy Sykes."

Elizabeth couldn't help herself. She said, "Oh, dear."

Sykes had been troublesome during the Gwadar affair while working with Elizabeth and another Raven, Beverly Mansfield. He was bright and had good language skills, but he was not the most subtle of intelligence officers. His views were more tuned to the 19th century Indian Army intelligence division which dispatched courageous — and sometimes reckless — cavalry officers to "go spy the land." And, he was completely befuddled by her own skills in mesmerism and other Tibetan mystic arts taught at the Viceroy's College.

Marian watched as Elizabeth's aura shifted like a kaleidoscope from blue to orange, then yellow and finally back to green. So far, she only saw evidence of a passionate young intelligence officer. She had not seen any sign of demons identified earlier by Naismith.

Elizabeth composed herself and said, "Master guru, you do know that Beverly and I had some … challenges working with Colonel Sykes?"

"Indeed, Elizabeth. Honestly, you are not the only ones. It turns out that the Viceroy, Lord Hardinge, is equally worried that Sykes may not be the man for the job. Sykes is currently in Kashgar in Chinese Turkistan and it will take time to get him back to India. Still, he knows Persia and especially southern Persia. For now, we will have to address the question of the threat to the Royal Navy oil fields in Abadan and rebels in southern Mesopotamia."

Elizabeth admitted, "I am not exactly an expert in tribal politics, and I am not fluent in Persian."

"Perhaps not, but Winslow-Heath wants us to be involved and so we shall be."

"We?"

Naismith looked directly into Elizabeth's eyes. She felt him peering gently into her mind. She heard, or perhaps felt him say, "Oh, yes, Elizabeth. This is absolutely a job for the Ravens."

Marian followed Elizabeth out of Naismith's office. She said, "Would you like a less formal cup of tea at the officer's mess?

I have been busy all day and would like to take tea without worrying about intelligence operations."

Elizabeth responded with enthusiasm as they walked out on the parade ground in the cantonment. "Absolutely. I am currently in small, temporary quarters in the barracks and I could use a bit of fresh air and tea."

As they walked, Marian started her effort to elicit details of Elizabeth's time in Bombay. She started with simple questions. "You said your work was not appreciated in Bombay. Please don't believe that to be true here in Rawalpindi. What about work challenges? Agent operations? Did we give you the tools to do the job?"

Elizabeth nodded. "My agent handling and even agent recruitment work has been good." She paused and said, "I wonder about my self-control sometimes."

"Eh?"

"Guru Marian, I seem to have powers that I can't control. Not simple things like *lung gom pa* or even complex things like the illusory body or telepathy. Honestly, I haven't used my skills in the illusory body in Bombay. What I mean is my anger."

They had reached the officers' mess and Marian was pleased to see there were tables set outside. They sat down and a waiter in an immaculate white uniform came up. Marian said, "Tea and cakes for two, please." The waiter bowed and disappeared. Marian said, "In another month, it will be too hot to eat outside and the mosquitoes would drive us inside even if the weather did not. But for now, outside among the jacarandas will be most pleasant."

She shifted the conversation, "Elizabeth, you said you have trouble controlling your anger?"

Elizabeth was quiet for some time. The waiter arrived with the tea tray and placed it on the table. He was about to pour when Marian waved him away. "I will take care of this. Thank you." The waiter was not used to seeing two women in khaki uniforms, but they were wearing the proper rank and seemed perfectly capable of serving themselves, unlike some of the young subalterns he often served. He nodded and left.

After Marian had poured a cup for each of them and placed a small pastry on Elizabeth's plate, she asked again. "Anger?"

Elizabeth sipped her tea and looked at Marian. "When I get angry, I seem to gain additional powers. Strength and the ability to extend my *chi* outside my body."

"Not uncommon abilities for any of us."

The distress and uncertainty had simmered inside Elizabeth for too long. Now, in the presence of her mentor, it all boiled over.

"I have killed men, Marian. More than one. When the anger takes hold, I seem unable to control the power."

Elizabeth paused. It was hard to continue. "In Gwadar and again in Bombay I killed the target rather than disabling the target. I did not wish it to be so. In fact, in the most recent case, I would have preferred it not to be so. I understand the ladder of consequences and I understand that we sometimes need to injure or even kill to escape. But I don't seem able to measure my powers. They are either full on or off."

"Have you asked Guru Naismith?"

"I do not wish to burden him."

"And you do not wish to reveal your worries."

Elizabeth blushed. "That as well."

"Elizabeth, your challenge is not unusual. As you mature in these skills, you will be better able to measure your powers. Remember when you first started to explore *lang gom pa*?" Marian remembered her student and her first experiment with the Tibetan leaping technique.

Elizabeth laughed. "I nearly fell down the mountainside."

"Exactly so. Now, here is something to ponder. Anger is an emotion that is dangerous. There is nothing wrong with a bit of fear to heighten your senses, but anger opens a dark side that can be chaotic. There is power there, but power without control is most dangerous. Think about this the next time you meditate."

Elizabeth nodded. "Thank you, Guru Marian. You are still teaching me, whether you like it or not."

Marian simply bowed her head.

That night in her quarters, Elizabeth decided to focus her meditation on controlling her emotions. She started slowly counting her breaths. Count of five inhaling, hold for five, exhale for five, then empty for the count of five. Repeat. Slowly, her mind cleared and she started to focus on how to keep control of her emotions, specifically anger.

Just as she reached the stage where her meditation was calming her, a voice invaded her mind. *Emotions are good, Elizabeth. Do not let these false gurus tell you otherwise. ANGER is useful. It gives you power. You should enjoy that power, Elizabeth. Do not avoid it. Do not avoid it.*

Elizabeth was jolted out of her meditation as the voice — no, more like a whine — disappeared. She looked around the room lighted by a single candle she used for concentration. Where did that voice come from? Who was it? Certainly not anyone she knew.

It took her some time to regain a calm state enough that she could return to her meditation. In the end, she decided it was a puzzlement that would not be solved.

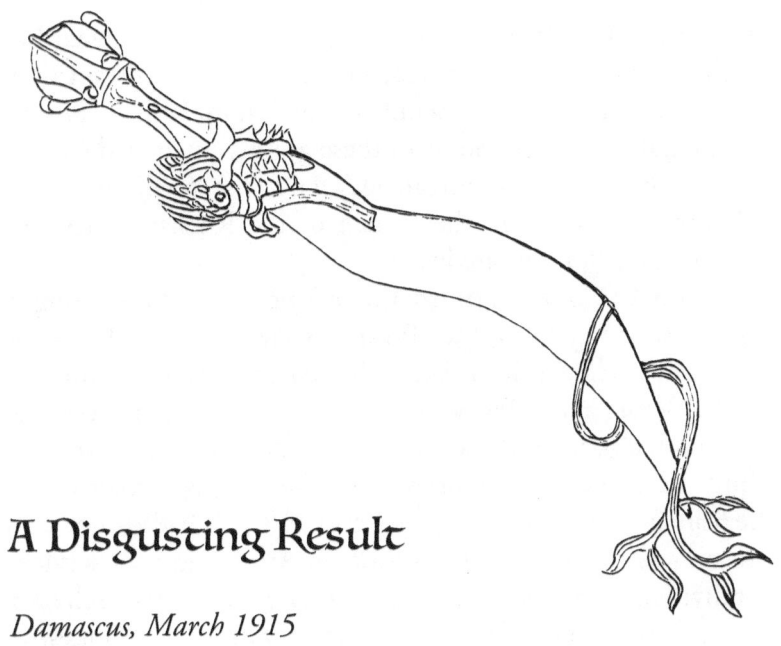

A Disgusting Result

Damascus, March 1915

Michael carried the head of the British officer back to Damascus. He knew that the Germans were unlikely to find such a trophy even close to appropriate. He also knew that the Turks in Damascus, especially the Turks who were working with his father, would find the delivery appropriate and satisfactory. Michael had spent enough time in the Ottoman Empire to know that the "young Turks" might present themselves as modern, but they were still sons of the great Ottoman fighters who once owned the Eastern Mediterranean and threatened Vienna.

After reporting to von Trier and commending both Lettow and Friehart, he returned to the house he shared with his father, who had been working with the Turkish secret police "special organization" that they discussed with von der Goltz three months ago. That group was hunting various elements within the Ottoman Army and civil administration who were considered disloyal. Michael had no idea what his father might have uncovered, but he knew for certain that the Ottoman Empire included many non-Turkish ethnic and religious groups. Some of these groups surely had chafed under the Ottoman bureaucracy and just might want to side with the British, the French or the Russians once the Ottoman caliph declared war.

James O'Connell arrived after a long day and even longer night working with the Turkish secret police. He knew through a telepathic message that Michael was waiting for him. Before reuniting with his son, he took time to drop his work clothes and use a bath to wash away the frustration built up through working on what he had expected to be a legitimate counter-subversion effort. What it had turned out to be was cleansing of the Ottoman Army and civil service. Individuals who were simply the wrong ethnicity or religion were now targets of the special organization and, honestly, James couldn't stand the mission. He had his staff run a luke-warm bath to wash away the street grime and pour him a large Irish whisky to wash the bitter taste out of his mouth.

When father and son were finally together on the veranda of their house, they were both clean and dressed in loose clothes that made them look like characters from the Arabian nights. They had matching black-and-white striped cotton overshirts that were not quite as long as the kamiz of the shalwar kamiz of India, but still long enough to cover the drawstring waist of their loose cotton pajama pants. They were both wearing leather, Persian slippers and over their shoulders were black wool shawls known as abayas. They were sitting in wooden chairs with rattan seats, looking out over the small flower garden surrounded by a ten-foot-tall brick wall. It was private and the only noise they heard were the cooing of doves in the trees and the occasional slap as a gecko fell from the wall into the yard.

"Father, I need to tell you about my trip and ask for your help."

James took a healthy sip of his whisky and said, "Michael, given your skills, I wonder what in the world I can do to help."

"Father, I need to deliver a package from the Rashidi tribal chief to the Turks. I would like to do so without showing the Germans what I have."

"What could be so important to the Turks that the Germans shouldn't know?"

"Father, it isn't what is so important. It is what is so disgusting that the Germans should not know."

"Disgusting?"

"Father, as you know, my mission was to ensure Shakespear was assassinated. That mission was accomplished." Michael paused long enough to take a sip of his whisky. While generally not fond of strong spirits, Michael thought he needed the fortification to spit out the rest of the tale. "The Rashidi tribal chief gave me Shakespear's head to give to the Turks. I suppose he saw it as proof of his loyalty and, perhaps, his power."

"You brought the head back to Damascus?"

"Indeed, I did. I wasn't sure whether it would be useful to us or not." Michael smiled to himself and offered what he thought might be an intemperate but useful remark. "After all, Shakespear wasn't going to need it anymore."

James O'Connell was shocked at the callous comment. He had raised his son to be a focused intelligence officer. To be sure, Michael had become that focused officer. What he had not expected was a level of blood thirst that this comment showed. James realized that his son often did read his mind — whether he had permission or not — so he buried his shock and disgust inside a mental fortress that he hoped Michael could not penetrate. He said, "We may find someone in the Turkish secret police who would value this ... gift. I cannot imagine that it will help in our personal goals of traveling to Ireland, but I suppose there might be some utility."

Michael nodded. He had noticed his father's aura flash from blue-green acceptance to hot red disgust or anger and back to blue-green. He wasn't certain whether that was due to the gift, his actions or something entirely different. Before he could say anything, a squeaky dream voice intruded his head.

Do not worry about your father, Michael. He does not understand yet how your new world will be filled with disgusting, violent things. You and I know that this is only the beginning. It is only the beginning.

Michael was puzzled by this intruder in his mind. Was it some part of his own personality? Was it something else? The Arabs spoke of djinns who were spirits that lived in a mystical world. Michael knew enough about the astral plane to know that there was something like a mystical world where such entities might exist. However, he also knew enough about the minds of men, including his own, to know that parts of the human mind were at least as malevolent as any djinn from a fairy story.

Just One More Mission

Damascus, March 1915

"I THOUGHT OUR ASSIGNMENT HERE WAS OVER AND WE WERE GOING TO IRE-land." Michael did his best to not sound like a complaining teenager, but he was just that: A disappointed teenager. He was looking forward to one event and found himself going to another. He was walking with his father toward the large, brick building that served as headquarters for the German intelligence contingent for the region. They were both dressed in formal European clothes which, for once, was a relief to Michael because his last two trips into the building had been in the stiff grey wool of the German officer corps.

James O'Connell smiled at his son's impatience. While he was regularly surprised by Michael's maturity, there were also times when he was reminded that his son was not yet twenty years old. Michael had accomplished much in the last few years, but he was still a young man with a young man's energy. He also had yet to receive orders that were disappointing or contradictory. James expected that he was about to receive both during this meeting with Colonel von Trier. He worried that Michael might say something that would disrupt his growing relationship with von Trier — a relationship that was beneficial to their current lives in Damascus and their future lives in Ireland. Before Michael left on the mission to Arabia, James had been confident that he could prevent any outburst from his son. Since his return and, most especially, since his delivery of the "gift" of Shakespear's head to the Turkish leadership, he was no longer certain. He was also no longer confident that he could keep any of his misgivings a secret from his son.

He said, "Michael, this is a world war. I have spent more time in Damascus than you have over the past few weeks. I know the Germans want to get us to Ireland so that we can fight for Irish independence. They wish this not because they care about Ireland, but because they want to disrupt the British war machine. The Germans have been supporting the independence movement for years including shipping guns to Ireland and providing some degree of political support. Even now, they are meeting with a senior leader in the movement in Berlin. Roger Casement ... *Sir* Roger Casement in Britain ... is in Berlin after spending last year in America arranging shipments of rifles to Ireland. He is working with the German intelligence departments to determine when he should return to Ireland. I suspect our German masters here wish to send us with Casement when he goes to Ireland. It is not so easy right now with the Royal Navy blockading German ports on the North Sea. My theft of the difference engine is helping German submarines to evade the blockade and attack British ships in the Atlantic, but it remains nearly impossible for regular ships to leave German ports."

Michael said, "So we are merely pawns in the larger games of empire?"

Again, James heard a level of emotion he should have expected from his young son. He remembered very well how he sounded when he was confronted with the prejudices of marrying what his fellow officers viewed as "a local." To him, his wife was a Persian princess who offered so much love and a Parsi family far more cosmopolitan than his peers. To the British, she was just another Indian. More than once he had expressed anger and dismay when he should have understood that their prejudices were so ingrained that they couldn't actually see them for what they were: hatred and perhaps some degree of fear of "the other."

He said, "The Germans are supporting revolutionary movements throughout the region. They are funding Indian revolutionaries. They are funding Persian tribals and, as you well know, they are funding one side of a civil war in Arabia. We simply must be smart enough to understand their desires and manipulate those desires to our own end. We are smarter than they are, we have skills they cannot imagine and we must use those skills to gain their confidence and then succeed in our own, personal goals."

Michael nodded. He knew what his father was trying to accomplish: he was afraid Michael would do something that would set them back in their long-term goal. He knew his father was right about one thing: they were much smarter than their German "masters." He said, "Father, I realize everything you say."

When they arrived, von Trier was at his desk grumbling to himself. He looked up from the paperwork and said, "Good day, gentlemen. Please have a seat while I complete the last of this intolerable paperwork from our Ottoman allies. I now know why in German and in English we often use the term 'byzantine' to describe paperwork that is overly," von Trier paused to look for an appropriate word in English, "baroque." He finished flipping through the pages, and closed that file.

He pulled an ink pen from its holder at the top of his desk and signed the top of the file with a flourish. He shouted to his orderly in German. "*Drei kaffeebohne, bitte!*"

From behind them, they heard a muffled "*Jawhol, Herr Colonel.*"

The coffee arrived and the three men sat drinking the black Turkish coffee. During his time with the Arabs, Michael had grown accustomed to drinking it while holding a sugar cube in his mouth. James and von Trier used the sugar in the glass sugar dish; James had one spoonful, von Trier three. Michael watched as the colonel drank his coffee. His aura shifted from green to yellow and back again. Clearly, there was something bothering the German, and Michael assumed it had to do with some upcoming assignment. After they had finished their first cup of coffee and the servant poured a second into their glass cups held in engraved silver holders, von Trier finally spoke.

"Gentlemen, I must apologize for delaying your trip to Berlin and onward journey to Ireland. There are complications at every end of the trip from Constantinople to the continent and then from Germany to Ireland." Michael watched the colonel's aura. As near as he could tell, the German was telling what he thought was the truth. Whether it was simply a fiction from von Trier's higher headquarters, Michael could not determine. It made him feel slightly better that their primary contact felt an obligation to them. He watched as von Trier continued and his aura changed again to yellow. Michael realized that this was not due to an effort to deceive but rather discomfort over the mission.

"Since you will be here for a time, Field Marshal von der Goltz has decided that there is a critical mission that both of you could perform for our Ottoman allies and, by extension, for the German Empire. The mission will be challenging and will put you in harm's way in a manner that I have not asked from you in the past. Still, we have to accept that when we receive orders, we must obey them."

Von Trier took a sip from his coffee cup and then reached into his desk drawer. He pulled out a small bottle and three small crystal glasses. He poured a clear white liquid into each of the glasses. The room filled with the gentle aroma of peppermint. Michael thought: Schnapps? This must be serious if he is going to ask us to drink with him at mid-afternoon.

"The British fleet is operating on oil, Persian oil. They have a partnership with the Qajar shah that allows them to maintain control over Abadan where they have a refinery. They are also occupying Basra on the Shatt al-Arab on that same coastline and it looks as if they are planning to invade Mesopotamia by traveling up the two great rivers, the Tigris and the Euphrates." Von Trier looked at Michael, "As with your previous mission, the reason we are so interested in these actions is because of our Ottoman allies. Honestly, as Germans, we are perfectly happy that the British intend to waste manpower in Mesopotamia and Persia, manpower that could be used in Europe. Still, I suppose they assume that their Indian Army troops who were previously on the Afghan frontier can be used to accomplish this mission. Perhaps they are right. Either way, our Ottoman allies are very upset that they might lose access to the Arabian Sea."

Von Trier stood up, taking his coffee cup with him and leaving the schnapps behind. He walked over to a large map unrolled on the library table next to the tall windows. "Please come with me, gentlemen." They stood and followed him to the table.

Von Trier put his hand on Damascus. He said, "We are at the center of the great Ottoman Empire which covers so much of this land of Mesopotamia and Arabia. The young Turks who control the Ottoman government wish to expand their empire. My seniors in Constantinople find this desire maddening. They know as well as you do that once you leave

Damascus and head either South or East, Ottoman control is a fiction. These areas are controlled by tribes and ethnic groups marginally loyal to the Ottoman government. General Liman von Sanders recommended the Ottoman expansion east should be limited to capturing Crimea. Instead, one these young Turks, Enver Pasha, decided to invade the Caucasus, in the middle of winter no less!"

Von Trier shook his head. "It is a nightmare." He took another sip of coffee and shouted to his orderly in German. "*Kaffe!*" The Arab servant returned with the silver coffee pot and dutifully poured coffee into their glasses and then brought the sugar to each of the Europeans. He disappeared with the tell-tale slap of leather slippers on the wooden floor.

"Now the Turks intend to invade Persia. We expect they should be able to capture Kermanshah with little difficulty. After all, the Persian army is even less capable than either the Turks or the Russians. But, this does not help any of our interests." He pointed to the Arabian Gulf and said, "O'Connell, you know all too well that the British maintain control over the Arab states along the Gulf."

James nodded and said, "Sir, control is probably a bit too strong a term. The British intelligence and diplomatic presence in Kuwait and the Trucial States work hard to influence the sheikhs. That influence is based entirely on British gold."

"Indeed, O'Connell. But, we have no influence there." He pointed to the southern end of the map toward the east coast of Africa. "Our influence only extends just past our port cities in German East Africa. Their influence has made the Arabian Gulf a British lake. And, probably most important, they control the oil fields in Persia." He moved his hand north and covered the area between Abadan and Basra. "I am no expert in this region. I am a simple hussar officer who grew too old to lead cavalry charges. So, now I am relegated to managing our intelligence collection here. But, I have just received a new mission and it is a difficult one to be sure." He took another sip from his now-full glass. "That mission is to erode British influence in southern Persia and to undermine the growing British invasion force that is amassing in Basra. In short, we are no longer focusing on intelligence, we are now focusing on subversion."

Michael cautiously spoke. "Sir, are we talking about operations in Mesopotamia and Persia similar to the one you sent me on last year in Arabia?"

Von Trier nodded, "Exactly, young O'Connell! The Field Marshal wants you and your father to engage tribals, convince them that alliances with the British will only result in the loss of their independence. If it means a few British troops killed by these tribals, so much the better. It will mean you traveling into areas where you have not been in the past. That is a risk I am asking you to take."

James O'Connell said, "Sir, I have worked with the Qashgai before and some of the Arab speaking tribes of southern Persia. It is not unknown territory."

"Excellent, O'Connell." The colonel walked over to his desk and handed two glasses of schnapps to the O'Connells. He took has own and raised his glass. "To my two agents of influence. May they succeed in ways beyond our imagination!" They downed their drinks in one gulp.

Michael was not used to the fiery liquid and had an embarrassing moment when he choked. Von Trier said, "Young O'Connell, I promise not to ask you to drink again. You are too important to our cause to choke in my office. Now, I want you to make a plan of attack. I will need you to report back to me tomorrow with how you intend to begin your work. Do not worry about how you will get to the area. We already have that plan in place. All you need to do is tell me where you want to start. The German Empire will do the rest."

As they walked away from the German headquarters, James asked his son, "Are you willing to do this mission? After all we have done for the Germans so far, it seems to me we could convince von Trier that we are not needed."

Michael knew that his father was alluding to their combined strengths in mesmerism. There was no doubt in his mind that either they could convince von Trier that they were not suited for the job or they could imbed in his mind a false memory that they had already traveled to Persia and had accomplished the mission. He smiled and said, "Father, I know what we could do, but I doubt that anything we might do with von Trier's mind would get us closer to Berlin and then onward to Ireland. I realize that I am by no means a Persian scholar, but many of the tribes in Fars Province are Arab speakers not Persian speakers. We have already demonstrated that we can work with Arab tribals. And, honestly, I think it would be especially rewarding to spend our last days here working to undermine the British effort to control yet another country. They already have more than their share. Von Trier never said that we would be working to expand the German Empire. Rather, we are to counter the British attempt to expand their empire. I believe we can do well for ourselves and do good at the same time."

Michael paused as they got into a carriage that would take them to their house in Damascus. He switched to telepathy: *And, there is no reason I can see why we couldn't fill our pockets with German gold while we are doing this mission. Regardless of who wins this war, gold is gold and we are going to need gold in Ireland.*

James pondered Michael's last comment. In his mental castle he used when he didn't want Michael to read his mind, he thought that Michael's experiences in Arabia had changed him. He seemed less to be pursuing the personal vendetta that James had against the Raj and acting more like a foreign mercenary willing to profit from the Germans and, perhaps, in the long run, from the Irish. He wondered how these changes would affect Michael's mental and physical health. He stepped out of his mental castle and sent Michael his own telepathic message. *We need to take care that the Germans don't use us and then toss us out into the world to be captured by the British or the French.*

Michael responded: *Father, that will never happen so long as I am a player in this game.*

The O'Connells returned the next day. Michael agreed that his father was better suited to provide von Trier their plan. This would allow him to concentrate on the colonel's aura and, if necessary, to use mesmerism and telepathy to ensure the colonel agreed — and possibly even believed he came up with the plan. There was only one sticking point that James thought likely and it would be at that point that Michael might need to intervene.

James O'Connell started with a brief summary. "Sir, we looked at the disposition of forces in the area. In November, an Indian Army contingent is based in the Iranian port of Abadan on the Persian Gulf. Later, a larger contingent landed 30 miles west in Basra, in Mesopotamia. That force is called the Indian Expeditionary Force D. It has moved gradually up the Tigris and captured Qurna at the junction of the Tigris and Euphrates rivers in December."

Michael could see the colonel was growing bored with the background so he sent a telepathic message to his father: *Focus on our plan, Father.*

James nodded and said, "Colonel, the secret to understanding the way to undermine the British both in Persia and in Mesopotamia is to attack their haphazard logistics. The Indian Army is designed as a policing force on the Indian frontier with Afghanistan. The units live in their cantonments, leave on raids and return after a few days. They simply don't have the sort of military capability that a modern army must have in the field. Further, in Southern Persia, the British have been most arrogant in their handling of the tribes. Again, they assume that the tribes, especially the Arab tribes, in Persia are like their tribal counterparts on the Afghan border and in Baluchistan. They have established political agents in the region and they are bribing some tribal leaders just as they bribe the Pashtun maliks."

James paused to see if Michael had noticed any serious erosion in von Trier's concentration. When he received none, he pressed on. "Sir, there are only two of us and we have considered our planning based on a prudent, realistic view on what can be accomplished. As Herr von Clausewitz correctly pointed out: a critical principle for victory is concentration of force. While Michael and I are just two men, we believe we can use our abilities to undermine the British. We have designed two different attacks on the British. Both are based on our abilities to work with locals, subvert any loyalty they might have for the British and then turn the locals into a resistance force." Another pause to ensure von Trier was showing interest.

As they had rehearsed in advance, it was now time for Michael to begin his part. "Sir, as you know I have been successful in working undercover as an Arab laborer. One of our possible choices is to engage the tribals in the area near Abadan. The British assume that there is a small threat to their Indian Army force there. It is their arrogance and their complete misunderstanding of the tribal politics that will allow us to create a troublesome environment for them and, by extension, for the British Navy which will worry that their oil fields are at risk."

James took over. "Sir, the alternative would be for us to infiltrate the area north of Basra on the border between Mesopotamia and Persia. Once there, we would move south building a network of locals willing to slow down and even stop deliveries of key supplies for the British troops in the field. While I do not know the specific commander in charge of Basra, I do know precisely how amateurish the British officer corps is about supplies and logistics. They are most interested in dash and intrepidity and have little interest in the hard work of the profession of arms. They also do not pay attention to the locals who do all of the hard work for them. In part, that is a function of the fact that most of the members of the officer corps of the Indian Army are individuals who have little formal military education. They receive their commissions by paying for the commission or through some family connection. I believe we can make their lives miserable by simply shutting off their supply lines."

Michael took over again. "Sir, we are prepared to take on either of these challenges. The decision, as always, is yours to make. Personally, we believe the greater strategic value is in Abadan, but the greater value to our Ottoman allies is in Basra."

Von Trier looked at the two men across from his desk. They were smart, experienced and clearly brave men. Anyone willing to disappear behind enemy lines with little more than his wits to stay alive had to be courageous and, in von Trier's mind, slightly demented. He recently received a similar briefing from another of the Empire's spies, Wilhelm Wassmuss, who had argued much the same thing. Wassmuss and a small band of German adventurers were already working in Southern Persia. The decision was clear. He would be sending the O'Connells to Mesopotamia. He said, "Gentlemen, thank you for your clear understanding of the challenges and your two courses of action. I need to let you know that we have already deployed a small contingent to attack the tribal problem in Southern Persia. For that reason alone, I need you to focus your attention on Basra." He paused and then shouted to his orderly. "*Drei kaffeebohnen, bitte!*"

"Jawohl!" came the reply.

Once the coffee was delivered, von Trier continued. "I can deliver you either by land or by sea. Our objectives are long-term, so it would not be a problem if you think a delivery by sea makes more sense."

Neither of the O'Connells had expected this question. They had always assumed they would be traveling by land. Michael said, "Sir, the distances are great in either case."

The colonel smiled and replied, "Not if you are traveling by airship."

Michael was the first to recover from this offer. "Sir, if we are traveling by airship, then I recommend we travel into the Khuzestan desert. I can use my contacts with the Al-Rashidis to arrange a rendezvous with the Beni Lam Arabs. The area is still considered a quasi-independent sheikhdom and the Beni Lam have traded there for centuries. From there, we will proceed south toward the British lines. We will do our best to disrupt the British troops."

"How soon will you be able to arrange someone to receive you?"

James O'Connell replied, "Sir, it will take some time to arrange couriers, but it shouldn't take more than a month to confirm a meeting site. All the Bedouin are hostile to the British and will be more than willing to help."

Michael added, "Of course, they will only do it for gold and rifles."

Von Trier laughed and said, "Gold and rifles. Where in the world are these not currency?"

Michael watched von Trier's aura carefully as he said, "Sir, I recommend sending a half payment of 250 marks in gold with the courier with a promise of 250 more marks to the Al-Rashidis and 100 Mausers. When we meet the Beni Lam in the desert, we will need to have an additional 50 Mausers and 100 marks when we meet them in the desert." He noticed no change in the colonel's aura. He realized that he should have asked for more funds.

"I will make that happen immediately. You will report back to me personally as you prepare for the journey."

James realized this was not a request but an order and before Michael could say anything he acknowledged the order. "Yes, sir. Would once a week be acceptable?"

"Excellent, O'Connell. Now, you are dismissed. Begin your work using whatever human sources you must to succeed. I will have a courier sent to your quarters with 500 marks in gold — 250 for the courier and another 250 for any other source operations you deem necessary here in Damascus to prepare for the mission. Before you depart, I will issue you an additional 500 marks."

Michael and James O'Connell stood and did a formal bow to the colonel. They turned on their heels and marched quickly out of the room. As they left, Michael sent a telepathic message to his father: *I should have asked for more.*

James replied: *Never fear. We have a month to ask for more.*

Riding with the Cossacks

Khoi, Northern Persia, April 1915

THE LINKUP WITH THE MANSFIELDS HAD BEEN EASILY ACCOMPLISHED. MARY identified a place on the map where the road from Baku crossed over the river Araz. It was a hard four-day ride for the Bankrofts and their Cossack protectors, but they made it well in advance of the scheduled meeting time. They found the Mansfields waiting at the bridge, looking like any of the thousands of Armenian refugees that streamed east in an effort to escape the Ottoman troops. The Cossacks made camp that night in a forested area well away from the road. They set up a perimeter which allowed Francis, Mary and Bektashi to take care of their beleaguered colleagues.

That night, Alexander Mansfield said, "I know we have business elsewhere, but I believe we have some unfinished business nearby."

Beverly looked at Mary. Her eyes shown bright in the fire-light. Mary had read novels describing characters with hatred in their eyes. That was how she would have described

Beverly's gaze. "We saw an Ottoman patrol destroy an Armenian farming village. The village was no threat to anyone. The patrol simply decided to wreak havoc on the village for fun. They aren't far way. We would very much like to pay them a visit."

Alexander nodded. "And, if you need a reason to help us, we promise that the Ottoman officer in charge will certainly have intelligence with him. As we watched from a distance, we saw a courier deliver dispatches to him."

Mary knew Francis was always up for an adventure. The question she had in her mind was whether the Cossacks would go along with a night raid. As if Francis had read her mind, he stood up and walked toward the Cossack officer's tent. He came back in short order.

"They are ready for a night attack. The Russian in charge was tired of what he saw as simply a protective detail. He was thrilled that he and his men would be able to return to Baku with something, anything, that showed they were fighting the Turks."

Bektashi had been in the shadows during the discussion. He whispered to Francis, "Master, do we attack the Turks tonight?"

Francis looked at his three companions. They all nodded. He whispered to Bektashi, "Indeed, Bektashi Bey. It would appear this is more than a simple search and rescue. We ride with the Cossacks tonight."

With a swish of his loose garments, Bektashi was off to saddle the horses.

Alexander asked, "Will he fight?"

"Like a demon," was all Mary said.

The glow of the cook fires was the only sign of life in the Turkish camp. The soldiers were settling in for the evening.

The success of the Ottoman Army at Van meant they were safe. Their probe into Persia had been successful and they were on the outskirts of Khoi. They had routed the Russians that protected Van and there was little risk from the Russians who were still stinging from that defeat. It had been a hard-fought winter with defeats in the Caucasus and then victories in the Anatolian plain. Their leaders in Constantinople, including the famous Enver Pasha of the CUP, made it clear that some of these setbacks were the result of Armenian treachery. As the Ottoman troops sat around the campfire, they joked that the Armenians were done now. Thousands were dead and the army and Turkish militias rounded up even greater numbers and were marching them to camps in Syria. Success seemed to surround them and they could finally relax. What they didn't see were five shadows moving just outside the firelight and heading toward their commander's tent.

The tallest of the four looked at the radium dial of his wristwatch. It was 2300hrs. They had fifteen minutes to accomplish their mission before the Cossacks attacked the camp. He used hand signals to move his counterparts to both the front and the back of the tent. The goal: to capture the Ottoman officer, take whatever dispatches he carried, and do so silently so that none of his troops were the wiser. They had already silenced the four sets of pickets sent out to guard the camp. Francis had planned to have the Mansfields and the Bankrofts handle the pickets. By the time he had silenced his target, Bektashi had already finished two more. Alexander handled the final picket. The guards never really had a chance when the shadows descended upon them. Now, it was time to engage the real target.

Mary and Beverly worked silently toward the main door of the tent while Francis and Alexander moved to the rear of the tent with Bektashi standing guard deeper in the shadows. Beverly gently opened the flap of the tent to find an Ottoman officer sitting on the edge of his cot, drinking raki in candlelight. Across from him was a young, terri-fied girl sitting on a camp stool awaiting whatever fate the officer intended. Mary looked down at the officer. The officer looked up just in time to see Beverly join Mary. The candle-light revealed two women in cloaks. He thought to himself: a gift from some local clan leader? How delightful.

Mary walked over and offered a hand that seemed to the Ottoman officer as an invitation. He was unsteady as he stood up, but eventually was in arm's length of this cloaked lady. He reached for her outstretched hand. She grabbed him by the wrist and twisted his arm while covering his mouth with her other hand. The officer resisted and Mary applied what she thought was the right pressure on his neck just below the mastoid process in the rear of his skull. Mary never knew for certain whether it was the raki or her anger at the thought of what the officer intended to do with the young girl, but the officer was dead in less than a second. Mary lowered him back down on his cot.

The sound of Alexander's knife slicing through the tent wall caught the attention of the three women. Francis glided through the opening to find three living and one dead. He whispered, "We agreed to take him prisoner."

Mary shrugged. "He resisted."

Beverly added, "It was an error on his part."

By now, Alexander was in the tent. He said, "So it would appear. Who is our other guest?"

Mary shrugged. Beverly spoke to the girl in Persian. "Who are you?"

The girl shook her head. Clearly, she had not understood.

Alexander addressed her in Armenian. "Who are you and why are you here?"

The girl could barely get out, "Captive."

"From where?"

"Van."

"Where is your family?"

"All dead."

Francis had located the officer's papers in a small, green leather dispatch case under the cot. He looked up. "We have some things here to keep." He gathered the papers, closed and relocked the dispatch case and put it back under the cot. "Just in case the Cossacks don't finish the job properly, I want it to look like this Turk died in his sleep. We need to get out now. Ask our newest colleague to follow us and be quiet."

Alexander turned to Beverly and said, "I suspect she would prefer your assistance rather than mine." He pointed to the rope that tied the girl to the camp chair. Beverly nodded and untied the girl's ankle.

She put her right forefinger to her lips and used her left hand to point toward the slice in the tent wall. Mary lightly touched the girl on the forehead. She passed a mental image of safety and security that the girl seemed to understand. Mary walked to the opening in the tent wall and beckoned the girl, who rose and walked slowly toward the tent edge. She bent over and spit on the officer's body, then nodded and followed Beverly and Mary. Francis, Alexander, and Bektashi had already disappeared into the night. Beverly grabbed the young girl by the shoulders and pushed her through the hole in the tent wall. They moved quickly out of the range of the firelight, sat down in the darkness, and waited. They did not have to wait long. The Cossack raid on the camp began precisely at 2315hrs just as Francis and the Cossack captain agreed. Just like their dead captain, the Ottoman soldiers had no chance of survival.

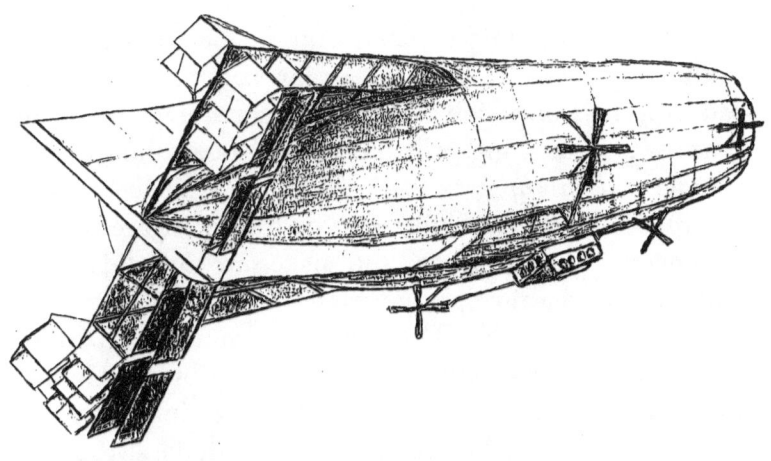

An Ideal Way to Cross
the Arabian desert

Khuzestan, Early May 1915

WHEN THE WAR STARTED, ENSIGN JAN SCHULTZ WAS WORKING ON HIS DOC-
torate in engineering at Heidelberg. He was not keen on
serving in the German Army though he was offered command of an artillery company. Instead, he volunteered to
serve on an Imperial Navy Airship. He never regretted his
decision.

The two passengers in the crew cabin puzzled him: a
young man dressed in the grey uniform of a German officer
and an elder gentlemen dressed in civilian clothes that looked
more suited to a construction engineer than a soldier. Neither were German native speakers — that was certain. As
was their role in the war: Schultz was certain they were spies.
Schultz had never known anyone serving in military intelligence, so his expectations had been colored by the mystery
of the trade and the few novels he had read while at university. These two men looked so ordinary. The one in uniform

looked so young, almost a child, and the man in the civilian clothes seemed older than the airship commander. Schultz had expected some sign of superhuman courage or intelligence or ... something. Still, orders were orders and the commander of *Luftshiff 9*, or the Lucky Lady as the crew called her, made it clear to Schultz that he was to engage the two passengers and, most important, make sure they did not get in the way of the airship's operation.

As he looked out the window and down nearly 3,000 feet to the desert below, Michael was captured by the German airship and its ability to sail over the sand dunes that had been his nemesis on the last trip to meet with the al-Rashidis. The German airship was easily twice the size of the ship that took him to the Viceroy's College, and certainly faster. There were few landmarks that he could use to gauge their speed, but it was certainly faster than the fabric and wood aircraft the Germans used to reunite him with his father in Afghanistan nearly two years ago. The German crew referred to their ship as a Zeppelin after its designer, Ferdinand von Zeppelin. They told Michael that this was a relatively new model known as the P class airship. Whatever its name, Michael was convinced this was an ideal way to cross the Arabian desert.

They were sitting in the canteen of the airship where the crew shared their meals. It was really little more than a 6-by-8-foot cabin with a small wood table anchored to the floor and metal chairs. Schultz served strong, black coffee and explained the airship as a means of passing the time until the two passengers were delivered to their destination. Well, they were on his ship after all, so why shouldn't they know about the ship?

"We are a naval Zeppelin based in a disguised field just north of Dar es Salaam. This is our first mission outside of Africa since we brought our airship from Germany. L-9 is a warship with the ability to deliver bombs on targets and we have machine gun positions for defense and for ground attack. We have bombed British supply ships in the Arabian Sea as well as served as a scout for our fast cruisers hunting British troop ships and their escorts. We have even practiced resupply operations like the one you have requested."

Michael could not help himself. He was fascinated. He asked, "What is your top speed and the highest altitude you have flown?"

Schultz smiled. "At one point, the gauges on our airspeed indicator have shown a top speed of nearly 100 kilometers an hour, but we did have a tail wind. The Zeppelin factory says our top speed is 65 kilometers an hour with a range of close to a thousand kilometers. As you can imagine, our range is based on the fuel for our engines not our ability to stay aloft. Honestly, we could stay aloft indefinitely."

Schultz chuckled, "Or at least until the crew got hungry. As to our maximum altitude, we generally cruise at 1,000 meters. On one mission, we did fly at nearly 3,000 meters to avoid detection, but at that altitude it was very cold, and our range was significantly reduced. Plus, we were very cold since we had left our wool clothes at our base. After all, Equatorial Africa is quite warm."

Michael had to do some quick mental arithmetic since he had been raised in the British system of feet, miles, and miles per hour. After he had made the calculations, he realized that the airship was well and truly a wonder and certainly life as a crew member must be quite enjoyable — even in wartime. As if reading his mind, Michael heard his father ask, "Is there any danger?"

"Sir, there is no danger to you on this trip. However, when we are hunting British warships, there is always a danger when they engage us with their guns. Remember, this airship is nothing more than a series of hydrogen gas bags wrapped in fabric with our wooden gondolas and engines strapped below. One lucky shot and our airship would explode and we would fall to our deaths. Of course, nothing like the dangers you face in your job or those faced by the German Army."

Michael recovered quickly and asked, "What are the losses in the airship squadrons?"

"We are considered a high risk. Not as high a risk as our *unterseeboots,* but our colleagues in Europe are currently suffering about fifty percent casualties." Schultz took a sip from his coffee mug. "When we were first sent to Africa, the crew was disappointed. Now, after nearly a year of war, they realize that we really are flying in the Lucky Lady. We are fighting a different war here in the East. More importantly, we can serve the Empire with far less risk of death than our colleagues in the west."

Schultz stood up, stretched to his full six-foot height and pulled out a large gold pocket watch. He said, "Gentlemen, we are two hours away from our rendezvous with your colleagues on the ground. What can I do to help you prepare?"

Michael smiled and said, "Ensign, we are ready. How will you deliver the cargo? There will be no landing dock in the desert like the one we used in Damascus."

Schultz nodded. "We have delivered cargo before in Africa. We have attached parachutes to the pallets of rifles and ammunition. As to your own arrival, we will hover above the ground at 20 meters, lower a rope ladder like you may have seen on regular ships and you will climb down. It won't be easy, but it is the only way we can safely make it so."

Michael nodded. He looked at his father and said, "You have made that sort of transfer before?"

James nodded. "It is as the ensign said. Not easy, but not as dangerous as it seems."

Schultz said, "If that is all, I will let the captain know you are ready. I will return to the canteen and then take you aft to the loading dock."

James said, "Thank you, Ensign. You have been kind."

"It is my duty, sir. Please stay in the canteen until I return.

This P-class ship has a complicated set of corridors and it is confusing to any newcomers, even other members of the airship squadrons. I would prefer not to play hide and seek with you as we approach our destination." Schultz turned and left the galley. Michael could see him at the end of a corridor climbing a set of stairs to what he assumed was the bridge.

James turned to Michael. He said, "Well, so far I am impressed with von Trier's support."

Michael nodded. "It is amazing what the modern age provides us when we wage war. Imagine how powerful it would be if the Lucky Lady arrived at a British garrison near Basra and started dropping bombs and firing machine guns? It would create havoc! Do you think there is any chance we might convince the airship commander to do so?"

At first, James thought Michael was joking. But as he looked into his son's eyes, he realized Michael was serious. He said, "Son, there is no going back on our plan. Von Trier has given us the resources for the plan that we proposed. We are obliged to do our best. If our best is not good enough, then the Germans may work in a more conventional way. I suspect if that happens, it will be a German cruiser or submarine that will do the damage. As the ensign said, this is the only airship in the entire region. It is based in Africa. I think they want to keep it available for emergencies. Such as … our rescue when we have accomplished our mission."

Michael nodded. In his mind, he could imagine how an airship at 3,000 feet could attack soldiers. They would look like ants and would be crushed like ants. But, as his father said, they had another mission entirely. Perhaps another day. He said, "Father when we arrive, please let me start the discussion. The Rashidis know me and these tribal folk are a suspicious lot. They will eventually warm to you and, I suspect, focus on your advice because they respect age. I will introduce you as my father and my teacher and that will go a long way."

"Not as long a way as our delivery of German Mausers, more ammunition, and German gold."

Michael smiled and said, "Indeed. These people have a tradition of raids and looting. More guns mean better raids and more power for the tribe. What I do not know is their connection with the Beni Lam. But, if the Rashidis are involved, we will be safe," Michael paused, "at least until they leave. But I suspect the Beni Lam will want no part of a tribal war."

Much later, a bell sounded in the canteen. Shortly after that, Schultz reappeared. He said, "Gentlemen, it is time for us to go down to the delivery deck. We are approaching the target."

They followed Schultz through several corridors and down two flights of metal staircases to the delivery deck. Once they arrived, they saw the open windows and the machine gun operators who sat in wicker seats looking out over the horizon. They wore leather coveralls, leather gloves and helmets, and green-tinted googles. Michael thought they looked more like insects, perhaps wasps, than men. Even though they were flying over the desert in May, at 3,000 feet and traveling at nearly 40 miles per hour, the deck was cool to the point of chill. Michael could see why the uniform of the day on this deck was leather. For once, he was glad of his German Army wool. He looked back at his father who pulled an Arab scarf known as a gutra around his head and neck and buttoned up his khaki cotton coat. They walked over to their luggage — two small carpet bags. Both Michael and James strapped on heavy leather belts with holsters. Michael reached into his bag and pulled out a large Luger pistol known among his German officer colleagues as a *lange pistole* or sometimes Navy Luger because of its long barrel. He placed it in the leather cross draw holster on his left hip. James reached into his bag and pulled out an American Colt revolver and placed it in a leather shoulder holster. They opened a metal arms locker that was near the skin of the deck and pulled out two Mauser carbines and slung the rifles around their back.

Schultz looked on as they prepared to depart. He knew what he did for the German Empire was important, but he wondered whether anything two men could do would matter to a larger world war. Still, if their mission was important enough to task the Lucky Lady to deliver them to this spot in the desert, he had to believe that their mission was critical to the Kaiser. One of the crew chiefs was laying on his stomach looking out a small hatch in the floor. He turned to Schultz and said, "Sir, we are approaching the target."

Schultz nodded and said to a second crew chief, "Open the gate!"

The second crew chief pulled a lever and suddenly the rear of the compartment began to open. Two clam-shelled doors opened with the sound of winches and gears pulling open the entire aft section of the gondola. Michael was entranced as the gondola switched from a dark wood world to a world of bright blue sky and deep khaki sand below. Schultz put his hands on the elbow of the two O'Connell's. He said, "Gentlemen, please take care. It is enchanting to see the world revealed like this, but it is also easy to make a wrong step and launch yourself to your death."

James turned to Schultz and said, "This happens?"

"Oh yes. If you haven't noticed, our crew chiefs are attached to the airship by a harness and rope system that looks like something you might see on a trapeze artist. After our arrival in Africa, we started to call them monkey harnesses because they allow the chiefs to walk out to the end of the platform like a monkey working gracefully through the trees. Now, please step back because the delivery of the cargo is about to begin."

Michael watched as two of the men he saw earlier began pushing a cart toward the platform. On top of the wheeled cart were two wooden crates strapped together with some type of thick rigging and on the top of these two crates was what looked to Michael like a large, folded sheet. The men pushed the cart off the edge of the platform and Micheal watched as the crates tumbled away from the cart and the sheet billowed open. It looked like a large umbrella attached to the crates by hawser lines that usually served to tie up ships to a dock. Michael noticed that there was a rope dangling over the edge of the platform. One of the crew chiefs began to reel in the rope and at the end of the rope, the cart reappeared. The crew chief in his monkey harness grabbed the edge of the cart and guided it back into the airship.

James was just as entranced as Michael. He said, "That was amazing."

Schultz laughed and said, "We do this sort of delivery regularly in Africa. Now, watch as the captain turns us around and takes us down to only ten meters above the ground. Once we are at that height, we will drop the rope ladder and you will leave us. I hope your reception party is waiting."

Michael said, "Given the fact that we are bringing them guns and gold, I doubt there is any risk of them not showing up."

Schultz nodded. "Guns and gold. It our standard delivery in Africa as well." Schultz came to the position of attention, saluted and said, "Gentlemen, I will leave you in the capable hands of our two crew chiefs. I have a job on the command deck that needs to be accomplished. I wish you safe travels and good success."

James took Schultz' hand and said, "Thank you for your work and safe travels to you as well. We will be living by our wits on the ground, but you face wind and storm as well as the enemy. I wish you a safe return to port."

Schultz did a courteous bow, turned on his heel and disappeared into the darkness of the forward part of the cabin. As he did so, one of the crew chiefs approached the O'Connells and tied what looked to Michael like a climbing rope around each of their chests and under their arms. Michael nodded and said to his father, "I don't think they trust us to climb down the ladder."

"I don't blame them. I have seen men crushed between a ship and a dock because of a false step on a rope ladder. Son, it never hurts to be careful."

Michael had not considered the risk of the climb down the ladder until this minute. The ship finally came to a stop and the crew chief escorted them to the edge of the platform. He motioned for them to sit down, carefully grab a rung from the rope ladder and place their foot on a rung two or three below that first one. As Michael gingerly made the turn, his boot slipped for a second. Though it felt like forever, Michael's boots eventually found the rungs and he started to climb down. Once Michael was on the ground and untied, James turned to the crew chief, rendered a salute and then grabbed the outside of the rope ladder with both hands and both feet and slid slowly down to the ground. Michael watched as his father made his graceful landing. He realized this might not have been the first time his father had made this sort of departure from an airship.

As they stood below the airship, its immensity overwhelmed them. They were in its shadow and the long tail section with the painted iron cross of the German Empire was dramatic. Suddenly, the engine noise increased, the four propellers began to carve the air and the ship pointed skyward and toward the west. They watched as the ship receded until it was nothing more than a dot on the horizon.

James said, "Well, so far so good. Where are our contacts?"

As if to answer, the Arabs appeared over a sand dune to the north and began to ride like madmen toward their two visitors and the two crates broken open on the desert floor. Michael said to his father, "And so, our war begins again!"

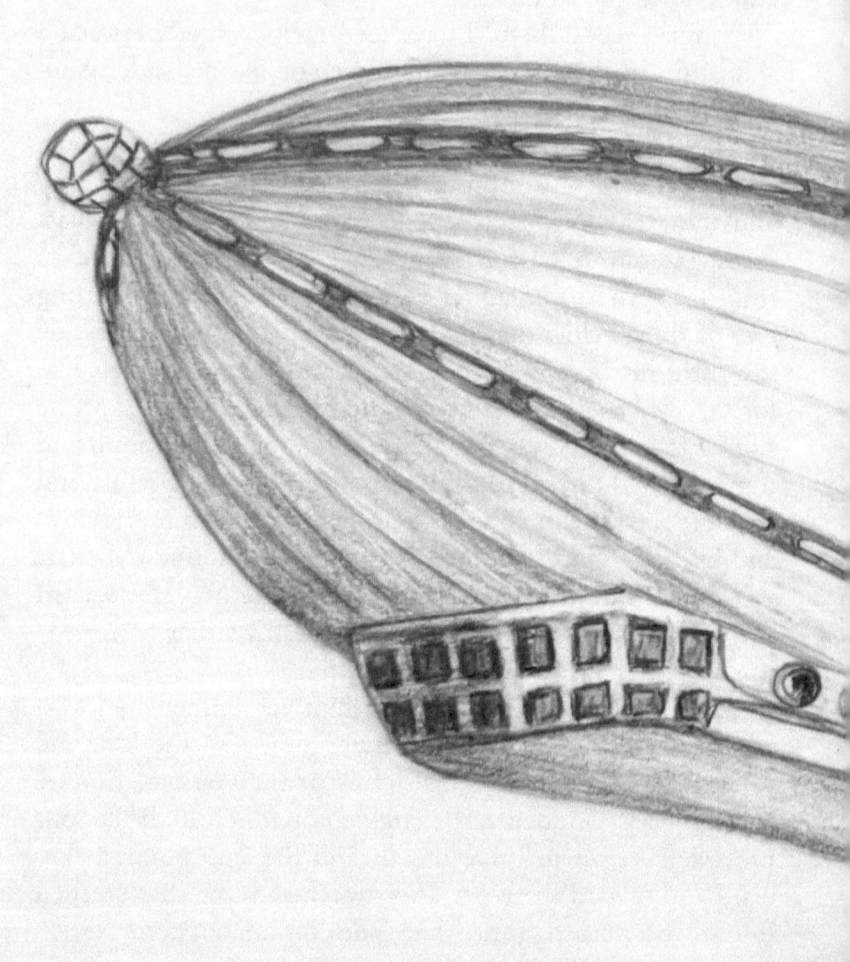

Part Three

Counterforce

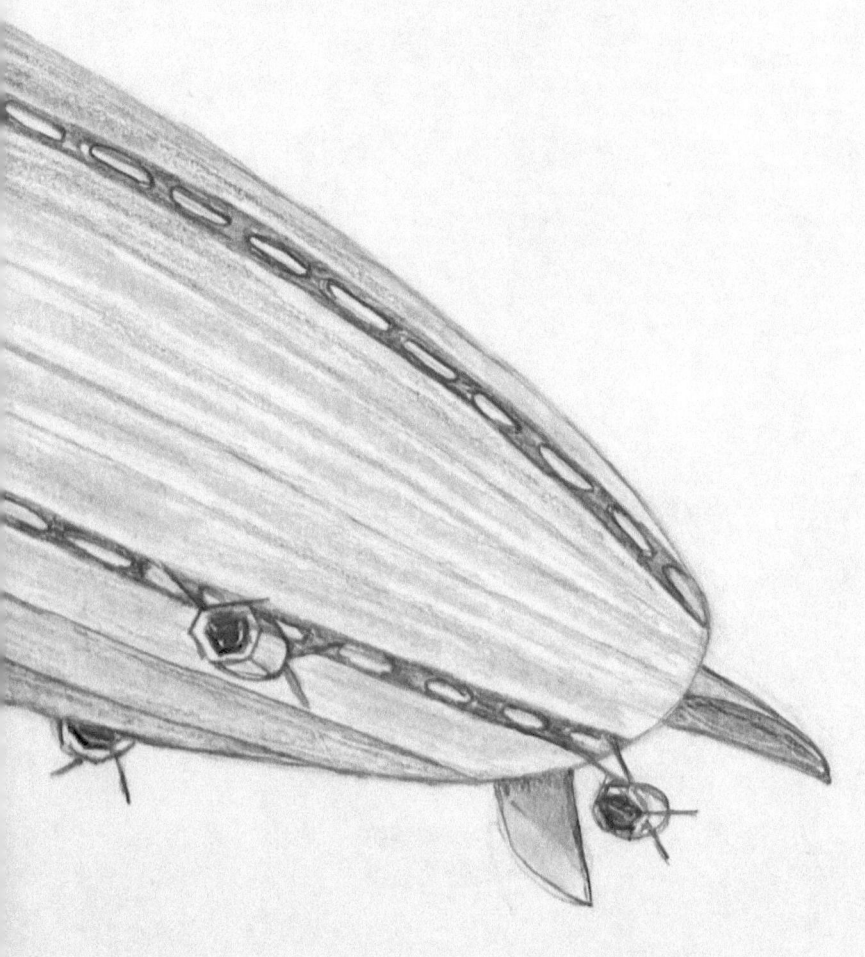

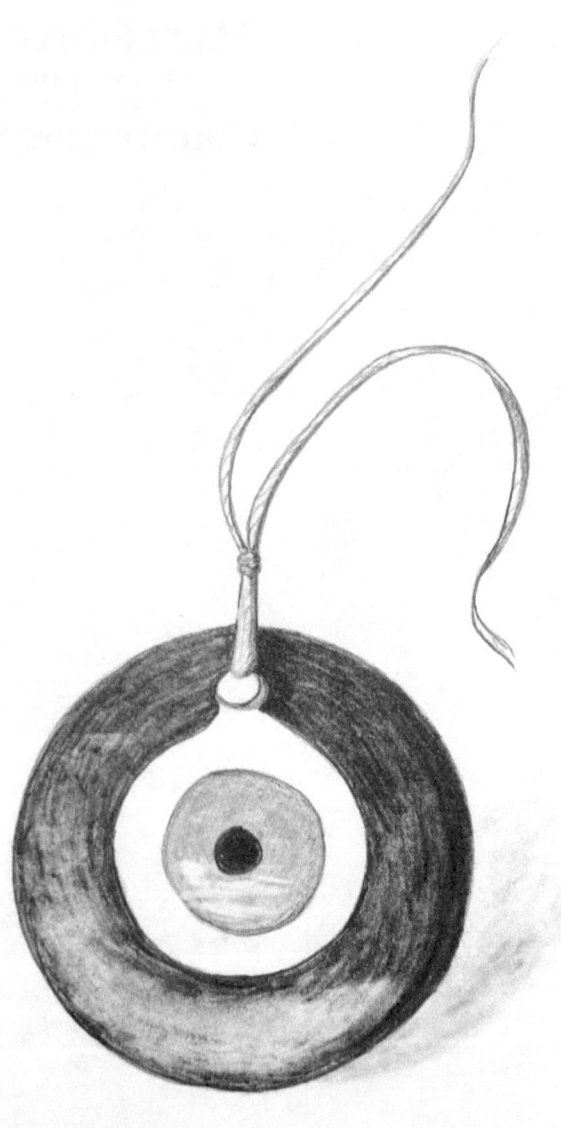

A Confusing Way to Get to a War

Muscat, May 1915

ELIZABETH, MARIAN AND NAISMITH TRAVELLED BY RAIL TO KARACHI HARBOR
and then by Royal Navy destroyer to Muscat. It seemed to
Elizabeth a most indirect way to get to Mesopotamia but
she knew by now that the British military was not always the
most efficient. She and Marian spent their days at sea in a
very cramped cabin that normally would have been the quarters for two ensigns on the ship. Naismith shared his own
quarters with two young ensigns. It was hot and unpleasant.

Naismith periodically joined Marian and Elizabeth in
their quarters. He and Marian used the time to teach Elizabeth additional meditation techniques that allowed her to
resist the stifling heat. Naismith said that the Tibetan meditation technique was designed to eliminate the stimulus
from the outside body to keep the inner core of the body and
mind at ease. He said the technique could be used for either
extreme heat or extreme cold. In an aside, he added that the
mind could prevent the body from suffering. He nodded to

Marian. She understood this was another teaching moment for Elizabeth's "demons."

Elizabeth looked at the grey-bearded man across from her. He was nearly a foot shorter than her father and easily fifty pounds lighter. For the past few years of her life, he had served as teacher, mentor and something like a beloved uncle. Elizabeth knew the world of shadows that she lived in took its toll on the players in the Great Game. Naismith's face was creased and his skin was darkened from years in the Indian sun. She wondered what she might look like in a few years. She hoped she would look more like her mother than Naismith, but then again, who knew? She smiled at Naismith and said, "So, this is the technique that the Hindu mystics use when they walk on hot coals?"

Naismith laughed. "No, Elizabeth. Do not confuse carnival tricks with mental discipline. The Hindu sadhus in the marketplace simply coat their feet with multiple layers of oil that prevent their feet from turning into cinders. Now, I suspect they may use some meditation to allow their mind to control the fear that must come with any risk of harm, but no amount of mediation is going to prevent the physics of heat or cold doing damage to human tissue. For this reason, you must take care not to burn yourself on the hot exposed pipes below decks or the railings and gun positions above deck."

The meditation techniques gave Elizabeth some comfort, but her impatience with the enforced isolation was enough to drive her to distraction. Marian sat next to her and whispered, "When your anger seems to take over, just imagine this meditation. Imagine a cool mountain stream. Imagine the trails near Nathiagali where you first found the Himalayan orchid."

Elizabeth had to admit that her two mentors were helping her gain more self-control, and even in the heat, she was less uncomfortable. As she sat in her bunk, she felt Naismith probing her thoughts and her boredom. She expected some comment about their work. Instead, she received another lesson in the mystic arts.

Naismith said, "So, since we can't move about, we shall make things move about instead." With that comment, Naismith raised his hand, palm down and closed his eyes. Elizabeth watched as Naismith began to levitate off the small metal chair in their cabin. As he did so, paper and pencils from the small writing desk rose up and began to circle around him like planets around the sun. Naismith opened his eyes and snatched the items out of the air. He settled back into his chair. As Elizabeth looked over at Marian, she had levitated her body and appeared to be sitting on the cabin wall as if gravity had been suspended. Naismith said, "Your turn."

To avoid looking foolish in any attempt to float items in the cabin, Elizabeth said, "My mother tried to teach me some kinesthesis on my last trip in a warship. We moved chess pieces on a chess board."

"A good start, but far less than I know you can accomplish. Let's start with something easy." Marian returned to her place next to Elizabeth.

She put the paper and pencil back on the writing desk. "Just write a small note."

Elizabeth stood up and started toward the desk when Naismith said, "No, Elizabeth. Write the note from where you are sitting."

Elizabeth wondered: *How is that useful?*

Naismith's voice came into her mind: *It isn't useful, it is simply an exercise. First, you move the pencil on the paper, then you can learn to move other items. A knife perhaps. Perhaps even changing the path of a bullet.*

Elizabeth nodded, closed her eyes, and imagined the pencil first standing up on its own and then scratching a note on the page. She decided to use cursive script so that she didn't have to lift the pencil off the page. When she opened her eyes, she found Naismith floating upside down sitting on the ceiling of the room. He was smiling.

She looked over at the desk. Words were on the paper: *Float, damn you*

From her new perch on the ceiling, Marian nodded. "Now you are beginning to see how much the mind can control. Far more than you thought."

Elizabeth said, "Are you going to float there all day?"

Marian said, "What do you mean?"

Elizabeth realized Marian was sitting next to her on her bunk. "Did you really levitate or did you just make me think you were floating?"

Naismith smirked and said, "Yes."

Elizabeth had spent enough time with experts in this field to know that there was a very short distance between what was real and what was illusion. She was tired of being the student in the cramped space of the warship cabin. She decided to change the subject. "I still don't understand how traveling from Karachi to Muscat is going to get us to Basra. I realize that the port of Muscat serves trade between the Arabian Sea and the Persian Gulf, but surely this ship could take us directly to Basra."

Naismith smiled at her impatience and her effort to avoid more training. There were times when Elizabeth showed herself as a mature young woman, but other times when she acted as a young girl. Naismith knew that was to be expected, but it remained a small amusement in what was the serious work of the secret service. As he was about to offer an answer, he heard or rather felt a voice in his head: *Keep training her. She is going to be important to my plan.*

Naismith's face tightened as he fought for control of his mind. He thought: *Chodak, you know nothing about this girl. She is a warrior that will easily defeat your schemes. She is the daughter of two masters of the mystic powers. She will not be your prey.*

The voice retreated. As it did, he heard a final, simple croak: *We shall see, soldier. We shall see.*

Both Marian and Elizabeth were shocked over the transformation of Naismith's face. One minute he was smiling and the next, his face went blank and his eyelids closed. It was distressing to watch. Elizabeth asked, "Master Guru, is something bothering you? You were about to answer me and then for a second, you seemed to be someplace entirely different."

Naismith recovered and smiled. "I was just thinking of our upcoming rendezvous with the Ravens."

"They are in Muscat?"

"They are coming to Muscat from throughout the region." He paused and said, "To answer your question directly, we are going to Muscat because that is the route of this destroyer's patrol. They are hunting a German cruiser as well as German submarines that are known to be in the Arabian Sea searching for our troop and cargo ships. The Royal Navy is patrolling a triangle among the ports of Karachi, Muscat and Bombay. As important as we might think our work is, the truth is the Royal Navy only offered to take us on as cargo for the leg of the patrol from Karachi to Muscat. Once I knew that was the case, I simply told the Ravens to assemble in Muscat. It will take them many days because they are traveling by horse and camel and Persian dhow."

"So, Muscat is nothing more than a rendezvous point for our onward travel?"

"Indeed. If my briefing from the Royal Navy in Karachi is correct, the port facilities that service Basra and the Abadan oil fields are awash with cargo and troop ships at anchor. No one seems to have considered how hard it would be to supply an Indian Army division in Mesopotamia. From Muscat, we will be traveling by other means to get to our final destination."

Elizabeth smiled. "By air, perhaps?"

Naismith responded, "We will have to wait until we get to

Muscat. I don't know how successful the colonel has been in arranging our onward travel." He paused when there was a knock on the cabin door.

In response to Naismith's shout to enter, a young sailor in white cotton duck pants and a cotton undershirt entered carrying a small tea tray with a teapot, three mugs, sugar and some biscuits. "Compliments of the captain, sir. He apologizes for the accommodations, but he said that the major and the lieutenant," the sailor paused and looked at both Marian and Elizabeth in khaki blouse and skirt, "would understand that it would not be proper to be seen on the ship."

Naismith nodded and used just enough of his mesmerism voice to control the sailor's impressions of them both. "Please send my thanks to the captain. By my calculations, we should be in Muscat by," Naismith looked at his wristwatch, "tomorrow morning. Is that so?"

"Indeed it is so, sir. We will anchor out sometime during middle watch and then enter the harbor at four bells on the morning watch. I realize it is hard to make out time inside your," the sailor looked around trying to find some adjective to use with the cramped cabin, "quarters."

"Thank you. That will be all then until dinner."

"Sir, dinner will be served at six bells in second dog watch."

"Excellent. Dismissed then."

"Aye, sir."

The sailor closed the door behind him. Elizabeth shook her head. She said, "Bells and dog watch?"

Naismith laughed. "Elizabeth, don't forget that sailors don't wear watches like we do or like the men you have met piloting our airships and aeroplanes. Only the seniors on ships will have watches. The bridge will have clocks on board, but sailors need to know what time to be at their duty stations. So, their world is divided into seven watches: first watch, middle watch, morning watch, forenoon watch, afternoon watch, first dog watch and second dog watch. Each of the first five are four hours long and the two dog watches are two hours long. Bells are rung at the half hour. So, time is divided in the first five watches by a total of eight bells. The two dog watches are divided by four bells."

"So, four bells in the morning watch is 0600hrs? And, six bells in the second dog watch is 1900hrs?"

"Well done!"

"A bit strange but I understand. How does this get sorted with the changing time zones?"

Naismith laughed again. "I forget sometimes you are a serious student of natural history. The ship watches would be adjusted each day at noon based on the sextant sighting at the end of the forenoon watch. So, the ship's time would be on a gradual shift. Luckily in our short bit of travel, the ship will remain in the same time zone between Karachi to Muscat."

Elizabeth nodded. "It was a challenge trying to sort out time changes when I flew from Constantinople to Alexandria, then to Aden and then from Aden to Karachi."

"Our world is shrinking because of our new means of travel. Still, you need to remember it is all a man-made creation. As the mystics would say, it is all *maya*. It is all illusion."

Inside his head, Naismith heard Chodak laugh: *It is all illusion until it isn't, soldier. You know that better than most. Teach her well because she will need all her skills to survive the fight ahead. I want her alive so that when I need her, she will be there.*

Naismith shook his head as if he was a horse trying to shake off flies trying to settle on his eyes. He wondered why Chodak was suddenly so interested in Elizabeth or, for that matter, why he was so interested in intruding into his own thoughts.

This time Marian asked, "Master Guru, are you unwell?"

Naismith returned to the present and said, "Nothing a little tea won't help. Will you pour, Elizabeth?"

Elizabeth dutifully poured a cup of strong, black tea into a mug and handed it to Naismith. For the first time, she watched as her guru picked up a cube of sugar, put it into his mouth and then slowly sipped the tea and passed it over the sugar cube. She knew it was a style of drinking tea most common among the natives of India, Afghanistan, and Persia. She had not seen Naismith drink tea that way. He rarely took any sugar at all. She thought to herself: Something is wrong. I wish he would tell me so I can help.

As she formed that thought, a voice inside her head spoke to her: *Do not worry about the master guru, Elizabeth. He will be fine. You need to focus on your own skills as you prepare for war. Prepare!*

This time it was Elizabeth who shook her head. Where did that voice come from?

A Long Ride Ahead

Tabriz, Persia, May 1915

IT WAS LATE AFTERNOON AND BEKTASHI AND THE YOUNG ARMENIAN GIRL Alia were sweeping the courtyard in their small compound. Their brooms raised small clouds of dust as they pushed the desert sand toward the far end of the compound. They had been here nearly two weeks since they rode in with the Cossacks. It was a small, walled compound with one main building that served as sleeping quarters and a dining room for the British officers. There was a second building that served as a kitchen and sleeping quarters for Bektashi and Alia. In the far corner of the compound was a small outhouse that connected to the open sewers on the other side of the wall, known in Persian as "the jube." It wasn't the palace they occupied in Constantinople nor the luxurious quarters they enjoyed in Odessa, but it was far better than the previous month of horseback riding with the Cossack patrol. Bektashi had lived in worse places, and he expected he would live in better in the future. For now, he was determined to keep the place as clean as could be managed in the hot, dry climate.

It had taken Bektashi more than a week of arguments with his British masters to convince them that this young woman would be safer with them than with either a Persian household or a Russian Cossack camp. Each night when they made camp, he argued his point. It didn't help that one of the Cossacks was ethnic Armenian and he wanted to take her with him back across the Russian border. Once they arrived in Tabriz, he decided it was time to make his views known.

Bektashi was adamant. "Madame, this girl needs a family now. Riding with Russians, Cossacks! Never, I cannot allow it."

Francis and Mary were surprised at his strident comment. Mary said, "Bektashi Bey, how will you take care of her? How will you even talk to her?"

Bektashi put his right forefinger next to his nose. "Madame, you know Bektashi is a man of the world. I speak Armenian. Of course, I do! And, over time, I will teach her English and Persian. She will be a perfect member of our little team. She will help me cook and clean, she will learn how to ride and how to shoot. I am sure you will teach her some of your wizardry. It will be a good thing."

Mary was quiet for a moment as she probed Bektashi's mind. What she saw were memories of his own childhood. Bektashi was an orphan of tribal war and knew the difficulty of burying hateful memories when you can't bury your dead family. Mary could see Bektashi's plans. Someday, Bektashi intended to return to his mountain village in Albania. He would be wealthy. He would be wise. And, he would be vengeful. For now, he was simply happy to be riding with these two mystic warriors and fighting the Turks wherever and whenever he could. Clearly, he was moved by the fact that their Armenian girl was in the same situation. Mary could see that he would not accept anything other than their agreement. She looked at Beverly.

All Beverly did was shrug. She could not imagine adding an untrained teenager to their already strange band of intelligence officers, Cossacks and one outspoken Albanian. However, she knew the Cossacks would leave soon enough, heading back to the Persian-Russian border and their endless patrols. She also expected she and Alexander eventually would receive their own set of orders and leave the Bankrofts behind. It would be their problem after that. Mary turned to Francis and said, "I agree with Bektashi. We could use additional help as we take on a new mission. He will be responsible."

Francis could see there was more to the story than he would know until much later when they were alone. He said, "Bektashi Bey, it is entirely up to you. If you believe she will be a help and she is willing to stay with us, then make it so. You will be responsible. You will have to arrange for proper traveling kit for her because none of us are going to be staying in Tabriz for long."

Bektashi did one of his deep bows and said, "I will do my best, master."

Bektashi watched as the four British officers walked back into the compound. He could see they were excited. They had a new mission! Honestly, he was tired of keeping house in the narrow streets of Tabriz. Trying to find food in the market and negotiating everything from cucumbers to lamb shanks. These Persians were tedious. It seemed they were ready to take the gold out of his teeth if they could get away by some clever ruse. Also, taking care of the two colleagues, Andrew and Beverly, resulted in double the normal work and twice the worry as he was certain that there were enemies somewhere in the city searching for these four British agents.

Once inside their compound, Francis said, "Bektashi Bey, we have a new mission!"

"Master, I could tell that from the lightness of your step when you returned from the British mission. Where do we go? What shall we do?"

"We ride south and into Kurdistan. We will meet agents there who will help us into Baghdad. There we will be operating inside the Ottoman lines. It will be most dangerous, Bektashi Bey. We cannot ask you to risk your life in such a dangerous mission."

Bektashi straightened to his full height of nearly six feet. He was still much shorter than Francis Bankroft, but he hoped to appear as strong. "Master, where you and Madame go, so shall I go. We are certain to complete our mission and will be rewarded!"

Mary Bankroft laughed and put her hand on Bektashi's shoulder. "Who could ask for a better comrade? It will be a long ride just to get into Kurdistan and we must prepare both ourselves and our horses for the journey. But, tonight, we must enjoy a good meal. I stopped along the way and picked up some lamb tenderloin. No shanks for us tonight, Bektashi Bey. We will dine like pashas!"

Bektashi smiled and said, "Madame, how did you get the Persian butcher to give up this meat? I know you must have paid a fortune."

It was Francis' turn to laugh. He said, "Bektashi Bey, you have been traveling with us now for months. You must know that Mary is a witch. The butcher never knew what happened."

Bektashi realized that his master was joking, but he also knew that indeed both of these English people were wizards or djinns or some sort of magicians. They accomplished things in ways that he could not imagine and made people see things that were not there. He was pleased to be on their side because he knew it was never good to work against wizards.

"Master, what of our two guests? Will they be traveling with us?"

"They will depart on a separate mission tonight. We will guide them to their meeting place and then watch to keep them safe."

Once again Bektashi stood at what he considered his most formal position of attention. "Master, you can count on me."

"We always do, Bektashi. We always do. Now, we must discuss our plans with our colleagues. You and Alia must prepare the meal. Our work tonight will keep us up for hours past midnight and we need to be ready for anything."

Bektashi nodded and disappeared into the house in a flurry of robes. Mary laughed and said, "He is a wonder, you know."

"Indeed, and he will be key to our success once we get into Kurdistan. We will need someone to maintain our base camp as we engage the Kurds. There will be no Cossack guides for this mission."

"Four can travel faster and with a much lower profile than four and a company of Cossacks. That is especially true as we ride farther south into Kurdistan."

"And, as you well know, that is only the beginning."

As promised, Bektashi prepared a meal that was hearty while not too extravagant. He wanted it to be a good farewell meal, but not something that would run well into the evening. There would be cleaning to do, weapons to prepare and horses to saddle. Bektashi knew the schedule and intended to keep to it. His prized possession, the gold hunter watch, remained in his cummerbund and he checked with regularly.

He had learned over the past years working with the Bank-rofts that timing was the key to any successful operation.

During the meal, the Bankrofts and the Mansfields discussed the future, at least as much as they knew. Beverly was the first to open the discussion. "So, Kurdistan? What in the world are you to do in Kurdistan?"

Francis stopped a fork of lamb and pilau that was headed to his mouth. He looked up and said, "Start a rebellion, of course."

Alexander said, "Just the two of you?"

Mary smiled and said, "Well, we only have orders to start one rebellion."

Beverly choked as she started to laugh.

"Seriously?"

Francis said, "The goal is to create a counterforce against the Turks so they have a two-front war in Mesopotamia. It isn't as if we haven't been involved in this sort of thing in the past. Of course, it helps to have a local guide. Our office in Tabriz has provided us with one of their contacts, D17, who is a Kurdish tribal leader based in Berazeh. D17 trades in Tabriz and has been a reliable reporter to the Tabriz office for five years. He has family connections in the mountains on the Ottoman side of Kurdistan and into the city of Suleimaniyah. We can only hope that his influence is as profound as he claims."

"And, if not?"

Mary smiled and said, "Then you will have to repay the favor and save our skins."

Beverly said, "From the message we received, it would appear we will be far away."

"It is never far for the Ravens."

"Then, you know?"

Francis said, "I only know that the office in Tabriz thought Raven was a code word."

Mary nodded and said, "Well, in some ways, it is."

Alexander said, "The message was vague. We are to be picked up tonight and then we will meet Naismith tomorrow night. The rest of the briefing will take place in a Navy compound in Oman."

"A long flight. I hope you are prepared for the trip."

"How can we prepare? We have our Raven uniform in our kit bags. Little more."

Francis smiled and offered, "Travel light, freeze at night."

Beverly said, "Not in May in the desert!"

They all laughed as Bektashi brought in the desert and the coffee. With a great deal of ceremony, he pulled the hunter out of his cummerbund and said, "Ladies and gentlemen, if we are to be in place at the proper time, we have approximately one hour before we should leave."

Francis smiled at Bektashi and said, "Thank you. It is easy to get distracted with old friends. We will be ready, I promise."

Once Bektashi left, Alexander said, "I would like to take him with us."

Mary said, "No chance of that Alexander." She used just enough mesmerism skill to both ensure there would be no argument but also no realization that she used her skills on her colleague. She knew all too well that Francis was committed to his men. An argument might end what would was a very pleasant final evening together. As she gathered the last of her fig and yogurt desert on her spoon she said, "He is a treasure to be sure. You both need to learn to find loyal allies in whatever assignment you have next after you have completed the Raven mission."

Beverly nodded. "It is a skill we need to improve. That said, we haven't had the experience you both have had in the trade. We are just barely journeymen." She finished her desert and added, "And speaking of journeyman, do you think we shall see Elizabeth in Muscat?"

Mary nodded. "I have received little in the way of communication from Elizabeth other than a brief message saying she was going to be working with Guru Naismith. I suspect that answers your question."

Alexander agreed. "There are no Ravens without Naismith. If Elizabeth is working with him, then she will be with us on our next assignment."

Mary looked across the table at her husband. Francis was proud of their daughter's accomplishments but was a concerned father when it came to her work with the Ravens. She decided to change the subject. She said, "And our son, Conrad, is currently on his way to Mesopotamia as well. He will be a staff officer working for what they are calling the Indian Expeditionary Force D. Honestly, I'm relieved he isn't headed to the Western Front or, for that matter, for Gallipoli."

Francis said, "It is all war, dear. It is all dangerous."

Alexander said, "True enough, Francis. But, so far, Mesopotamia is not paying the butcher's bill that we are hearing about on the Western Front. For heaven's sake, there is talk that the Germans used poison gas!"

Mary could see that the conversation was about to take a turn that no one needed as they prepared for travel. Again, she used a calming voice on her guests and her husband, "We can only focus on what we need to here and now and hope for the best."

Beverly could see what Mary was trying to do. She stood up and said, "Amen to that. Now, I am going back to our rooms to do one last check of our packs."

Alexander nodded: "I believe I have received my instruction."

Francis smirked and said, "So have I. We will leave the table for Bektashi and Alia and spend our time getting ready." As he stood up, he noticed Bektashi was lurking in the shadows with a rolling cart, ready to clear the table. He raced in as they departed. Alia followed. They had more than enough to do before they left and Bektashi could see no good reason for his English masters to be focused on wars that had nothing to do with them. They had their own wars to fight.

Bektashi turned to Alia and said, "I will need to go to the stables to prepare their horses. Can you complete the cleanup on your own?"

Alia smiled: "Yes, uncle. I am more than capable. In fact, if you need me in the stables, the dishes can wait."

Bektashi stopped and thought for a moment. This girl was strong willed and would be a good companion on the road. She needed to feel a part of the story so that she would remain loyal. He said, "You can go with me and help in the stables and when we ride tonight. But, you must remember to keep still and never, ever talk about what you see tonight or any night in the future. Our lives may depend on our silence!"

Alia was a teenager who was used to adults speaking to her as if she was a child. Still, the British family and their Albanian servant had been kind and she understood they were fighting the Ottoman Army. That was enough for her to be obedient. At least until she could find a way to avenge her family. She said, "I promise, Uncle. You can trust me to remain silent."

A Monster in the Desert

Tabriz, May 1915

THEY LEFT TABRIZ IN THE DARK. SIX HORSES AND RIDERS HEADING WEST. They passed traders who were happy to be inside the boundaries of the city. The traders knew that the desert at night was filled with terrors: bandits, packs of wild dogs, even the occasional pack of lions. The most dangerous were the bandits — a blend of Persians, Arabs, and Kurds who wandered the borderlands looking for caravans that were poorly armed and poorly led. As they passed the six riders, they shook their heads and thought: there go six riders to their death.

Bektashi was not in the least worried. He rode at the end of the six with a Mauser rifle across his saddle, always at the ready. He watched Francis load his pistols and place them in shoulder holsters. He also wore a sheathed short sword, wickedly sharp and heavy, and carried his own Mauser across this saddle. Bektashi asked once where the sword came from since it looked like nothing he had seen in his days across the Ottoman Empire. Francis Bankroft simply said,

"Afghanistan." That was enough for Bektashi. The only thing he knew about Afghanistan was the population were demons.

Mary Bankroft's weapons were far less obvious, but he noticed she was also wearing a brace of pistols in holsters on her hips. Bektashi was certain that there were other weapons somewhere under her abaya. Still, she was a wizard, so why should she carry weapons at all? The two other British agents looked to be prepared for war as well, but a strange war indeed. Under woolen shawls they were wearing strange, blue-black garb that seemed to change color in the moonlight. Sometimes blue, sometimes black, and sometimes absorbing the available light so that they were close to invisible. They had pistols and knives but what captured Bektashi's attention was they carried crossbows on long straps across their backs. Crossbows? It was both arcane and terrifying.

Alia rode next to Bektashi. He was pleased that she was a good rider. She never complained, and she understood how to care for horse — her own and the horses of their British employers. He also liked that she rarely spoke when they were on the road. This allowed him to focus on the safety of their little caravan. When they were riding with Cossacks, it was of little importance. Now, Bektashi felt their security was his responsibility. When they departed the compound, Francis told him that they would ride for an hour out into the desert. After that, they would stop and their colleagues would leave them. If it all went as planned, they would return well before dawn. All Bektashi said was "Inshallah, master."

While Bektashi had no chance to check his treasured hunter pocket watch, he knew from the movement of the crescent moon that they were approaching an hour and that meant they would stop soon. He turned to Alia and said, "Little one, you need to be prepared to see magic and wizardry. So, no matter what you see or hear tonight, I need you to promise you will keep silent. Our safety may depend on it. And do not fear, Alia, because our masters are humans but they have the power of djinns." He watched as a wide-eyed Alia nodded her assent.

The five Arabs sent to kill the British agents were hiding in an alley when the six riders left the walled compound. At first, they were unsure if the British would return. If they could have been certain, they would have waited inside the compound and finished them on their return. They had ridden north to Tabriz under instructions from the Germans. It had been a long trek, but they were well paid and further reward was promised when they returned with proof they had killed the British agents. So, not knowing whether these riders would return to Tabriz or continue traveling south, the assassins decided to follow. The British had small packs on their horses and they were definitely heading south. Were they making good their escape? If so, to where?

The lead Arab decided as their targets disappeared in the dark. They would follow. If the British continued, they would ambush them somewhere on the road at dawn when they were tired and the sunrise blinded them. If they returned, then they would ambush them in the dark just outside the city walls of Tabriz. There were three men and three women. They would be easy prey for men used to the violence of night work. They would earn their German gold and they would be able to sell whatever they found on the Britishers. It was certain to be a good night's work.

Francis stopped his horse. He looked at the radium dial of his wristwatch. 0150hrs. They had arrived at the right time and based on his reading of the terrain, at the right place. He dismounted and the others did as well. Bektashi and Alia took the reins of all six horses and pulled their mounts next to a small hillock that offered both cover and a small bit of grass for the horses. Francis whispered to Bektashi, "We will only be here for a short time so do not loosen the saddles. We will be returning to Tabriz within the hour."

Bektashi nodded and relayed the message to Alia. Once the horses were collected, Bektashi sat down in the sand of the hillock and rested the Mauser on the legs. He turned to Alia and whispered, "Child, do you know how to use a knife?"

Alia smiled. "Yes, uncle."

Bektashi pulled a six-inch blade from his belt. The Damascus steel shined briefly in the moonlight as he handed it to Alia. He said, "I do not expect trouble, but if we have trouble, I want you to use this."

Alia nodded. She was not afraid. Sad perhaps, but not afraid. She had witnessed how easily and willingly Mary Bankroft had killed the Ottoman officer. These were dangerous people. They would protect her.

Bektashi said, "Remember what I told you, little one. We may see some things tonight that make no sense. You need to be prepared for wonderment. But you must witness in silence."

Alia could not imagine what Bektashi was hinting. He was a good man and was protective. Clearly, he was also a teller of tall tales. Her opinion of Bektashi and the Bankrofts changed in the next few minutes.

She heard a small rumble, like the distant noise of a locomotive that she had seen once when her father took her to Angora to sell their wool. But not quite like a locomotive and certainly not coming from the ground. As she looked around to determine where the noise was coming from, Alia suddenly noticed the stars in the sky were no longer visible. Something was obscuring the sky! It was a grey monster; a sort of flying monster making a growling noise. Alia looked over to see the four Britishers standing together looking up at the monster. Had they called it? Did they control it? She looked over at Bektashi. He was sitting there with his mouth wide open. This was not something he had expected. Alia was suddenly afraid. Perhaps it was as Bektashi said. She was traveling with djinns.

Francis watched as the airship approached. He turned to Alexander and Beverly and said, "These pilots are nothing if they are not punctual."

Alexander nodded. Beverly said, "It is time to bid our farewells. Thank you both for taking care of us when we thought we were finished. Now, we are heading to another adventure, but healthy, well-fed, and well-armed. All because of you. Good luck in your mission."

Mary said, "And good luck to you. When you see Elizabeth, please tell her we love her and wish her good fortune. Also, send our regards to Guru Naismith. If Naismith is in charge, there is nothing the Ravens can't accomplish."

Francis took Alexander's hand, shook it, and then did the same to Beverly. He said, "Godspeed." After that, he turned and opened a small box. The glow from the radium painted ball lighted the four adventurers in a blue-green glow and marked the spot for the airship.

On board the airship, the navigator watched from the observer's position in the front of the ship. He said, "Sir, our passengers are about 100 yards dead ahead."

The captain of the airship was standing next to the airman managing the ship's wheel. He turned to the flight engineer and said, "All stop."

"Aye, aye captain. All stop."

The sound of the ship's engines changed to a murmur and

the men on the bridge felt, more than heard, the large propellers slow and then stop. The ship gracefully came to a stop
as it passed over the radium glow of the signal. The captain
said, "Smythe, please tell the mates to drop the pilots' ladder
and make ready to take on passengers."

"Aye, aye, captain."

The transfer took place in a few minutes. The Mansfields
climbed the ladders with no difficulty at all and as soon as
they were aboard, the airship began its slow return to altitude. In less than ten minutes, it was invisible in the night
sky.

Francis turned to Mary and said, "Well, I'm sorry to see them
leave. We could use some partners if we are going to accomplish the mission of raising a Kurdish rebellion."

Mary nodded. "Still, I am happy to know that they will be
working with Elizabeth. They are experienced agents and
while Elizabeth is capable, she could always use a little
assistance."

Francis nodded. Bektashi returned with the horses. He
was obviously affected by the arrival of the airship. Francis
said, "So, Bektashi Bey, what did you think of the airship?"

Bektashi smiled and said, "Master, it was a marvel. I do
believe Alia is a bit worried that it was some sort of monster
rather than a mechanical beast. But, I have something else to
report."

Francis said, "And?"

"Sir, we have been followed. There are men out in the
desert. I do not know their purpose, but they are not good
for our work."

Mary heard Bektashi's comment and said, "Then we shall
have to make sure they are handled properly."

Bektashi bowed and said, "Madame, those are my thoughts exactly."

Francis nodded. He said, "Give me a few moments and then ride back along the trail. Bektashi, please be careful when you decide to use the Mauser. I shall be among our visitors and I would prefer you did not shoot me."

Bektashi was not entirely certain what Bankroft meant, but he responded simply. "Yes, sir."

The five Arabs were still wondering what in the world had just happened. The sky had turned grey, the stars disappeared, and a sound like thunder had filled their ears. Just as quickly, the stars returned and the noise disappeared.

"Mohammed, I don't like this. We were paid to kill the Britishers. I was not paid to kill wizards."

The leader of this small pack of thieves shrugged. "Wizards, djinns, witches, Britishers. They will all die if you stick them with cold steel. We were paid to do a job and we need to finish the job."

Number three of the Arabs was considering the debate between his two colleagues when he died.

Francis had used a well-practiced skill of silent killing after he crept up out of the shadows. As his victim fell to the ground, the leader turned his wicked gaze at his colleague. He thought for certain that the noise was from his friend deciding to sit down in the sand and ponder whether he should run away or follow orders. The leader already had his hand on the hilt of his knife when he realized that next to the body of his friend was a shadow. His eyes widened as the shadow rose in height while he seemed to be an ant staring at the soles of a human foot. Inside his head, he heard a voice say: *"You chose killing over flight. That was a dangerous choice on the ladder of consequences."*

The leader shook his head as if to clear the noise that was echoing inside his mind. He pulled his knife from its sheath and struck out at the shadow. His knife passed through the shadow as if he tried to cut smoke from a fire. The voice said, *"Not quick enough, villain. Not quick enough."* The voice faded in his mind as he realized he was dying from a knife that was sticking in his chest, passing through his ribs directly into his heart. He fell to his knees and made no sound as he died.

By now, the living Arabs realized there was an enemy among them. They turned to face their new adversary when the crack of a rifle and a pistol sounded simultaneously. The Mauser round passed through one of the Arabs as he fell face first on the ground. The .45 caliber round from the pistol in Francis' right hand ploughed into the chest of his partner, dead before he fell backwards. Francis raised his hand to signal Bektashi to cease fire. He turned and focused his attention on the smallest and slowest of the five and the only one still alive.

That man had witnessed the deaths of his counterparts through what seemed a mental and visual fog. Their deaths were somehow less important than the voice that echoed inside his mind. He stood still, knife in his right hand. He stared up at the shadow that seemed to surround him. The voice said, *"Who are your masters?"*

The Arab tried to speak but he could not make a sound.

Again, the voice echoed both inside and outside his head. *"Who are your masters?"*

He bowed his head and spoke, "I am a simple thief and, sometimes, I kill. Whoever pays me it is my master."

"Who paid you this time?"

"I do not know his name. He was an Englishman dressed in a German uniform. He spoke Arabic, but with an English accent. No German speaks this way. He paid us in German gold. He told us to ride north until we heard of British spies on the border. It was a long ride, but he was right. You were there."

"What did this man look like?"

Before the Arab could answer, a thin dagger blade appeared from this chest. A young girl stood behind him and watched as he crumpled at her feet. She put one sandaled foot on his back and pulled the dagger out. She wiped the dagger clean on his clothes and looked up at Francis. He realized that while he used mesmerism to confuse the Arabs, all Alia had seen was Francis standing among armed men. She heard none of the conversation because it was passed telepathically. She knew only one thing: He was fighting alone. Francis looked at Alia and said the one word shared by Armenian, Persian, Turkish and Arabic, "Shukran."

Alia nodded and walked back toward Bektashi and Mary. Francis spent a few minutes working through the pockets of the Arabs. He found notes in the leader's pocket and German gold coins in all of their pockets. Nothing more. He had intended to interrogate the Arab until he gave up everything he knew. Now, that would not happen and all Francis knew for certain was their travels into Kurdistan would not be without danger from the Germans or the Ottomans or both.

He quickly caught up to Alia and walked by her side as he approached the horses. Francis shouted to Bektashi, "It is all over. We are coming back." He kept his thoughts to himself. There would be time enough in the future to consider what just happened. He would share the story with Mary. Perhaps she would have a better understanding of what it all meant.

The Gathering of the Ravens

Muscat, June 1915

THEY SAT IN A CIRCLE AROUND A LARGE MAP TABLE IN A BASEMENT. THE summer heat did not penetrate the room which was a blessing because June in Muscat could easily reach well over 110 degrees Fahrenheit. Nighttime temperatures were only slightly better at 90 degrees. Colonel Winslow-Heath had arranged the room specifically for the Ravens when he received the request from the Royal Navy and the Indian Army for their services in Mesopotamia. He knew that the human brain wilted in any temperature over 100F. He needed the Ravens at their best if they were going to work on this problem.

The colonel looked around the table at the faces illuminated by the glow of several oil lanterns borrowed from the British consul's house. Not all the Ravens could make the rendezvous. One of the Ravens, Eugenia Waterson, was in Tashkent tracking a German effort to engage the Afghan Emir. Winslow-Heath thought: More power to her. If she could disrupt those ne'er do wells, she would have done great service to the Raj. If only seven of the Ravens were available, then seven would have to do.

Winslow-Heath looked across the table at Naismith. He was Winslow-Heath's most trusted colleague. A hero in the silent war fought across a world of battlefields over nearly thirty years. Naismith looked worn, like a trusted pair of boots — trusted for the battle but about to give out at the seams. To Naismith's right was Elizabeth Bankroft. Young, impressionable, but brave. To Naismith's left was his deputy, Marian Sandusky. Next was Beverly Mansfield. Also young. A woman who could easily be his daughter and next to her and to Winslow-Heath's left sat her husband, Alexander Mansfield. Like many of the men who graduated from the Viceroy's College, he was intrepid and ready to join a fight at the drop of a pin. Winslow-Heath knew from Naismith that Mansfield had few of the skills in mysticism that Elizabeth or Beverly had mastered. Winslow-Heath suspected that Mansfield probably could build those skills, but he used other skills to gain the necessary intelligence and, when needed, to win a fight. To the colonel's right and completing the circle were two other Ravens. Jonathan and Martha Sanderson, another married couple, newly arrived from Calcutta. Winslow-Heath was always bemused by the fact that many of his officers ended up being married. Still, he thought of their dangerous lives and how it might be a relief to know your spouse was at your side at those moments of high risk. He smiled as he considered the fact that it also might arouse great passion. Well, so be it.

The Sandersons were working with Indian Special Branch when they received the call. The Indian police, through their political security arm known as Special Branch, were tracking a German-funded Indian separatist movement operating in Siam and Burma. The "Siam Scheme" as it was known in the shorthand of the secret services, was a dangerous band of revolutionaries who received funds, training and even arms from a Hindu separatist group based in the United States. The Sandersons' work had revealed links between German intelligence operations and Indian revolutionaries that were more robust than anyone had expected. Winslow-Heath wondered if eventually he would have to dispatch one or more of his people to America to counter this effort. He had been loath to pull the Sandersons from their work on the other side of India, but he needed a full complement of Ravens if he was going to accomplish this critical mission.

He looked down at his tea mug and realized it was empty. He turned his head and using his standard "parade ground" voice, he shouted, "TEA!"

A muffled voice from another room said, "Absolutely, sir. Right away, sir."

Winslow-Heath shook his head and mumbled, "Civilians."

In less than a minute, a young consular official rolled a cart into the briefing room. The colonel looked up and said, "Leave the tea, son. I will do the needful. YOU ARE DISMISSED."

The young man did what he thought was a proper about turn and left the room, quietly closing the door. The colonel said, "I don't know how the consul survives with these ... people."

Naismith smiled and said, "Sir, the truth is that the consul has good people now and even more before the war, but they are all either up the country supporting the Navy or they are in uniform facing German Mausers."

Naismith's comments were presented in a gentle voice, but they did their job. The colonel harrumphed in his mustache and began to pour tea to all and sundry at the table. As he did so, he started the briefing.

"We are faced with a challenge that I have not expected nor do I have any good solutions. However, it is clearly a challenge that calls for both sophisticated intelligence operations and the type of ... action that have been the hallmark of the Ravens from the beginning." Winslow-Heath took a deep drink from his white ceramic mug, made a face and said, "Who in the world would call this tea?"

Naismith smiled and said, "Sir, it is the sort of tea that the Arabs drink. It is green tea with cardamom in it. It is not drunk with milk, but with sugar."

The colonel put down his mug and simply said, "Bah." He stared at the mug as if it had insulted him. Eventually, he continued, "The Indian Expeditionary Force has made good progress going up the Tigris. They have been hampered by many logistical challenges due to poor planning by the force leadership, but the soldiers have persevered, and they have shown the Turks the power of British cold steel. In the most recent battle, in a town north of Basra called Qurna, the Indian Army crushed a force led by one of the Ottoman "young Turks" known as Suleimani Askeri Bey. His force was devastated and rather than report his defeat, he committed suicide."

Naismith nodded. Beverly said, "Sir, we heard about this as far north as Kurdistan. It was a triumph."

"Indeed Major, a triumph but also a surprise. You see, the Indian command was prepared for the Ottoman forces, but what they were not prepared for was what we estimate were fifteen thousand tribals who came out of the Eastern Desert to fight for the Turks. Luckily, the Arabs had not previously faced our soldiers with modern weapons and a century of discipline. They charged, received significant fire, faced cold steel, and retreated into the desert wastes of Khuzestan. And that, my friends, is the problem we have. We know they retreated into the land of the Beni Lam tribes and disappeared. The Indian cavalry commander wanted to give chase, bless him, but the overall commander kept his focus on the Turks."

Naismith decided it was time for him to jump into the

discussion. "Sir, what do you imagine the Ravens can do to help? We have our skills but hunting thousands of Arab raiders is not one of them."

"No, but hunting a few leaders is precisely what the Ravens have done over the years. And this is particularly difficult for all of you, because we know something of these leaders and it is most … disappointing."

Elizabeth noticed for the first time that the colonel's aura had shifted in color to bright orange-red. He was angry. No, he was furious.

"Ladies and gentlemen, the problem we face is the leaders of these tribals are two British traitors. Worse still, they are traitors who attended the Viceroy's College. They are James and Michael O'Connell."

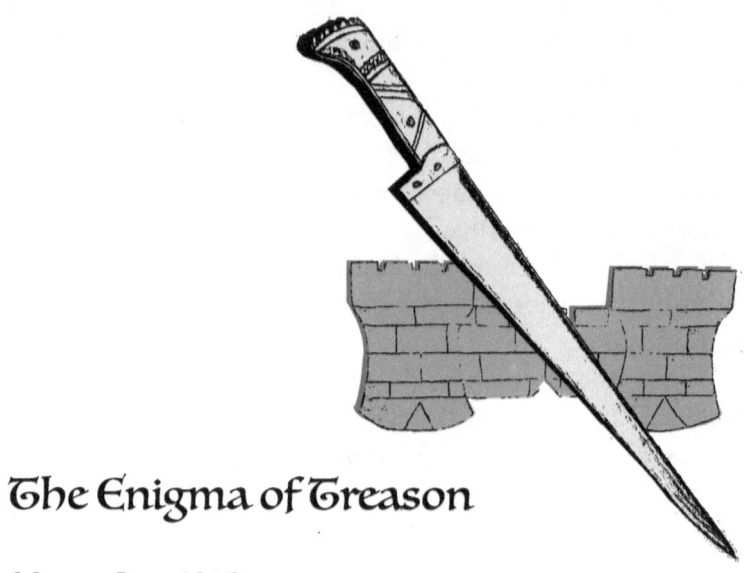

ᚷhe Enigma of ᚷreason

Muscat, June 1915

THIS WAS THE WORST NEWS POSSIBLE FOR NAISMITH. HE HAD LONG SUS-pected that the O'Connells were working as mercenary intelligence officers in Mesopotamia. There were intelligence reports that suggested a man who met James O'Connell's description was working with the Ottoman security police in Damascus. The reports said even the Ottomans were willing to admit, albeit reluctantly, that it was O'Connell's agent operations that allowed them to arrest and execute dozens of Arab military officers who gathered in Damascus to discuss the possibility of an independent Arab state. Long before that report, Naismith was certain James O'Connell was the thief who stole the Royal Navy plans for a new computing device known as a difference engine. The difference engine could revolutionize naval gunnery. At a minimum, it could speed navigation by sea and by air, allowing navigators to make course corrections faster and more accurately than before.

As to Michael O'Connell, there was no solid reporting on

the young man, but Naismith had detected hints and he was concerned. Even during his first term in college the young man had been a special student, with significant abilities in what Naismith referred to as the "mystic arts." William Shakespear, the British military intelligence attaché in Kuwait City, had reported that a young man fitting Michael O'Connell's description travelled into the Nejd before the war to meet with the Shammar tribals. And then, Naismith heard the sad news that Shakespear was killed in a battle. It seemed likely there was some role Michael played in the tragedy.

Shakespear was the finest Arabist in the Indian intelligence service and a close personal friend of both the Emir of Kuwait and the tribal leader Abdulaziz bin Abdul Rahman al-Saud, known to British intelligence as Ibn Saud or son of the Saud, who was in command of the entire central desert known as the Nejd. Shakespear's relationship with Ibn Saud was based on years of work. There would always be some relationship between the Empire and these Arabs, but it would not be the same now that Shakespear was gone.

Even if the O'Connells had served as intelligence entrepreneurs before the war, Naismith was incredulous that they would be working with the Germans after six months of world war. Had they not read about the catastrophic losses in the trenches of Europe or the unrestricted submarine warfare taking place in the world's oceans? Had they not heard of the sinking of the passenger liner, RMS Lusitania? He could understand a German staying loyal to his homeland, but what could possibly motivate these British subjects to serve the German Empire?

Winslow-Heath looked at Naismith and said, "Colonel, are you unwell?"

Naismith refocused his attention and returned to the briefing. He said, "Sir, I fear I was trying to understand the puzzle of this treachery. The O'Connells were both raised to be loyal to the Crown. And now, you have reporting that they are traitors to the Empire and guiding enemy forces against Indian Army troops. This treason is a hard pill to swallow."

"Naismith, you and the Ravens must swallow this pill and move out smartly. We want ... no, we absolutely need these two traitors to be taken off the battlefield. If you can capture them, you should. If you must kill them, you must. The lives of thousands of our troops are absolutely at stake here. It is going to be hard enough for our forces to take Baghdad and Damascus without the worry of tribal rebels coming out of the desert to raid our supply trains and kill our leaders while they sleep."

Winslow-Heath looked down at his abandoned cup of tea. "Naismith, both you and I have seen what it is like to be at war with tribals." Winslow-Heath looked up at the Ravens. "I am not speaking of the little conflicts, the small wars that we have been fighting with various small tribes led by mad mullahs. I am talking about war. The Afghan war when both Naismith and I were with Lord Roberts. It was terrifying for the troops and, honestly, for me, to think that any time we laid our head down to rest, the Afghans might infiltrate the camp, cut a few throats, and escape with a few of our horses. Therefore, we must put a stop to this and do so immediately."

Like it or not, Winslow-Heath took another sip from his mug of green tea. The bitter brew did not improve his disposition. He continued, "I will not make any attempt at determining how the Ravens will do this mission. I know you have special skills and I wish you luck as you use them. All I can say for certain is that I have an airship on standby to take you into Mesopotamia in two days. You have two days to decide where that airship will take you and what you will do once you get to your destination. Now, I will take my leave." Winslow-Heath looked at Naismith and said, "Colonel, I will expect an update from you tomorrow at 17 hours. After that, we will act on whatever you have decided must be done. Good evening."

Elizabeth had not had such a formal meeting with Winslow-Heath before, so she was the last to rise out of her chair as the colonel stood up and walked out the door. She expected the Ravens to sit in silence for a few moments while they considered their new mission. She was completely wrong.

A Plan Fit for the Ravens

Muscat, June 1915

As soon as Winslow-Heath left the room, Alexander Mansfield spoke. "I see no reason to design a plan to capture these two. If we bring them back to Basra or Muscat or even Rawalpindi, the Army will just shoot them. The extra care we would have to take to capture these two alive could put us all at risk. It seems to me that our mission is to end their operations with the tribals. My vote is to end their operations permanently and bury them somewhere in the desert."

Beverly was less blunt but no less angry at the O'Connell's treachery. "I would prefer to capture them and bring them back to trial. We need to know what they did, who they did it with, and who are their masters."

Jonathan piped in, "We know the Germans are working hard to destroy the Empire. That they are working to kill our troops in Mesopotamia should come as no surprise. Martha and I have been working with Special Branch on a German conspiracy that runs from America through Thailand into

Burma and India. They are determined to wreak havoc on the Raj. What I am not clear on is how in the world we are going to infiltrate into tribal lands in the middle of a war-zone. Guru Naismith, what do you suggest?"

Naismith was dismayed and realized he wouldn't be able to pretend that he wasn't hurt by the news. "I know we have very little time to come up with a plan, but I need some time to comprehend this enigma of treason,' he said. "Further, I need to consider Jonathan's question of how to infiltrate into Khuzestan to find them. I am … at a loss at present. If you will be so kind, I need to spend a few minutes in deep meditation considering this new problem. I will go to the next room for this meditation. If I do not return in a half hour, please come next door to get me."

With that, Naismith slowly got up from his chair and headed to the door. Elizabeth was about to follow when Marian placed her hand on Elizabeth's arm. She said, "Elizabeth, I believe the guru really wants to be alone. In the meantime, we can consider what resources we have here and how they might be useful."

Martha said, "I'm afraid Jonathan and I have been out of the picture for so long as we chased the Siam Conspiracy." Martha looked up at her colleagues and said, "Any thoughts?"

A dismayed set of four faces looked at her and shook their heads. "Our work against the Ottoman intelligence service in Armenia doesn't offer much hope," Beverly said. "After our operation in Gwadar, Alex and I were focused on Northern Persia and Armenia."

Elizabeth was lost in thought as she remembered the young face of Michael O'Connell as he sat smiling at her in Russian language class at the Viceroy's College. How in the world could things have changed so much that now Michael was a traitor? She noticed everyone in the room was looking at her. Elizabeth realized that her work in Bombay was probably the closest thing they had to leads into Khuzestan, so she said, "I have had several reports over the last year of hostility to British interests by both the Beni Lam in Mesopotamia and the Lurs in Southern Persia. The primary perpetrator seems to be a German adventurer named Wassmuss."

Alexander smiled for the first time. "Adventurer? Elizabeth, I think that is a wonderful turn of phrase for all our work. Adventurers!"

Martha said, "I've been called a witch and a spy and even a djinn. Never an adventurer."

Elizabeth began to blush. She didn't think her colleagues were enjoying a joke at her expense, but she wasn't quite sure. Just to be certain, she did not offer anything else about her Bombay reporting.

Marian was the first to see that their lighthearted banter had hurt Elizabeth's feelings. She said, "Dear, please don't think we are making fun. All in this room have had long journeys and now we have heard terrible news. A small bit of levity is welcome and your identification of Wassmuss was just a chance to break the ice. On a serious note, please tell us more!"

Elizabeth looked over her colleagues. Their auras were all blue-green. It was as Marian said, they were interested and waiting for her to say something. Perhaps she had been too hasty in assuming they were making fun of her work. Perhaps they really did want to hear what she had to say. She decided to relate what she knew and what she thought. That would be the true test of whether they accepted her as a colleague instead of a junior officer who was included simply because of her skills in the mystic arts. She thought back through the months of collection and began.

"The Arabian Sea may be part of the world war, but it is also the trading network for dozens of city states. Bombay is one of the hubs. Zanzibar is another. Aden is the third and where we are today, Muscat is the fourth. Probably the most important link is the city of Bandar Abbas. It is an ancient

Persian trading center, and it is very close to the oil fields of Abadan. Many of my Bombay sources are linked to the trading network. All of them have been reporting efforts on the part of the German Empire to undermine British power in the region. In the case of India, the Germans have been supporting Indian revolutionaries." Elizabeth nodded to Martha and Jonathan.

"In the case of Arabia, the Germans have been in a direct battle with the British Empire to control the Arab tribes in Central Arabia, most specifically the tribes led by two chieftains: Ibn Saud who has his headquarters in the remote city of Riyadh, and Mohammed Al-Rashidi who has his power farther north in an area that extends to the border with Mesopotamia. The death of our colleague, Captain Shakespear, took place when these two chiefs had a major battle earlier this year. Major battles among the Bedouin are actually quite rare. They are a raiding culture. My sources who traveled to Kuwait City were convinced that the Rashidi tribesmen would not have faced off against the Saudi tribesmen without a major delivery of German Mausers."

Elizabeth paused again to see if she was being helpful. It seemed so. "Persia is primarily a Shia country, but the borders that we draw are not borders that the tribes acknowledge. Just as the people in Southern Mesopotamia are primarily Shia Muslims while their Ottoman overlords are Sunnis, so it is that the tribes in Southern Persia pay little attention to the Persian monarch and the Shia clerics who command obedience from them. Before the war, Wassmuss traveled in the region as an ethnographer, academic and writer. Several of my sources met him in 1913 and 1914. They saw him as a charming man with excellent Arabic and Persian. None of my sources suspected he was a German spy. Clearly, he must have been at the very least a German collaborator and today he is most definitely involved in creating tribal unrest in the region."

Jonathan said, "But how does that fit into the colonel's instructions for us to use any means necessary to stop the O'Connells?"

Beverly said, "I think the O'Connells were most probably the ones who killed Shakespear and that is enough for me to call them traitors."

Elizabeth could see they were all beginning to focus on revenge rather than the mission. This was hard for Elizabeth because she still had a soft spot in her heart for the Michael O'Connell she knew from the Viceroy's College. He was a young man with a sense of humor and a wonderful set of blue-green eyes that melted Elizabeth when they spoke together at the College. For once, Marian could sense Elizabeth's concern for Michael and her ambiguous view on their mission.

Marian said, "Based on my reading all of your reports, I believe the problem is that Wassmuss is only one man and his focus appears to be on creating tribal unrest near the Abadan oil fields. The Royal Navy needs that oil. In the case of the O'Connells, I think their role in raising the tribes allied with al-Rashid and the Beni Lam tribes of Khuzestan makes them an obstacle to the Indian Army plans to capture Baghdad and, perhaps, Damascus. That is why they need to be stopped. If we can capture them, we can interrogate them and make them explain their plans as well as give up the names of their tribal allies. Just like Wassmuss, if we eliminate the German support of guns and gold, any of the Arab tribes most probably will wait out the conflict in hope of siding with the winner."

Alexander said, "Marian, I think your assessment is correct. And, while I remain convinced that the O'Connells will face a firing squad if we do capture them, I understand now why it makes sense to try to capture them rather than kill them."

Elizabeth was relieved that someone was taking her side

on this point. The Ravens were a highly skilled and deadly team. If they decided to kill the O'Connells there would be nothing that the O'Connells or for that matter, Elizabeth could do to stop them. She said, "It is all well and good for us to debate the end result. But how in the world are we going to find the O'Connells in the first place?"

Marian smiled and said, "I believe that is precisely what Guru Naismith is doing right now using his own skills on the astral plane."

Ḟuntinɡ in the Astral Plane

As HE FOCUSED HIS MIND, NAISMITH TRIED TO USE HIS MASTERY OF THE mystic arts to probe the minds of the O'Connells. His consciousness was disrupted by the question: What made his two students choose treason? He suspected they were always less patriotic than most of his students, but still treason was something that he found entirely confounding. It was not as if he had never been angered by someone in the Indian Army, particularly when they treated him or one of his Gurkha soldiers as some lesser human. The British officers in the line divisions were certainly prejudiced and egotistical. But Winslow-Heath demonstrated daily that he did not share these prejudices and it was Winslow-Heath that they all worked for now. This was the same man the O'Connells had worked for before they disappeared. What sort of anger or hatred would make a man choose to betray his countrymen? And, at what price?

Naismith had been an intelligence officer for years. He recruited sources and ran sources. He had worked with men who were interested only in their own profit and he had

152

worked with men who were motivated by revenge. These motivations were not unexpected in a region where tribalism and sectarian violence were as common as the change of the seasons. Adding to those challenges, many of the local emirs were petty despots. Their actions incensed many and, from that incensed population, Naismith and his students selected a few that would be willing to take the risks necessary for espionage. Naismith also remembered more than a few of his sources who were willing to take the risk simply because they thought the British government in India was the best possible government they could expect. They were loyal to the Raj because they saw only potential chaos if the British government left India. So, what motivated the O'Connells? Self-interest? Revenge? Certainly not loyalty to the German Kaiser. It was well and truly a puzzle.

Naismith opened his shoulder bag and pulled out a single candle and placed it on the floor. He sat on the floor next to the candle and used a match to light it. He focused his attention on the flame and forced the conflicting images of treason out of his mind while counting his breaths. Inhale to a count of five. Hold to a count of five. Exhale to a count of five. Hold empty for a count of five. Repeat. The breathing and the counting pushed the annoying thoughts out and allowed him to bring forward his advanced mental skills.

After a few minutes, Naismith first tried to reach into the minds of the two O'Connells. This might not be the most direct way to identify their location, but it would help him access questions that simply would not go away. Unfortunately, he found both O'Connells created mental fortresses, mind castles, preventing him from penetrating their thoughts. It bothered Naismith greatly that he could sense a power in Michael O'Connell that he had not seen when the boy attended the Viceroy's College. It was as if he had absorbed strength from his anger and then translated that anger into power coming from someplace inside the mystic sphere. Naismith shook his head and returned his focus to the candle and his breathing.

Naismith smiled. He remembered a quote from Appian of Alexandria. Naismith was certain it was one of the few quotes remaining from his Latin studies as a young man. During the Second Punic Wars, Hannibal was attributed to have said, *Aut viam inveniam aut faciam.* "If I cannot find a way, I will make one." With that thought, Naismith relaxed and launched his illusory body toward Mesopotamia.

Travel in the astral plane is not limited in time or space. It is only limited by the concentration of the user. For that reason, Naismith did not actually sense a flight to Mesopotamia or any rush as the distance between Muscat and Khuzestan folded like a woman's fan. Rather, one second he was in his small quarters in Oman and the next he was floating over a tribal encampment of the Beni Lam. Naismith debated for a moment whether he needed to find the precise location of the O'Connells. It would be useful to know which of the black tents served as their quarters. However, Naismith also knew that he ran the risk of warning the O'Connells if he stayed too long. In the end, his conservative side conquered his curiosity and he returned to Oman. He now knew where they were, at least close enough that he could guide an airship to the camp. Once on the ground, the Ravens could do the rest.

As Cold as Ice

Beni Lam encampment, Khuzestan, June 1915

MICHAEL O'CONNELL AWOKE FROM A DOZE. IT WAS HOT, AND LIVING INSIDE the black tents was like living in an oven. They traveled early in the morning, camped well before midday and then waited until well past sunset to hold meetings with the Beni Lam tribal leaders. There was really nothing to do either outside in the blazing sun or inside in the stifling tent, so both Michael and his father leaned against their pillows made from the camel saddlebags and dozed on a sweat-soaked goat-hair carpet.

Michael was pleased with their actions so far. They had roused the Beni Lam into action. While the tribesmen had not defeated the Indian Army troops, they had harassed the troops, killed a few and raided the Army supply trains. The tribesmen were satisfied with the loot gained from the raids and pleased that they had only suffered a few dead and fewer wounded. Both the dead and the wounded were young men who had taken risks that their leaders avoided. The wounded were now in camp telling anyone who would listen of the bravery under fire. The dead had been left on the battlefield. By now, they were probably buried by the Indian Army troops simply to avoid the disease and the carrion feeders that were part and parcel to land littered with dead men and dead horses.

Michael and his father had been careful to stay with the Beni Lam leadership. Michael learned the lesson of William Shakespear — guide the tribesmen but do not get involved in the fight. War was cruel and random. Good men died for no reason other than by chance. Michael knew Shakespear hadn't died by chance, but he witnessed enough fighting on that day in Arabia to know there was no reason to take risks for some opportunity to brag about your bravery under fire. That was simply a fool's game.

He did wish he had a troop from the Shammar with him. They were slightly more disciplined fighters simply because they had been at war for years with the Wahhabis under Ibn al-Saud. The Beni Lam were raiders, now armed with German Mausers and fueled by German gold. They were reasonable tools for the current job, but it would take some work to convince the tribal elders to allow Michael and his father to train some of the Beni Lam fighters. Michael was not certain that he had the ability to make those changes among the tribals. Perhaps the best plan would be to declare victory after this skirmish and return to Baghdad. The Germans would already have heard of the Ottoman defeat in Qurna. It might be best to return with a report of their small victory.

As he pondered this thought, Michael slowly fell back into a light sleep. The heat was enough to make any man tired and there was really nothing to do until sunset. Michael's head dropped back into the pillow. His father was already snoring. A gentle rasping rhythm that made it progressively more difficult to keep his eyes open. His last thought before he went to sleep was how he would convince the tribal elders to let them return to Baghdad to get more guns and more gold. That would be the perfect excuse.

Michael was not sure how long he had been asleep when he woke with a start. It was as if a glass of ice water had been thrown on his face. He was sweating, but he was always sweating. The difference was that this time, it was a cold sweat. Michael had no explanation for what had just happened. It was as if some second sight warned him of impending doom. He looked over at his father. James O'Connell was still asleep next to him. He seemed to be undisturbed by whatever had caused Michael to wake up. Like most of his dreams, Michael could not remember any of the details — only the dread that followed the dream.

Michael poured a small cup of water from a goatskin bag that slouched against their makeshift bed. He took a sip and then woke his father. He said, "Father, I have a plan that I need to discuss. I think the time has come for us to leave this place."

James O'Connell was puzzled. Just a few hours before, they had talked about how they could create a small raiding force from the Beni Lam that could harass the Indian Army troops stationed along the river. What could possibly have changed his son's mind in just a few minutes? He reached into the single pocket in his robe and pulled out his gold hunter pocket watch. He had been asleep for three hours. It would be sunset soon and after prayers there would be a meal. This was a good time to talk to his son and to decide a good plan before they shared the meal with the Beni Lam elders. He took a sip from the shared cup of water and said, "Son, what has changed from our last talk?"

Michael shook his head. "A premonition?"

James looked at his son. Michael's aura was a bright orange which suggested extreme emotion. He wondered whether this was fear or anger, but he knew better than to dismiss the possibility of a premonition. James was sufficiently schooled in the study of the mind to know that most premonitions were simply the unconscious mind synthesizing facts in non-linear ways that the logical brain dismissed. The problem with premonitions is that they are often both incomplete and affected by emotions coloring reality. To determine the value of the premonition, James asked, "What did you see?"

Michael concentrated. He tried to assemble a logical order of his thoughts. He did not want to admit that his concern was based almost entirely on fear. What made him afraid was less clear. Certainly, his direct participation in the death of William Shakespear showed him the permanence of death as well as the cruelty to the wounded in desert warfare. It was important to him that he provided a logical answer for why he wanted to leave and leave soon. Something more than just dread. Michael did not want his father to think he had childish fears.

After a minute, he said, "Father, I believe we have accomplished as much as we can with these tribals. They understand the value of raiding against the British troops. Armed with Mausers and funded with gold, they will continue their raids. After all, it is their nature to do so. What concerns me is the nature of our relationship with the tribals. My experience with the Shammar tribesmen proved to me that Arab culture values raiding and young men will take high risks to show their elders that they are warriors. That may have been reasonable in the last century when they were raiding undefended villages and fighting with matchlock rifles. It is even a reasonable strategy in a war between tribes. It is not as reasonable when facing a determined adversary like the Indian Army. I saw with my own eyes how easy an outsider can die in these conflicts. After all, Shakespear was playing the same role we are when he was killed."

Michael paused and then said, "Father, in my view, this is not our fight. We have accomplished our mission for the Germans. It is now up to the Turks and the Germans to sort out the conflict and it is now time for the Germans to live up to their end of the bargain. We need to get out of Arabia and back to Ireland. If we were German soldiers or Ottoman soldiers, then we would have to stay. We are neither. We have created a resistance movement and now they can find someone else to proceed with their plans. I suspect there will be more than enough German adventurers willing to accomplish this next stage."

James laughed. "Adventurers? That's what you think is needed here?"

"I do not see us as anything but mercenaries. We are trading our skills in exchange for a chance to liberate Ireland. And, I might add, I think the Germans view us as expendable mercenaries. That is what worries me."

"Will we be able to convince the Beni Lam elders that our time here is over?"

"Father, we will simply tell them that we need to return to Baghdad to get more guns and more gold. I doubt they will care one bit about us; what they care about are guns and gold. And, if the Germans decide they want to send more guns and gold, they can do so with their own men."

"And what do we do about the Germans when we arrive in Damascus?"

"We tell them what they want to hear: that the Ottoman troops are dismal failures, but the Arabs were brilliant. And, honestly, who knows what successes or failures will happen on this battlefield in the weeks that it will take for our return to Damascus. Perhaps the Indian Army will take Baghdad. Perhaps they will be defeated somewhere along the Tigris. If the former, we will be able to explain precisely why that happened. If the latter, then we will claim we played a role."

"My son, it would seem you have already designed a plan. I think it is a good one. Now, all we need to do is execute that plan."

"Well, we can start tonight by guiding the conversation

toward a plan to deliver more guns and gold. It won't take more than a few days for them to decide they need to dispatch us to get those guns and that gold. Once they have come to that plan, we will agree." Michael smiled, "Of course, we will be reluctant at first, but we will agree."

"How long do you think this will take?"

"No more than a few days, father. Still, we cannot rush them. We must make them certain that they are ordering us. That way, we can insist on guides, camels and food when we head north. They will begrudgingly provide these items because they will see it as the only way for more guns and gold. Meanwhile, I have another chess piece to use to add to the challenges the Indian Army faces in Mesopotamia. It will be a long ride, but easy work. After that, I will return and we will leave for Baghdad and, eventually Berlin."

James shook his head. His son was proving to be a master manipulator. His only hope was that he was able to be as good at manipulation when meeting with the Germans.

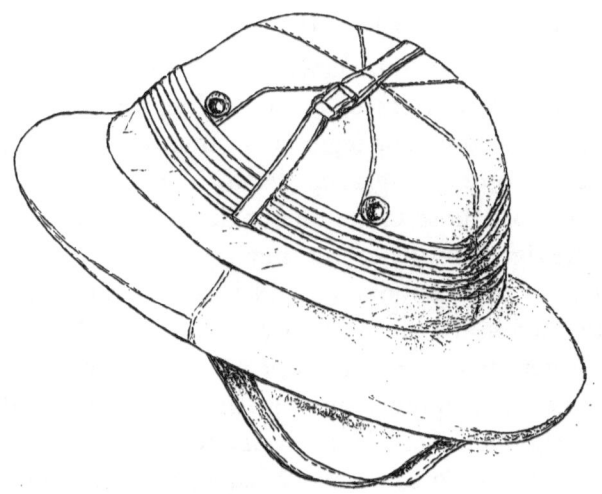

The Price of Ambition

Basra, June 1915

CAPTAIN CONRAD BANKROFT WALKED ALONG THE DOCKS. THERE WERE small boats piled in every direction unloading supplies. The locals were used to small boats carrying small crates. Now, the boats were larger, ferrying in very large crates of ammunition, rifles, clothing, medical supplies and food from the ships anchored out in the harbor. It was a logistical nightmare. The British Indian Army was using a small dock with an equally small local workforce to bring in supplies for thousands of men. Those men required equipment. They were using up everything rapidly and all these supplies had to come from India. Conrad was slowly learning the lesson of war: Winners often were not the most brilliant tacticians. They were the ones who were quickest at delivering equipment to the battlefield. And the supply chain was ready to collapse.

Food was critical. The Indian Army was made up of soldiers from multiple religions. Feeding the English troops was not a problem. They might grumble, but they would eat whatever was available. That was certainly not true for the Muslims, Sikhs, and Jats who would rather starve than break their religious strictures. It was madness on the docks as crates marked for different regiments came off the transport boats in every order imaginable. And, it was Captain Bankroft's job to sort those crates and make sure they were delivered to the right unit wherever they might be along the occupied portions of Mesopotamia and Persia. It was a daunting job especially in the blistering heat of summer.

When he volunteered to leave the relative comfort of his regiment's temporary quarters in Karachi, Conrad expected an assignment leading a cavalry scout squadron at the forward edge of a great Army. What he found on arrival at Basra was an Indian Army that was stuck in the desert awaiting orders to advance and awaiting supplies. The Indian Army commanders were either still on the Royal Navy flotilla anchored out in the harbor or they were based in occupied buildings formerly the headquarters of the Ottoman Customs and Police.

Conrad understood now his arrival was poorly timed. He was one of three senior captains from Northwest Frontier regiments with no direct affiliation with the divisions assigned to the Indian Expeditionary Force. The three captains reported to a lieutenant colonel serving as one of the two adjutants for this force. The lieutenant colonel was in foul spirits, sitting in a room infested with flies. He guarded his teacup with herculean vigor while using a fly whisk to keep the infestation from landing on his mouth and eyes.

"Gentlemen, I understand you have volunteered to serve our mission and I commend you for that. However, at present we do not have any billets for cavalry officers. We do, however, have a critical need for officers focusing on the logistic madness at the harbor." He went on and on about the various challenges and the shortcomings of the local stevedores working the docks. Finally, he said, "Gentlemen, it may not be glamourous work, but it is essential work. We need men willing to untie this Gordian knot. Those are your orders. Fix this problem!"

So, here he was. Marching from quay to quay, shouting at Indian levees in Urdu, local levees in his rudimentary Persian, and in less than polite English at the Royal Navy boatswain. In the latter case, the Royal Navy personnel were interested in one thing and one thing only: get offloaded and return to their ships as soon as possible before something ugly happened to their boats. That meant that they had little interest in the safe offload. Conrad watched as more than one crate of rifles or ammunition crashed onto the docks. One of Conrad's peers walked up to him. Bruce Macintosh was dressed in dirty khaki shorts and shirt, and wearing a sweat-stained cork helmet known in the Raj as a topee. He said, "This is the price of my ambition. I have arrived at the gates of Hell and these are the boatmen who will carry me away."

Conrad smiled. He said, "Of course, it might be worse. I have heard that the vast majority of the troops are digging trenches in the swamps north of here. At least we aren't hip deep in muck."

Macintosh said, "Speak for yourself. One of the Arabs was too vigorous with a block and tackle and I ended up in these infested waters. Heaven only knows what sorts of vermin live on me now."

Conrad laughed. "Why don't you take a break, Bruce. Go wash off. I reckon I can handle this chaos on my own for an hour. An hour, mind. Not the rest of the day."

Macintosh was already walking away when he said, "Did I tell you my watch fell into the drink? I have no idea how to keep time now."

Conrad shook his head.

Leaning against a stack of rifle crates, an Arab laborer watched the exchange. He was still not certain why he was there. Was it a djinn who visited him last night in his sleep?

Whoever he was, the Arab knew that his night visitor was the master and he was his servant. All he knew for certain was he had to follow the instructions. And those instructions were to go to the docks, observe and then report back. While he couldn't understand the British officers when they spoke to each other, he fully understood what was happening. The British were trying to receive ten times the material that the docks could hold.

The Arab was no friend of these invaders. He thought a small explosive charge might cause one or more of the docks to collapse. It wouldn't stop the British, but it would certainly terrify the local laborers and that would mean the British would have to unload and stack their supplies on their own. A slow process would come to a stop and when it restarted, it would be an even slower process because no Arab would want to work for these invaders.

Mission accomplished, the Arab slipped away unnoticed. His orders were to return home and wait. The djinn had told him to wait. He would obey.

The shadow appeared in the corner of the room in the Arab's house. An image of a man, perhaps, but almost transparent. The Arab feared for his life as he listened to the djinn.

"Did you do as you were told?"

"Yes, master."

"What did you find, my friend." The djinn's face was as white as death. Still, the Arab took some comfort in the fact that the face was smiling at him.

"Master, the British are overloading the docks and the wood frames can barely withstand the weight. The workers are overworked and angry with the British and Indian troops who order them around as if they were slaves. The foreigners do not speak Arabic. They use Persian. The dock workers understand Persian but are insulted that these foreigners will not speak in their language. It is as you said. The docks are dangerous and the dock workers are ready to revolt."

"Can you plant the explosive?"

"I can. It will not be hard. But where will I find a bomb?"

The djinn smiled again. "Look at the corner of the room. There is a wooden box. You simply place the box near one of the ammunition crates, light the fuse and leave. You can do that."

The Arab was in what Michael's instructors at the Viceroy's College called "the waking dream." Michael could see in his eyes that he would obey to the best of his ability. He waited in silence.

"Master, I will obey."

"Excellent. Now, take the gold coins that are on top of the box and put them in your pocket. Then you can rest. Tomorrow night you will place the box on the docks. Now, rest."

The Arab did as he was instructed. The djinn disappeared.

Michael had a long ride ahead of him back to the land of the Beni Lam. He was pleased with his little excursion. If the Arab did his job well, there would be chaos on the docks tomorrow night. If the Arab was caught, the British would have to shut down the docks as they searched for more bombs and more saboteurs. No matter what, the Indian Army's supply chain would be damaged. A small victory which Michael could use in his discussions with the Germans. Perhaps he would exaggerate the success slightly. Perhaps not. It wouldn't matter when he used his mesmerism skills on the Germans.

฿ow to Build a Resistance

On the Persian border in Kurdistan, June 1915

FRANCIS SAT BY THE FIRE DRINKING TEA WITH A KURDISH TRIBAL LEADER. Mary and Alia sat in the darkness near their tent while Bektashi walked back and forth from the tent to the fire, serving tea and dates. The Kurdish tribal leader had been a contact of the British service for over a decade. Like many of the maliks on the Afghan frontier, he received a small stipend in gold from a member of the service who traveled a circuit throughout northern and western Persia. The gold allowed him to gain status among his fellow tribesmen and it helped him buy the guns and ammunition for his young men. In exchange, he passed information to the British. Mostly observations on the day-to-day operations of the Ottoman government as well as periodic tidbits of intelligence about Russian or, more recently, German travelers.

Francis was struggling with the conversation. The Kurd spoke heavily accented Persian and Francis would be the first to admit that Persian spoken in this region was far different from the Afghan Persian he had used over the years from Mashhad to Chitral. Still, they were making themselves understood through patience and, in the case of Francis, his skills in reading minds. Francis was not as adept as Mary, but he had the training and some of the skills. Better still, he had spent a career working with men just like this tribal leader. He had a good understanding of what the man desired and what he might find intriguing.

"Daryan Khan, do the Ottoman threaten you and your people?"

"*Dust-e-aziz,* they know better than to threaten us. We could come out of the hills and squash their little outposts in Mendeli like bugs. All the land on the Diyali used to be ours. Of course, that was long ago, but we remember."

"How long ago, Daryan Khan?"

"Perhaps a thousand years, my friend. We have been mountain people forever."

"Would you be willing to do so for your independence and a return to the Diyali?"

"What does that mean? We are already independent. The Ottomans don't bother us and we don't care about what they wish to do in the river valley."

"Have you heard of what they did to the Armenians?"

Daryan Khan paused for a moment. He shook his head. "That was truly a sinful act. I know most of the Armenians are Christian, but we are all people of the book. How could the Ottomans think it anything but an act of the devil."

"The Armenians thought they were safe from the Ottomans because they were also mountain people. You saw the girl traveling with us. She was the only survivor from her village."

Daryan Khan looked toward Mary and Alia. "That one? I thought she was your daughter."

Francis smiled and said, "No, my friend. My daughter is

fighting the Ottomans and the Germans on another battlefield."

The Kurdish tribal leader laughed long and hard. "Ah, I misjudged you, British. A warrior family. Where is your son?"

"Fighting as well. When I last heard, he was fighting Afghans but he will be fighting Ottomans and Germans soon enough."

"And your wife?"

Francis leaned over toward the Kurdish tribal leader and whispered, "She is a witch who can kill men without laying a hand on them."

"Truly?"

"I have seen it with my own eyes. We were fighting together. I was using my knife and she was using her hands. I never saw what she did, but the man died silently."

The Kurd laughed again and said, *"Dust-e-aziz,* you had best keep her happy or you will see an early grave."

Francis laughed as well. "I know it well, my friend. For now, I am safe because she is focused on killing Ottomans and Germans."

"Then perhaps we need to talk about how we can work together. We have always wanted Mendeli with its orchards and river. Perhaps we could even stretch across all of the Diyali district and return to our long-lost lands. With a witch on our side, how can we possibly lose?"

Later in their tent, Mary said, "You haven't told me what you said to Daryan Khan that made him laugh."

Francis said, "I told him you were a witch."

Mary gave Francis a stern look. "You did not."

Francis smiled and said, "Oh, yes I did."

"What was the precise reason for that?"

"Mary, my dear. It is how you create a resistance. You

make it clear to the oppressed that you are here to help and that with your help, they can't lose. He asked me why you were here and I told him that you were here to kill Ottoman and German soldiers with your witch powers. It isn't exactly a lie."

"I will admit that I have used my powers over the years to assist our work. I'm not sure I like being called a witch."

"Well, to answer your question properly: Daryan Khan made it clear to me that I had to keep you happy or I would be visiting hell sooner than I hoped."

Mary smiled, "He is wise."

Francis said, "Now, we need to pass a message to Winslow-Heath. If this project is going to work, the Kurds are going to need rifles, ammunition and, perhaps, more than a little gold."

Mary smiled and said, "I will use my witch powers to send that message to Guru Naismith. He will have to send the message on to Winslow-Heath. After all, we don't really want to scare the good colonel, do we?"

"No, we do not."

Mary said, "Then you need to leave me for some time, while I reach out to Naismith. Leave the candle burning and please make sure I am not disturbed."

Francis nodded and left the tent. He was always amazed by Mary's skills but preferred not to watch as she did whatever it was that she did. She called it the "illusory body," but he found it disturbing to watch as she sat in a full lotus position and then began to levitate. Francis understood what she was doing, but that didn't make it any less worrisome.

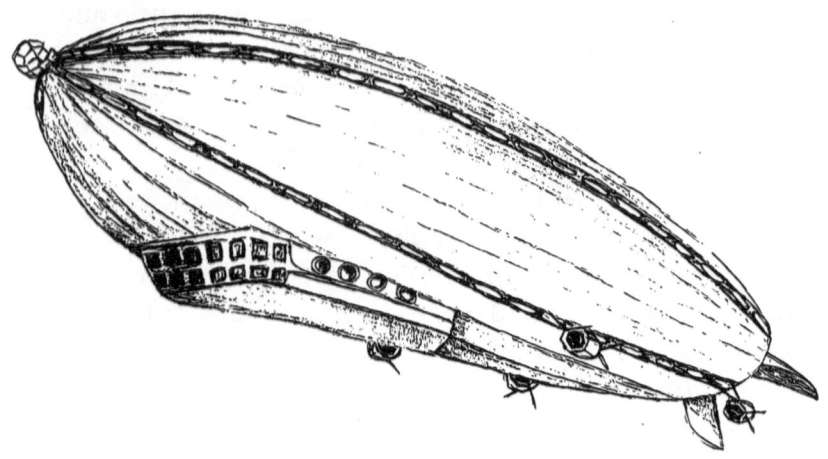

A Raid Plan

Muscat, June 1915

WINSLOW-HEATH ENTERED THE ROOM. THE RAVENS WERE ALREADY IN place, and they stood when he arrived. Behind him were two staff officers. One to take notes and one to carry the large tea tray. The colonel expected this meeting to last some time and he had decided that he would have a proper mug of tea even if he had to make it himself. He sat down. The staff officer with the tea tray put it in front of the colonel, poured him a cup, added a small bit of milk from a tin of condensed milk and stepped back.

"Ravens, please help yourselves." Each of the Ravens, starting with Naismith, walked to the tray, poured a mug of tea and then returned to their seats. Elizabeth was pleased to have tea, though she missed the biscuits that the colonel usually served in Rawalpindi.

"Naismith, what is the plan?"

Naismith put down his mug and said, "Sir, first I need to pass on a message from the Bankrofts."

Elizabeth's head snapped up and she almost spilled her tea. She had not heard from her parents in weeks. Her father used ciphered telegrams when they were in Baku and Tabriz and mother had been good about sending brief telepathic messages until she headed into Kurdistan. Since then, her mother had been silent.

Winslow-Heath turned to his aide and said, "Take this message down. It will be critical to our overall plan." He turned to Naismith and said, "Continue."

"Sir, Francis and Mary Bankroft are now working with the Kurds north of Baghdad. They are convinced the Kurds are ready to resist the Ottoman forces there. But, they will need some bona fides to prove they represent the Crown."

"I suppose they are requesting guns and gold."

"Sir, you know our ways too well. They need 100 rifles, 10,000 rounds of ammunition and 100 gold sovereigns. They have sent me a precise location for the delivery."

"After this meeting, please give the location to McKinley." Winslow-Heath nodded to the aide. "We will make that happen as soon as possible. Now, about the plan for the Ravens?"

"Sir, I have located the encampment where the O'Connells are staying. It is the headquarters for the Beni Lam tribal leaders in Khuzestan. Khuzestan is a borderland between southern Mesopotamia and southern Persia. The Beni Lam are nomads. They move back and forth across the border. I was surprised how close they are to Basra, but honestly our forces have stayed close to the river and the Beni Lam territory runs east from the Tigris well into Persia."

"How close to our forces?"

"Perhaps a day's hard ride in the desert. I doubt our cavalry squadrons could arrive before the Beni Lam were long gone."

"Precisely why this is a job for the Ravens. A raid into an enemy camp. Capture the traitors. Return to base."

Naismith nodded. "I think we have a plan for just those orders. We will need support from an airship and, perhaps, an aero plane. And, we will need to move quickly. Perhaps as early as tomorrow night."

The colonel nodded. "We can certainly make those available and the schedule will be yours."

Naismith nodded. "Sir, then here is our plan.

Sabotage on the Docks

Basra, 01 July 1915

CONRAD BANKROFT ONCE AGAIN WALKED THE LENGTH OF THE DOCKS. THE setting sun was on the horizon and the muezzin call to prayer had just started. Conrad knew that the dock workers would be leaving for the day, using prayers as their excuse for leaving work undone and equipment splayed out along the docks. Unlike many of his Basra colleagues who had worked in headquarters cantonments in central India, Conrad knew the power of the evening prayer. It was powerful enough that he could not remember a single time on the frontier when Afghans raided his outposts nor a time when his men would push forward at sunset.

A slight breeze came off the Tigris and stirred the large fronds of the date palms that lined the various canals that fed into the main channel. It had been another tedious day walking a patrol, engaging the locals in his barracks Persian, and generally trying not to melt from the beastly heat and humidity. The breeze carried with it the fetid scent of human waste, rotting vegetables, and the ever-present smell of green swamp. More than once in the last few days, he wondered about his choice to jump into the warzone ahead of his unit. In discussions at his command, he heard that they should be arriving in another three weeks. Perhaps once they arrived, he could be free from this tedium. He knew the docks and the supplies were critical to the larger Mesopotamian campaign, but he could not remember a time in his entire army career when he felt so useless. And hot.

Conrad wondered how the Indian troops were surviving. Most of the soldiers on the front lines were troops reassigned from duties on the Afghan frontier. This time of year, it would be hot on the frontier but there was always some cooling breeze. Also, on the frontier there was never this humidity. When he was on patrol in the Bolan Pass, his biggest challenge was to keep his men hydrated. The dry air sucked water out of a man long before he knew that he was in trouble from dehydration. A man could march in one-hundred-degree heat and not see any sweat on his uniform or his helmet. The Indian Army's khakis were designed to keep sweat against the soldier's skin and keep him as cool as could be expected.

In contrast, here in Basra Conrad was always soaked to the skin. His blouse and shorts were sweat-stained and the sweat from his legs ran in rivulets into his socks and boots. His cork helmet was stained a dark brown. Conrad coveted the floppy headgear the Gurkha troops were wearing. Large brims and crowns meant their headgear kept them far cooler than his cork helmet. He could imagine the defensive positions along the Tigris had to be hell on earth for the troops, including those who wore turbans as part of their uniforms. He wondered who in the world would want to live in this place? He heard some of his more erudite colleagues use an Arab proverb that said: When God made hell he did not think it bad enough, so he made Mesopotamia. As Conrad swung his left hand in front of his face to drive away the biting flies, he thought the proverb must be true.

As the sun set and the air cooled, Conrad noticed a man dressed in a long robe acting most peculiarly. At this time of day, the Arabs were all long gone from the docks, yet this one had just placed a wooden box next to one of the cranes on the docks. A thief? Perhaps not a thief since he was placing something on the docks rather than taking something away. As Conrad puzzled over his observation, he noticed the man run away in a flurry of cotton robes and leather sandals. Later, Conrad could not explain why he came to the correct conclusion. But in that instant, he knew: saboteur!

He ran at full speed along the dock until he came upon the box. As he caught his breath, he heard a hissing sound. Conrad was not a member of the Royal Engineers, but he had spent enough time with the sappers to know that explosives were charged using a long fuse and a blasting cap. The hiss coming from the box was precisely the sound he had heard in the past when the sappers blasted a new road in the Bolan Pass. Conrad looked in all directions for someone, anyone who might help. There was no one.

Conrad picked up the box and ran to the end of the dock, away from the cranes and away from the crates piled high with ammunition, rifles and food. His only thought was to get it away from the military stores and, if he had time, to throw the box into the water. He barely had time. The box exploded just as he tossed it into the river. He did not remember the sound of the blast or the pain as shrapnel hit his face and his right shoulder. That would come later.

Mary sat up with a start. She and Francis were having tea awaiting further news from Naismith on their requested delivery of supplies. Bektashi was pouring the tea when she jerked upright from the pillows in the tent that served as their bedroom, dining room and office. Bektashi barely avoided spilling tea over everyone. Alia was sitting in the corner of the tent awaiting her regular session with Mary learning to read and write. She gave a little squeak as she watched Mary sit upright and grow exceptionally pale.

Francis touched her arm and said, "My dear, what is it?"

"Something terrible has happened to Conrad." "Conrad? How can that be? He is an adjutant back in India."

"I have no idea. All I know is that he is injured."

Now it was Francis' turn to grow pale. He had long ago accepted that Mary and Elizabeth would travel in harm's way and there was little he could do about it. He worried when Conrad was in a cavalry squadron chasing bandits on the Afghan frontier, but that was long ago. He was supposed to be an adjutant in his regiment serving in their headquarters in Karachi awaiting transfer. Of all the things he needed to worry about right now, he had no idea one of those things was his son. He whispered, "Is there any way you can find out more?"

"I will do my best." She looked up at Bektashi and said, "Can you please take Alia outside for a few moments. I fear I have a headache and need to lie down."

Bektashi knew that something else was afoot. He had lived with the Bankrofts for nearly two years now and he suspected that they had their own skills, perhaps even black magic. He accepted their white lies as part of the exchange for their kindness and the excitement of working for two British officers. Still, there were times when their skills, most especially the skills of Mary Bankroft, worried him. It did not seem proper to work among shades and shadows. Ghosts and djinns. He bowed and turned to Alia and said, "We need to leave our masters alone for a few minutes. Madame is unwell." Alia stood and followed Bektashi as he left the tent.

"What can I do?"

Mary looked into her husband's eyes. He tried to be the unemotional military officer who faced danger with no care. She knew better. She said, "Dear, you need simply to be quiet while I make my journey in the illusory body."

Francis nodded. Telepathy was one thing, but when Mary or Elizabeth took off traveling in the astral plane, he was always terrified they might not return.

Mary laid down flat on the carpet. She assumed the yoga position that was known as *savasana*, the corpse pose. She began by counting breaths and clearing her mind of her concerns. It would take some discipline, but Mary knew the breath counting would eventually focus her attention. Francis watched as her breathing slowed and her body relaxed. As if lifted by an invisible hand, Mary began to levitate. Only a few inches, but her body was as rigid as a board. She had entered the astral plane and was traveling in the illusory body, in Tibetan *sgyu-lus*. Francis had never been able to concentrate hard enough or clear his mind of what Naismith had told him years ago were his troubled thoughts. He stared in amazement as Mary's body began to slowly spin anti-clockwise. It terrified him.

Mary departed her earthly body. She knew that time and space were not real in the astral plane. She just needed to concentrate on Conrad's soul and she would be beside him. And, so it was.

Conrad was lying in a hospital bed. His right shoulder and the top of his head were covered in bandages. He was awake and talking to a doctor. The doctor said, "A good piece of luck, Captain. If the bomb had exploded closer to you or if there had been more shrapnel, you would have lost an eye and your arm. As it is, you will have a rather dramatic scar on your right cheek and one running down your right arm, but otherwise, you should be able to return to duty in a month. I suspect you will look quite dashing once it heals." Mary could feel the concern in the doctor's mind as he smiled at her son. He was worried about infection in this primitive hospital. "You need to rest and heal, son. I know the commander wants to see you, but I've put him off for another day. By then, you probably won't be on quite as a high dose of morphine and you might actually avoid saying something foolish. Now, rest. You are young, you are strong, and you were exceptionally lucky."

Mary looked down on her bandaged son and thought he was not so lucky. Still, he would mend. But where was he? She concentrated and began to float away from the hospital bed. She heard Conrad say, "Mother?" She wondered if that was the morphine or if she was projecting a ghost image of herself in her son's mind. Regardless, she needed to leave him and find out where he was.

Mary felt herself float through the walls of the building that was serving as a field hospital. She rose higher and higher and began to see the city streets and the river as it flowed south toward the sea. Mary had been in this city before. Years ago, she had traveled by steamer up the Tigris on a mission for Winslow-Heath in search of James O'Connell. She now knew her son was in Basra.

Francis watched as Mary's body stopped rotating and slowly settled on the carpet. He knew she would be exhausted and would be thirsty. He stood up and walked out of the tent. Bektashi was standing guard at the tent flaps. Francis said, "Bektashi, I need some cold water for Madame as well as some hot, sweet tea. She will be well soon, but she needs refreshment."

Bektashi bowed and disappeared into the darkness.

Francis returned to his wife. She was sitting up. He said, "I have some tea coming soon."

Mary smiled, "If there's tea, there's hope."

"Winslow-Heath has said so many times."

Mary said, "Francis, Conrad is wounded but will recover. He is in Basra."

"Basra?"

"He must have volunteered."

"Madness."

Mary smiled, "Perhaps, but he is his father's son." Mary looked up to see Bektashi bringing a cup of tea. She said, "Bektashi, you are a marvel." Francis wasn't sure, but he thought Bektashi was blushing.

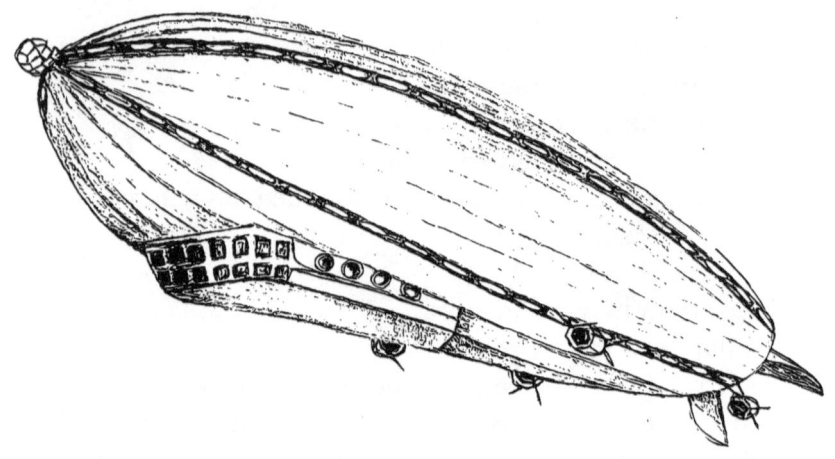

Underway by Airship

Somewhere over the Persian Gulf, 02–03 July 1915

NAISMITH SAT ALONE AT THE END OF THE PASSENGER COMPARTMENT IN *HMFS Falcon*, one of the combat airships operating from the Royal Navy port of Muscat. They were underway and headed toward the Beni Lam encampment in the desert north and east of the Indian Army forces north of Basra.

Their mission to capture the O'Connells was simple enough — assuming everything went according to plan.

The airship would approach silently from the east. It would operate on battery power for the last few miles and arrive at the location at three in the morning. The Ravens would slide down the rope ladders and approach the Beni Lam encampment on foot. Naismith knew from his reconnaissance that the Beni Lam were keeping their "guests" in a tent on the edge of the encampment. They might appreciate the German guns and gold, but not enough to treat the O'Connells as members of the tribe. The team should be able to reach the O'Connells tent, accomplish the mission, and slip away without raising any alarms.

After the Ravens moved away from the camp, two aeroplanes from the Royal Flying Corps based in Basra would attack, using machine guns and some aerial bombs. The attack might or might not do harm, but would certainly create havoc among tribesmen, their horses and their camels. While chaos reigned in the camp, the airship would meet the Ravens at the designated pickup location and drop the rope ladders for their ascent. From there, it would be a straightforward return to Muscat where they would turn the O'Connells over to Winslow-Heath and the security personnel for interrogation and, most likely, trial and execution.

It was not as if the Ravens hadn't accomplished a similar mission in the past. In fact, it was how they rescued the Bankrofts from Mazar-e-Sharif in 1913. Still, Naismith knew that in wartime, things rarely go according to plan. So, he quietly reviewed all the possible parts of the plan that might fail. As he was working through the possibilities, he received another telepathic message from Mary Bankroft.

Telepathy was not like a telegram or a dispatch. A master in telepathy could not be ignored. You might not choose to reply, but the message drilled into your mind. Mary Bankroft was a master of these mystic skills and she knew precisely how important it was to avoid frivolous use of such a powerful skill. *Guru, I need you to know!* The message echoed in his head. It was Mary's voice to be sure but with a level of urgency that he simply could not ignore.

Naismith concentrated and focused his inner thoughts away from the matter at hand and established the telepathic link with Mary. *Mary, I am here. I have little time. The Ravens are in flight.*

Guru, I need you to know that our son, Conrad, is in a Basra hospital. He was injured. Sabotage, guru. Sabotage. Can there be any doubt who did this?

Naismith did his best not to allow his emotions to carry him away. If he lost concentration, he would lose the link with Mary. He had no time to spare and he needed to pass his own message back to Mary and Francis. *The Ravens are about to address this threat. We will finish this tonight and Conrad will be avenged.*

God speed, Guru. Farewell, farewell, farewell.

Mary's telepathic link to Naismith disappeared. He was certain that Mary wanted him to inform Elizabeth but now was not the time. The Ravens, all the Ravens, needed clear heads if they were to accomplish tonight's mission. As he returned to his contingency planning another voice crept into his head. *Soldier, you will not succeed tonight. I have other plans for your targets. They have a purpose that you cannot understand. You will fail, you will fail, you will fail.* Before Naismith could reply, the voice of Chodak was gone and with it the eerie feeling of a monstrous presence that engulfed him anytime Chodak's spirit reached out to him.

It left Naismith with dread. How could Chodak know their mission? Why would he care about their mission? What was Chodak's single focus on this small piece of the world where Naismith and the Ravens traveled? He shook his head and stood up and walked to the opposite end of the compartment, toward the ship's galley. If nothing else, a cup of tea might distract him from these horrid thoughts and focus his attention on the present. He looked at the radium dial on his wristwatch. It was 0130hrs. Ninety minutes to go. Little time to prepare and no time at all to come up with some sort of contingency plan.

As he walked along the aisle of the compartment, he touched each of the Ravens on the shoulder. As they departed Muscat and headed out to sea, he encouraged them to sleep. They would need to be ready for battle soon and a few hours of sleep would help. As he woke them, he said to each of them, "It is time. Feel free to take tea and then return to the cabin. We will do our final preparations and then head to the cargo cabin for our weapons and to await our arrival."

As Naismith walked past Elizabeth, she looked up and said, "What did my mother tell you?"

It has been years since Naismith had used a mental castle to protect his inner most thoughts. None of his colleagues or his students had the ability probe his mind. Once again, he had misjudged Elizabeth's growing skills. "Mind reading" as it was called in the carnivals was simply a mix of understanding the body language and speaking cues as well as a clever use of a partner in the crowd. If a person had telepathic ability, it also meant they had the ability to probe a person's mind. Unbeknownst to Naismith, Elizabeth had probed his. This unnerved him. Where would these powers take Elizabeth?

Before he could answer, he heard her voice inside his head: *Do not worry, Master Guru. I will not steal your secrets.*

He responded in kind. *Your mother wanted to know when the supplies they had requested would arrive.*

There was a different tone in Elizabeth's response, *Master Guru, DO NOT TREAT ME LIKE A CHILD. YOU MUST NOT LIE TO ME.*

Naismith was shocked. The message had a veiled threat that he had not felt for years. In fact, the last time he felt such a concern was back in the Viceroy's College and the individual was one of tonight's targets: Michael O'Connell. He responded: *She told me your brother was in hospital in Basra. He was injured due to sabotage. Your mother believes the sabotage had to be planned by the O'Connells. She does not know, she only suspects. Remember what we always say: Before we decide we have to know, not suspect.*

As soon as he sent the telepathic message, he felt Elizabeth's blazing anger. Anger might have a purpose among conventional army soldiers, it had no place in the world of the Ravens. Elizabeth nodded. *I will manage this anger, Master Guru. Guru Marian is helping ... I promise. But once this operation is over, I will have my time with the O'Connells. Do not try to stop me. It is only proper that I should have my time with them.*

Naismith desperately needed his tea. He needed time to focus his attention on the operation and the Ravens. He sent a curt reply, something that he tried to avoid, but now was the time to make sure this powerful, young mind understood she was about to play a very dangerous game. *We must accomplish this mission and we must do so in a way that allows all the Ravens to return safely at the end of the mission. DO NOT FORGET THIS!*

This time it was Elizabeth who was taken aback. It had been years since she faced a telepathic message this powerful. It drilled into her head and seemed to echo over and over again. When she was a student and her concentration had faded, both Guru Marian and Guru Naismith often sent a message that demanded obedience. Now, this was the same type of message. She knew both Marian and Naismith would be watching, looking for a sign that she was not compliant. Not working as a member of the Raven team, but rather on her own accord. She bowed her head and said out loud, "Master, I will obey."

Naismith was already walking down the aisle and heading for the galley, but he heard Elizabeth. He smiled and thought that he often forgot that Elizabeth had already seen war and already proven herself capable as a Raven. If she said she would obey, then he was convinced she would obey to the best of her abilities. That was all he ever asked from any of the Ravens. Still, he would ask Marian to keep a close eye on Elizabeth and after the operation was over, he would bring Elizabeth back to the Viceroy's College. Her abilities far outstripped her control. That would be very dangerous in a world at war.

Ravens Attack

Khuzestan, 03 July 1915

THE RAVENS FELT *HMFS FALCON* COME TO A HALT. FOR THE LAST TWENTY minutes, the only noise in the airship had been the sound of the propeller blades. When these fighting ships used their batteries, they were absolutely silent. Now, the engines briefly switched to reverse pitch to stabilize the airship. The cargo master slowly cranked open the clam-shelled doors at the rear of the airship. The cabin had been bathed in red light so the Raven's night vision was ready for the image of the desert sands receding to the horizon and the sky awash with stars. The moon had already set, so the only light was the reflection of the stars on the sand. The cargo master and his deputy threw two rope ladders out of the open doorway, dropped to all fours and slowly crawled to the edge to make sure the ladders were not fouled and that they touched the ground. They backed away from the doorway and the senior of the two walked up to Naismith: "Sir, the hatch is yours. Please take care as you initially grab the ladder. Thirty feet is a long way to fall, even if you are going to land on a sand dune."

Naismith noticed the slight smile from the cargo master. He responded in kind and said, "Not to worry. This is not the first time we have enjoyed an airship delivery." With that, Naismith raised his right hand and pointed to the door. He walked to the left-hand ladder while Marian walked to the right. Now the team was split in half. Behind Naismith, Beverly and Elizabeth followed. Behind Marian, Alexander, Jonathan and Martha followed. The cargo master noted that these soldiers were dressed in a blue-grey uniform that matched the night sky. Strapped on their backs were weapons that seemed to belong to medieval knights rather than modern soldiers. Crossbows, long swords, and some sort of short pike. Each had a small shoulder bag filled with heaven only knew what and each had a pistol in a black leather holster. He watched as they slipped away into the darkness. Once they were gone, he and his partner crawled to the edge of the doorway and confirmed these night soldiers were safely on the ground. Though their uniforms had appeared black in the red light of the airship, he noticed that on the ground, they seemed to blend into the shadows of the desert sand. The cargo master shook his head and decided it was just his imagination.

When he looked again, the Ravens had disappeared. He turned to his two airship mates and they reeled up the rope ladders and closed the clam-shelled doors. As the cargo master walked toward the speaking tube to let the commander know they were away, he thought to himself: God speed, you creatures of the night. You are brave indeed.

Naismith gathered the Ravens together in a tight circle as they watched the airship disappear on the eastern horizon. Naismith looked at his watch. It was 0315hrs. He knew in

July, the false dawn sky would reveal itself in two hours. They had enough time but needed to move quickly. He said, "We need to move out. We use *lung gom pa*. Follow in a single line. I will lead, followed by Elizabeth, Alexander, Beverly, Jonathan, and Martha. Marian will be at the end of our column. Do not break the link. Now, we must go."

With a simple nod of his head, Naismith began the effortless leaping of *lung gom pa*, covering 10 yards in single stride. In order, each of the Ravens followed. They crossed the Khuzestan dunes as shadows in the darkness and made their milelong approach march with little difficulty and faster than any animal could have travelled in the desert.

They stopped at the edge of a dune overlooking the Beni Lam camp. Again, Naismith checked his watch. 0330hrs. The aeroplane attack would take place at 0500hrs, coming out of the eastern horizon. They had ninety minutes to accomplish their task. Enough time if all went well.

As he pulled his hood up over his head, Naismith took three deep breaths to wash away his concerns and focus his mind. He pulled a small staff from his belt and gave it a vigorous snap. The staff expanded in size from less than a foot to over four feet long. At one end of the shaft was a small, razorsharp hook. This weapon, a modified *guru danda* or monk's staff, had served Naismith well over the years. It was less obviously a weapon than the sword or crossbow, which in his mind made it all the more deadly because of the shock factor when an adversary faced the blade. Each of the Ravens pulled their weapons out. Marian had a similar *guru danda* and carried a crossbow over her shoulder. Beverly held a curved blade in her right hand known as a *kartrika*. Normally used as a symbolic flaying knife, this knife was razor sharp. Angled across her back was a large three-foot-long *kukri* commonly used by the British army Gurkha regiment. Elizabeth and Alexander had crossbows and Martha and Jonathan had curved swords known as *khadags* or fire swords. All were for silent killing. They each carried pistols for more conventional combat. Naismith had his old Webley service revolver. Elizabeth had the Browning given to her by her mother. The rest of the team were carrying the new Colt automatics.

Naismith saw that all was in order: "Remember the plan. From here, we approach the tent. Marian, Elizabeth and Alexander will serve as our protectors. Your crossbow bolts must kill any who approach the tent. Beverly and I will enter the tent while Martha and Jonathan will prevent anyone from escaping our attack. We will use mesmerism to gain their compliance. Our goal is to capture these two traitors silently and take them back to India. Our mission requires more stealth than force. That said, you all know that if force is needed, it must be swift and violent."

Naismith paused and looked directly at Beverly. "I do not expect trouble from James O'Connell, but Michael O'Connell is another story entirely. Beverly, you must be prepared for Michael to use his own powers to confuse us. Keep focused and all will be well. Success to you all." With that, Naismith disappeared down the slope.

Each of the Ravens now pulled up the grey-blue hoods on their Raven uniform. They were invisible along the dune as they approached the tent. At one point down the slope, Naismith pointed to Elizabeth and Alexander to stop and take up their positions. Marian stood to their rear. They took a knee, pulled out their crossbows and loaded the first bolt, forming a triangle so they could cover any direction. A few yards later and Naismith pointed to the sides of the tent where he wanted Martha and Jonathan to wait. With his defenses deployed, Naismith used the razor-sharp knife on his *guru danda* and silently sliced the tent wall. He and Beverly entered as wraiths in a nightmare.

A screech filled both Michael and Naismith's ears. It was some sort of war cry and Naismith knew the source at once: Chodak! That demon had decided to intervene. To Beverly, there was only the sound of their feet on the sand until she heard Michael O'Connell stir from his slumber. She had no warning of trouble.

Michael jumped up from the pillows and carpet that made his bed on the far side of the tent. He was dressed in pajama pants and a grey undershirt. He faced his two attackers in a fighting stance as taught in the Viceroy's College. In the circle of decision, the instructors taught a blend of fighting styles from the East and the West. More importantly, they taught the importance of the first strike as a means of breaking contact and flight. They also taught their students how to face up to three attackers at a time. Michael remembered two things from his training. First, standing and fighting might be the honorable thing to do if you were a soldier, but as an intelligence officer, you were not paid to win fights. You were paid to escape and live another day. Second, pick the most dangerous of your targets first and strike as hard as you can.

Michael was still waking from a deep slumber so from his perspective, he faced only one opponent. A woman in dark clothes. In the first few seconds, he assessed her to be about his size and certainly a few years older. An assassin from some rival tribe? A member of the Beni Lam who wanted to slice their throats and steal the German gold? It hardly mattered to Michael. He assumed he had the advantage of skill, and with that in mind, he stepped forward to dispatch this intruder with a single punch to the temple. Michael knew it was a killing punch. In this situation, the attacker was likely in the business of assassination and had already climbed the ladder of consequences.

As he threw the punch, it felt as if he was trying to punch through a wall of water. There was resistance slowing his arm. It was well and truly a puzzle to Michael. Beverly had watched Michael prepare to fight and as he did, she extended her *chi*. The power of her concentrated mind far exceeded the power of his well-toned muscles. Just short of his targeted strike to the temple, his arm froze in space. He could push no farther. At that point, Michael knew that he faced an entirely different sort of adversary. He withdrew his fist, focused his mind and extended his own *chi*. Beverly was pushed by the force of Michael's mind, back toward the hole in the tent wall. Michael smiled as his power grew with his confidence. He would push this woman back as far and as long as he wished. She could not stop him.

What did stop him was a scissor kick at his ankles that dropped him to the ground. Naismith had used the Tibetan reclining boxing technique known as *panxuanshe qanji*. Naismith had made himself invisible to Michael and crossed behind him while Michael focused on Beverly. Michael fell face-first onto the carpet and struck his head on a stone that had been swept away from their sleeping space in the tent.

James O'Connell was finally awake. As the sleep left his eyes, he realized that they were under attack. While not as adept as Michael in the mystic arts, James had years of experience in street fighting. As an intelligence officer, he often travelled alone and regularly met sources in alleyways and cafés where villains made their living by killing and robbing single men and women. In the bedlam, he understood immediately that they were fighting for their lives. He bellowed for help, first in English, then Persian and finally in Arabic. He expected the Beni Lam camp to be asleep, but certainly someone would hear. As he cried for help, he noticed that he had made no sound at all. These were not normal attackers. These were masters of the mind and his mind was the battlefield.

If he could not speak, at least he could move, so he raced toward the grey figure near the edge of the tent. He hoped his weight and his speed would carry them both through the gaping hole in the tent and into the desert. If he could accomplish that feat, he might make an opening for Michael to make good his escape. Beverly's voice filled James O'Connell's mind: *Traitor, you are finished. Do not force me to kill you. We intend to take you back to India.* This sound inside his head filled his mind with dread. It made James realize he was doomed. He might not escape, but he intended to do his best to save Michael.

He tried to shout, "Son! Run from this ambush. Escape! I will take care of this attacker." Once again, no sound came from his mouth. It was like many of the nightmares he had over the years. He knew his son was in danger but could do nothing to warn him. With all of his strength, James closed on Beverly and pushed her through the hole in the tent wall.

As he did so, he seemed to rise above the ground. Beverly had closed her arms around his body and using her levitation skills, she lifted them both in the air, spun them around four times, and dropped them to the ground. They landed in a heap on the desert floor with Beverly on top and James on the bottom. She had spun them in a manner so that James landed with his own fists on his solar plexus. He fought for breath as he saw two more wraiths close in on him. In his mind, he felt a cold blade at his throat and heard a soothing female voice say, *Relax! You need fight no more. Relax.* Even as he feared for his life, the mix of the voice and the fact that he could not catch his breath made James compliant. In seconds, his arms were bound and Beverly and Jonathan carried him away toward a dune in the distance.

Naismith had let go of Michael's ankles as he moved quickly up the young man's torso, hoping to bind his hands before he regained consciousness. Michael recovered just in time to realize what was happening. He used every bit of power he knew to extend his *chi*, spinning himself like a top and sending Naismith flying to the edge of the tent. Michael was coming to his senses as he watched his father and Beverly flying through the slice in the tent wall. Michael was deciding how to attack when a voice inside his head said: *You must escape! You will not win this fight, Michael. You must escape to fight another day.*

A second voice inside his head intruded. *CHODAK. Leave the boy. He has played the game and lost. Let him face the world as it is not as you wish it to be!*

Chodak's voice now filled the minds of both Naismith and Michael. *Soldier, what do you know of the world? The world is chaos. No one can be its master and as humans strive to control each other, there will always be chaos and war. On this side of the mystic plane, we demons grow in strength every time there is conflict, we feed on the souls of those killed in violence. This time it is an entire world at war and millions dying violent deaths. We are growing in strength every day as we devour the souls of the dead and dying on the battlefield. I NEED THIS ONE AND WILL NOT LET YOU TAKE HIM.*

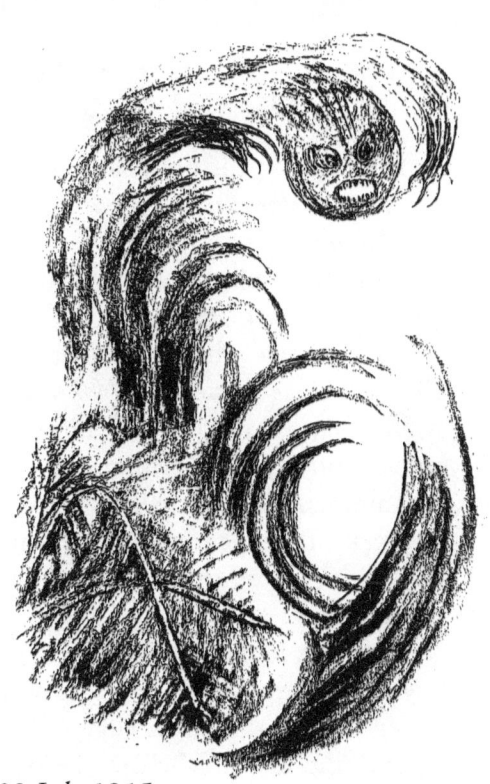

Symbols
of the Game

Beni Lam encampment, 03 July 1915

MICHAEL COULD MAKE NO SENSE OF THIS BACK AND FORTH TAKING PLACE IN his head. One voice was clearly Guru Naismith. The other sounded like no man or woman he had ever heard. It was a sound as if a screech owl could speak. He could not determine who the voice was or, for that matter, where it came from. And Naismith seemed equally confused. Michael was no longer confident that he could win in any battle of minds or body with the master guru, and now he felt the presence of multiple masters of the mystic arts. This was not a battle he could win. That other voice was right. He had to flee. This was not a day to fight to the death. This was a day to escape to fight another day.

Michael summoned all his mental energy, pushed his hand out in front of him and sent a blinding flash toward Naismith. While Naismith easily dodged the flash, the energy lighted the tent and the walls burst into flame.

The voice in his head said, *You are wise for such a young one. Run north, run north. Take a Beni Lam horse and escape! I will protect you.*

Naismith's voice receded, crying out, *Michael, do not take this path. Return with me.*

Michael used what little mental energy he had left to reply, *You have chosen your path, Naismith. I have chosen mine.*

Martha, Alexander and Elizabeth watched as the tent quickly turned into a torch, lighting the entire Beni Lam encampment. The camp dogs began to bark in unison waking everyone. The quiet raid was turning into a run for their lives. Naismith escaped from the tent just before it became a solid wall of flame.

Elizabeth looked away from the flames and saw a figure leaving the tent and heading toward the Beni Lam horses staked out on the north edge of the encampment. She recognized the figure. Michael O'Connell, her colleague at the Viceroy's College, a traitor against the Crown, and most probably a man who just tried to kill her brother. As he ran, he passed the first of the Beni Lam running toward their position behind the tent. Elizabeth aimed carefully and shot the man with her crossbow bolt. He dropped with the bolt in his forehead. Instead of reloading, she dropped her crossbow and used *lung gom pa* to pursue her target. The last thing she heard was Marian's voice saying, "NO!"

With a final leap, she landed in front of Michael. Elizabeth extended her *chi* and brought Michael to a halt. He stopped as if he had hit an invisible wall. She said, "Michael, you must come with us. Your work here ends now!"

Michael laughed. He snarled, "Elizabeth Bankroft. Why do you think your side of the fight is righteous and mine is treason? We are merely symbols in the chess game played among empires. You are a pawn in the hands of your English masters. On the other hand, I have decided to have self-will and move as I choose. I have chosen to be the master of my own game rather than the pawn. And, now you think you can stop me from exercising my will? I refuse to accept your pitiful mutterings."

Elizabeth saw Michael point his open hand to the ground and extend his *chi*. The power of his mystical energy carved a trench deep in the sand which headed directly toward Elizabeth. The earth seemed to crack open at his instruction. The soil turned black as oil gushed up from the rift in the sand. Michael put his hands on his hips and started to laugh as Elizabeth gazed in horror as the crack and the oil headed toward her. As it approached, Michael pushed the palm of his right hand down to the ground and the oil burst into flame.

At the last second, Elizabeth focused her concentration on the sand at her feet. A column of sand formed, raising her above the flames. From twenty feet above, she looked down upon Michael O'Connell. She stepped out with her left foot, swung her left hand across her hips while her right hand passed above her left in a tai chi move known as parting the wild horse's mane. As her two hands scissored across her chest, a gust of wind pushed the oil and the fire towards Michael. She felt his concern over this movement and could see his aura shifting quickly from a confident green to a concerned yellow-orange.

Marian finally caught up to the two young antagonists. She was completely puzzled by what she saw in front of her. It seemed as if Elizabeth and Michael O'Connell were standing a few yards apart doing nothing at all. If anything, they seemed to be as still as statues. She thought: What sort of mystic battle is taking place in their minds? Suddenly, Michael spun on his heel and ran on a diagonal away from Elizabeth and Marian. He headed straight toward the Beni Lam horses. Marian looked around to see dozens of men coming out of their tents. She and Elizabeth were silhouetted against the fire. Elizabeth started to run after Michael. Before she could begin her first leap, she heard Marian's voice in her head. *Elizabeth, return to the Ravens. We must leave now! Remember your promise. Discipline, Elizabeth. Discipline!*

Elizabeth took one last fleeting look at Michael as he rushed toward the horses and then turned back to see Marian drawing her pistol and facing the new attackers. Elizabeth did the same and suddenly the camp was filled with the sound of the two automatic pistols sending hot lead into the crowd. As they finished their first magazine and before the Beni Lam fighters could recover, Marian and Elizabeth fled. They arrived next to Naismith and the rest of the Ravens in two leaps. As she passed the burning tent, Elizabeth picked up her crossbow. She stopped, dropped to one knee, loaded another bolt and sent it into the chest of a young Beni Lam tribesmen. She climbed to the top of the dune; Elizabeth gasped, "Guru, I was trying to prevent his escape."

Naismith nodded. He said, "This is a day when accomplishing half a mission will be enough for the Ravens. We need to return to our rendezvous with the airship."

Martha joined them at the top of the dune and said, "And the Beni Lam fighters?"

Naismith looked up at the lightening sky. "The Royal Flying Corps will deal with the Beni Lam."

Martha shook her head, "Guru, I meant those men running at us."

Naismith smiled and said, "Ah, those men. Well, I will have to deal with them myself. You two join the rest of the Ravens. I will be fine here."

They begrudgingly joined the others, including the bound James O'Connell, leaving Naismith. When last they saw him, he was standing on the edge of the sand dune as at least a dozen young men ran toward him waving scimitars.

To the Ravens, Naismith seemed to make no move at all.

To the young men, he appeared as a giant sand monster rising from the dune. It looked like some sort of hooded man. When it finally reached its full height, it was taller than any palm tree they had seen in an oasis. It had red eyes and sharp teeth and waved its bloody claws at them. In their heads, they heard a voice scream, *TODAY IS NOT YOUR DAY TO DIE! LEAVE THESE INTRUDERS TO ME! I OWN THE DESERT.*

The Beni Lam dropped to their knees and bowed their heads. The eldest behind them took a knee and looked at the monster. All his life, he heard tales of djinns of the desert that ate men simply for pleasure. They had no interest in testing the truth of these tales just to capture a small group of raiders. After all, they only set fire to the infidels' tent. They had stolen no horses or camels. Yes, the raiders had killed some of their tribesmen; now those same raiders would have to answer to the djinn. The Beni Lam could deal with any intruders who survived until sunrise. As for the night time, why not let the djinn take them?

When they looked up, the djinn and the raiders were gone. The leader said, "Good riddance. We have our new guns and gold. We don't need infidels to tell us what to do with either of them. We have dead to bury. We will extract revenge later." As the leader turned, he saw a single rider leaving the camp. He smiled and said, "It would appear at least one of the infidels intends to make good his escape. I suspect the djinn will soon be eating his heart as well."

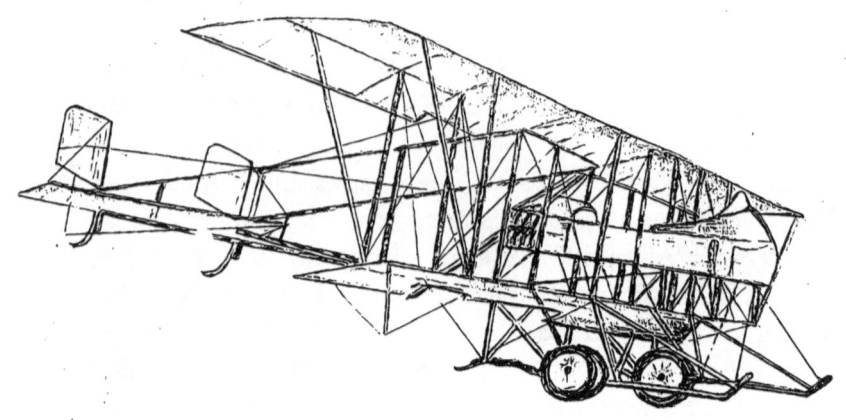

The Sound of the Future

Beni Lam encampment, 03 July 1915

As they walked back down the dune and toward the encampment, the sky shifted from black to maroon on the eastern horizon. The leader said, "It will soon be time for prayers. Let the tent burn. It needed to be cleansed of the infidels and fire is the best way to clean their stench."

As they reached the main tent to report to the elders, they heard a noise like the buzzing of flies in oasis waters where an animal had died. They wondered at the sound of such flies. They had seen none in the encampment.

The pair of Maurice Farman "Shorthorn" aircraft from 30 Squadron, Royal Flying Corps, circled the Bedouin camp at 3,000 feet. Flight Lieutenant Gerald McAlpine knew flying the pusher engine aircraft in the heat of the desert was a challenge, but dawn flights were a perfect mix of clear sky, cool air and light winds. He was the pilot in command of the two-ship mission and thought it was far better than most of the training flights they had completed in the few weeks since their arrival. He enjoyed the flying and knew it was this was the future, but he was a soldier and he wanted to use his skills for King and country. Finally, they were going to war!

He reached forward and tapped the observer/gunner on the shoulder and gave a thumbs up. The gunner acknowledged. McAlpine then signaled to his tentmate and wingman, Stephen Beedle, pointing to the target below. He pointed the aircraft toward the circle of black tents, making sure that he was traveling out of the eastern sky so that any ground observer might miss the silhouette of their flimsy brown aircraft in the false dawn.

He leveled the aircraft at 200 feet, angling the track across the camp. As soon as they reached the edge of the camp, his forward observer opened fire with his Lewis machine gun sending .30 caliber bullets into the tents and into the men as they ran from the tents. As he gently pulled up, he looked back and saw Beedle conducting his own gun run. He slowly spun the aircraft around. His aircraft was far less advanced and far less maneuverable than any of the aircraft they trained on in England. It flew just like it looked — a bathtub sitting between two canvas wings with a propeller in the back. Not a proper aircraft at all, but at least he was flying and not leading some infantry platoon in the trenches in France.

McAlpine headed back across the camp. As they crossed over the tents the second time, both he and his gunner tossed hand grenades over the side of the aircraft and watched as they exploded below. He pulled up and watched as Beedle did the same. Mission completed, he headed back toward Basra and what he hoped would be a hearty breakfast and some tea. During his briefing last night, he was told that these tribals had attacked the Indian Army forces at Qurna. Now that they had a taste of the future, he expected they would leave well enough alone and let the Ottoman Army do its worst against the forces of Empire. At that point, it would be the job of 30 Squadron to conduct reconnaissance with these kites. Not an ideal option for a member of the Royal Flying Corps, but still a job far better than most.

As they reached cruising altitude of 3,000 feet and headed south towards Basra, McAlpine noticed an airship on the same heading. It had Royal Navy markings. That meant it was clearly part of the larger British effort in Mesopotamia, but McAlpine wondered why a Navy airship would be so far from the ocean. It was clearly heading toward the Arabian Sea at an altitude twice the height of his aircraft. He wondered, was it blown off course? He shrugged and thought no matter how fragile his Shorthorn might be, it was not likely to be blown that far off course. Of course, who knew what challenges an airship crew faced with their hydrogen gas bags and large outboard motors?

Shadows in the Mind

Somewhere over the Arabian Sea, 04 July 1915

ELIZABETH WOKE WITH A START. AS WITH ALL OF THE RAVENS, SHE HAD BEEN exhausted after they embarked on the airship and headed away from the Beni Lam and the fighting in Mesopotamia. Naismith had walked along the aisle of the passenger compartment and congratulated each of the Ravens for the mission's success. He told them that they were headed back to India and it would be a multiple-day flight. He offered to help them relax and rest. He warned that this operation was unlikely to be the last for the Ravens.

Elizabeth fell into a deep sleep shortly after Naismith passed by her. Later in the flight, she expected that this first sleep was helped by Naismith's mesmerism skills. As the hours turned into days, her subsequent sleep was disrupted by nightmares of every shape and size, from classic childhood terrors of being pursued by monsters to more adult dreams of failing at some mission. She remembered the faces of the men she had killed and the agent she had lost to German treachery. Each time she woke, she walked over to what the airmen and sailors called "the head," washed her face and then walked to the spartan canteen where she made herself a cup of tea.

On this occasion, Marian sat down next to her with tea. Elizabeth was not yet accustomed to the white ceramic mugs with no handles. She found it curious but assumed it was a style created specifically for airships. In the dim light in the cabin, Marian's face seemed as welcome as the tea. Elizabeth was unsure of the day or the hour as the airship made its way east. She said, "I fear I have lost track of time."

Marian smiled, "It is the 4th of July and it is late evening. We are flying over Baluchistan."

"I slept most of the day?"

"Yes, and well-deserved sleep to be sure."

Elizabeth stared into her mug of tea. The cream created a series of rings on the surface of the tea. She said, "I almost died there."

"Elizabeth, we would not let you die."

"Eh?"

"The Ravens are mission first, of course. But we do not let our colleagues face mortal danger alone."

Elizabeth whispered, "But what about the confrontation with Michael? He almost burned me alive."

"Elizabeth, tell me what happened."

With that Elizabeth proceeded to describe her anger at watching Michael get away, her leap in front of him and then the fight with Michael somehow bringing up oil from the ground and lighting it on fire.

"Elizabeth, whatever you saw when you confronted Michael was in your mind. It was not real."

"I felt the heat. I smelled the burning oil."

"Elizabeth, I was there. I saw nothing except you facing Michael. You were both still as statues and nothing like you described happened."

"He created all of that in my mind?"

"He has powers. He accesses those powers through the astral plane and projects them into the minds of his adversaries."

"So, I was not at risk?"

"Elizabeth, you were absolutely at risk. If you believed you were going to die, you might have died. That part is absolutely true."

"Do we all have these powers?"

"Dear, you already know you have these powers. You have used them over and over again these last few years."

"But not creating terror."

"Michael is reaching into a dark space in his mind. That unleashes power. It is not power he controls."

"I have felt that way before. We talked about my anger."

"Controlling your anger is important. Michael's power does not come from anger. It comes from something...."

This time it was Marian staring into her mug of tea. She was searching for a word. "I am reluctant to use the word evil because that leads us to a religious discussion. I certainly believe Michael is capable of harmful acts that are based on his own dark personality. Some would call it evil and imply involvement of some deity. I prefer not to allow the individual an excuse. We have free will. Michael is choosing a path that will do great harm to others and, more likely than not, to himself."

Elizabeth looked up and said, "But what about me?"

Marian said, "We all have darkness in us. It is up to you to keep that darkness locked in a corner of your mind."

Elizabeth wondered if she could keep the darkness away.

Marian had read her mind and said, "We can help you, Elizabeth."

Part Three

Chess Pieces on the Board

Small Lies with a Purpose

Baghdad, 05 July 1915

MICHAEL O'CONNELL STOOD BEFORE VON TRIER. HE HAD EXPECTED THE German officer to be waiting for him in Damascus. That would have given him time to make a credible story and a follow-on plan to save his father from what he was certain would be a British firing squad. Instead, when he arrived in Baghdad, he was summoned to the provisional German command headquarters. There, in a far less comfortable set of quarters, he faced his German master.

Michael was still in the Bedouin clothes he had stolen from the Beni Lam. He was wearing sandals, and even after a bath and a shave he looked precisely as bedraggled as he felt. Still, his mind burned with anger and embarrassment at the events of two days ago. He had lost his father to the British. And he had lost the influence over the Beni Lam. How could he now argue that he and his father had fulfilled their bargain and could comfortably leave the battlefield and head to Berlin? Michael had always been a resilient. He had lived

through the heckling from the other children in the cantonment school, calling him a half-breed or worse. He had lived
through the regular beatings in the Circle of Decision at the
Viceroy's College. He had even lived through the hard times
of undercover work playing an Arab boy in Carchemish. Still,
the loss of his father to Naismith was almost too much. If he
intended to save his father, he would have to craft a story that
von Trier would understand — a story which would not have
any discussion of actions in the mystic plain.

Von Trier looked at the young man. He had led soldiers in
battle and he recognized the signs of battle on this ... boy.
For all his skills and achievements, von Trier realized that
Michael O'Connell was not yet twenty years old. In a normal
world, he would be a cadet in one of the military academies
and, in time, lead hussars into battle. Instead, he had been
living with Bedouin nomads, convincing them to fight irregular warfare against a British army, serving as the flanking
attack on a badly run Ottoman campaign. Now, he had
returned alone. There was a story to be told and von Trier
intended to give the young man a chance to tell it on his own
terms. He said, "Captain, I think we could both use some
strong coffee before you begin your tale."

Michael nodded. It was a good opening move on von Trier's part. It meant that he would be willing to listen and,
perhaps, open to suggestion. He squared his shoulders and
answered, "Yes, sir. I could use some strong coffee."

After von Trier had bellowed orders to his staff and they
returned with a large silver coffee service and a plate of pastries that Michael thought looked better than anything he
had eaten in weeks, von Trier surprised him by pouring the
coffee himself. Michael had always been suspicious of the
German's interest in him, but he had to admit, he had not
expected such a simple courtesy from this Prussian.

Von Trier opened the conversation by saying, "We were
very pleased with the work you did with the Beni Lam. I

know the Ottoman troops were defeated in the battle of Shaiba, but they would have been decimated if your Beni Lam raiders had not conducted a flanking attack. As you said before you left, the nomads are a powerful force even if they are not exactly a disciplined force. The guns and the gold we provided were resources well spent. Congratulations."

Michael bowed his head to appear embarrassed by the praise. In fact, he knew full well that the Beni Lam had delivered what they promised, no more and no less. They were raiders at heart and once they knew they could raid the British lines at will with few casualties, they did so with determination. They would continue to do so for as long as the British were in Mesopotamia and the cost was not too great. Still, he also knew that if he was going to gain any traction with his new plan, he would have to exaggerate the influence that he and his father had on the Bedouin. He began, "I believe German Mausers and German gold influenced the battle."

"Led by two German agents."

"Sir, we did our best to organize them and point them in the right direction. After that, we had little control over what they did. The Beni Lam are brave, but they are raiders at heart. They will never be willing to stand and fight."

"Well, the Ottoman troops proved they were even less willing to stand and fight." Von Trier shook his head and poured Michael another cup of the strong coffee. "Now, I need you to tell me what happened at the encampment a few days ago."

Michael watched von Trier's aura. It was a blue-green. The colonel was sincere in his questioning. He did not intend to turn this into an interrogation. For that reason, Michael knew he would have a good chance of turning the discussion to his advantage. He started, "Sir, I have no idea how the British raiders knew we were in the Beni Lam camp and, most especially, how they knew which tent was ours. During the fight I only saw a few of the raiders. I believe they were

Gurkhas from the Indian Army." Michael paused to sip his coffee and waited to see if the colonel would accept this first lie.

Von Trier nodded. "The Gurkhas have been used on raids across this entire campaign front. They are conducting operations capturing Ottoman commanders on the Red Sea coastline and there are rumors of Gurkhas conducting similar raids as far north as al-Kut. I feared that might have been your fate."

"Have you determined if there were any Ottoman commanders who knew of our actions with the Beni Lam? I do not believe the Gurkhas attacked our tent by accident."

"Nor do I, Captain. I have expressed my disappointment to the local Ottoman leadership and they intend to dispatch their special force, the *Tashkila'at Mahsusa,* to search for traitorous officers in their midst. I fear they will only look for officers who are not Turks, but there is little more I can do."

"Sir, I understand. The Ottoman Army in Mesopotamia is made up of Turks and Arabs as well as a mix of some other nationalities. I suspect the Turks will always choose to distrust those who are not their own."

"Exactly so. Tell me about the raid."

"My father and I had been working late with the tribal leaders of the Beni Lam, designing the next raid and determining what, if anything, they needed in resupplies from our side." Michael used the phrase *from our side* as a tool to underscore his own loyalty to the Germans. He had no such loyalty, but this was not the time to suggest that he was an independent agent. "One of the reasons why I believe there must have been an outside agent involved was the tribal leaders made it clear that they were interested in a resupply of ammunition for the Mausers. Surely, they would not have given us up to the British if they were hoping for more ammunition and, perhaps, more weapons. I would be more willing to accept Beni Lam treachery if we had just delivered the second tranche of arms."

"I defer to you, Captain. I have no expertise in the Arab mind and, sadly, some of our own experts are now deployed further east in Persia, so you remain our only surviving expert."

This bothered Michael because in the long run, he did not wish to stay in Mesopotamia as an "expert" for the German command. Still, in the near term, it meant he would be able to speak with some authority. He continued, "Sir, the raiders came out of the eastern desert. I have no idea how they bypassed the Arab pickets set up to protect the camp."

"These Gurkhas are famous for their stealth and, I fear, the Bedouin are famous for their lack of discipline."

Michael countered, "I think the Beni Lam pickets were in fear of their lives if anything happened to us. I saw the tribal leaders make that clear when they found one of the pickets asleep. He was short a finger the next dawn."

"I stand corrected. As I said, you are the expert in these matters."

Michael continued, "The Gurkhas attacked our tent and immediately set fire to it. They grabbed my father. I fought two of them to a standstill, but there were reinforcements coming when my father shouted to me to make good my escape. He said that our mission was more important and needed to be continued. As they dragged him off, I continued to fight. Suddenly, two aircraft attacked the encampment using machine guns and grenades. One of my attackers struck me with the butt of his rifle. I was dazed. In the confusion, he must have thought I was dead. When I recovered, the camp was under air attack and the raiders were gone. I took one of the Beni Lam horses and tried to pursue the raiders, but I never did find at trace. I wonder if they used the aircraft to cover their escape?"

Michael used just the right amount of emotion mixed

with mesmerism to ensure the colonel accepted his tale. It was, after all, mostly true which was the centerpiece of any successful lie. And the emotions he expressed were real. After a pause to sip his coffee, Michael shook his head. "The Bedouin were useless in any pursuit. They were convinced that the attack was a result of desert djinns who were somehow cleansing the camp of infidels. They remain interested in attacking the British, but it was clear they were no longer interested in working with me. I decided to leave and report back."

Michael paused again and decided to change the topic. He asked, "Sir, why are you in Baghdad instead of Damascus?"

Von Trier nodded. "I will answer your question after I make a brief comment. I appreciate your intrepidity, young man. Living with the Bedouin had to be a challenge. You and your father were walking a tightrope with them. We could expect no help from them if they had decided desert spirits were cleansing the camp of infidels. I am pleased that you made it out safely even if your father did not." The colonel paused to take a sip of his coffee. He said, "I am also pleased to hear that you think the Beni Lam will continue to raid the British. I suppose it is their nature to do so and the addition of our guns and gold simply enhanced their willingness."

Michael watched the colonel's aura very carefully to determine if there was anything but sincerity in his speech. It appeared that the colonel was being truthful.

Von Trier continued, "As to my move, after the battle of Shaiba, the baron decided that we needed to provide additional support to the Ottoman command. You may or may not know that the Ottoman commander in charge, Suleiman Askari, committed suicide after the battle. He blamed your "irregulars" for his loss. Well, of course he did." Von Trier shook his head. "Askari was close to Baron von der Goltz. It was the baron who picked Askari as the first head of the *Tashkila'at.* The death was a disappointment for the baron to be sure. So, he instructed myself and a half dozen senior operational officers to follow him to Baghdad and provide direct support — honestly, direct command — to the Ottoman commanders, Nureddin Pasha and Halil Pasha. So far, it appears to have worked. The new commanders are less audacious and far more realistic in their understanding of the capabilities of their troops. The British may regret their victory at Shaiba. I personally think the new commanders are far better than Askari."

Michael said, "Sir, I am sure that will be the case. The British are demonstrating the feckless nature of their military planning."

Michael used this as an opening for his own adventure tale. "You probably have not heard of the logistics tangle in Basra. Just before the raid on our camp, I made a short reconnaissance to Basra to determine how badly the British are bungling their supply efforts. It was far worse than even I expected. The Indian Army is not used to what we would call expeditionary warfare. They fight in India from established bases. Suddenly, they had to move men, materiel, and horses from India to Arabia. They did that in reasonable form, but they did not think about their supply chain. Their troops are suffering shortages in nearly everything. There will be significant death on the Tigris before they are through."

Michael paused simply for effect. He wanted von Trier to push him for more details.

"Captain, you went alone?"

"Yes, sir. It was not more than two days ride from the Beni Lam camp to the outskirts of Basra. It was there that I used a disguise to move along the docks to see what was happening. I saw the mess with my own eyes. I also added slightly to the mess by using an Arab to plant a small bomb on the docks."

"And the result?"

Michael could see that his story was playing on von Trier's imagination. It was precisely the reason why he mentioned it.

He hoped this would give him leverage when he pushed his real purpose. "Sir, I never expected to have any great results. I believe the bomb was moved and exploded harmlessly at the docks. However, it accomplished the mission. The British had to shut down all operations while they conducted a thorough review of all the dock workers. They did not find my saboteur, but now they are using their own troops to move material from the docks. They will probably return to using local labor ... eventually, but for now, front line troops are being used as stevedores. That should slow things down some."

"Bravo, Captain! That is precisely why our operations are so important to the larger campaign."

Michael looked down at his sandaled feet and used his most obsequious tone when he said, "I am only doing my duty, sir."

"On your own initiative and at very high risk. It is precisely the sort of work the baron expects of our little contingent. I can't wait to let him know of your success."

Michael decided the moment had come, "Sir, I have a request."

"Captain?"

"I would like to return to Basra and kidnap a British officer. Someone of importance so that we could arrange a trade for my father. As you know, the British most certainly will execute my father. I would try to rescue him myself, but I have no idea where they are keeping him. I doubt it is Basra, given the chaos there. If not Basra, it could be anywhere. The British lines are porous. I could do this with as few as two or three good men. Before we made that trade, we could interrogate the officer to determine their next set of plans." He paused to see if von Trier would take the bait.

The colonel bellowed to his staff for another pot of coffee. Michael could not determine if he simply wanted more coffee as they changed from reporting to planning or if he was stalling as he thought of some way to refuse Michael. The only good news for Michael was that von Trier's aura had not changed. Whatever he eventually said, it would be truthful or, at least, what von Trier thought to be true.

There was a pause in the conversation as both locals and staff officers passed through the office. Von Trier instructed one of the staff officers to bring him a map and a recent report. Michael took this as a positive sign. He did not realize how positive it was until von Trier started his discussion.

Knight's Cross Gambit

Baghdad, 05 July 1915

MICHAEL GENERALLY WAS A PATIENT YOUNG MAN. AFTER ALL, HE SPENT A good portion of the last two years working with Arab sheikhs who, if nothing else, thought hard before they spoke and had time on their side. And, when they spoke, it often began with a parable from the Koran or some story from the long distant past. Still, it seemed to take forever for von Trier to respond. First, the coffee. Then, he had his staff officers carefully place a map on a side table, using weights on all four corners to hold the map in place. After that was accomplished, von Trier had an officer bring a brown paper file that was filled with what looked like reports or summaries. Von Trier made a serious effort to prevent Michael from seeing the reports. The pace and the limited information drove Michael to distraction. He wondered if that was the point or if von Trier was simply demonstrating his own painstaking commitment to accuracy. Whatever the cause, Michael was nearly ready to use his mesmerism skills to force the colonel to speak when the colonel finally did speak.

"Captain, you have identified an interesting challenge and I have no doubt that you would have a good chance of success in capturing a British officer in Basra. However, I am not certain that you would be able to find a British officer of significant importance, nor do I think we would have the leverage necessary to arrange for your father's release. After all, the British know that we play by the same rules as they do. We treat uniformed officers as prisoners of war and we treat individuals who operate out of uniform as spies who will be tried and shot."

Michael's heart sank at the cold-blooded nature of von Trier's comments. He knew that the colonel was simply stating the facts, but that hardly made any difference. Michael was willing to do whatever it took to gain his father's release and he had to move quickly before the British executed his father for treason during wartime. He kept his concerns to himself and simply responded, "Sir, I fear you are correct."

"Michael...." Michael was taken aback by the colonel's use of his first name. This had not happened before and he wasn't certain if it was a good sign or bad. "Michael, I am as convinced as you are that we need to move heaven and earth to get your father released from the clutches of the British command. I just believe we need to do it in a different way. And, it so happens that we have a possible alternative. Please come over to the map while I explain."

Michael followed orders and walked toward what he now saw was a German engineering map. He had seen a similar document when he played his role as the young Arab boy in Baghdad. The German engineers designing the Berlin-to-Baghdad railway were thorough in their cartographic skills. The scale of this particular map was listed as 1:50,000. Michael did quick mental calculation and sorted out that one centimeter on the map represented approximately 500 meters. The map was of the area west and north of the city of Baghdad, including the village of Mendeli. Michael could not remember exactly, but when he was living undercover in Baghdad, he heard Mendeli was famous for date orchards. It seemed like a strange map to use for this discussion, but Michael suspected there was a tale that von Trier wanted to tell.

"Captain, when you were living undercover in Baghdad, how did you find the Kurds?"

"Colonel, they are an independent sort. They reminded me of the Pashtuns I knew in India. They walked with their heads held high and woe be it for any Baghdadi trader who got in their way. They seemed dangerous folk."

"And so they are. The Turks fear them more than they fear the Armenians. Of course, we both know what their troops have been doing to the Armenians, but so far, they haven't been foolish enough to stir up a rebellion of these mountain people. From our perspective, we hope they do nothing to cause trouble. It would be exceptionally difficult to defend along the Tigris if they must defend Baghdad from Kurdish raiders."

"Sir, is there some risk here? My little experience with the Ottoman bureaucrats in Baghdad showed them to be hardly the sort to pick a fight."

"It depends, young captain. It really depends on who in the Ottoman hierarchy you talk to about the Kurds. Askari, for one, was determined that the Kurds would bend to the will of the CUP. He was all about modernization and pan-Turkic enculturation. It annoyed the Kurds."

"But Askari is dead."

"Indeed, but his campaign lives on. And, just as we see the risk in a Kurdish rebellion, the British see a gain if they can foment rebellion."

"They are doing so?"

Von Trier put his finger on the map close to the foothills

near Mendeli. "At least two British agents are working with the Kurds in the mountains and have encouraged them to raid the village. They are working in the same manner as you and your father with the Beni Lam. They are using guns and gold and encouraging the myth of independence."

Suddenly, Michael understood the point of this discussion. "If we could capture these agents …"

"Exactly so. If we could capture these agents, we could trade them for your father. Plus, we could eliminate this flanking threat to Baghdad. Perhaps even end this small rebellion before it becomes a danger to the overall campaign."

"And the baron?"

"Ah, the baron understands the strategic value. He cares little if the British agents are killed or captured. But, I suspect you would prefer we capture them in hopes of a trade."

"Yes, sir. I would like that very much."

Von Trier handed Michael the brown file. "Here are all the reports we have on the activities of the British agents. I suspect you will want to move quickly on this and I will give you all the resources you need. I have a troop of German hussars at my disposal and would very much like to use them for a coup of this sort. I also have received approval to expend as much German gold needed to subvert the Kurds and capture the British spies. Read the file and report back to me tomorrow."

"Yes, sir!" Michael saluted and turned toward the door.

"And Captain …"

Michael stopped in his tracks and turned.

"If you would be so kind, please come tomorrow in uniform."

Michael smiled and said, "Sir, I will do my best to find my uniform which I put in storage before we left for the Beni Lam. I promise to be more presentable, to be sure!"

"It is all I ask." Von Trier smiled as he said it. "Now, dismissed!"

Michael raced out the door and headed toward the small quarters that he and his father had shared before they departed for the Beni Lam. He wondered if he had been wrong all along about the colonel. The Prussian seemed to have a heart as well as a sharp mind.

As Michael O'Connell left, von Trier sat down and considered the situation. He was a chess player, and this seemed like a classic knight's cross gambit. If O'Connell succeeded in capturing the British agents, so much the better for him and for James O'Connell. But even if all he did was kill the agents or disrupt their operations, then from the German perspective, it was a success. Rescuing James O'Connell was not a strategic goal for Germany.

He knew that the young man thought he was smarter than any of the German staff. As much as von Trier admired the young man's courage, he had been warned long ago that Michael O'Connell would do what he could for himself rather than for the imperial cause. Well, now, von Trier had offered him a mission which he would not refuse — a chance to do both. It had been a long day and von Trier decided he deserved a glass of Schnapps.

Running Guns

Eastern Diyali Province, 07 July 1915

FRANCIS RODE WITH THE SMALL KURDISH DETACHMENT AS THEY ENTERED the deserted valley. The drought had turned what should have been a wheat field into a dusty dirt patch. From Francis' perspective, a dusty dirt patch was preferable. It was that early morning period that sailors called BMNT or begin morning nautical twilight: the hour before dawn when a cloudless sky shifts from black to midnight blue to grey. Francis looked at his wristwatch. It was 0420hrs. They had precisely twenty minutes before the first delivery of guns and ammunition.

Darya Khan looked at his British comrade. A tall man with a dark black beard just starting to turn grey at his chin. Wrinkles near the eyes from years of staring into the sun. He was dressed in classic Kurdish warrior clothes: loose pants tucked into high boots, a long green shirt with a broad leather belt that held…? Well, Darya Khan would have called it a very long knife, but he noted that some of his men thought it was a very short broad sword. Francis Bankroft called it a Khyber knife. Whatever it was, it looked deadly. Under the woolen vest, Bankroft had two holstered pistols, one below each armpit. They were not revolvers and Darya Khan wondered how they might work. Across the pommel of his saddle, Bankroft had a German Mauser. Darya Khan coveted that rifle and thought that after the first successful raid on an Ottoman camp, he would ask Bankroft to give him that Mauser. With any other man, he might have simply taken it, but Bankroft looked like a man who could kill with guns, knives or his bare hands. Worse still, he was married to a witch. Better to ask and hope Bankroft would make it a gift.

Francis got down from his horse and pulled what looked like three small cannon balls out of his saddle bags. His Kurdish partner watched as Bankroft paced out a triangle on the ground, thirty steps on each side. He then appeared to open the balls and place on them on the corners of the triangle. In the false dawn, suddenly the three balls glowed a ghostly green. Darya Khan pulled a necklace out from under his shirt. At the end of the silver chain was a large *nazar* — a circle of blue glass with a small circle of white at its center. It was designed to ward off the evil eye but, in this case, Darya Khan hoped his small incantation might protect him from this British warrior's wizardry. Cold light from black iron? Not only was this man married to a witch, but he was a wizard!

Francis walked back to the horses and said, "All we need do at this point is wait. Please tell the men to dismount and hold the horses to keep them calm. The guns will arrive soon."

True to their promise, two Royal Flying Corps aircraft arrived precisely at 0440hrs. They made one pass to identify the marker and then returned to land with little difficulty on the rough field. The pilots did a quick ground loop and paused while each of their observer/gunners reached into the small cargo bay of their aircraft and dropped off two large canvas bags and ten crates of ammunition. Delivery complete, the lead pilot looked to Bankroft for instructions. Bankroft provided a formal salute and the lead pilot responded. With that, he opened the throttle on the engine, bumped down the field and was soon airborne. The second pilot followed his commander and as the sun rose, the only evidence that the aircraft had ever been in the area were the bundles and the crates.

Francis said, "As promised, we have received our delivery. Tell the men to load the crates on the donkeys. Darya Khan, please come with me to inspect the first canvas bag."

As they walked toward the bags, Darya Khan noticed his British counterpart picking up the cannon balls, threading the two halves together and putting them in a small satchel on this side. Bankroft did this as if it was nothing special. The Kurdish leader was both amazed and pleased to see that he was traveling with a man with such skills and yet such a common way about him. When they arrived at the first canvas bag, Francis slowly unbuttoned that bag. The first thing he pulled out was a leather pouch.

He handed it with some ceremony to Darya Khan and said, "This is a gift from my government to you for your willingness to work with us." Darya Khan took the bag, realizing immediately that it contained gold coins. From its heft, he suspected it was a small fortune. When he looked up, he saw Francis holding a brand new Mauser rifle. Francis said, "And this, my friend is my gift to you. The rest of the rifles are as good, just not new. This one is brand new. The first person to fire a round through this weapon will be you. I hope you make it a good shot!"

This was not the first time that Francis had delivered guns to allies, and he tried to make each delivery a ceremony. Running guns to irregulars could be a dangerous business. It was important to make sure that the effort was tied to a more personal rather than professional relationship. Otherwise, the intelligence officer might be simply a tool that could be discarded when the irregular was offered a higher price or a better weapon. Francis' experience with Pashtuns on the border taught him that once he gained a personal relationship with a tribal chief, the chief saw it as a debt of honor that he would respond with loyalty.

Francis had read files and heard from colleagues of the fickleness of tribal loyalty. Certainly, there were plenty of specific examples where British officers were treated more as a commodity to be traded or even killed when the opportunity arose for greater profit. He suspected those stories revealed more of the failures of the British officers than the perfidious nature of the tribal leaders. Honor was a vital commodity for tribal leaders — an important element in gaining and keeping their leadership positions. Far more than any value that could be placed any action, it was an honorable relationship that Francis always worked to establish and maintain. So far, it had proven successful. He hoped this would be true with Darya Khan.

The Kurdish leader took the rifle in his hands. The gun oil on the barrel and the varnish on the stock gleamed in the morning light. It was the finest weapon he had ever held in his hands. As he watched his men pull the rest of the rifles from the two sacks, he realized that Bankroft had not exaggerated. The other rifles were in good working order and they would serve their new masters well. But this rifle ... this rifle was special. It was new! It was something that would be a powerful symbol of Darya Khan's leadership for years to come. More importantly, he knew that Bankroft selected the weapons for his tribe. He could have delivered weapons from the British inventory. The Lee-Enfields were common enough in Mesopotamia and Persia. They were satisfactory weapons, but they were not works of fine engineering. On the other hand, every Kurd in the Ottoman Empire knew of the German Mauser. It was accurate, it had an action that was clean and swift, and the stocks were made of the finest hardwood. This was a weapon that any warrior would covet. And now, he had a brand-new Mauser. He spoke slowly and carefully to his British colleague, "This is a fine weapon and a gift from one warrior to another. I shall not forget this. From today onward, you are my brother."

Francis knew he had been successful in gaining Darya Khan's trust. Now, it was essential that he turned that trust into action. He said, "Brother, now we need to get back to camp and decide how we are going to use these weapons."

Darya Khan smiled and turned to his men, "*Yahla, yahla.* Let us return with our friend and decide how we shall use these fine rifles!" As he walked back to his horse, Darya Khan wondered if there were enough Mausers for all of his fighters. If so, that would be good. If not, he would have to be responsible for their distribution and that would be a challenge. Not the first one that he had as their tribal khan and certainly not the last. He smiled as he pocketed the gold and looked at his new Mauser. It was probably the best challenge he had for some time.

Keeping It in House

Nathiagali, 08–11 July 1914

JAMES O'CONNELL WOKE AS THE SUNBEAMS WANDERED ACROSS HIS CELL. IN the past, he had always relished the early morning light in the foothills of the Himalayas. The sounds of birds and the gentle swish from the tree leaves offered a degree of romance to his decidedly unromantic life in the espionage trade. Less romantic now as he sat in a bare cell. He looked around the cell: a rope bed known as a *charpoi* — the Urdu name describing the four legs of the bed. Next to the bed were a small writing desk, a single carved wooden chair with a wicker seat, a small sink with a bowl and pitcher of fresh water, and a lidded bucket for his excrement emptied once a day. James had already washed using the water in the pitcher and rolled up his mattress and sheet at the foot of the bed, his only real chore of the day. He had no idea when the interrogator would arrive but he wanted to be prepared. He decided to practice a few yoga positions to calm his nerves and to keep his body limber. After all, he knew it was only a matter of time before he would be shot for treason against the Crown. Best to take the time he had to keep calm and accept his life was at its end.

In another part of the compound, Naismith sat his desk pondering how to structure today's interrogation. He was pleased that he had been able to accomplish one task: after capturing O'Connell and returning to India, Naismith was able to convince Winslow-Heath to keep the news of O'Connell's capture "in-house." He knew all too well that the traitor would quickly face a firing squad if news of the capture reached the seniors in the Indian Army. Naismith was no stranger to military law, but he would prefer to keep O'Connell alive. He wanted to know everything that had transpired since O'Connell decided to switch to the German side. A decision that took place well before the war. Naismith wanted to know O'Connell's reasoning, what he had passed to the Germans, and how the Germans had used O'Connell since the beginning of the war. A .303 bullet in O'Connell's chest would not reveal any answers and, in Naismith's estimation, would do no one any good.

With his plan outlined on a small set of notes, Naismith straightened his desk, and walked over to the Persian carpet that covered most of the floor in his office. He sat down in the center field of the carpet, known as a *gul* or flower, and began a series of deep-breathing exercises which would lead him into a cleansing meditation. He wanted his mind clear of all the anger he had over O'Connell's treachery, as well as his concern over how the Ravens would react when they heard that he was keeping O'Connell alive — possibly avoiding military justice forever. As he settled his mind, he imagined the snow fields of the Himalayas that were visible in the far eastern horizon. Cold, clear, clean snow.

How are you, soldier? Are you pleased with yourself? Can you imagine how little you have accomplished by capturing James O'Connell? Chodak's high-pitched voice interrupted his meditation and forced him back to his present challenges. Naismith looked up to see a translucent skull appearing to float directly in front of his face. *You know his son is totally in my control. He will do whatever I ask, especially when I offer his father in exchange for his servitude. Your world is such a small one, soldier. Still, it is always amusing to me to watch as you slowly twist in the winds of time. Enjoy your day, soldier.*

As suddenly as Chodak appeared, he disappeared. In just those few seconds, Naismith had broken into a sweat as if he had run a mile in these mountains. Given his study of Buddhist scripture, he rarely allowed himself to become emotionally attached to anything happening that he could not control. He only focused on what he could control, which was his own emotions. But Chodak's regular appearances terrified him. Naismith had no idea how to fight this ghoul or, for that matter, where to fight him. He stood and walked to a small bowl and pitcher near the office window. He poured a little water into the bowl, saw the sunlight race through the rippling water and then watched as small waves moved from the center of the bowl to the edge. He stopped to watch the last of the waves and then placed his cupped hands into the bowl and splashed the water over his face. The water was cool and refreshed him. Naismith decided that today would be a day to ignore his concerns, ignore Chodak's intrusions, and focus his attention on O'Connell.

James O'Connell never heard Naismith enter the room. In fact, he never heard the cell door open at all. It was as if one moment he was alone and the next Naismith was in front of him looking down as he finished his yoga breathing routine.

Naismith's voice was gentle, barely a whisper. "I suppose you realize you are in serious trouble."

"Guru Naismith? I had not expected to see you today."

"The previous interrogators were not to your liking?"

"They were ..." O'Connell searched for a word as he stood up. "They were vigorous in their questioning."

Naismith laughed. "Vigorous, eh? Well, I hope they did you no physical harm. We have no intention of that sort of punishment."

"Just a .303 in the chest."

Naismith looked at O'Connell and said, "Only if you are ... tedious."

"Tedious?"

"I have bought us some time. Winslow-Heath has agreed to keep your capture a secret for now. The military justice system, the trial for treason, and your execution are all likely but not certain. What is certain is that you will answer my questions. How you answer them could easily mean you live to see old age." Naismith pulled up the single chair and motioned for O'Connell to sit on the *charpoi*. In normal circumstances, that would have meant O'Connell was sitting far below his interrogator's eyes. However, Naismith was a slight man and when he leaned forward in the chair, he was face-to-face with O'Connell.

"Let us begin. When did you first decide to work for the Germans?"

O'Connell could feel the old man reaching into his mind. He realized that it would take all of his concentration to avoid lying. And, even then, the lie would be so weak that it would be revealed immediately. James O'Connell understood now how Indian, Persian and Arab locals felt when he used his mesmerism powers on them. He would obey, whether he wished to or not.

"Excellent, James. There is no good way to avoid the questions. If you try, there will be pain. Not pain I will create. Pain your own body and brain will create in resisting my questions. What's the point? Really, just start telling the truth and it will be so much easier and quicker that way. And, as I said before, who knows, it might mean the difference between life and death for you and for Michael."

This comment startled James. He was certain that Michael had made good his escape. What sort of reach could Naismith have that would threaten Michael? Since James had no real idea of the limits of Naismith's powers in the mystic arts, he accepted that Michael could possibly still be in danger. He nodded and began.

"It all begins with the death of my wife. My colleagues could have saved her. They chose not to do so because she was not ... British. They left her to die in Bombay. Worse still, she might have been saved if I was not on a collection mission. I had been doing my part for the Raj, but the Raj decided not to do the same for me or my family."

Naismith knew this sort of pain. He was, after all, the son of a British officer and a North Indian princess. The level of prejudice had followed him throughout his military career. It was one of the reasons why he had leapt at the chance to serve in military intelligence. His work rarely involved other British officers. Now that he was near the top of the military intelligence hierarchy, no one spoke of him as a "half-breed" or as an "Anglo-Indian" — which Naismith knew was the same thing. Rather, they spoke of "the colonel" who ran the school in the mountains and commanded the Ravens. Still, that early prejudice would never have taken Naismith into the world of treason. It was a puzzle. He said, "Continue, James."

"I dropped Michael off at the college and was back in Bombay. Winslow-Heath dispatched me to the Gulf to expand our collection in the Arab sheikhdoms." Naismith nodded and noticed that James still used the term "our collection." Perhaps he was not as far gone as they all thought.

"I was in Aden during a ship visit. I was invited on board. There were a number of Royal Navy dignitaries on the cruiser as well as diplomats from the consulate. They all used derogatory terms for the locals as well as for any "half-breeds." They scoffed at the idea that an Englishman could possibly love a local. Rape a local, certainly. Even keep a local woman as his mistress. But love a local? Impossible! I was furious. I left the event on the fantail of the cruiser. As I wandered the ship, I got lost. I ended up in a room where I saw a small version of the difference engine. I had read about it in various scientific journals that made it out to the Raj and here it was. Better still, sitting next to the engine unguarded was a rolled-up set of plans for the engine and its use. It was clearly labelled. I don't know what came over me. Often you read children's books that talk about the angel on one shoulder competing with the devil on the other. I suppose the devil spoke more eloquently that night because I took the plans. I'm not certain what I intended to do with them, but I took them."

Naismith thought about the story. It was plausible, especially if you believed — as Naismith did — in the power of demons who live in the shadows of our world. He could imagine Chodak pushing James to take this first step. Especially if he had plans for young Michael O'Connell. Naismith shook his head as if to clear this malign and absurd thought. James O'Connell simply decided to somehow profit from his actions. To guide the conversation, Naismith said, "Did you know someone who could engage the Germans?"

James smiled and said, "Sir, if you recall, that was one of the taskings that you gave me yourself before I left the school after dropping off Michael."

Naismith thought back to that day. "So I did, James." He said, "Would you take some tea?"

O'Connell laughed at the polite offer, as if tea would help the situation. Still, it sounded like a good thing. He said, "Sir, I would very much like to take some tea."

Naismith nodded. "I will have some made up and then I will return. We will continue this conversation." With that,

Naismith stood up and, to James' amazement, he simply disappeared.

Naismith returned on a regular basis for several days. Each time he arrived, James worried that it would be the last. Very much like Scheherazade in *One Thousand and One Nights*, he hoped that his stories of work with the Germans would extend his life just one more day. He had no expectation that he would end up anywhere but against a wall facing a firing squad. However, if he could extend his life just one more day, that might be one more day that Michael would be able to make good his escape. To where? Well, ideally James hoped the Germans would transfer Michael to Berlin, perhaps to work in their oriental department under Max von Oppenheim. James had no reason to believe Michael would end up in Ireland. That was a dream that had no chance of becoming real.

Just before dawn one morning, James was daydreaming as he watched the first light of dawn creep into his cell. Suddenly, he heard Michael's voice as clear as if his son was sitting next to him. The telepathic message echoed in his mind.

Father, I can see you. You are in the Viceroy's College. Are you well?

Michael, so far, I have been well treated. I have been interrogated by Guru Naismith. I have not tried to resist. If I did, Naismith would only need to probe my mind to force me to tell the truth. My goal has been to string the story along so that you were eventually safe.

Father, I am in Baghdad. I am designing a plan to free you. Continue to engage Naismith. He will do his best to keep you alive. I will do my best to free you.

But how? Certainly not a raid into India.

A trade, father. A trade. Now, I must go before Naismith arrives. He might feel my presence. Farewell, father. Farewell.

And, just as suddenly as he arrived, Michael was gone. James knew that Michael's plans created some hope that he might survive. He needed to hide that hope deep in his mind and bury it. Surround it with despair and compliance. Naismith might notice some hope, but James was determined that Naismith would not notice that he had been in telepathic contact with Michael. He focused his mind on these matters as he started his morning meditation.

Once again Naismith arrived as if he had floated through the walls. He appeared while James sat in the full lotus position counting breaths.

"So, James. I will have tea delivered soon. Shall we begin again? What was your first operation with the Germans? I suspect it was before the war. Where?"

James nodded and began to spell out his efforts in Afghanistan building tribal alliances supporting the Germans. The more he spoke, the deeper he buried the conversation with Michael.

O'Connell couldn't protect his mind from Naismith. Naismith knew of the exchange with Michael and thought about the consequences. He returned to the thought: focus on what you can control. And, right now, he could control James O'Connell.

A Simple Kidnapping

Baghdad, 10 July 1915

MICHAEL ARRIVED IN VON TRIER'S OFFICE PRECISELY AT 10 HOURS. HE KNEW the German appreciated precision and it was precision that Michael would offer. Over the past three days, he had met with von Trier and two staff officers to discuss the details of the files he received. Michael wore the German field grey uniform, and, over time, he realized that while it was uncomfortable, it did provide him with a bit of social armor. On 08 July, von Trier had presented Michael with the Iron Cross, First Class, for his work with the Beni Lam and his personal actions in Basra. The black and white ribbon and the black and silver cross was rare in the provisional headquarters in Baghdad. In his travels to and from the headquarters, Michael noticed only one other Iron Cross on an officer and that one was the second class. Still prestigious, but not as much as his. Of course, he was aware of von Trier's awards which included an Iron Cross on his chest and the *Pour le Merite* or Blue Max that he wore around his neck. The Iron Cross meant that even with his lesser rank of captain, the staff gave him far more privileges than he would otherwise have deserved. Michael had to admit, he had grown used to those privileges that came with wearing the uniform.

As he entered von Trier's office, he was surprised to see Baron von der Golz sitting behind the oak desk with von Trier standing to his left. To his right was a young staff officer with a notebook. Von der Golz was in an Ottoman uniform with his rank as field marshal. Michael did not need anyone to tell him that a conversation with "the Pasha" was filled with risk. Still, he proceeded to the desk, came to the position of attention, and saluted. He remained at attention and held his breath. He had planned a less formal discussion. Now, that plan had gone awry. He hoped that he could salvage something from this meeting. He was pleased when von der Golz said, "Captain, please take a seat. We have work to do and I don't think you can accomplish this work standing at attention."

Michael bowed, slowly exhaled and sat in the chair across from the field marshal.

"Captain, von Trier has told me of your actions and I was pleased to award you the Iron Cross. Now, you have another audacious plan and before we agree, I wanted to be certain that we were clear on the operation. While I recognize the importance of family loyalties, I want you to be clear that this operation you are suggesting is not about arranging a trade for your father. It is about removing a threat to our flank. Hundreds, if not thousands, of Ottoman troops might be saved if we can concentrate our effort against the British advance up the Tigris. If we must address a rebel attack from the Kurdish mountains, our operations simply will not succeed. Do you agree?"

Michael paused for what he assumed would be the appropriate amount of time to ensure that the field marshal was asking a real question and not a rhetorical one. He said, "Sir,

I agree with you completely. One reason we aroused the Beni Lam was precisely to force the British troops to focus on multiple threats. I have no idea if the British spies can have the same level of success if they are allowed to do so, but we simply cannot allow them the opportunity to build that capability. I have been working with the colonel's staff to design a plan that will neutralize that threat."

"And if that means killing the British spies?"

"It will be my duty to do so." Michael hoped that his immediate response would disguise the fact that he had no intention of killing the British agents. From his perspective, it would be a simple kidnapping. Not as dramatic as the one that resulted in his father's capture. Rather, it would be as simple as finding a Kurdish fighter susceptible to both German gold and his mesmerism skills and watching the events unfold.

Von der Golz nodded. He had seen men who were truly heroic and men who posed as heroes. The young man before him seemed to be truly heroic. He knew that if the operation failed, it might still result in the death of one or more of the British spies. And if it also meant the death of this young hero, then that was the price of war. Heroic Germans were dying in France every day. He said, "Then I will leave the planning to von Trier and the execution to you, Captain. I wish you good luck." The baron stood up and everyone, including Michael, came to the position of attention until the baron had left the room.

This time it was von Trier who slowly exhaled. Michael had not focused on his primary German contact. Clearly, von Trier was at least as worried about von der Golz as he was. As he took his place behind the desk, he turned to his aide and said, "Coffee for three, Manfred. I think we could all do with some refreshment."

The young man did a stiff bow and headed out the room. When he was gone, von Trier looked over at Michael and said, "It was a near run thing, my friend. The baron was not sure you had the will to accomplish the mission. Clearly you do and he was impressed. This will open resources to us that were otherwise not possible. I hope that makes you happy."

Michael remained cautious whenever talking to any of the Germans. "Happy is not precisely the word, sir. I think encouraged is a better way to phrase my understanding of the future mission."

Von Trier laughed and said, "Encouraged? Well, yes. We can be encouraged that the baron did not put us in irons because he thinks we are mad. Now, we must prove to him that we are not mad."

"Sir, I will do my best, though often my operations have appeared … unconventional."

"Unconventional is splendid, so long as it delivers success."

Before Michael could reply, the staff officer came in with a tray of coffee and pastries. Von Trier said, "Well done, Manfred. Now we can get to work."

A Raid on Mendeli

Western Mesopotamia. 13–14 July 1915

FRANCIS RODE WITH THE KURDS AS THEY APPROACHED THE OUTSKIRTS OF Mendeli. It was just before midnight; they were skirting the eastern boundaries of the oasis town and heading for the Ottoman compound on the road to Baghdad. Before they left the camp, Mary, Bektashi and Alia had approached Francis to wish him good fortune and to focus his attention on the larger picture — the capture of information that would help them decide which Turkish outpost to attack next. Both Francis and Mary understood that their work with the Kurds was designed to bleed off some Ottoman resources so that the Indian Army could conduct more effective operations along the Tigris. The only way to build the capability was to start on the periphery and slowly work toward Baghdad. Mendeli was the first step.

Bektashi initially insisted that he ride with Francis. It took some persuasion, but he eventually accepted that he was needed to "protect" Mary and Alia. Francis also pointed out that Mendeli was just a test run, hardly a complicated operation. He promised Bektashi that on the next raid he could ride with him. The Albanian was disappointed but accepted his orders. Mary smiled at the thought that she needed protection, but used a small bit of mesmerism to reinforce Francis' position. She also informed Bektashi that they would be planning a special mission into Baghdad and he was central to the plan that would not include any of the Kurds. His honor appeased, Bektashi rendered a formal salute as Francis mounted his horse.

One hour later, Francis looked over at Darya Khan. Darya Khan rode a grey stallion; his bridal, reins and saddle blanket were all multi-colored wool, woven by his wife years ago. When Francis had asked if it was appropriate to ride into battle with horse tack that was as special as this, Darya Khan just laughed.

"Francis, what is the point of having such things if they stay wrapped in some bag inside our tent? My wife worked for weeks on this and two of my daughters helped. My three sons are just behind us with their own festive garments. Why not? It is not as if these Turks and Arabs are going to be worried about what we are wearing when we start to cut them down with our new rifles and our old swords." Darya Khan laughed. "And, if we die tonight, then why not die looking like a pasha?"

For most of his life, Francis had been involved in shadow wars where usually he was the on his own or with one trusted companion. He had to admit Darya Khan had a point. Once they were conducting the raid on the Ottoman outpost, it seemed unlikely there would be any difference between his garments in greys and blues and Darya Khan's in bright green, turquoise and carnelian. At that point in time, it would be close-in fighting. Everyone would be focused on their own sword and the sword of their adversary.

As the thirty riders closed on the Ottoman compound,

Francis was reminded of the first couplet of Lord Byron's poem *The Destruction of Sennacherib.*

The Assyrian came down like the wolf on the fold,
And his cohorts were gleaming in purple and gold;
And the sheen of their spears were like stars on the sea,
When the blue wave rolls nightly on deep Galilee.

Francis also hoped that the raid would not turn out like the end of the poem. Like many of the operations before, Francis took comfort in the detailed plan and his effort to check and double check every step. He still knew that once any operation started, the gods of chance took over. He reached over for the tenth time to check that his two pistols were safely tucked into their holsters and the Khyber knife was in its sheath. He had left his Mauser with Bektashi. Once the fighting started, there would be no time for carefully aimed fire. It would be close combat where pistols and blades would carry the day.

They deployed their riflemen along an embankment that overlooked the Ottoman camp. The Turks apparently did not believe in using defensive positions, known as pickets in India, to protect from rifle fire. On the Afghan frontier, more than one soldier had died from an Afghan sniper. The Afghans were famous for accurate fire from distances that few in the Indian Army could believe. It only took one such incident for a young officer to move his pickets to well beyond the range of the Afghan jezails. With their new Mausers and well-practiced mountain rifle skills, the Kurdish raiders would teach the Turks this same lesson tonight.

After placing the riflemen, Francis joined Darya Khan with the remaining dozen Kurdish riders who would ride directly into the compound through a poorly guarded gate. Earlier, Francis had asked Darya Khan if he was confident that his riflemen would follow orders. The Kurdish tribal leader laughed and said, "Two of them are my sons. They will follow orders."

Francis looked at his watch. It was nearly one in the morning. By now, most of the guards assigned for the night watch would be dozing at their posts and those who were on the day shift would be sound asleep. He looked over at Darya Khan and said, "It is time to wake up the Turks."

Darya Khan's white teeth gleamed underneath his sumptuous moustache. He walked over to his riflemen and said, "We begin. Take care as you fire. We will be among them very soon."

The riders moved quietly along the ridge line before reaching the road to the west of the compound. Surprise would be essential, so they walked their horses in the shadows of the orchards and irrigation ditches that made Mendeli famous for dates. After taking care to get as close to the compound as possible, the riders broke into a gallop and rushed the Ottoman guard post. The sleepy guards woke to the sight of Kurdish swordsmen racing down the road toward them. They felt as well as heard the horses' hooves as the raiders descended on their position. As conscripts, the guards were poorly trained, poorly paid and poorly fed. They had no intention of losing their lives tonight. They abandoned their post and their rifles, and disappeared in the darkness.

Francis and Darya Khan were in the lead and rushed the now-unguarded compound. Francis reached the first tent, drew his Khyber knife and sliced through the tent ropes which dropped the tent flat. When no one ran from the collapsed tent, he realized: A trap! He shouted to Darya Khan, "Treachery! We are in an ambush!"

Darya Khan pulled his stallion up short. He had his sword in his hand and was looking for adversaries to his left and right. None appeared. A shot rang out and the Kurdish leader dropped to the dirt, dead from a pistol round to head. Francis looked for the assassin and could find no adversary.

He looked behind him to find Darya Khan's eldest son brandishing a still-smoking German Luger. The young man turned to Francis and said, "It was time for a new generation to lead the clan."

Francis was surrounded by the raiders who suddenly turned their weapons on him. Francis knew resistance would be foolish. His only thought was of Mary, Bektashi and Alia. He was no expert at telepathy, but in extremis, he was convinced he could send a message. He concentrated as the riders came up to him, took his pistols and his Khyber knife. As they threw a rope around him and pulled it tight pinning his arms to his side, he sent a message: *A trap. Escape!*

As the young riders grabbed the reigns of his horse, the Ottoman soldiers arrived from the village huts where they had waited. Francis was surprised at the coordination of Kurdish rebels and Ottoman troops. As the Ottomans entered the compound, three men in German grey wool walked up to him. The leader of the small group, a young man wearing an Iron Cross around his neck looked up at his captive. He said in perfect English, "Welcome to Mendeli. Tomorrow morning, we will decide what we are going to do with you." With that, the German officer did a formal about face. He shouted to the Kurds, "*Yahla!*" His two colleagues brought three horses from their hiding place in the compound and they all mounted up. Francis was surprised when they turned and rode east rather than west.

As they rode through the night, Francis received a tele-pathic message from Mary. *We escaped. Are you safe?*

Francis responded as best he could. *Darya Khan is dead. German ambush.*

German?

Most certainly. Francis noticed the more he worked on his telepathy, the better he got. He wondered if Mary was doing all the work in this link inside the astral plane. Just as sud-denly, another voice entered his head.

Lieutenant Colonel Bankroft and Major Bankroft. We need to be clear. I will trade your husband for my father.

Mary's voice intruded. *Your father? Who are you?*

Michael O'Connell. To be precise, Captain Michael O'Connell of the Prussian intelligence service. Naismith captured my father. Reach out to him. Let him know. A one-for-one trade. And, by the way, you need to move south quickly. I think the Kurds are pursuing you.

This last line was filled with sarcasm and ended with a small giggle. Francis could barely understand what was happening in this communication. James O'Connell in custody? Michael O'Connell a German officer? It was almost too much to bear as he rode through the night to some future prison. Francis had been in many dangerous situations, but never in a world where he faced an adversary operating both in the real world and the mystic world. His skills in the mystic plane were limited to telepathy and a bit of mesmerism. And now, he was riding toward some German headquarters in Mesopotamia. He knew he needed to escape, but at present, he couldn't imagine how to make that happen. Francis was a practical man. Surrounded by armed guards, bound both to his horse and with another loop leading to one of the Kurdish traitors, he decided to do the one thing that he could do at present. He decided to sleep. He used a breathing technique to calm his jangled nerves, closed his eyes and hoped to awake when they arrived wherever they were headed. Perhaps in the light of dawn, he could make up a better plan.

Are You Comfortable?

German compound, Kermanshah, 15 July 1915

FRANCIS WAS SUSPENDED BY ROPES THAT WERE ATTACHED TO HIS WRISTS AND threaded through two large iron eyelets in the wall of his basement cell. The ropes were pulled tight and he was just able to balance on his toes to avoid taking his entire weight on his shoulders. It was a painful position, which was precisely why the Ottoman interrogators had created the method. Francis had heard stories of Ottoman torturers trussing up prisoners in this position so they could more effectively use the lash on a back. Some tales of torture were likely exaggerations, but experience taught him that humans could be imaginative fiends. So far, he had not felt the taste of the lash and that surprised him. He was, after all, a captured spy rather than a legitimate military prisoner of war.

Francis expected an extended, painful wait over the next few days before they finally decided to put him against the wall and shoot him. He used his limited mystic skills to detach his mind from his body. Pain, after all, was simply nerve endings sending signals to the brain that something bad was happening to an extremity. Francis worked to block that message and keep his mind focused on one thing: escape. Sooner or later, his captors would bring him down from this modified crucifixion and switch to some other type of torture. When that happened, he intended to be ready to strike. He knew escape was unlikely. But since he assumed he was already sentenced to death, it hardly mattered if he died trying to escape or died standing in front of a firing squad.

When he turned to more optimistic thoughts, he considered what he knew of his surroundings. His captors had made no effort to prevent him from seeing where he was: a low-walled compound with buildings on two sides, stables on a third side and access to the cellar where he was imprisoned. In more peaceful times, he could imagine that this room might have been a place to protect food from the summer heat and the winter's cold. Now, he was the only occupant. If the guards should release one or both of his arms, he would do his best to kill them and then make his way to the stables. After that, he would ride hard and fast, heading south toward the front lines of the battlefield where the Ottoman and Indian Army soldiers were fighting. Francis accepted that the plan was filled with speculation and almost certainly errors, but it was a plan and that made him feel better.

As Francis rocked back and forth between taking his weight on his toes and taking his weight on his shoulders, he suddenly heard a telepathic message. Mary's voice filled his mind.

Darling, we are going to rescue you. I can see where you are. Naismith knows where you are. You need to delay any German plan for as long as possible. Do you hear me?

At his best, Francis was an amateur in telepathic messaging. He concentrated. *Do my best. Stay strong.*

Buy us a little time, dear. We are coming.

As Francis contemplated this message, he began to consider whether he should choose hope over despair. It was his nature to remain optimistic and he knew in his heart that there was always a chance so long as he did not give up hope. It was at that point that the door opened and light flooded in. After living in the dark for so long, it took Francis minutes before he could focus on the figure in the doorway. He had to turn his head to see the doorway. All he could identify was a man in uniform.

The voice from the doorway spoke in perfect English. "So, Lieutenant Colonel Bankroft, are you comfortable?"

Francis knew that he should not antagonize his captor, but he could not help himself. "So far, I have found the accommodations a bit spartan. And, I will admit I would like a cup of tea."

The voice laughed. "Tea, always tea for you British. Well, the good news is that we have some use for you alive. The Ottoman *Tashkila'at* are disappointed that they are forbidden from using their exquisite methods to extract information from you. I have made it clear that I would expect you would prefer to die rather than talk. That would be unfortunate because, as I said, you are of use to me. Honestly, once the Turks start to torture people, there is only one ending. Death."

"I have assumed I was a dead man already."

"Perhaps so, but perhaps not. It will all depend on what happens next."

Francis smiled and said, "In the meantime, would it be possible to change positions? I am finding the current one rather tedious."

"Would you prefer St. Andrew's position?"

Francis knew that St. Andrew was crucified upside down. He smiled as best he could and said, "No, thank you. I had hoped for a chance to sit down."

The voice laughed again. "Perhaps later. When we get a chance to take tea."

Michael O'Connell sat in his small office above the cellar. Several months ago, the Turkish forces had pushed into Persia and occupied Kermanshah. How long they would stay there was anyone's guess, but it was a perfect place for what he hoped was a successful operation. He did not trust the Turks and worried that they might disobey von Trier's orders and start to torture Bankroft for no other reason than their own amusement. He needed a chance to concentrate, and this small space was the only one he could use without distractions from the Turks. He closed his eyes, focused his mind and began a series of mantras that his father had taught him in their years together. He imagined himself sitting next to Naismith in the Viceroy's College. He focused his mind on an image of Naismith. When that image became clear, he started his telepathic message. *Guru, do you remember me? Your long-lost student.*

Michael was surprised when Naismith responded immediately. *Michael, of course I remember you. I miss you. I want to talk to you.*

As well you might, Guru. But for now, I need to send you a message. I have Francis Bankroft in my custody. The Turks want to torture him. The Germans want to execute him as a spy. I want to trade him for my father.

Michael, how do I know you have him?

Guru, come visit him. Or have Elizabeth visit him.

Michael, how do you think this can work? I don't know if the British will release your father.

Michael could feel his temper rising. He wanted to be in control, but for a moment he snapped. *I don't care if the British agree or not. This is between you and I. We both travel in the astral plane. We both know that all things are possible. I know you could move my father anywhere and none of the British would know about it. So, listen carefully. Here is my plan. This is not a negotiation.*

Michael could feel Naismith surrender to his will. He smiled and continued to send the rest of his message.

Part Four

The Final Problem

Need to Know

Nathiagali, 16 July 1915

NAISMITH CALLED THE RAVENS BACK INTO HIS OFFICE AT THE COLLEGE. THE college training had been suspended since August 1914. When they returned from the raid in Mesopotamia, he asked the Ravens to rest in their old student housing while he determined their next mission. In fact, he had always expected that they would not return to their previous operations. The Ravens were too valuable a collective for Winslow-Heath and the Raj. The war in Mesopotamia would need special operations to succeed and the Ravens were the most special of all the forces that the Indian Army possessed. Now, he was about to ask them to work on a project that would risk everything they had for something that was precious to Naismith and to at least one of the Ravens, but that would not be sanctioned by Winslow-Heath or by any of the Indian Army leaders. How would they respond? He wasn't entirely sure.

As the Ravens entered his office, Naismith thought about how important and how powerful a team he managed. The

Ravens had been his creation from the beginning. They were more than just graduates of the Viceroy's College. They were specialists in their trade and all of them had demonstrated skills in the mystic arts that made them more than just intelligence collectors and more than just skilled military professionals. More importantly, the mix of men and women in the Ravens meant that he could deploy them in any environment, and they would be invisible to their adversaries who assumed that only men, and exceptionally fit men at that, could accomplish sensitive tasks.

He had arranged the map table so that the six Ravens could be comfortable. Plates, napkins, tea, fruit, biscuits were all arranged by him. He would let them sit where they pleased, but he made sure he was at the head of the table with the windows behind him overlooking the mountains. This would allow him to gauge their responses. He would see their faces clearly and, equally clearly, see their auras as he outlined his thoughts. His entire plan would be a very near-run thing. Still, he could see no real choice. Once he realized that he had only one way to proceed, he knew he would have to engage the Ravens.

Naismith began slowly. "Your work in Mesopotamia was excellent. We faced a real challenge in infiltrating an enemy camp, capturing an enemy spy, and leaving. No losses and, honestly, no real evidence that the Ravens were even on the ground. We only captured one of the two targets, but we did capture the senior of the two. That meant we have gained intelligence that was crucial to our understanding of German involvement in the region."

Naismith looked up at the team. All except one was pleased. Elizabeth was clearly dismayed. He said, "Elizabeth, you did your best to capture Michael O'Connell. None of us doubt that and I, for one, believe that losing you in the battle would not have been worth the gain of capturing Michael."

Elizabeth nodded. When she did speak, she did so in a soft voice. Every one of the Ravens had to lean forward to hear her. "He has a powerful understanding of mystic ways. He nearly destroyed my mind during the confrontation." Elizabeth did not wish to finish her thought: this was the first time she had ever battled someone in the mystic plane, and she had lost.

Beverly spoke next. "Michael O'Connell is a dangerous individual to be sure. He nearly killed both Guru Naismith and I while we were in the tent. I still don't quite know how he did it."

Naismith said, "He has tapped into a darkness inside his mind. The mystic plane is simply your own mental energy, which you can use for good or evil. Whether he was working for us or the Germans wouldn't really matter. What matters is he is using a side of his personality that is unbounded by care for any other human being. I believe the psychologist Sigmund Freud uses the term psychopath to describe a person focused on his own interests and disinterested in the effects it might have on others. In Tibet and Nepal, the term would be useless because the Tibetans attribute this sort of action to someone possessed by demons within their pantheon of spirits. I can only say that when a person has decided to engage that darkness, whether it comes from their own mind or from demons, they have unleashed power which is destructive — both to themselves and to those around them."

Jonathan asked, "Guru, have you seen this manifestation in the past?"

Naismith worked hard not to go pale when he said, "Yes, Jonathan. I have seen this unleashed by another in the past. I only survived because the evil one became over-confident. Over-confidence is something we might expect from Michael O'Connell." He paused for a sip of green tea. "It was terrifying then, and I find it terrifying now that Michael O'Connell is walking on the knife edge of this possibility."

Naismith looked at Elizabeth and said, "It was a near-run thing that you survived, Elizabeth. While you have extraordinary skills, he has similar skills unbounded by any moral compass. That means, his skills would always defeat your own."

Elizabeth looked more determined than ever when she said, "So, we can do nothing about this?"

Naismith had not expected this comment from Elizabeth, but it served its purpose. He said, "Those of us who avoid this dark path will always be less capable. That does not mean we will be defeated. It simply means we have to understand that our efforts must be collective, not individual."

When Naismith finished speaking, Marian turned to Elizabeth and whispered, "This is how we are going to defeat Michael. We are going to do it together."

Naismith continued, "We can do something about this, but it will mean taking great risks including taking actions that would never be sanctioned by our Indian Army superiors. That was why I called you in for this meeting."

Naismith poured himself another cup of green tea. He looked into the teacup as if it would help him see the future or perhaps serve as a talisman against bad fortune. There was a long pause. The Ravens were not used to this level of silence in their own planning meetings, but they all recalled one-on-one sessions with Naismith while attending the Viceroy's College. There was no point in speaking because Naismith would only speak when he was ready. The mantle clock over the fireplace in Naismith's office was the only sound, the ticking of the clock passing the time first for a minute, then two, and three. Elizabeth thought her mind would explode when finally, Naismith spoke.

"I must ask you to decide whether you are willing to take this journey with me. We may not succeed and even if we do succeed, there is a chance the commanders in the Indian Army will see us as insubordinate. Most of what I will tell you is strictly for you alone. Our masters in the Indian Army do not need to know it and, honestly, if they did hear about it, they would not believe it. I will not ask you to make the decision to help me unless you know the consequences. So, I ask you now, will you follow me."

Beverly was the first to speak. "To the gates of Hell, if need be, Master Guru."

Martha nodded. "I too will follow you."

Jonathan smiled and said, "I am not a poet. I simply say yes."

Alexander said, "Who would protect all of you if I didn't go?"

Finally, Elizabeth said, "I will follow as well."

Naismith looked across the table at Marian. She nodded. He wasn't sure if he should be pleased or dismayed. He turned to Elizabeth and said, "One thing you need to know is that this path will take you down a very dangerous knife edge of your own emotions. You will need to be disciplined. You will need to follow orders and you will need to be part of the team. The Ravens will only be able to succeed in this mission if we all work as one. Like the fingers in a hand. A fist is only strong when all five fingers are joined together. One finger operating apart and the fist is compromised."

Elizabeth wasn't sure what this all meant. Was this Naismith warning her about what she did at the Beni Lam camp when she chased after Michael? Was it something else he knew she had done in the past? She still carried in her mind the deaths of the men she killed. She wasn't sure that she could have controlled herself when she killed in Bombay. Since she had no information that allowed her to understand, she simply said, "Yes, Master Guru. I promise."

Naismith said, "Then we can continue." He took another sip of tea. Marian realized that Naismith had stage managed the entire discussion. He knew she had spent the previous week working with Elizabeth on controlling her emotions. He just needed to hear it from Elizabeth herself. At the end of the table, both Beverly and Jonathan noted that Naismith drank as if he was dying of thirst.

"This mission has to do with both the O'Connells and the Bankrofts." Naismith looked over to Elizabeth and watched as her aura fluctuated from bright red-orange, to blue and back to yellow. Even with Marian's help, Elizabeth was having trouble managing her emotions. He decided there was no way to describe the situation but to state it clinically with all the detail he possessed.

"After we captured James O'Connell, I arranged for his interrogation here at the Viceroy's College. In part, I wanted to use my skills to gain as much information as I could about the German plans in Mesopotamia. In part, I wanted to keep O'Connell away from the less open-minded members of the Indian Army who would have run a short show trial and shot him in the square in the Rawalpindi cantonment within a day of his arrival. They would have cared little about what we might gain from O'Connell, instead focusing on punishing him for his treason." He paused again and realized this next part of the story was going to be far harder to tell.

"Last night, during my evening meditations, I received a telepathic message from Michael O'Connell. He stated that he had captured Francis Bankroft in Kurdistan and was holding him in a Turkish compound in Kermanshah." He looked over at Elizabeth. She had gone pale. Naismith looked at Marian who reached over and put her arm around her colleague. Naismith continued, "Francis and Mary Bankroft have been working with the Kurds to foment a rebellion east and north of Baghdad. Francis was captured after Michael recruited a senior Kurdish rebel to join the German side. Mary and the rest of their household escaped and are in the mountains in Kurdistan protected by another clan of Kurds."

He looked around the room. Except for Elizabeth, the faces had hardened and were a deep blue-green. These Ravens intended revenge.

"Michael O'Connell has offered a prisoner exchange. His father for Elizabeth's father. He has identified the place and the time. The place is an ancient rock-carved relief known as Taq-e-Bostan in Kermanshah. Kermanshah is recently occupied by a Turkish intrusion into Persia. Many would say that the Shah in Tehran had no control over the city, and I suspect the Turks have little control now. Michael has insisted that we meet in eight days. He understands that we will be hard-pressed to get from Nathiagali to Kermanshah in that time, but he expects us to accomplish this mission by whatever manner possible. I see no way to avoid the exchange. I have debriefed James O'Connell thoroughly using my own … methods. From my perspective, it serves no purpose to execute him when we can use him to recover one of our own. I expect perfidy from Michael O'Connell and that is why I need your help, Ravens. I need your help to make sure we recover Francis Bankroft and to capture Michael O'Connell. The most important factor is Francis. Michael and James O'Connell can be captured another day."

Alexander was the first to speak. "How are we to get the entire team to Kermanshah in eight days? It took us nearly three by airship to get to Basra."

Naismith nodded. "This is why I need your willingness to operate on the edge of insubordination. We need to convince Colonel Winslow-Heath that we need an airship. The operation we will propose will be completely true, just not truly complete. And, I will use a deft touch of mesmerism to convince him that it is his idea to release an airship for us. However, every Raven must be in agreement if we are to succeed in this complicated deception."

Elizabeth spoke for the first time. When she did, she surprised Beverly because her colleague had wondered if

Elizabeth was even breathing. "Guru, I would like to make that appeal to the colonel. I think he would be on our side and my family has been very close to the colonel for years."

Naismith thought about the offer. On the one hand, it would be easier to use mesmerism if Winslow-Heath was in an emotional state. On the other hand, it would mean Elizabeth would be a direct participant in insubordination. He said, "It would mean working hard to explain the situation without revealing the trade."

"Guru, I can do this."

"Then Elizabeth, you and I must go to Rawalpindi immediately. Ravens, prepare for battle and await the arrival of an airship. If we are successful, we should have an airship in a day, two at most. If we are not successful, I will need you all to consider some alternative means — perhaps aeroplanes? Now, we must make haste. Dismissed!"

With that, the Ravens stood and watched Naismith and Elizabeth leave the room. Once they were gone, Jonathan said, "This is going to be a near-run thing."

Martha smiled. "If everything was easy, they wouldn't need the Ravens."

Whatever It Takes

Rawalpindi, 16 July 1915

ELIZABETH AND NAISMITH ENTERED THE OFFICES OF COLONEL WINSLOW-Heath. They were both wearing their Indian Army uniforms. They had sent a telegram requesting an immediate meeting and he had been more than willing to see them. Winslow-Heath was in good humor as he welcomed them into his office. He had already arranged a full tea service around the polished-oak map table that had served as the planning session for so many of the Raven operations as well as the individual operations of each member of his cadre of intelligence agents. After pouring tea for the three of them, the colonel opened the conversation. "First, I wish to congratulate you on your mission against the O'Connells and the Beni Lam. I realize the young O'Connell made good his escape, but I suspect he will be less of a headache than his father."

Naismith opened the gambit by saying, "Thank you, sir. And also, thank you for allowing me time to interrogate

James O'Connell. While I am not yet done with my efforts, he has been most compliant."

The colonel smiled and said, "Most would be compliant if they are facing a British .303 as the alternative."

"Sir, one thing that we have determined based on this interrogation is a bit of grave news."

Elizabeth watched as Naismith began to weave his story which was completely true, even if not truly complete. She wondered if she would have been willing to take the risks that Naismith was about to take for another Raven or perhaps the parent of one of her colleagues. Naismith continued, "Sir, it turns out that the Germans have captured Francis Bankroft in Kurdistan. I understand the Bankrofts were working to foment a Kurdish rebellion. Francis was captured because of an agent operation they ran inside the Kurdish tribes."

Elizabeth watched as the blood drained from the colonel's face. His hand shook as he put his mug of tea down. Elizabeth was afraid that he might collapse right in front of them. She reached over and touched the colonel on the forearm and said quietly with a small bit of mesmerism thrown in, "We can fix this, sir."

Winslow-Heath took a sip of his tea and recovered his composure. Whether it was simply the tea or Elizabeth's comment wasn't clear to Naismith, but he knew that it was time to make his plan clear. He said, "Sir, time is of the essence. I doubt the Germans or the Turks will be as gentle with Francis as we have been with James O'Connell. Based on the interrogation, we know where they are holding Francis. It is on the Mesopotamian border with Persia. I recommend we dispatch the Ravens again. I have not released them to return to their individual missions. They are still waiting for us in Nathiagali."

The colonel had recovered and looked Naismith in the eye and with his most formal military expression, he said, "Whatever it takes, Naismith. Whatever it takes."

Elizabeth said, "Sir, we are going to need the fastest airship in theatre. There is no time to spare."

Winslow-Heath nodded. "I can offer you something else, but it will be difficult to take the entire set of six Ravens in a single craft."

Naismith said, "Sir?"

"We have five test boats in Karachi. They are basically fast coastal patrol boats. We are experimenting with them in use against the German submarines that are operating in the Indian Ocean. They are fast, but I suspect they can only take three Ravens on board. That would mean the Ravens would travel on three boats, no?"

Elizabeth asked, "How fast, sir?"

"Fully armed with one torpedo, they travel at 35 knots."

Naismith said, "Sir, none of us are Navy."

"Ah yes. I asked that question as well. They said 40 miles per hour."

"Not too much faster than an airship."

"True, and you would still need to get to Kermanshah once you docked in Bandar Abbas."

"One other alternative which might make sense for an advanced party. We have two Avro something or other trainers here in Rawalpindi. They are fast, two-seater air-craft. No guns, but then again, we don't expect a fight here in India. They cruise at about twice the speed of an airship. Approximately 70 miles an hour. I think we might be able to break free one of those trainers and a pilot. You could put a man ..." Winslow-Heath paused and corrected himself, "... or a woman, on the ground in Kermanshah to do a recce before your raid."

Elizabeth smiled and said, "Or I could fly the aircraft with another Raven with me."

Winslow-Heath said, "I heard you can fly, but the real question is, can you land? The trainers would require multiple stops for fuel. Most probably Quetta and then God-knows-where."

"Sir, it is my father. I am willing to take the risk."

"Then I am willing to get you our canvas crates as well as an airship."

Naismith bowed his head and said, "Sir, it is another high-risk Raven mission. I hope you understand what we are trying to accomplish."

Winslow-Heath nodded and said, "Naismith, I suspect I know precisely what you are trying to accomplish, and I will support you whatever happens." The colonel's comment surprised both Elizabeth and Naismith. For a moment, no one spoke.

Finally, Elizabeth said, "Sir, I believe I left my flying suit here the last time I came to Rawalpindi. With your permission, I would like to recover it and go immediately to the airfield. I will need something that extends your authority, but other than that, I will spend the day making sure I can take off ... and land."

Winslow-Heath said, "Well, you may have a bit of luck there. The Royal Flying Corps instructor is a Major Joshua Marshall. I believe you have met him on a previous Raven mission."

For the first time in two days, Naismith noticed Elizabeth was smiling.

Come with Me

Kebir Koh, 14–16 July 1915

MARY BANKROFT LED HER SMALL CARAVAN THROUGH THE PASS IN THE MOUNtains toward Persia. She was not entirely certain her final destination, but she received telepathic instructions from Naismith to travel east and so she headed east. She was still suffering from the shock of her husband's capture in the early hours of the 14th and, worse still, her own escape from the Kurdish camp.

That night, Bektashi proved himself once again to be priceless. When she came out of their tent after the telepathic exchange first with Francis and then with the traitor Michael O'Connell, Mary told Bektashi and Alia that they needed to leave immediately, Bektashi nodded. "Madam, the horses are loaded already. I never trusted these tribesmen and their grumblings last night when the master and Darya Khan left for their raid made me even more suspicious. We can leave as soon as you have your riding clothes on. All is ready."

Mary put both hands on Bektashi's cheeks and kissed his

forehead. "God bless you and your entire family. Now, mount up and I will be ready in minutes." She had rushed back into the tent, grabbed her travel pack, her weapons and pulled on her boots. She mounted her horse, and they were off at a gallop. The camp dogs seemed to be the only ones who noticed their departure. Mary was uncertain who was friend and who was foe, so they rode like demons deeper into the mountains, heading east toward Persia.

By dawn, they were miles away from the camp and working their way through a deserted caravan trail. This route would be busy in a few months, but in the heat of the summer there were neither crops nor handicrafts to sell in Mesopotamia and no copper pots or dried fruit to sell in Persia. Along with the three horses they rode, Bektashi had tied lines on three other horses from the camp to bring them along. He also released the rest of the horses from their ropes as they rode away. With luck, it would take time for the Kurds to find their horses and to decide whether it was worth the effort to pick up their trail.

At noon, Bektashi recommended they halt and rest the horses. There was a small clearing with a stream that would allow the horses to be watered off the trail. He and Alia immediately removed the saddles from the first set of horses and put them on the second set. Mary took a moment with her back to a pine tree and prepared herself for travel using the illusory body. It was through her illusory body that she followed her husband to his cell. She saw his captors tie him and torment him, though thankfully, they did not torture him. She also heard the discussion between Francis and Michael O'Connell. She realized that Francis had no idea he was talking to a former colleague, now traitor. But, from her perspective in the illusory body, she knew. She also heard Michael dispatch a telepathic message to Naismith. Normally, telepathy was between individuals, but since Mary was already gently probing Michael's mind to determine his plans, she managed to understand the telepathic conversation between Michael and Naismith.

After she recovered from her mental effort, they mounted and rode until it was too dark to proceed. They might be in a hurry, but riding in the pitch dark in treacherous terrain was simply not going to help. Once the moon set, they pulled their horses together and settled in for an uncomfortable night in the mountains named after the highest peak in the chain, Kebir Koh. As she slept that night of the 15th, Naismith came to her in a dream. He promised that he would free Francis and that all would be well. He instructed Mary to ride east into Persia to a small village named Harounabad. He would link up with her there. Before she could ask anything in her dream, she awoke. In the darkness, Bektashi had a small spirit stove going, already boiling water.

"Madam, tea will be ready soon. I'm sorry, I forgot to bring any canned milk." His white teeth shown in the darkness. At the very least, Bektashi had not lost his sense of humor.

"Bektashi, hot tea will be most gratifying. I have a plan that I need to share with you and Alia after we take tea."

Bektashi walked over to Mary with a tin cup full of steaming hot tea. He whispered, "Madam, please do not reveal your witch skills to Alia. She is just a child."

"Bektashi, I believe Alia is more than a child and probably has more *witch* skills than I."

Bektashi nodded and pulled out a nazar that he kept with his prayer beads. He mumbled some prayer as he walked away.

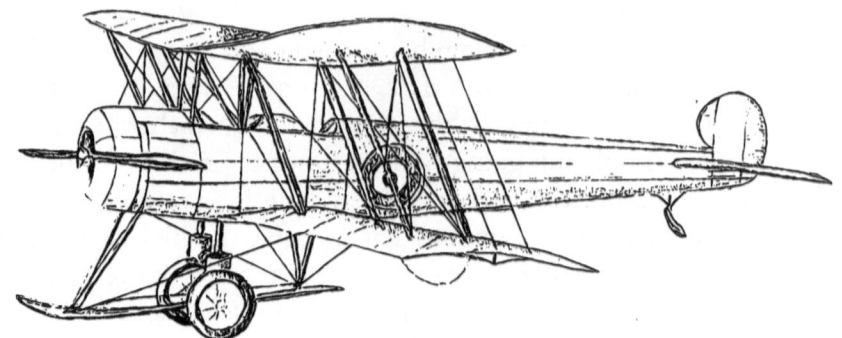

ᴛhe ᕼidden ᕼand

Basra RFC military aerodrome, 20 July 1915

THE TWO AVRO AIRCRAFT CIRCLED THE AERODROME AND LANDED WITH
little drama and even less ceremony. As they taxied to the
mix of brick buildings and green military tents, support
personnel from the Royal Flying Corps stepped out in the
blast furnace heat and guided the airplanes to two empty tin
shelters. In front of the shelters, the pilots shut down their
engines and climbed out. Their passengers slowly followed.
The RFC ground crews noticed that in the back seat of the
lead aircraft were two men, one of whom was in handcuffs.
The two men were cramped, but Naismith was the smaller
of the two and had ensured his captive was as comfortable as
possible strapped into most of the wicker seat.

If that wasn't enough of a shock, the ground crew realized
that the pilot of the second aircraft was a woman and her
passenger was also a woman!

The senior sergeant looked his men and said, "Well, what
are you waiting for, you muckers! Get the aircraft under

cover and start your maintenance. It's as if you have never seen pilots before."

One of the ground crew wearing corporal stripes said, "But sergeant, one of the pilots was a woman!"

The senior sergeant had never heard of such a thing, but he was not about to show any doubt or misgivings in front of his troops. "MacIntosh, you highlanders live in the last century! Women have been flying these crates for a decade. Why wouldn't the RFC want them flying their training birds? It's not as if they are going into combat."

Elizabeth and Beverly were walking side by side toward the command shed. Beverly said, "It's not as if!"

Elizabeth giggled and said, "Well, it's not the first time we've had this sort of reception. Each leg of this journey, we've watched as the ground crew were gob-smacked as we crawled out of these Avros. Luckily, we've had Major Marshall to explain that indeed I am certified to fly the Avro trainer. Let's leave them to ponder who we are and get some tea and a stop at the loo."

A few minutes later in the tent that served as the RFC canteen, Elizabeth, Beverly, and Joshua Marshall shared a cup of tea. Beverly asked, "Where is Guru Naismith?"

Marshall shrugged and said, "I honestly haven't a clue. One minute we were all crawling out of the bird, and the next, Naismith and your prisoner were gone. They can't have gone too far. The compound is fenced with barb wire to keep out curious locals and any Turkish saboteurs. I understand we are transporting this man to Mesopotamia for some sort of trial. Was he a deserter?"

Beverly decided that Marshall deserved a reply, even if it was not an entirely accurate answer. "He abandoned his intelligence post before the war. We have been hunting him for all that time. Desertion in wartime is a capital offense. In peacetime, it is an entirely different story."

Elizabeth took up the tale, "Lieutenant Colonel Naismith

decided that the deserter needed to see war up close and personal. He needed additional manpower and we needed to get back to work here in Mesopotamia. It turns out the RFC needed two of the Avros transported to replace two of their aged aircraft. So, here we are!"

"Lucky for me that you are such a quick study. I will admit, I was surprised at how fast you built up the skills. Of course, that doesn't make you an RFC pilot … yet."

Elizabeth smiled and said, "I never expected to be in the RFC."

Beverly said, "But surely she deserves pilot's wings after this, doesn't she?"

"I will put in the paperwork. It seems to me that Captain E. Bankroft has accomplished all the necessary hours for wings. Let's just keep her forename out of the records, ok?"

Beverly laughed out loud. "Heaven forbid the RFC should have a woman pilot!"

Marshall nodded. "We will just keep the system in the dark on that one." He took a sip of his tea and nodded to the entrance to the tent. "Did you see the ancient kites the poor blokes are flying here? Shorthorn pusher aircraft? Well, some lucky chap will be flying Avro 2A soon enough."

"And 1A?"

"Ah, that will be yours truly. I'm taking over the small detachment here. I've done my part for the Indian Army Air Corps. It's back to the RFC for me."

Elizabeth and Beverly spoke at the same time, "Congratulations!"

"I would rather be flying on the Western Front. That is where the real war is. But one accepts the job given. And it occurs to me that there may be more special missions like this one before too long if you are in theatre."

Elizabeth thought she had obfuscated their role the last time she flew with Marshall. Clearly, he had heard something from one of his airship mates on the role of the mission. She said, "Intelligence operations from the air are changing the face of war on the Western Front."

Marshall smiled and said, "And imagine how important it might be to deliver an agent behind enemy lines. The Avro is a robust bird. It can land just about anywhere. Just remember that for any future use."

Beverly smiled. "I'm sure we will pass on the recommendation."

"I hope you do more than pass it on, I hope you use my recommendation."

Elizabeth couldn't suppress a grin. "We are merely cogs in the wheel of intelligence."

Marshall laughed and said, "I always thought of you two as cogs."

Their tea party was interrupted as Naismith and O'Connell arrived at the table. Marshall, Elizabeth, and Beverly stood up. Beverly asked, "Are we ready?"

"As much as anyone can be ready for this mission. We have horses and a small Indian escort to the Persian border, after that, it will be camels and desert. We get the escort for only a few miles, but an armed escort is always handy."

Marshall looked down at the table. He was clearly sad when he said, "Sir, I guess this is farewell."

Naismith smiled and said, "This is the second time you have helped us, Major. I have no doubt there may be third time in the future."

Marshall nodded. "I just said the same thing to your two subordinates. Aerial delivery of people and equipment is something these Avros could do if there was someone with the right need and the necessary imagination. And, of course, the power to influence the RFC."

Naismith leaned over the table and offered his hand. "I hope to see you soon, Major."

"Likewise, sir.

Naismith reached into his pocket and handed Marshall a

small brass coin. One side had an image of a raven. On the other was a simple Latin phrase: *Invisibilia manus*.

Marshall looked at both sides of the coin and said, "I will be ready if you need me."

Naismith nodded and said to Beverly and Elizabeth, "It's time to go."

What Is the Price of Independence?

The route to Kermanshah, 22–23 July 1915

THEIR CAMP WAS BASED IN A SMALL WADI ON THE EDGE OF THE DRY LANDS
between the mountains on the border between Mesopotamia
and Persia and the Zagros Mountains to the east. For at least
a thousand years, caravans bypassed this land between the
mountains on their way from Esfahan in Persia to Baghdad in
Mesopotamia. Instead, they traveled north of the two ranges
where more reliable sources of water meant better graze for
the caravan horses and camels. And, where there was water,
there would be oasis. Kermanshah was one of those oases and
it was their destination. They had to make Kermanshah in
two days which meant very long hours on horseback.

Their approach from the south was designed in part to
obscure their travels, though Naismith had no doubt that if
Michael O'Connell wanted to find his father, he could do
so using the illusory body. They tried to hide their travels by
blindfolding James O'Connell, but in evening campsites it
seemed unfair to torture the man any more than they already

had. During the days of hard riding, James O'Connell rode blindfolded and strapped to a wooden nomad saddle with no control over his horse. Even Elizabeth, who had good reason to hate the O'Connells, seemed unwilling to keep him blindfolded.

O'Connell sat next to Naismith while Beverly and Elizabeth tended to the evening chores including hobbling the horses and their two camels, cleaning the tin plates after the evening meal and taking the first guard mount. In this remote part of Persia, they rarely saw anyone during the day except for the occasional farm family out in their irrigated fields. There was no way to predict if those families reported their travels to local bandits who might want to cut their throats for the chance of treasures that might be in the saddlebags. It was during this post-dinner interlude that O'Connell talked to his captor.

"Naismith, what is your plan?"

Naismith leaned against the camel saddle and stared at O'Connell. "You ask me this every night and every night I say the same thing: I have no plan. I am simply following your son's plan. He has Francis Bankroft and said he would trade him for you. We believe that is a fair trade since Bankroft is an important agent of the Raj and you are a traitor who would have been shot shortly after you were captured if it hadn't been for me."

"But why didn't you turn me over to the military?"

"I wanted to know what you were doing for the Germans and why in the world you decided to change sides."

"And did you find the answers to your questions?"

"James, I found the answer to the first set of questions. You tried to lie to me about your work with the Germans and the Turks, but you can't lie to me. I have probed your mind, captured your memories and know your actions from the time you stole the plans for the difference engine to the time you were working with the Beni Lam. I know your thoughts as well as you know yourself. I even know about your hatred for the Raj based on the injustice of the death of your wife. Even so, I do not understand your willingness to turn to the Germans. You must know that they will never fulfill their promises."

O'Connell was taken aback by Naismith's blunt reply. He had worked hard to keep some of his actions and all of his motivations hidden in his mind castle. He hadn't felt Naismith's probes into his mind castle where he kept his darkest thoughts under lock and key. Now, given what Naismith already knew, he decided to try an explanation. He started slowly. "Naismith, the Germans may or may not live up to their end of the bargain. Michael and I want to get back to Ireland and work for Irish independence. The Germans have a vested interest in that same effort. You probably already know they are trying to undermine the entire British Empire. Whether they will succeed or not will be based on the people they dispatch to the various corners of the Empire. I think we will have demonstrated to them that we are valuable and can accomplish much in Ireland."

"Do you really think they will ever let you leave Arabia? Both you and Michael are established agents. You understand the cultures of the Arabs, the Kurds, and even the cultures of India. Long before the war started, in Berlin they had an Oriental Bureau run by Max von Oppenheim. Do you really think these Prussian officers will trade a known entity in Arabia for an unknown potential in Ireland? It seems to me that they will squeeze as much life out of you as they can. And, in the end, when the Indian Army defeats the Turks in Mesopotamia and the Egyptian Army defeats the Turks in Arabia, will they leave you to find your own way out of the collapsing Ottoman Empire? I think there is a good chance that they will do just that."

O'Connell had little time for Naismith's lecture. He already knew that he couldn't hide his views from Naismith, so he decided to be equally blunt. "Naismith, the difference is that Michael and I have the advantage of our skills you taught us in the Viceroy's College. We have had some success manipulating the Prussian officers in Damascus and Baghdad. They are professional soldiers, good at what they do, but they are not aware of the games we play with their minds. We will convince them that we need to go to Berlin to help von Oppenheim. In Berlin, we will convince others that we will be best suited to help them support the Irish resistance. Step by step is the way you always taught us at the Viceroy's College and step by step we will win our freedom in Ireland."

Naismith nodded. "And if winning Irish independence means a violent civil war? What is the price of independence?"

"We will pay that price. If it means civil war, then that is what will happen whether we are in Ireland or not."

Naismith was saddened that one of his earliest students might have become so committed to unrestricted violence. As he considered O'Connell's position, Chodak's voice interrupted: *You see, soldier? They are ready to kill for their beliefs. You kill for the Raj. Do you believe in the Raj?* The voice ended with a long cackle and then evaporated from his consciousness.

Naismith said to O'Connell, "It is time for you to return to your shackles. We have work to do tomorrow and you have no place in the work." He pulled out the metal shackles and bound O'Connell's hands behind his back and then ran the attached chain between his legs and shackled his ankles. He ran a separate chain to the tent frame. Finally, he put a loose canvas hood over O'Connell's head. He realized it was uncomfortable, but he was certain it was more comfortable than a .303 round to the chest.

After binding O'Connell, Naismith walked out from the tent and looked at the night sky. The clear sky was awash in stars. The moon would rise in another two hours and it would be clear enough at that point to navigate toward his rendez-vous with Mary Bankroft. By dawn, Mary would be reunited with her daughter and they could all move toward their final destination on this trip, the stone caves of Taq-e-Bostan.

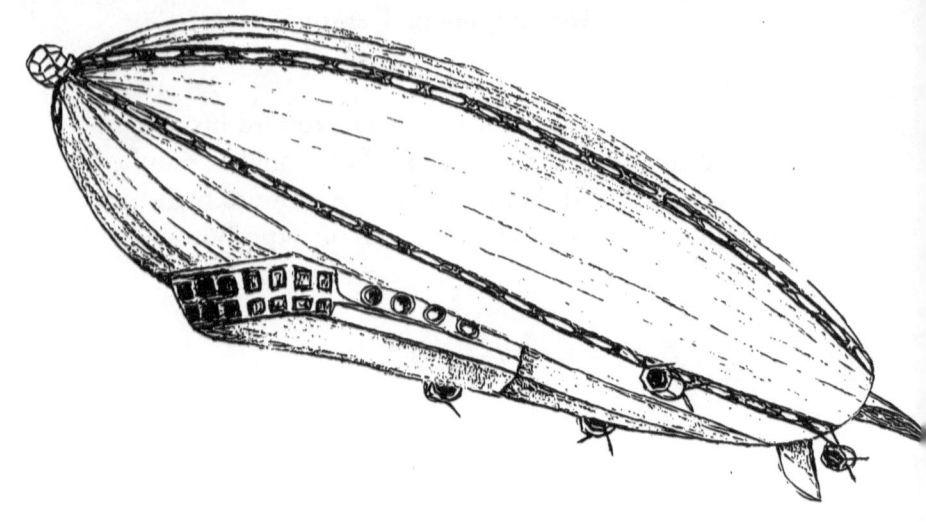

A Flight of Ravens

Somewhere over central Persia, 23 July 1915

JONATHAN PACED UP AND DOWN THE PASSENGER CABIN OF THE *HMFS Sam-itar.* He had been pacing like that since the airship crossed into Persia long before dawn. Martha looked up from her seat at one of the porthole windows and said, "Will you please stop that pacing! The airship is traveling as fast as it can fly. The captain has already said we will be at the rendezvous on time. You are not making the wait any easier."

Alexander smirked and added, "And you are wearing out shoe leather that you might need if we have to walk out of Persia."

"I'm just worried that we won't arrive on time. The entire plan requires us in place well before tomorrow evening." As if to point out his concern, he looked down at his wristwatch. It read 1100hrs.

Martha asked, "Have you reset your watch now that we are in Persia?"

"No."

Alexander shook his head. "You are well and truly a madman. When did you last set your watch?"

"Rawalpindi."

"So, you are one hour later than you should be."

"Really?" Jonathan seemed puzzled by the entire question.

"Jonathan, you are just not used to traveling by air. We have already covered over a thousand miles since we boarded the *Scimitar*. It may be a smooth flight, but we are covering the distances faster than an automobile or a horse and in areas where there are no railroads. We don't need to stop for petrol or for anything else. We just keep flying."

"So, it's 1000hrs?"

"On the ground, yes. Here on the ship, they keep their watches on Greenwich Mean Time so that changing time zones matters little to the crew."

Jonathan made a face. "That makes it 0600hrs?"

Martha nodded. "In London."

Marian looked up at her fellow Ravens. They had all been her students at the Viceroy's College and had been successful both individually and collectively. This operation was the biggest challenge in their careers. She decided to end the conversation. "Will you please sit down and rest. We have hours to go before we get to our destination. We all need to rest. Please?"

Jonathan finally gave up and slumped along one of the long benches in the compartment. Martha added, "And don't go up to the command deck again. The navigator said if you go up there again, the captain intends to either put you in irons or throw you out of the airship. Neither is going to help us!"

Jonathan just grumbled. In less than a minute, he was asleep.

Alexander walked over to Martha and said, "Did you cast a spell on him?"

"A small one. It was either that or find something to use to hit him."

"Bruised ego is one thing, bruised body something entirely different."

"Indeed. I haven't asked. Do you think Naismith's plan will work?"

"If you mean, will we all get out of this alive and rescue Francis Bankroft? I believe so. If you mean, will we accomplish all that he set out for us? I am less confident."

"Well, if it is the former, that's good enough for me."

"I agree. If we can save Francis Bankroft, then the rest can be some future mission."

Marian had feigned sleep to listen in on the conversation. She smiled. The operation might or might not succeed, but the Ravens were ready.

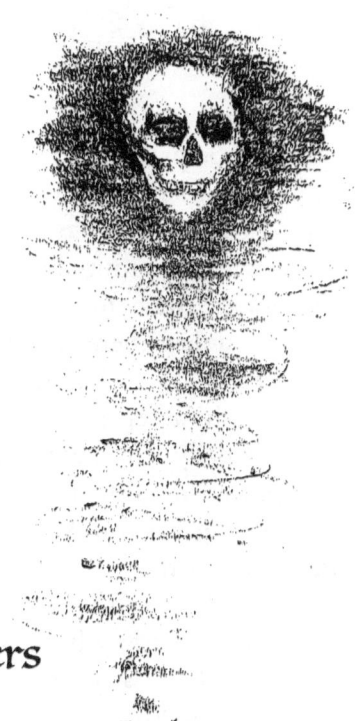

Confronting Monsters

Taq-e-Bostan, 24 July 1915

THE REUNION BETWEEN MOTHER AND DAUGHTER HAD BEEN BRIEF, IF EMO-
tional. Naismith led them back to the camp were Beverly and
O'Connell were waiting. Mary had to use her mesmerism
skills to prevent Bektashi from punishing James O'Connell
for the crimes of his son, Michael. As they rode to their destination, Mary made sure she was always between O'Connell
and Bektashi. She wasn't certain that her previous instructions would prevent Bektashi from pushing O'Connell off
his horse with painful consequences for everyone. All Bektashi knew for certain was that they were on a rescue mission
for his master and he needed to do whatever it took for its
success. They arrived at their camp on the outskirts of Kermanshah at sundown.

Naismith wasn't pleased with Bektashi's insistence on
joining them as they moved forward to the meeting with
Michael O'Connell. Mary and Elizabeth informed Naismith
that short of shooting Bektashi, there would be no way that

he could be prevented from moving with them. And, if Bektashi went forward that meant Alia would go as well. Finally, they all came to a compromise. Bektashi and Alia would travel with the group, but they were assigned to maintaining the horses away from the meeting. He and Alia would be on site; unless there was an emergency, they would not be involved in the exchange.

Bektashi accepted the tasking with a small bit of grumbling. Finally, Elizabeth came to him and, using a modicum of mesmerism said, "Bektashi Bey, there is only one man for this job and it is you. We must be confident that we can make good our escape."

He offered a slight bow and spent the rest of the day ensuring that everything was in order for their ride to the meeting. He insisted on cleaning and reloading each of their weapons and sharpening each of their blades. Beverly was more than a little amused when Bektashi asked if there was anything he could do for Naismith's ancient *guru danda*. Once she showed him how the blade extended from the staff, Bektashi accepted that Naismith had everything he needed.

The ride north to Taq-e-Bostan was direct along the wadi that once had been a formal irrigation channel for this fortress. Taq-e-Bostan encompassed two stone arches dating back to the Fourth Century before Christ. There was a small, silted-in pond in front of the arches and then what had been a *maidan* or formal entranceway, though now it was little more than an empty, dusty space. The arches were already in shadow when Naismith, his captive, Mary and Elizabeth rode up. They could not see any of the stone reliefs below the arches and carved into the mountain. Naismith researched the Sassanid Empire structure before he left the Viceroy's College. It was supposed to be quite wonderful. Naismith was certain he would not enjoy this relic tonight. One thing for certain was they were far enough away from Kermanshah to be undisturbed and far enough that Turkish troops would have no role in this exchange … whether it ended peacefully or not.

They pulled up their horses at a distance that was out of pistol range but easily within shouting distance. They dismounted and Bektashi and Alia took the six horses behind the rest of the party. On the ride up to Taq-e-Bostan, Naismith pointed out to everyone that if Michael O'Connell intended treachery, this would be the moment when it would happen. Naismith also told James O'Connell that if his son intended treachery, he would die first and die painfully. O'Connell understood and used his telepathic skills to let his son know he hoped the exchange would go precisely as planned. Michael had not responded which made James more nervous as they rode toward the stone arches. Bektashi made eye contact with O'Connell and made a slashing gesture across his throat. James understood the message.

Naismith shouted, "Michael O'Connell, we are here and have brought your father. It is as promised. Mary and Elizabeth O'Connell are looking forward to seeing Francis." The only sound was the echo as Naismith's voice bounced against the entrance of Taq-e-Bostan. Naismith looked to his left and right and said, "We need to be patient. He is here. I can sense his presence."

Mary and Elizabeth nodded. Bektashi carefully pulled Francis' Mauser from the scabbard. He had been careful to protect it throughout their escape. He was certain he would need it tonight.

Beverly had separated from the four riders before they left the wadi. She rode on her own to a spot on the northeastern side of the hill. It was there that she waited for her fellow Ravens to arrive. They had landed hours before dawn two miles north of the site and well east of Kermanshah. They walked to the rendezvous and waited in the pine forest. Beverly tied up her horse, changed into her Raven uniform, and began to walk into the forest. The only way that she could be seen by her colleagues with her careful approach was the small green glow of the radium dial of her watch. It was enough in the darkness to ensure a linkup. Once reunited, they made their approach to the edge of the forest and waited slightly above and to the east of the stone arches. Beverly in the lead with Marian and the rest of the team following. They saw no one and they were confident they were not seen. They watched as the six horsemen approached the arches and they heard Naismith's call.

Just as the moon rose above Kermanshah and began to bathe what had been a formal courtyard of the past, the voice of Michael O'Connell echoed from inside the arches. "Guru Naismith, I am pleased you have been so punctual. Walk forward so I can be sure my father is with you."

"Michael, not until we see Francis O'Connell."

"Always demanding! Do you think you are still my instructor? Look up to see my powers." A dazzling display of electricity arced across the reliefs and then encircled the arches. The blue-green flame illuminated the courtyard and the six dismounted figures.

"Michael, most impressive party trick, but we have not come here tonight to debate your powers. We have all accepted that you have become a master in the astral plane. We are here for a very basic exchange. Your father for Elizabeth's father. Nothing more."

If Naismith had hoped for a reaction from his comment, he received one that was more violent and far sooner than he expected. Naismith fell to the ground and landed on his back in the dirt. Michael had extended his *chi* across the courtyard with the force of an invisible fist hitting Naismith in the chest. Naismith slowly got up and said, "As I said, we are not here to argue of your powers. We are simply here for an exchange of prisoners."

"Not until you all have suffered as I have suffered under your domination."

Elizabeth did not understand what was happening. She understood Michael had decided to support Germany and not the Crown. That was treason. Naismith had explained the O'Connell's plan was to return to Ireland and fight for Irish independence. But what sort of mind would demand they suffer as the result of some unexplained domination? Naismith could feel Elizabeth's anger growing and he sent her a telepathic message: *Not now! Not yet!*

He spoke to Mary and Elizabeth. "We need to approach on foot and we need to keep calm." He turned to James and said, "And you need to calm your son so that this ends well. Right now, he seems uninterested in carrying out the exchange."

James O'Connell had never heard his son express such venom. He knew his son was angry, but after all, so was he. This was not the time nor the place to extract some small payment for the way the British had treated them. These people might be his enemy, but they were nothing more than pawns in the larger game of colonialization. Their plans were to checkmate the British King in Ireland not in Persia. To do that, they needed to get to Ireland and, to do that, they needed to accomplish this exchange and make good their escape. James sent another telepathic message: *Michael, let us complete this bargain like honorable adversaries and leave!*

Father, you don't understand. We need to punish them first.

James turned to Naismith and said, "I have tried. He isn't listening."

Naismith nodded. "Michael, before you deliver your punishment, can you please let us see Francis. We need to see that he is alive and well."

From inside the arches, there was a loud and long laugh. Michael said, "I find it amusing that you are willing to ask a favor. The last time we met, you and Elizabeth were determined to capture me by stealth. Now, I am expected to be kind." There was a pause from the voice. Naismith, Mary and

Elizabeth all held their breath. "All right then. Here is my proof that I am a man of my word."

Francis O'Connell was thrown out from the arches. He was shackled using a sophisticated torture technique. His hands were tied behind his back and then tied to his ankles. The ropes bent him back like a bow. A second rope ran from his wrists to a noose around his neck. If Francis struggled at all, he would slowly strangle. Naismith knew it was painful to see Francis in this degraded manner, but he also knew that this image would likely cause Elizabeth to explode in anger. Once again, he sent a telepathic message to Elizabeth and to Mary. *Not yet!*

Naismith shouted to Michael, "So this is what an honorable man does to his adversary?"

"It is better than shooting him!"

"But Michael, we have your father here. We did not let the Raj execute him as a traitor. We brought him here to you. Now, can I send Elizabeth to free her father while I take James to you?"

Michael's voice echoed from inside the chamber. "What makes you think that I intend to let any of you leave here?"

Mary finally spoke up, "Because you are an honorable man and you have given your word!"

Michael finally decided to walk out from the shadows. He was joined by a dozen tribesmen. Naismith found himself thinking about their clothing and their weapons. They were in desert garb and carried swords that flashed in the moonlight. He thought: are these Arabs? Persians? Kurds? It might not matter when he finally decided to unleash the Ravens. Naismith nodded and said, "Do we end this here? Is that what you have decided?"

"I have arranged with the Germans for our departure to Ireland. But only if we bring them English secret agents. And by the way, the agreement is to bring the English spies to Baghdad dead or alive. Your choice, Guru."

The Enigma of Treason

Naismith had expected treachery and Michael's last remarks came as no surprise. He sent a telepathic message to Marian: *GO, GO, GO!*

Marian received the message and waved her hand to her four colleagues. They had already donned the hoods on their Raven uniforms so their movement was both invisible and silent in the shadows of the rock face. In less than a minute, they were standing in the shadows of the archway behind Michael and his dozen swordsmen. Marian began the fight by using her *guru danda* to slice open the neck of the fighter farthest from Michael. He fell first to his knees and then forward into the sand. His neighbor had heard no sound and could not imagine why his cousin was on the ground until he saw the pool of blood. By that time, it was too late. Jonathan had the man in a headlock and, with apparently no effort at all, broke his neck by twisting his head 180 degrees. Alexander held his curved blade with two hands and with one swing, beheaded another of Michael's henchmen. Beverly used her *kartrika* and another Arab fell.

Bektashi watched as the tribal fighters seemed to die one after another. He concentrated and finally saw the five wraiths working their way down the enemy line. He dropped to one knee, carefully targeting the tribal at the opposite end of the formation. He squeezed the trigger and felt the comforting recoil of the Mauser. The man dropped with a bullet in his brain. Elizabeth looked back at Bektashi. He smiled as he worked the bolt action of the rifle. She raised her hand and said, "Wait. We are soon to be among them." Bektashi nodded. He looked for Alia. She had disappeared.

It was as they fell to the ground that Michael finally realized that the ambusher had become the ambushed. He was about to turn to face his new attackers, when Naismith's voice pierced his mind. *You have forgotten the ladder of consequences, Michael. This is the final problem. It is now the play of the Ravens!* Following that intrusion into his mind, Michael heard, no actually felt, a high-pitched sound revolving inside his skull. He dropped to one knee as he looked back at Naismith.

While all the attention was on the tribals and Michael, Elizabeth and Mary ran to Francis. They found Alia using a small, damascene-bladed dagger to cut the ropes binding Francis from head to foot. As the last of the ropes split, Francis bounced up on his feet and with a roar attacked the closest of Michael's surviving swordsmen. His target looked at the berserk Englishman headed his way. The man he faced was easily a half foot taller and 50 pounds heavier. The tribal had come to Taq-e-Bostan tonight to kill, but he had no intention of being killed. He dropped his blade, turned to flee and ran directly into the curved blade at the end of Marian's *guru danda*. Francis grabbed the blade dropped by the dead fighter. He said, "My Khyber knife!" He smiled as he joined in the battle. Right behind him were Elizabeth and Mary brandishing their own blades in the moonlight. The remaining fighters realized that they were now in a struggle for their lives.

Their raiding culture respected courage and honor, but only up to a point. That point was when they had to stand and fight on even odds. Their honor did not require them to fight spirits of the night. Who knew how many of these spirits were among them? The few survivors ran from the fight in a flurry of robes and headdresses. Elizabeth killed one of the fleeing men by throwing her damascene dagger into his back. He fell to the sand and the archway was suddenly quiet. The Mauser barked again and another of the Arabs fell into the sand.

In the confusion, Michael ran toward his father. The only thing standing in his way was Guru Naismith. Naismith showed no hostile motion as Michael ran to his father. Michael reached his father and quickly sliced his rope bindings. Michael and James ran to the horses that Michael had hidden at the entrance of Taq-e-Bostan. As they prepared to mount up, Naismith's gentle voice reached them.

"Do you really wish to have a life where you will be pursued from one end of the earth to another?"

James replied, "Better to escape than face a firing squad."

"And if that was not the alternative?"

Michael snapped back, "As if there were other choices with you British."

"If you swore to end your work with the Germans?"

James felt Naismith's probe into his mind. Along with Naismith's voice, he was hearing the same voice driving deep into his mind. That voice said: *Michael does not want to listen, but you might. What is the point of working with the Germans if your goal is to work in Ireland? What is the point of any violence other than self-defense? What would it take for you to return to the fold? A trip to Ireland? That can be arranged. All you must do is agree to our intelligence service offer: You will both be double agents. You can work for Irish independence and defeat the Germans at the same time. Reporting only to me as the Germans send you to Ireland.*

Michael looked at his father. He could sense Naismith was asserting mind control over his father. He had no idea of Naismith's goal but he decided at that point that he hated Naismith with a passion. All he needed was to escape with his father. Michael pulled a small dagger from his coat sleeve. It was shaped like a *phurba* with a pommel molded into the shape of three demonic Tibetan spirits. But unlike a normal spirit knife used only for ceremonial purposes, this one had three razor sharp edges on the triangular blade. Michael used his kinesthetic powers to dispatch the blade toward Naismith's forehead. At the last second, Naismith realized what Michael had done and deflected the blade ever so slightly so that it landed deep in his shoulder.

As the dagger hit home, a small whirlwind rose in front of Taq-e-Bostan. More like dust lifted from a small breeze. But it grew quickly until it engulfed the maidan. Inside the whirlwind the white skull's voice crashed into the minds of everyone left alive at Taq-e-Bostan. *WE ARE DONE HERE. THE O'CONNELLS COME WITH ME. NAISMITH, YOUR LIFE IS OVER. ELIZABETH BANKROFT, YOU WILL BE MINE ANOTHER TIME. NOW, FEEL MY POWER!* The whirlwind swirled over all in Taq-e-Bostan. The Ravens, Naismith, the three Bankrofts, Bektashi and Alia were swept up and thrown to the ground. The two O'Connells and their horses were swept away as the whirlwind traveled west into the night. When it was gone, all was calm.

Slowly, everyone remaining in Taq-e-Bostan got up, except for Naismith. Elizabeth was about to pursue the whirlwind when she saw Naismith on the ground. Blood was streaming from his shoulder. She focused her attention on her allies and, for a moment, forgot her enemies. Francis and Mary arrived and began to help Elizabeth treat Naismith. Marian arrived next. She pulled a small package from her shoulder bag. From the package she took a large cotton bandage and then a vial of green, foul-smelling fluid that she poured on the bandage. With Elizabeth's help, she extracted the *phurba* from Naismith's shoulder. Marian spoke directly to Elizabeth. "Take the blade, walk among the dead Arabs and drive it into the ground. Focus your energy on driving the evil spirit in the blade into the soil and freeing the *phurba*. We must assume Michael placed spirit energy on it before he launched it at Naismith. GO!"

Elizabeth took the blade in both hands. It seemed to have a life of its own. It twisted and turned as if fighting to get free from her hands. She walked past Bektashi and Alia. He had put his hands in front of the girl's eyes so that she would not see what he was certain must be the blackest of black magic. Finally, Elizabeth reached the entrance to the caves. She was surrounded by the bodies of Michael's men. She calmed herself and extended her *chi* so that her concentration was focused on controlling the blade. Beverly was right, there was an evil spirit embedded there. Once she concentrated, the blade was no less confrontational, but now Elizabeth could control it with two hands. She began a slow Tibetan mantra as she walked, "*Om mani padme hum.*"

The farther she got from Naismith, the more vigorous was the blade's effort to get free. Finally, in the darkness of the archways, in the midst of the dead Arab bodies, Elizabeth drove the blade deep into the sand. Suddenly, the blade became the inanimate object that it should have been in the beginning. Elizabeth could feel the spirit knife surrender to the soil. As she stood up and watched the blade slowly twist into the soil, she heard a voice, more like a whine from the whirlwind, fill her mind.

Tonight, you have killed again. This time with a blade in close combat. Every soul who died tonight fed my power. I thank you for the meal. Your comrade Michael understands the power I offer. He is already on my side and will deliver more souls for me to feed on. In exchange, he will get what he desires. The question is will you join me so you can have what you desire?

Elizabeth shook her head as if that action would drive the voice from her mind. She was devastated by what she had seen tonight. What was the whirlwind? And what was this voice? She had heard it before but had never been able to put a face or a name to the telepathic voice. She could not imagine who might be speaking to her with such vile thoughts. What monster was this?

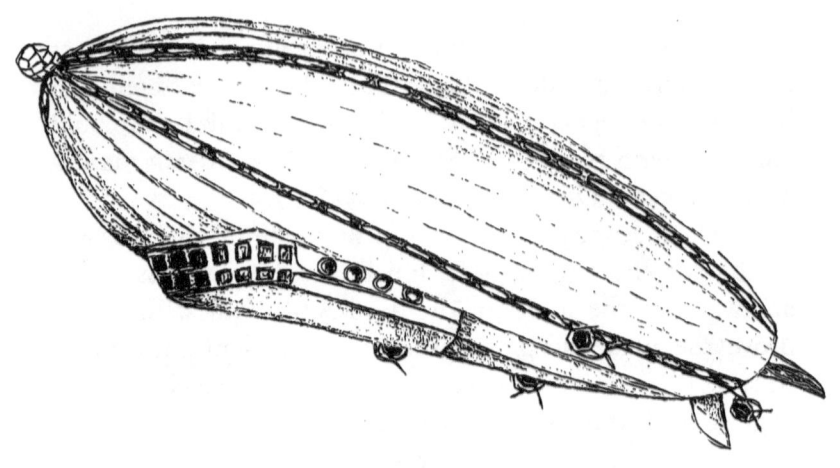

ꝋomeward Bound

On the outskirts of Kermanshah, 24 July 1915

As they waited at the rendezvous, it broke Bektashi's heart when
Francis told him to release the horses. First, he could not
imagine how they would get back to what he thought of as
civilization. On foot? Through the desert? Impossible. Also,
he could not imagine any Persians in Kermanshah would
treat the horses in a proper way. When Francis asked if he
had ever met a Persian, Bektashi acknowledged that he had
not, except for the thieves in the markets of Tabriz. But he
had read more than a few tales about Persians in the *One
Thousand and One Nights*. Francis finally had to order Bektashi to walk their horses to the outskirts of Kermanshah
and release them into the city before they walked back to the
link-up with the airship.

When he returned, Francis came to Bektashi and said,
"You saved my life tonight and Alia freed me from my bonds.
You are family now. My gift to you is the Mauser you used

to save me. It is the only thing I can give you. I have nothing more."

Bektashi bowed and said, "Master, I see you recovered your sword!"

Francis smiled. "One of the Arabs thought it was worth stealing from me. My pistols are long gone, but are easy enough to replace. This on the other hand is something that has seen miles and adventures." He raised the blade and it flashed in the moonlight. "I am glad to have it back." Francis turned to Bektashi and Alia and said, "We are returning home by air."

Bektashi gasped, "By air! A magical flying carpet?"

Francis laughed and Mary calmly said, "An airship. Something that is new to this world. You and Alia will be the first from your countries to travel in this new type of warship. It will be comfortable and you will see the world in a different way."

Elizabeth spent her time with Marian nursing Naismith while they waited at the rendezvous point. He looked pale and drawn, consumed with fever and delirium. Marian said the medicine that she placed on the wound had drawn out the poison. "He will recover, there is no doubt. He will be weak for a time, but the Master Guru will return to lead the Ravens again!"

Elizabeth looked puzzled and said, "Poison?"

Beverly walked up in the dark. "You already know the *phurba* was filled with an evil spirit. But, its power to kill was based on some sort of plant poison that Michael placed on the blade. You must remember your training at the Viceroy's College on poisons? It was in second year when you studied Kautilya's *Arthashashtra*."

Elizabeth had to admit she had missed training on poisons and she had not spent enough time with the *Arthashashtra*. She said, "My studies were focused in the second year when the Master Guru handed me over to Guru Marian. We studied alone in a separate building. I am still not entirely certain why he did that, but soon afterwards I joined the Ravens."

Beverly chuckled. "Well do I remember your arrival. None of us thought you were of any use until we heard you were a master of the illusory body. I suppose that is why they pulled you aside. You have proven yourself essential to the Ravens. But you must return to the basics. When we settle in 'Pindi, you must spend some time with me on poisons. I know you favor the subjects in natural history, so it will take no time. You need to know about poisons and antidotes. And you need to read the *Arthashashtra* as well as Asian classics from T'ai Kung to Sun-Tzu to the master Japanese swordsman Musashi. You have gained much in the way of the spirit world, but you need to temper it with an understanding of how we as Ravens fit into the real world. This world war of ours may be fought with modern weapons, but our shadow war will be fought with ancient weapons that kill and kill silently. We are the dagger in the darkness where artillery cannot reach."

Naismith began to talk in his delirium. He kept repeating the same word over and over again. "Chodak, Chodak, Chodak."

Elizabeth asked, "What does it mean? I know no word in any of the languages I speak that sounds like chodak."

Beverly nodded. She looked over at Alexander. "Do you know of any words in Nepali or Tibetan that sound like chodak?"

When Alexander shook his head, Marian said, "Chodak could be a name rather than a word. It isn't a common name in the great mountains, but it is a name. Could it be that whirl-wind? Was it natural or from the spirit world? I have always assumed that tales of the spirit world were simply myths that the Tibetans used to explain their mystical powers. I have heard him speak of this before. I never understood what it meant. And, I am with you. I always thought evil spirits were creations of parents to keep children in line."

Before they could continue the conversation, Jonathan came up to the group and said, "I have placed the markers and the ship should arrive soon. Let's get the guru ready."

They had made a litter out of material from the saddles and some of the ropes they always carried on Raven missions. The six Ravens carried Naismith to the edge of the dunes northwest of Taq-e-Bostan and far from the prying eyes of Kermanshah. Francis, Mary, Bektashi and Alia followed.

Mary used a calming mesmerism voice on Alia so that she did not panic when she saw their way home. To Bektashi, she simply said, "Watch and wonder, Bektashi Bey. This airship will take us home."

As the sky turned from dark blue to purple and a faint hint of light appeared on the horizon, the grey airship appeared. Every time Elizabeth saw an airship in flight, she was amazed at the wonders of the 20th century. Most of the new inventions were clearly weapons of war and this airship was no different. But she could imagine a world without war when people would fly from continent to continent simply to see the world just as they did before the war on fast steamships across the Atlantic and the Pacific. The sound of the gasoline engines eventually filled the dune fields, but to Elizabeth, this machine was near magic.

The ship stopped its engines and hovered thirty feet above the small group. Two rope ladders dropped from the rear of the crew compartment and Francis and Jonathan immediately climbed into the airship. They needed to inform the master crew chief to send a litter down for their wounded colonel. Once Naismith was on board, the rest of the Ravens climbed into the ship. Mary was the last one, guiding Alia and Bektashi up the rope ladders into the behemoth. When all were aboard, the crew recovered the ladders, closed the rear doors and the airship turned on a course to India.

It took a little gentle persuasion for Mary to convince Alia and Bektashi to look out the portholes as the world fell away from them and the airship flew up to its cruising altitude of two thousand feet above the ground. Eventually, both Alia and Bektashi traded their fear for wonderment as they watched the world slip past them. Once they were calm, Mary moved to the bench next to her husband. She said, "I was so worried."

Francis nodded. "I would be lying if I told you I wasn't worried. And you would know if I was lying."

"You know me too well."

"Do you have any news on Conrad? I understood he was in Basra. Foolish young man leaving his regiment to join the fight. There are plenty of fights on the frontier and this war is not going to end anytime soon."

Mary said in a calming voice, "He is fine, but we do need to talk about Conrad when we get home."

Francis knew when Mary used "the voice" on him, there was no good way to argue, so he didn't argue. Instead, he took a deep breath and watched the world slip past. It was a world he had not been certain he would ever see again.

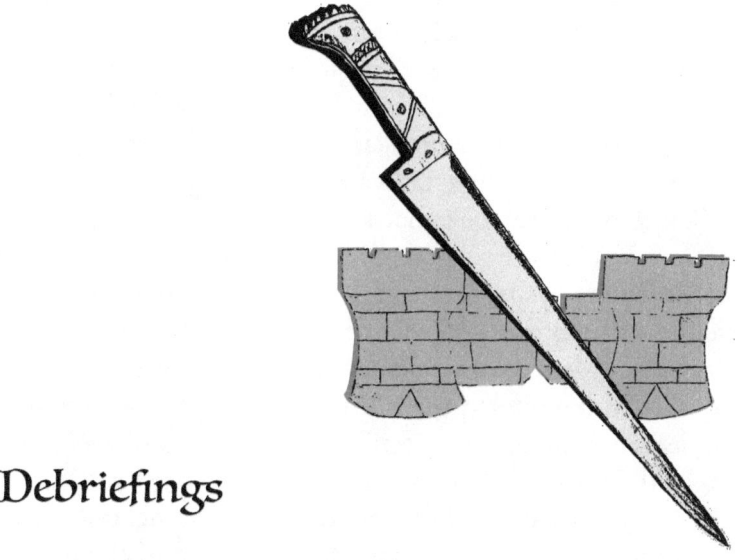

Debriefings

Rawalpindi, 10 August 1915

THE DEBRIEFING WITH COLONEL WINSLOW-HEATH WAS FAR LESS TROUBLE-
some than any of the Ravens expected. After all, they had
been involved in the escape of a traitorous intelligence officer.
However, Winslow-Heath looked at the far more positive
result of the operation: the recovery of Francis Bankroft. Each
of the Ravens, as well as Mary and Francis, were debriefed
individually by the colonel.

The first two were Mary and Francis Bankroft. The colonel wanted that business taken care of so that he could send
them back to their bungalow in the cantonment for the first
time in over two years. No one told the colonel of the whirlwind that Naismith called Chodak. They had seen it with
their own eyes and still didn't believe it. How could they
explain this to Winslow-Heath?

The colonel did find Michael O'Connell's treatment of
Francis beastly, but mostly he was interested in Michael's
ability to convince the son of Darya Khan to kill his father,

take over the tribe and establish an alliance with the Turks and the Germans. Equally interesting was how Michael had convinced local tribals in Kermanshah, most likely Persian tribals, to help him. Francis stated categorically that he would be ready to return to Kurdistan with a small contingent of Ravens simply to avenge Darya Khan.

Winslow-Heath took that recommendation as a possible future irregular warfare operation but he said that he had more pressing needs for the entire family of Bankrofts. However, he refused to reveal this new mission until Francis and Mary had at least two weeks rest. As they departed from his office, Winslow-Heath said, "In the old days, I would give you leave for six months to recover and, perhaps, even visit England. However, there is a war on and we need your assistance now not six months from now. So, go home, rest, write down your adventures so that I have a record of them, and come back to me in two weeks."

Mary and Francis did not argue. They admitted to each other that their months on the road in and out of enemy territory had tired them a bit. Francis smiled and said, "It will take us at least two weeks to get Bektashi and Alia settled in our bungalow in the cantonment. The staff will likely have something to say about our new additions to the family."

Mary agreed as they walked out of the headquarters building and across the parade grounds toward their house. It was hot and humid. The monsoon had arrived with a vengeance, and all were complaining about the rain. After nearly two years in the desert, Francis and Mary were happy to take a walk in the rain.

Winslow-Heath debriefed Naismith last. He would have planned to debrief Naismith last in any circumstances, but these were not ordinary circumstances. When the airship arrived in Rawalpindi, they had already used the Marconi wireless to inform the hospital that a wounded man was on board. The ancient, wooden wagon that served as an ambulance arrived on time and immediately took Naismith to the cantonment hospital. Marian traveled with him and informed the Army surgeon of Naismith's maladies: the deep shoulder wound and the poison on the blade that caused the wound. For once, the Army surgeon was willing to engage a local homeopathic doctor as well as a local botanist that was researching the plants of Asia. The homeopathic doctor determined the nature of the poison was derived from the fruit of a South Indian tree known in Kerala as the suicide tree. Elizabeth immediately went to the Rawalpindi medical library and found the taxonomic name: *Cerbera odollam*. With the toxin identified, the doctors crafted a mix of herbal and modern medicines as a treatment which they delivered into Naismith's body by way of a daily injection. By the end of the first week, Naismith was walking, and after ten days he was released from the hospital on condition that he would remain on light duty until the end of August.

Winslow-Heath spent very little time focusing on the events of Taq-e-Bostan. By the time Naismith finally visited him in his office, the Ravens had already reported on that encounter. More than anything else, the colonel wanted to know about Naismith's discussions with James O'Connell. After two large mugs of tea and an hour discussing the entire story from the Beni Lam raid until the events at Taq-e-Bostan, Winslow-Heath asked, "Do you think he will take our offer?"

Naismith nodded. "I do think James will consider our offer. There are several reasons why: First, I don't think he wants to spend the rest of his life looking over his shoulder waiting for the Ravens to find him. Secondly, I believe he has seen the atrocities committed by the Turks and the fact that the Germans don't seem to care so long as they have a solid partnership with the CUP. O'Connell told me that he was especially disturbed by the actions of Baron von der Golz. Von der Golz is a Prussian through and through, but James' assessment of the German is that he has been in the East too long. O'Connell believes the general, who is also a field marshal in the Ottoman Army, is aware of the worst atrocities, and may even encourage them, whether against the Armenians or against Arabs that the Ottoman secret police identify as enemies of the state."

"So the Germans have revealed their true side?"

"At least one has. O'Connell told me during interrogation that he found your counterpart, a Colonel von Trier, to be thoughtful and committed to collecting intelligence whether it was good or bad news. Honestly, if the O'Connells never met von der Golz, I think we would have no chance of recruiting James. But events played out in our favor. I also think James is growing increasingly worried about his son's mental health."

"His treason is weighing on him?"

"Sir, sadly not. James thinks Michael is totally dedicated to the German cause. What worries James is that he has seen Michael's behavior change toward extreme violence. He thinks it all started when the Germans dispatched Michael to the Shammar and during that time, Michael was involved in the death of William Shakespear."

"What?"

"Indeed, I was surprised as well and it took some serious mental probing to get James O'Connell to reveal what he knows. Which, by the way, isn't all that much. Michael was nearly a closed book to James after he returned. When he returned, he had the gruesome task of delivering William's head to the Turks and von der Golz as proof of the Shammar leadership's fealty to the Ottoman cause. James said after that trip, Michael was never the same. He was easily angered and quick to use his substantial skills to maximize terrorist operations in Mesopotamia. Whether James is correct about the why, he is certainly correct about the what. I'm sure you heard Francis' account of his time in Michael's hands. On the one hand, this helps our task of turning James O'Connell back to our side. However, Michael seems adamant in this desire to punish us for our prejudices and actions in India."

"What could that young man possibly know about India. He was a teenager when he abandoned India."

"Sir, there is a backstory you need to know. On one of his collection missions for us, James was out of town when his wife fell ill. No one in the British Lines in Bombay was willing to help because she was Parsi. The doctors and administrators simply did not accept that an Indian could possibly be the wife of a British officer. Michael was young, but he witnessed the prejudice. And, it was prejudice in the long run that killed his mother. James believes modern medicine could have saved her. As Michael grew, he was regularly criticized and bullied as a half-breed. And, his time in the Viceroy's College simply reinforced the fact that he would always be treated poorly."

Naismith took a sip from his tea and added, "As you know, the first few weeks of the College are quite vigorous and, honestly, designed to be tough on the first-year students. We want to be sure the students are ready for a life that will be challenging. It is only in the last few weeks of the first year that our students really learn why that program is so challenging. In the second year, we focus on both classical education and intelligence skills. Michael left after the first year believing that he had been singled out for additional punishment."

"And had he?"

"He was a student with great potential and I know his teachers pushed him to reach his potential. As you have probably heard from Elizabeth Bankroft, we made her life fairly unpleasant as well for the same reasons. I just think he came to us as a wounded boy and he is now a wounded man.

Whether we can do anything about that should be left to mentalists. I have no idea."

"So, what is the second reason why you think James may agree to our bargain?"

"It is precisely because he is so worried about Michael's mental health that he might agree to our offer. I think he realizes that Michael is on a very dangerous path and staying with the Germans will only accelerate his travels on that path. It is that point I intend to continue to raise when I speak to James again."

"When and where will that be?"

"Sir, I believe you know I have certain powers of my own. Those include telepathic communication ..."

Winslow-Heath raised his hand to prevent Naismith continuing. "Naismith, I trust in your actions and your capabilities. You do not need to reveal these skills to me. I fear I am too old and too settled in my ways to be open minded about such things. Just make it so. We will need James on our side."

Naismith bowed his head and smiled. Winslow-Heath was always ready for solutions even if he really didn't want to know how those solutions happened. In a sense, it was precisely what Naismith found so wonderful about working for the colonel. He did not ask hard questions that would force him to accept there was a world outside his military world. If Naismith had a commander who was more rigid, he was certain half of the successes for the past ten years would never have happened. He said, "Leave it to me, Colonel. I will find a way."

Winslow-Heath looked at the short, lean man sitting next to him. He trusted Naismith implicitly and he knew that his creation — the Ravens — was central to the war in the shadows. He said, "Burgess, I think you need to go to your quarters and rest. Tomorrow is another day and we have much to accomplish."

Naismith hadn't noticed how tired he was until

Winslow-Heath spoke. For once he wondered if the colonel had his own mesmerism capabilities. He said, "Thank you, sir. I am a bit tired and will return tomorrow morning for our planning session."

"Excellent. Take some of these fine biscuits with you. I will make sure the staff boxes them properly for you."

Naismith could only smile as he walked out.

In his quarters that evening, Naismith sat cross-legged on a silk prayer carpet. In front of him was a single candle providing the only light in the room. Naismith was staring at the candle flame as he calmed himself, ignoring the pain in his shoulder and focusing his breathing. When he was mentally ready, he dispatched his illusory body outwards, away from Rawalpindi in search of James O'Connell. As with his previous endeavors in the astral plane, his concentration transcended time and distance. He was immediately in the same room as James O'Connell.

O'Connell was sleeping in a house in Damascus. While the room was small, the décor was that of a wealthy Ottoman home. There were silk Persian carpets on the floor and hung on the wall. A carved chest of polished cedar was across from the bed. On the chest was an intricate embroidery and on that embroidery was a carved silver bowl and pitcher with fresh water. Small candles burned low providing just enough light for the owner to navigate the room if he should awake. And Naismith was about to awaken the owner.

James, I've come to talk to you.

O'Connell woke with a start. At first, he thought the voice had been a character in his nightmare, but as he sat up in bed, he saw a shimmering figure at the foot of his bed. He had no need to speak, he had to simply imagine his response: *Naismith!*

Yes, James. I've come to ask. Have you considered our offer?
It is difficult.

Life is difficult, war is difficult, but I am only asking you to decide if you want to live a life where you are a renegade or a hero. You cannot be both. We can help you with your desires or we can block them. It is a simple choice.

And Michael?

Michael will make his own decisions regardless of which route you choose. He is on a dangerous path that could drive him to madness. We can prevent catastrophe together or you can watch him self-destruct.

You saw?

Indeed, I saw. Michael is sliding away from you. He needs help. I can provide that help.

And Ireland?

None of us can know the future, James. We can only act on what we know in the present.

How do I do this?

Tonight, simply say yes. I start working on the how. I know you are planning to go to Berlin. We will be able to meet in Berlin. After that, we can decide the next steps.

Naismith, can I trust you?

James, can you trust yourself? Can you trust Michael? Can you trust the Germans? I think you need to have faith that we can work together.

Guru, I agree.

Then, rest. Keep our meeting in your mind castle apart from your son. He has a powerful mind. Keep it hidden.

O'Connell saw the apparition disappear and his mind was clear. Naismith was right. There was only one way to save Michael from himself. He would do whatever it took to make that happen. Since they had been protected by the whirlwind, Michael had been even more remote and unwilling to talk. James assumed the whirlwind was some apparition that

Michael created to save them, but Michael would not reveal his secret. That alone troubled James.

Naismith returned to his physical body. It was exhausting, but he was pleased that he had made a good first step with James O'Connell. He knew in the world of espionage that getting a potential agent to agree was one thing, it was an entirely different thing to determine what that agent was willing to do. But it was a good first step. He would meet with Winslow-Heath at dawn and let him know. He had an arrangement to walk with the colonel on the cantonment parade grounds. They both knew they were playing a deep game and it was important that no one should know how deep.

Michael O'Connell awoke with a start. Once again, he felt a hand at his throat. The lightest of touch, but ice-cold.

Michael, there is treachery afoot. Treachery! You need to keep focused on your goal: Ireland! Whatever it takes.

Michael could see no one in the room. The voice was in his head. It was more an animal-like whine than a human voice. It was at the same time clear and unclear. What in the world did it mean? He knew that the same voice had warned him of the attack at the Beni Lam camp. Was it simply his own mind warning him? Or some other being operating in the astral plane? Whatever it was, he was prepared for the challenge. The Germans promised that they would move from Damascus to Constantinople and then from Constantinople to Berlin. He realized every step of the way there was a risk. It was a risk he was willing to take.

Missions to Be Accomplished

Rawalpindi, 30 August 1915

THEY SAT AT THE LARGE OAK TABLE IN COLONEL WINSLOW-HEATH'S OFFICE.
They left the two ends of the table open. One for Naismith
and one for Winslow-Heath. At the far end, closest to the
chair reserved for Naismith, Elizabeth and Martha sat across
from each other. Next to Elizabeth sat Beverly and Jonathan.
Alexander sat next to Martha. At the end of the table closest to
the chair that would be occupied by Winslow-Heath sat the
two Bankrofts. Everyone at the table was in military uniform.
Elizabeth had not seen her mother in her own FANY uniform in the past. Based on the formality of the meeting and
its location, Elizabeth expected this would be an important
meeting. She was surprised to see her parents.

After all, just a day before, they had been lounging in
wicker chairs in Indian cotton shalwar kamis watching the
last of the monsoon rains thunder across the sky. Elizabeth
knew she had only one day left in her leave, but her parents were on rest and recovery leave for at least another week

when a runner from the Intelligence Department headquarters came to the house to inform the Bankrofts that their presence was requested at the colonel's office at 1000 hours the following day.

As the runner departed, Francis stood up and stretched and said, "Well, they always say a change is as good as a rest."

Elizabeth looked over at her mother. Mary smiled and said, "Let's hope it is a slightly less vigorous change this time."

Francis yelled into the bungalow, "Bektashi Bey, please tell the dhobi I will need a clean uniform tomorrow."

"Master, dhobi?"

"Apologies, Bektashi. The washerman."

"Of course, master."

Winslow-Heath and Naismith arrived together followed by two staff officers and an orderly with a large rolling cart of tea and pastries. Elizabeth smiled at the thought that the colonel never really held any formal meeting without first making sure there was enough tea and food to supply twice the number in the room. In part, that was because the colonel had an unsurpassed capacity to drink tea. Elizabeth had an unsurpassed capacity to eat pastries so she was well pleased.

The colonel opened with a simple greeting and instructions for each of the attendees to come to the cart and take tea and sustenance. He smiled as he noticed Elizabeth was quick to the tray and left with a full mug of milky tea and two different pastries. She returned a few moments later and gathered a mug of tea and a small mincemeat samosa for Naismith. The rest of the attendees finally settled down and Winslow-Heath filled his tea mug and sat at the head of the table. He nodded and the orderly left. Elizabeth had no doubt he would return with more tea in the large silver samovar that the colonel used for such occasions.

J.R. Seeger

Winslow-Heath was never one for preambles and this discussion was no exception. He started by stating that there was no time to waste in their work in this war. "We have been tasked to focus our attention on two matters: first, military operations in Mesopotamia and second, German efforts to undermine the Raj. The first mission will be a challenge because conventional military minds have trouble understanding how or even if good intelligence can help them. We have already demonstrated how we can use the Ravens behind enemy lines to counter German and Turkish operations with the tribes."

The colonel paused to take tea and look around the room. He thought about the challenges ahead and the risks he would ask of the men and women in front of him. He realized there was no way to avoid risk in wartime and if there was any chance of success for the operation, these were the people who could accomplish the mission.

"The general in charge of operations in Mesopotamia is Charles Townshend. He already demonstrated a degree of bold thought. With a small flotilla of armored tugboats, he led a force that drove the Turks out of Amara with few casualties. It seems likely that the next move up the Tigris will be to capture Baghdad. We have been tasked to support his mission."

"As a first step, we need to neutralize the tribal threat to Basra and Abadan. For that mission, I have requested Percy Sykes return from Chinese Turkestan and revisit his ties to the Persian tribes in the south. Soon enough, he will be promoted to full colonel and likely take no heed of my interests, but I am sure he will follow the instructions of the viceroy."

At the mention of Sykes, Elizabeth and Beverly looked at each other. They had previously worked with Sykes and found him to be an excellent linguist, good at the job as a political agent — meaning working with local potentates and tribesmen — but a man who had no use for women. Their work at Gwadar should have demonstrated their worth, but they doubted the man could change.

"In advance of Sykes' arrival, Elizabeth, Beverly, and Alexander will move to Basra and take up positions inside the small intelligence staff that Townshend has in the city. You will be working for a different Sykes. This Sykes, Mark Sykes, is the viceroy's political agent in Mesopotamia. Mark Sykes has been the viceroy's political agent for the entire Persian Gulf. He knows of your peculiar skills and, I suspect, will make good use of them until Percy Sykes arrives in the region."

Winslow-Heath looked over at the Martha and Jonathan. "Now, for you two, I have a special mission. I want you to travel with Francis and Mary to the frontier and then on to Kabul to support your fellow Raven, Eugenia Waterson. She has been tracking the travel of a German military delegation dispatched to Kabul. Their goal is to convince the Afghan Amir to side with Germany and attack the Raj using the Pashtun tribes on both sides of the border. We know this plan based on our capture of a notebook from one of the delegation. Our Russian allies are currently pursuing these Germans in Northern Persia. I want you in Kabul. If the Germans do arrive, I want to be sure they do not gain any traction with the Amir. Do whatever it takes to accomplish this mission. We must not have a tribal war while we are dispatching the best of our Indian Army regiments to fight in Mesopotamia, in the Dardanelles, and on the Western Front."

Winslow-Heath turned to his staff officers and said, "I think that is enough of serious business for today. Now, we come to a much more pleasurable job."

Awards and Decorations

Rawalpindi and Basra, 30–31 August 1915

THE COLONEL TOOK A SIP OF HIS TEA AND TURNED TO HIS TWO STAFF OFFI-
cers. Elizabeth recognized that this was far more formal than
previous occasions. Winslow-Heath smiled and began, "I will
start with awards that each of you at this table have earned.
I would be remiss if I failed to mention that all the Ravens
at the table should be officially mentioned in dispatches.
That is, of course, if there were dispatches describing your
operations."

Winslow-Heath smiled at his own joke. "Eventually, your
story will be told and I have it on good authority that you
will be rewarded."

Winslow-Heath took another sip of tea. "Personally, I
believe you all deserve more recognition for this secret operation, but the biggest challenge for me was to balance the
fact that the Ravens are a secret organization with the level of
heroism that you regularly demonstrate." The Ravens looked

at each other. They shared one thought: Not a bad way to end a tea party. Winslow-Heath was not finished.

He looked at Francis and Mary Bankroft and said, "You two have been awarded the Distinguished Service Order for bravery in action against the Ottoman Turks and the Germans in Armenia, Kurdistan and Mesopotamia. I will admit, it took some doing to make sure that Mary received the same award as Francis, but when I explained to the viceroy your actions together, Lord Hardinge was pleased to agree. So, what the viceroy instructs, the Army delivers." He paused to sip his tea. "In a normal military unit, this would have been a great ceremony with a band and colors and all of that. However, we are not a normal military unit, so I will simply pass the medal to my most favorite agents and thank them for their service."

The room erupted in applause. Francis and Mary both looked stunned.

Winslow-Heath turned to one of his staff officers and received a small box. He said, "Now, this is another small award that took some wrangling. Again, we can thank the viceroy for sweeping away bureaucratic madness to make this happen."

He handed the box back to his staff officer who walked over to Elizabeth. Winslow-Heath continued, "It is not the policy of the Royal Flying Corps to authorize pilot's wings to women, regardless of their flying skills. For this reason, the viceroy decided to create his own device to be issued to Captain Elizabeth Bankroft. Please pin the device on Captain Bankroft."

The staff officer looked at Elizabeth and motioned for her to stand. As she did, he opened the small box. Inside was a silver pin embossed with the Roman god Mercury. A set with wings extended from the god's helmet. The staff officer pinned the device on the left shoulder of Elizabeth's uniform jacket. He also handed Elizabeth an embroidered patch with the same image on a red, white and blue field similar to the rondels painted on the wings of RFC aircraft.

Winslow-Heath continued, "Captain Bankroft, you are now the first woman to have been awarded the viceroy's flying certificate. You are authorized to sew the embroidered patch on your left sleeve and when you are in mufti, you are authorized to wear the silver pin on your blouse." The colonel smiled. "Of course, the viceroy asks that you avoid any lengthy discussion on how you earned your flying certificate. He believes there are some ... irregularities that might cause some in the RFC to complain. You should just say that you received your certificate as part of your work with the FANYs."

Another round of applause followed.

Winslow-Heath slapped the flat of his hand on the table to get their attention. "Now, there is one last award which I am honored to deliver today. Again, it should be one given directly by the viceroy and, I believe he will eventually be able to take the time to deliver the full and fair accounting. But, for today, I have the privilege to be the one who awards Lieutenant Colonel Burgess Makepeace Naismith with the Order of British India."

Winslow-Heath looked to the other end of the table at the stunned Naismith. He smiled and continued, "The certificate reads as follows: For long and distinguished service to the Crown and to the Viceroy, Lieutenant Colonel Naismith is awarded the Order of British India. Lieutenant Colonel Naismith's service ranges from the Second Afghan War through the Great War and his efforts to train multiple generations of Indian Army intelligence officers has come to the attention of both the Viceroy and His Majesty, the King."

The second of the two staff officers walked over to Naismith and handed him a small box with a simple maroon ribbon. Winslow-Heath said, "The viceroy will eventually award the full ribbon and insignia in a ceremony when it will be appropriate to do so without fear of compromising your role as a senior intelligence officer. In the meantime, the ribbon will have to do. Congratulations, Naismith!"

Until this moment, in his entire life Naismith had not been shocked by events. He was stunned and had nothing to say. He knew the Order of British India was a recognition that dated back to Queen Victoria and was a tribute to long and distinguished service. He recovered long enough to say, "Sir, I hope this does not mean you expect me to retire from service."

When the laughing ceased, Winslow-Heath said, "No, Naismith. We are not through with you. There is a war on and we need men and women like those at this table to continue to risk their lives for the Empire." He turned to one of his staff officers and said, "Let's have more tea, clear the table of the food, and get to work."

Elizabeth stood next to her mentor and said, "Master Guru, congratulations! It is well deserved and long overdue."

Naismith looked at the Ravens who wished to shake his hand. He simply said to them all, "Thank you for being my colleagues."

For the first time in weeks, Conrad Bankroft dressed in his single remaining clean uniform. His arm was still in a sling and there was a substantial bandage on his cheek, but he convinced the doctors that his recovery would be speeded by a return to normal life. He was released for what the doctors called light duty, which Conrad understood to mean tedious work at the logistics command at the port. He wasn't looking forward to this work, but it was far better than walking around the small garden at the hospital.

When he arrived at the logistics command, he was instructed to go immediately to the command offices of the

Indian Expeditionary Force. Conrad was not certain why he needed to report to the higher command, but order were orders. When he arrived, he was guided into a large map room where General Townshend was working with his staff. Townshend looked up at the interruption. He bellowed, "Yes?"

Conrad came to the position on attention and rendered his best salute. "Captain Bankroft, sir."

Townshend's demeanor changed completely. He walked over to Conrad and shook his hand. "Son, I wanted to thank you for your intrepidity. Initiative and bravery! That's the spirit, son. I put you in for a gong of some sort, but for now, I wanted to ask you in person if you would like to join my staff. We are planning the next push north. Probably in Baghdad by Christmas! What do you say?"

Conrad was puzzled but said with as much enthusiasm as he could offer, "Yes, sir! I would very much like to join your staff."

"Good show, son. Join us at the map. We are planning our first move. We are going to attack the next Ottoman position. It should be easy enough. It's a small river town called Kut al-Amara. Just north of our current front lines."

Author's Postscript

While this story is clearly a work of fiction, it is placed in the real world of the British and Indian Army operations in the Middle East in 1914 and 1915. Other than the named general officers and the Viceroy, all of the British and Indian characters are the author's creations.

The German intelligence operations designed to undermine the Raj described in the book are set in the appropriate time and place including the German-Indian conspiracy that had its joint headquarters in Berlin and in San Francisco. The death of the Indian Army political agent William Shakespear during a fight between the warring Shammar and Nejdi tribes is also true as is the fact that the Shammar sent his head to their Ottoman allies as proof of their allegiance.

While the German intelligence officer von Trier is a fictional creation, Baron Colmar von der Goltz and Max von Oppenheim were both orientalists who were central to the German outreach to the Ottoman Empire. For further reading regarding these orientalists, probably the best single book is Lionel Gossman's book *The Passion of Max von Oppenheim. Archaeology and Intrigue in the Middle East from Wilhelm II to Hitler.*

My references for Tibetan mysticism were relatively simple. I used Gyrume Dorje's translation of *The Tibetan Book of the Dead* and a reprint of J.H. Brennan's *Magic and Mysticism in Tibet.*

For those interested in further reading on the Middle East intrigue during World War I, there are dozens of books focusing on these aspects of the war. Regarding the German-Indian conspiracy, probably the most detailed is the recent work by Tim Harper titled *Underground Asia: Global Revolutionaries and the Assault on Empire.* Equally well researched is Donald McKale's book *War by Revolution.*

315

Germany and Great Britain in the Middle East in the Era of World War I. Jules Stewart's *The Kaiser's Missions to Kabul* captures the nature and difficulties of German operations in Persia and Afghanistan as does Peter Hopkirk's book *On Secret Service East of Constantinople.* The role of the CUP in the conflict is well outlined in Sean McMeekin's book *Ottoman Endgame. War, Revolution, and the Making of the Modern Middle East, 1908-1923.* Another book I used in my research is *Arabs and Young Turks* by Hassan Kayali.

The adventurous life and tragic death of William Shake-spear is best described in Alan Dillon's *Captain Shakespear: Desert Exploration, Arabian Intrigue and the Rise of Ibn Sa'ud.* British intelligence operations in the region are well covered in Priva Satia's book *Spies in Arabia: The Great War and the Cultural Foundations of Britain's Covert Empire in the Middle East.*

Of course, no list of books on this subject would be complete without *A Peace to End All Peace: The Fall of the Ottoman Empire and the Creation of the Modern Middle East* by David Fromkin. It is the book that generated my own interest in the Middle East and remains a dog-eared reference book that I have used in all three of the Steampunk Raj novels.

Finally, I wish to thank my wife, Lise Spargo, for her patience and assistance as I probed deeper into the mysteries of the Raj and Tibet and for providing the wonderful illustrations to all three of the Steampunk Raj books.

About the Author

J.R. SEEGER is a western New York native who served as a U.S. Army paratrooper and as a CIA case officer for a total of 27 years of federal service. In October 2001, Mr. Seeger led a CIA paramilitary team into Afghanistan. He splits his time between Western New York and Central New Mexico.

About the Illustrator

LISE SPARGO has been an archaeologist, an intelligence officer, and the manager of a conservation charity. She is a formally trained botanical illustrator and splits her time between New Mexico and western New York focusing on capturing plant species using graphite and watercolours.

Bibliography

For those interested in further reading on the Great War in the Middle East and/or some of the individuals involved, the following reading list offers a start. There are many others worth reading, but this list should help.

A Peace to End All Peace by David Fromkin. While over thirty years old, the book remains the best possible start point for anyone interested in Middle East history in the first three decades of the 20th century.

Setting the Desert on Fire by James Barr. This work focuses on the Arabia and the desert war made famous by T.E. Lawrence in his two works, *Revolt in the Desert* and *Seven Pillars of Wisdom.*

Gertrude Bell: Queen of the Desert, Shaper of Nations by Georgina Howell. While there are nearly a dozen biographies of Bell, Howell's book in the best start for anyone interested in this brilliant and courageous woman.

Persia in the Great Game: Sir Percy Sykes, explorer, consult, soldier, spy by Anthony Wynn. This is the best single biography of this exceptional British intelligence officer.

The Berlin-Baghdad Express: The Ottoman Empire and Germany's bid for World Power by Sean McMeekin. This book covers both the geo-political and engineering challenges associated with the German-Ottoman alliance prior to the Great War.

The Ottoman Endgame: War, revolution, and the Making of the Modern Middle East, 1908-1923 by Sean McMeekin. This book covers in detail the complexity of the CUP-German relationship and the inner workings of the "Young Turks."

War by Revolution by Donald McKale. This is the most detailed and most readable account of the German operations against the British colonies.

Discussion Points for Teachers and Book Clubs

In this series, I have tried to keep the fantasy tied to the reality of colonial Britain in the first few decades of the 20th century. In that sense, the reader sees the British Raj through the eyes of a young woman who is coming to terms with what her life will be like in this new century as well as what will happen to her world when great powers go to war. Here are a few questions/discussion points.

- How does Elizabeth cope with the role of women in the military? Does she see the limitations she is facing?

- What does Elizabeth know about the structure of the British Indian Empire? She is the daughter and granddaughter of military and intelligence officers who have been in the Indian government for decades before she was born. Does she understand any of the tensions that exist between the governing powers and the governed? How does her mother express these tensions in her stories?

- In both books, we listen to characters who are "Anglo-Indian" talk about their lives. What did it mean to be an Anglo-Indian and what limitations did it put on their lives? How did the Germans use this to their advantage? How does Chodak intend to use this?

- Elizabeth must face death in this book. Both the threat of death and killing. Does she understand what has happened to her because of this? What would it be like to be a teenager who has seen this and who has the powers that Elizabeth demonstrates?

- Control becomes one of the issues related to Elizabeth's mystic powers. Does she understand her powers? How do others see her powers? What are the differences between Elizabeth and Michael O'Connell regarding their powers?

A School
for the
Great Game

J.R. SEEGER

"... a plot that twists through the shadow and shade
cast by the British Crown." —Toby Harnden
war correspondent and author of *Dead Men Risen*

A Steampunk Raj Novel

Book One
in the Steampunk Raj Series

How far will a teenager go to save her parents?
To the ends of the earth.

"Seeger transports the reader into the era of the Raj with a rollicking tale that reeks of authenticity."
—Toby Harnden, war correspondent

J.R. SEEGER
A Steampunk Raj Novel

Book Two
in the Steampunk Raj Series

In a game of move and counter-move between the Russians, the British, the Germans and the Turks, Elizabeth and Michael must survive a world going to war.

ALSO BY J.R. SEEGER
THE MIKE4 SERIES

TOP 50 SPY NOVELS RECOMMENDED BY SPIES
SPYSCAPE

"Author J.R. Seeger, an ex-CIA division chief and paratrooper, writes hard-edged spy novels including the MIKE4 series involving Sue O'Connell. The Special Operations Force surveillance specialist is part of a team that 'finds and fixes' terrorists in place so assault teams can 'finish' the target. Seeger's books are highly recommended by SPYEX consultant Kenneth Dekleva for their 'realism and topicality.'"

"The writing, the 'feel,' and behaviors of the characters are authentic, with plenty here to engage both the veteran operator, as well as the casual reader interested in better understanding the actions [and] courage of our OSS heroes."

LTG (RETIRED) JOHN MULHOLLAND, former Deputy Commander, US Special Operations Command and former Commander, US Army Special Operation Command

"Seeger has crafted a fast-paced narrative which carries the reader to multiple hotspots during WWII... This book may be fictional, but the accuracy and attention to detail yields a fine overview of the extraordinary contributions of a heretofore under-appreciated wartime agency."

ANN TODD, author of *OSS Operation Black Mail: One Woman's Covert War Against the Imperial Japanese Army*

"If you like good tales of the shadowy, often hard-edged world of counter- terrorism, read Mike4! Written by a veteran of 'the community,' it will teach while it entertains."

GENERAL STANLEY MCCHRYSTAL, author of *My Share of the Task: A Memoir and Team of Teams: New Rules of Engagement for a Complex World*

www.jrseeger.com

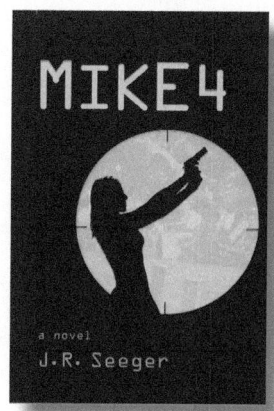

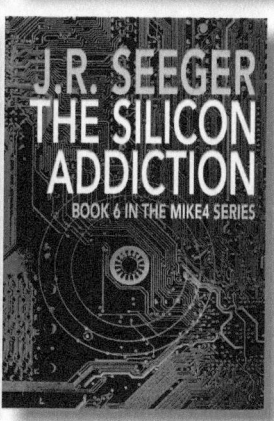

"With so many espionage and special ops thriller writers out there, Seeger is unique in that he lived and thrived in both worlds. *Playground for Ambition* captures that professional experience in a highly entertaining and well-crafted espionage tale."

MARK KELTON, former chief of the CIA Counterintelligence Center

www.ingramcontent.com/pod-product-compliance
Lightning Source LLC
Chambersburg PA
CBHW020401260626
47156CB00007B/2191